D0714259

Grange Abbey

First published in 2017 by
Liberties Press
140 Terenure Road North | Terenure | Dublin 6W
W: libertiespress.com | E: info@libertiespress.com

Trade enquiries to Gill Distribution
Hume Avenue | Park West | Dublin 12
T: +353 (1) 500 9534 | F: +353 (1) 500 9595 | E: sales@gillmacmillan.ie

Distributed in the UK by
Turnaround Publisher Services
Unit 3 | Olympia Trading Estate | Coburg Road | London N22 6TZ T: +44 (0) 20
8829 3000 | E: orders@turnaround-uk.com

Distributed in the United States by
Casemate-IPM | 1950 Lawrence Road | Havertown, PA 19083
T: +1 (610) 853-9131 | E: casemate@casematepublishers.com

Copyright © David Delaney, 2017
The author asserts his moral rights.

ISBN: 978-1-910742-40-2
2 4 6 8 10 9 7 5 3 1

A CIP record for this title is available from the British Library.

Cover design by Karen Vaughan for Liberties Press
Internal design by Liberties Press

This book is sold subject to the condition that it shall not, by way
of trade or otherwise, be lent, resold, hired out or otherwise circulated, without
the publisher's prior consent, in any form other than that in which it is published
and without a similar condition including this condition being imposed on the
subsequent publisher.

No part of this publication may be reproduced or transmitted in any form or by any
means, electronic or mechanical, including photocopying, recording or storage in
any information or retrieval system, without the prior permission of the publisher
in writing.

All characters in this book are fictitious, and any resemblance
to actual persons, living or dead, is purely coincidental.

Printed in Ireland by SPRINT-print Ltd.

Grange Abbey

David Delaney

LIBERTIES

There's a breathless hush in the close tonight,
Ten to make and the match to win,
A bumping pitch and a blinding light,
An hour to play and the last man in

Sir Henry John Newbolt

'With a bit of luck, she might have made it on Broadway or in Hollywood. With a bit of luck,' he repeated like a man who had none. 'The luck is nearly as essential as the talent, you know.' Then he gazed into his empty glass.

James Crumley

I stood before the ancient iron gates and gazed at the driveway beyond, its path meandering gracefully through the windswept meadowlands, then fading into the hills on the misty horizon. On either side of me two giant stone eagles stared out from their perches on massive, marble pillars, silent custodians of an era that lay buried in a far-distant past.

It was early autumn and the breeze had begun dislodging the leaves from the majestic oaks lining the estate walls. Those walls seemed to reach out endlessly, their shimmering scale leaving an indelible mark on my soul when I first set eyes on them during that hazy summer almost thirty years before. My gaze lingered on the dusty grey granite rising from the grassy roadside bank, enclosing an idyllic world I could not possibly have envisaged.

I turned and nodded to Patrick my driver, who had transported me into the heart of Kildare to this remote place on the southern outskirts of Straffan. I had flown in as the dawn was breaking over Dublin in the company's jet from Gatwick, on a mission for the man who was both my employer and lifelong friend. I raised a hand and waved to Patrick to acknowledge that this was indeed the location, and watched him sink into the seat as if anticipating a long wait. He would have known neither to offer assistance, nor ask questions of someone so close to the man who owned the sprawling company of which he was a part. I placed a key in a door under an ivy-clad archway and was surprised how effortlessly it turned in the midst of that surrounding neglect and decay. A thousand memories flooded my mind as I stepped away from the gates on a journey into a long-forgotten world.

When I first visited this place I was just fourteen, alone in Ireland, dispatched by my parents from our home in Sussex to board at Dublin's famous rugby school, Saint John the Baptist College. The year was 1964, and the school summer vacation was about to commence.

My parents, who had spent the greater part of their working lives in the Foreign Office, and were at that time seconded to the British Embassy in Cairo, concluded that it would be impractical for me to join them in the searing heat of Egypt. Their most recent assignment had been shrouded in secrecy and entailed endless travel across the Middle East, which was why an understanding had been reached with the college whereby I would remain there in residence for the summer. This was considered the best solution available.

During my first term at Saint John's, I had, in somewhat traumatic circumstances, befriended Paul Bannon, youngest of three sons of the wealthy Bannon construction dynasty. When word spread through the college of my vacation predicament, Paul nonchalantly suggested that I should come and spend the summer at their palatial home in Kildare. An invitation I at first declined, being then a rather shy, solitary type, stating that I wouldn't dare impose on such generosity. He replied that the decision was of course up to me, casually adding that he doubted I'd even be noticed among the crowd. That, and the prospect of spending yet another summer alone seemed to sway it, and so, with my parents' tacit approval, and the belated blessing of Monsignor Charles Ingram, the school's austere headmaster, the matter was settled, and I ended up spending that glorious summer at Grange Abbey, the sprawling Bannon country estate in the hills beyond the sleepy village of Straffan.

I pushed those memories aside and continued on my way, lingering briefly to gaze back at the entrance gates, now only a dot in the distance. Ahead of me loomed the shadows of a dense forest, its ancient trees barely allowing the light of day to penetrate. I walked through this melancholic cocoon and emerged into a valley with a broad lake, the wind whipping its waters, the sunlight shimmering across its surface. But it was to the far side that my gaze was inextricably drawn, for there in all its glory stood the great mansion itself, a towering bastion dominating the skyline and all that lay before it. Its splendour forced me to recall the sense of awe I felt on the day I first set eyes on this sprawling domain.

I continued past the lake house to the bridge beyond, its span dissecting the waters in five sweeping arches, and watched the great house draw steadily closer, a brooding presence straddling the grey cobalt sky. This was indeed Grange Abbey, once home to the Bannon family in Ireland, its shutters nailed closed, its doors locked to the world outside, its halls and corridors abandoned to the ghosts of a bygone era.

Rising three storeys above a cavernous basement, Grange Abbey had stood empty for almost a generation, but now all of that was about to change. A thousand men would arrive here during the coming months to sweep away the dust of half a lifetime, and restore this abandoned place to its former glory.

The master of the house, Paul Bannon, had decided that it was time to come home.

1

On a cold October Tuesday at the end of morning prayer, the fifteen hundred students of Saint John the Baptist College gathered in the Great Hall to mark the beginning of yet another new term. It was 1963, the eighty-ninth year of the great school's existence, and the entire teaching staff sat assembled on the stage in rows of tiered seating.

Then, moments later, the murmur of conversation slowly began to dissipate with the brisk arrival at the rostrum of the school's headmaster, Monsignor Charles Ingram. He was a tall thin man in his fifties, with penetrating blue eyes, a slender classical nose, and a mane of longish greying hair. He spoke with a rich Scottish accent, his thin, military bearing conveying the air of a man who both commanded and demanded the respect of colleagues and students alike.

Run by the Jesuit order of Catholic priests, Saint John's, one of Dublin's most prestigious schools, had first opened its doors to boarders in the spring of 1874. Housed in a rambling, ivy-clad structure, the complex stood on a tree-lined hill seven miles west of the city on the outskirts of Castleknock village, an affluent suburban location favoured by wealthy business types. The school prided itself on instilling a Catholic ethos, infused with a uniquely broad-minded twist, cleverly achieved by mixing clerical and lay teachers drawn from the best available in their specialities.

The classrooms and dormitories were arranged in a series of spacious quadrangles; a meandering jigsaw of atmospheric old buildings interconnected by a series of paved walkways and stone-clad arches. A granite wall separated the school buildings from the farm complex, a shabby conglomeration of converted stables and sheds serving as milking parlours, poultry houses and storage barns for winter fodder.

Beyond the farm complex the school's twelve rugby pitches stretched all the way to the outer boundary, their measured symmetry encapsulating the embodiment of all sporting activity throughout Saint John the Baptist's fabled history. The old trophy room bristled with the spoils of a hundred years of rugby glory. Its oak-panelled walls were adorned with the faces of Irish internationals who had first learned the rudiments of the game out on the playing fields of this school.

'Good morning to all of you,' the Monsignor began his address. 'It befits me as your headmaster to welcome you through the doors of Saint John the Baptist. On this day we stand together, all for one and one for all, as part of a unique, lasting friendship grounded on strength of character, courage and unfailing loyalty. This is the day on which we begin to look out for one another, a tradition we will endeavour to maintain through these, our school days, and for all the days of our lives, as did our fathers and grandfathers before us.

'Facing into the unknown is the supreme challenge for every man, and our paths through life will be immeasurably smoother if we embrace wholeheartedly the Jesuit ethos upon which this school is predicated. Should anyone wish to confide in me, my door will always be open. I give you my solemn assurance that our discussions will remain a secret between us and that all matters brought to my attention will be treated with the utmost sensitivity.

'When you look back in years to come, you will realise that your days within these walls were the greatest days of your lives, and when you leave and face life's challenges, the enduring wisdom of this experience will remain with you for ever more.'

And so began the roll-call in alphabetical order, the school bursar, a Mister Peterson, bawling out the names in a high-pitched rasping whine. The interminable list, beginning with the yawning, comatose hulk of Peter Joseph Abraham, who seemed abruptly to doze off following a distinctly bored, lack-lustre delivery, eventually reached Jerome Patrick Sedgwick, and then, Anthony Robert Selwyn.

Anthony stood immediately and responded audibly, 'Yes sir, present sir.' And that was it really, those few words providing confirmation of his presence, and signalling the beginning of a mesmerizing roller-coaster ride with the Bannons that would span a generation.

★

Saint John's proved from the outset to be a daunting experience for a boy whose childhood years had been divided largely between the rarified, genteel atmospheres of the British Embassies in Paris and Rome. Anthony's father, an old Etonian and a decorated Second World War, Sandhurst-trained officer, had spent four years as British Ambassador serving both those locations. A framed photograph of him receiving a George Cross at Buckingham Palace for exceptional bravery in the North African campaign against Rommel was judiciously hung on the wall of his office upon arrival at each new location, and removed on the day of departure to accompany him on life's journey.

Anthony and his sister Natalie received their early education at the international schools of those cities, mixing with children from other expatriate families. Their memories of those childhood years were certainly happy ones, their homes palatial, the wonder and excitement of two of the most glamorous cities in Europe laid out at their doorstep.

The geographic location of Anthony's education seemed always to be pre-determined by his parents' diplomatic whereabouts, and so it proved when it came to deciding where he should begin his secondary education. Some six months earlier his father had been advised that his next assignment would be as British Ambassador to the embassy in Dublin. Following consultation with his counterparts at the Irish diplomatic service, it was decided that his son should attend the boarding school of Saint John the Baptist. When, later, Anthony's father discovered that Saint John's had nurtured several current Irish ambassadors, including Paul Kavanagh, then Ireland's ambassador to Washington, whom his father knew and liked, that seemed to swing it.

The decision to complete his education in Ireland was influenced by one other interesting, if unrelated, matter. While in

Rome his mother had converted from the Church of England to Roman Catholicism and was therefore anxious that her son should receive a Catholic education. Where better, she thought than under the watchful eye of the Jesuits, whose motto, 'Give me the child . . . and I'll show you the man,' influenced her profoundly.

As matters transpired, his father received an eleventh-hour change of brief from the Foreign Office, and was instructed to prepare instead to travel to the embassy in Cairo, amid growing tensions in that region, which had some years earlier culminated in the Suez crisis dominating the international stage. The ambassador's prior military experience in the region during the North African campaign was a key deciding factor in the change. The family's move to Cairo was swiftly concluded. In too short a time to reconsider the merits of a less peripheral location for the completion of Anthony's secondary education. His sister Natalie subsequently enrolled at Roedean, the famous girl's boarding school on the south coast of England near Brighton in Sussex, a decision predicated on their father's insistence that at least one of his children be brought up in the tradition of the Church of England.

During those early weeks at Saint John's, Anthony heard reference to the Bannons from time to time. There was no doubting that this family was held in considerable awe by students from all levels, their wealth and influence spoken of in reverential tones, their family history and sporting prowess on the playing fields ingrained indelibly into the annals of this illustrious school.

Frank Bannon was undoubtedly the more famous of the three brothers. His captaincy of the school's rugby team and larger-than-life personality had placed him firmly at the centre of a boisterous group of rowdyish types who seemed to follow his every step.

Simon, the antithesis of his populist elder brother, seemed a vaguely troubled type, aloof and unapproachable, invariably accompanied by one or two faithful hangers-on, introverted, like-minded individuals who rarely seemed to participate in the mainstream.

The youngest of the three brothers, Paul Bannon, had been a boarder here for two years prior to Anthony's arrival, and had progressed through the college's junior preparatory system to join what was for both of them the first year of the senior school. Paul was lean, fit and even then considered tall for his age. His demeanour radiated a natural confidence and ease born out of a lifetime of privilege.

The 'Prep' students traditionally tended to congregate together, and while Paul made little apparent effort to court popularity, others seemed to gravitate towards him and seek to be a part of his considerable entourage. Here was a boy who would someday be a leader of men, whether in business or possibly the armed forces; somehow it seemed inevitable. Anthony, on the other hand, felt isolated and lonely in this vast school of cliques and groups, where one's popularity seemed to bear a direct correlation to the level of one's success on the school's rugby pitches.

During those first weeks he saw little evidence anywhere of the application of that lofty sentiment articulated by the school's illustrious headmaster on that opening day of term, 'All for one and one for all'. For him it had a hollow ring. His fellow students mostly regarded him as something of a curiosity, a foreign boy from a foreign country who spoke with a funny accent.

Anthony was a quiet type, shy and outwardly distant by nature, a spectator rather than a player. He found it increasingly difficult to adjust in this boisterous teeming atmosphere of underlying aggression. So much so that he gradually felt marginalised and increasingly the target of some of the nastier bullies who roamed the corridors and quadrangles unchecked and uncontrolled.

Survival in this fraught atmosphere was always likely to be a challenge for a slight, nervous type such as he, the product of a cocooned, nomadic upbringing, where the opportunity to formulate long-lasting meaningful friendships simply didn't exist. He was then small in stature, barely touching five feet in height, and found it a daunting experience to be thrown headlong into the game of rugby, obligatory for all students in this school, and played with an enthusiasm bordering on the reckless. How he survived those bitter lonely days, far removed from his parents and sister, isolated, ridiculed, bullied remorselessly by his peers, alone, defenceless and at times suicidal, was in the end down to a chance encounter with a boy who was subjected to none of these cruel taunts.

A boy who never knew the hurt and despair that haunted his every waking hour. Instead, a boy idolised and hero-worshipped, with a family name to which his name would be indelibly linked across a generation. He would witness their triumphs and disasters, their fortunes and misfortunes and would stand beside them on the day they fought what would become universally recognised as one of the most ferocious corporate battles in living memory.

But during those first tentative weeks at Saint John the Baptist, it was a boy named William 'Bunter' McKenzie who became his tormentor. A boy Anthony grew to fear and loath as the days passed and his life descended into a living hell. McKenzie spearheaded a dissolute group known as the Westies, comprising some fifty students originating from towns west of the Shannon river. The Westies had existed in the school for generations as a social group, whose numbers traditionally congregated daily in the school yard between classes, and gravitated towards one another during time out after school. But under McKenzie's leadership they had developed into an altogether more sinister and threatening faction.

The eldest son in a family of cattle-dealers from the Golden Vale region east of Limerick city, the 'Bunter' had since his arrival at Saint John's systematically bullied and fought his way to the pinnacle of this group. A psychopathic, unpredictable personality, with a long line of bruised and broken bodies scattered in his wake, the Bunter had developed a reputation for wanton brutality. His irrational cruelty marked him out as an individual to be feared and avoided in equal measure.

Anthony was the unfortunate one singled out to become the focus of the Westies' attention during those early weeks of the term. McKenzie and his companions began mimicking what they considered to be his upper-class, fastidious mannerisms, refined accent and impeccable attire. All traits which had been drilled into him since childhood, but now served to brand him as little more than a whimpering sissy. As time went by his punishment progressed to the more serious levels of verbal abuse and intimidation. He was taunted remorselessly by this group. Their behaviour, unhindered and unreported to the school authorities, who tended to treat such matters with little sympathy. Saint John's unwritten ethos was grounded on the principle that as part of life's preparation, boys should learn to look out for themselves in their formative years or else suffer the consequences in later life.

Anthony had previously sought a degree of solace in the gloomy stillness of a disused classroom at the end of a shadowy corridor leading to the cavernous rooms of the old section. He first began to seek refuge there having discovered it purely by chance, and identifying it as a quiet place, rarely frequented, a solitary vestige of tranquility in the harsh reality of his lonely predicament.

It was a Monday morning late in the autumn term, and he was beginning to feel he had reached a particularly low point, with not the faintest idea how to extricate himself from the misery he was forced to endure. He sat cowered in a corner, his slight frame hunched in the shadows of a curtained window, head in hands, immersed in the depths of his own private hell. Then he heard the sound of the door opening, and closing again, and as he lay crouched and scared, a shadow crossed the room, and a figure stood beside him. He didn't dare look up until he heard a familiar voice.

'Oh, it's you, Selwyn. I was passing and thought I heard a funny sound.'

This was the last thing he needed. He wasn't particularly enamoured at Paul Bannon or anyone else seeing him like this.

'Yeah it's me,' he responded tentatively. 'I just needed to be alone a while.'

'You've been crying,' he remarked matter-of-factly.

'Yes, I have,' he answered

Paul leaned against the wall and folded his arms. 'What's the matter?'

'Nothing that's any of your business,' he blurted a little too quickly.

Paul stared at him and shrugged.

'In that case, I'll leave you in peace.'

Anthony prayed that he was about to go, but he stood and pondered him pensively.

'It can't be easy adjusting to the hustle of a place like this.'

He nodded miserably.

'You must miss home,' he added. 'Most of the new guys do, but they soon get used to it.'

'I expect so,' he replied, gazing about self-consciously. He tried to put on a brave face, but his voice began to falter and tears welled in his eyes. He stared into the gloom, not knowing what to say next. Paul knelt beside him and placed a hand on his shoulder.

'What's this all about, Anthony?' he inquired softly.

He rested his head on his arms and slowly began to blurt it all out.

'I hate this fucking place,' he sobbed bitterly. 'I'm frightened out of my wits here most of the time and I really don't know how much more I can take. I promised my mother I'd telephone this morning, but McKenzie has me so scared I'm afraid to cross the yard. Life's been a misery since the day I set foot in this dump.'

He sat there hunched, a haunted look on his face, eyes glazed, his slight frame shivering. Paul leaned down and took him by the arm.

'Let's cross the yard together and I promise you'll have nothing to fear. C'mon. Let's do it.'

Anthony shook himself free.

'I'm sorry,' he replied, 'but what little courage I used to have when I arrived in this place has deserted me. I don't have any left.'

He knelt beside him.

'Anthony, look at me.'

When eventually he got the courage to look up, his eyes were glazed in terror. Paul stared at him, momentarily startled.

'You seem surprised by my state of fright,' he said almost in a whisper. 'But then you've never been on the receiving end of an orchestrated bullying campaign. I wouldn't wish it on you.'

'All the more reason we should face this together,' Paul replied, giving him a reassuring smile, his ice-blue eyes showing not a hint of fear.

'I'd really prefer to stay here.'

'Anthony . . . let's just fucking do it!'

They emerged from the corridor into the bright sunlight of the crowded main school yard and began walking in the direction of the administration building on the far side.

Paul could sense his anxiety as he watched him staring glumly in preparation for what must inevitably lie ahead, and as they approached half-way his step began to falter.

'I should have known it would happen,' he whimpered bitterly. 'Looks like I've been rumbled.'

McKenzie and his group sat in a line beneath some windows away to their left, quietly staring in their direction.

'Selwyn, get your ass over here, you fucking faggot!' McKenzie bellowed.

'Don't look around,' Paul prompted quietly. 'We're almost there.'

He faltered but a reassuring hand propelled him onwards.

'Look straight ahead,' Paul whispered.

'Don't make me ask again, Selwyn!'

In their peripheral vision they saw McKenzie mutter something to Robbie Dixon, seated on his right. Dixon, a dour thug from the outskirts of Limerick city, smirked at some private joke, then hopped to his feet and strolled across the yard in front of them.

'Are you fucking deaf, Selwyn! Do what you're fucking told and do it fucking now!'

Dixon never really saw it coming until it was too late. The fist seemed to materialise from out of nowhere, a single precision blow delivered fast and hard into the ball of his left eye, catching him unawares. He looked vaguely surprised and staggered backwards in slow-motion, trying desperately to hold his balance but failing in the end. The impact seemed to suck the wind out of him; he tumbled backwards and crashed onto the limestone cobbles, then crawled on his hands and knees and struggled to his feet, but suddenly fell back and lay still.

A silence descended across the yard as they set off again, with all eyes focused on the two of them. Anthony sensed a blanket movement on the left and saw the Westies rise together and move in their direction. Just then the siren sounded the end of morning break, and in an instant they were surrounded. McKenzie sauntered up to them and levelled his eyes inches from Paul's.

'The Wall – end of class today.'

That was all he said. It was all he needed to say. He backed slowly away and disappeared in the crowd.

2

All morning the news of an imminent fight at the Wall spread like wildfire through the corridors of Saint John's. The wall in question was the old stone boundary that divided the playing fields from the outer farm buildings, and down all the years, for as far back as anyone could remember, it was here that matters of dispute were ultimately resolved.

Although the Wall was far enough away from the school buildings to render it immune from prying eyes, the school's administration still afforded a degree of 'understanding' to such extra-curricular activity, treating it as an almost inevitable consequence of life in a community of fifteen hundred boarders. Turning a blind eye to a certain letting-off-steam was informally considered to be a helpful, if somewhat unconventional contributor to the smooth functioning of the famous school.

The siren sounded the end of morning classes and the corridors reverberated with the noise of students dispersing, some to the playing fields and others to the comforting atmosphere of the school canteen. When Paul entered the old oak-panelled library, he noticed a group of senior boys lounging on leather couches, his elder brother Simon sprawled in the middle of them, their presence confirmation that news of the fight had spread to the senior classrooms and dormitories of the upper house.

Now in his final year at Saint John's, Simon had recently been nominated head boy, a decision considered by most to have been political rather than popular. He gave his younger brother a withering stare.

'Just tell us it's not true what we've been hearing about you and McKenzie at the Wall today, and we can all be on our merry way.'

He sat on the only available chair.

'You heard correctly. It's true.'

Simon regarded him dispassionately.

'This could be embarrassing for me. I am the head boy of this college. You ought to be mindful of the way you behave.'

'There's nothing I can do. It's all set up.'

'Then you're out of your mind! You'll be lucky to last a minute in the ring with the mad bastard. He'll destroy you.'

'I didn't have a choice. McKenzie called it.'

Simon shrugged dismissively.

'You *gave* him no choice.'

'He gave himself no choice.'

'That's rubbish and you know it – you idiot.'

There was no answer to that. Paul stared with indifference at this elder brother who always seemed distant and cold-hearted. His eldest brother Frank might have been equally disparaging in the circumstances, but he would never have ridiculed him in front of an audience like this. Frank Bannon had been hero-worshipped in all the houses of the school. His captaincy of the senior team had been the catalyst to a famous run of thirteen consecutive wins, a record never previously matched in the history of Saint John the Baptist. Frank's icy riposte would always have been preferable to Simon's self-serving rant.

'And I'm presuming you're aware that the Bunter has a charge of aggravated assault hanging over him. The psychopath you're taking on at the Wall today practically clubbed a guy to death in broad daylight.'

'I *did* hear something about that.'

'Then you really *are* out of your mind.'

'Save your breath, Simon. This conversation's going nowhere.'

His brother stared at him, exasperated.

'Just listen to me this one time. You don't need to do this.'

'I don't have a choice, and you know it. Our parents always taught us to stand our ground – it's the way we were brought up.'

'We were brought up to use our brains,' Simon rasped, then turned and stared at no one in particular.

'My brother's acting like he's Jack Dempsey, and even that big mutt had the brains never to take on a fight he couldn't win.'

'Aw, let him get on with it,' Andrew Bradley drawled. 'We're never gonna change his mind. So let's get down to the Wall and at least make sure the Westies don't spring any unpleasant surprises.'

Bradley was the school's head prefect and one of Simon Bannon's closest friends.

'Keep your opinions to yourself, Andrew,' Simon snapped, the palpable anger in his voice bringing the discussion to an abrupt end. Bradley threw his eyes to heaven and nobody said very much after that. Simon stared grumpily at his brother, then kicked his books off the lectern and sighed.

'It seems there's nothing left to be said. We'll be there to make sure it stays one-against-one, but after that you're on your own. I wish you luck, because guess what – you'll need all of it.'

He stood abruptly and the others did the same. At the door he hesitated, then turned to his brother.

'Oh and by the way, I telephoned Jamie this morning. He left the Grange an hour ago. Not telling Jamie was a risk too far. I value my life too much!'

★

The temperatures dropped steadily as the day wore on, and when the chapel bell sounded for two o'clock, the thermometer on the yard wall was already hovering below zero. The wind had turned icy and the clouds were black and low when the last siren of the day sounded the end of class. Distant peals of thunder heralded an approaching storm and the first drops of rain were spattering off the window panes as the classrooms emptied out and students from all houses joined the march to the Wall. A few with prior commitments didn't get to make it that day, but as the clock struck four, a thousand boys were gathered to witness the day's most anticipated event.

McKenzie pushed his way through the crowd to the centre of a large clearing, flanked by his army of Westies, calm and confident, stalking the space in front of him. Then, just as Paul emerged from the far end, Simon Bannon and a group of sixth-formers spread out and positioned themselves along all sides.

McKenzie's face darkened. He stared at Simon and sneered.

'What brings you here, you fucking girl?'

'I'm here to make sure you play by the rules.'

McKenzie stared at him with a look of bemused contempt.

'There are no rules under this Wall, head boy, but guess what. I'm actually pleased you're here, because when I hammer the shit out of your short-on-brains kid brother, I'll have the satisfaction of knowing you'll be there to witness every blow that lands. I've just realised I've got you to thank for the great feeling I have about this.'

Simon felt himself wilting under McKenzie's unblinking stare.

'I'll report any misdemeanours to the school authority, McKenzie.'

McKenzie stepped forward and eyeballed him.

'Do that and you'll soon find out what happens to a snitch.'

Rob Morgan, the senior team captain, pushed his way through the crowd.

'McKenzie, I'm backing Bannon to hammer the shit out of you all day, you fat fuck.'

Nobody ever spoke to McKenzie like this. His mood turned sour. He didn't bother to look at Rob Morgan. He kept staring at Simon.

'Stick around head boy because when I'm finished inflicting permanent brain-damage on your kid-brother, you're next on my list. Two Bannons for the price of one. It doesn't get any better.'

Ben Pearson, a sixth-form prefect, strode into the middle of the square and cleared his throat. His hoarse, commanding baritone resonated across the expectant gathering.

'Are you two guys ready!'

Just then a newcomer pushed his way to the front of the crowd and stood calmly staring ahead. The sour-faced stranger, dressed in jeans and T-shirt, was plainly not of this school. McKenzie glanced curiously in his direction, but Jamie Sinclair just gave him a cold, unsettling stare. Ben Pearson raised a hand in the air.

'Last call, gentlemen. Are you ready!'

They both nodded. The crowd went quiet. Pearson gazed around dramatically.

'Three . . . Two . . . One, and . . . Go!'

There was a deafening roar as they moved from their positions, McKenzie closing the gap fast and screaming, 'C'mon, take me if you can, you lily fuck!'

Paul struggled to focus his mind on his opponent and on all that lay ahead. Undoubtedly McKenzie was an experienced street-fighter, his toned arms and legs evidence of regular visits to the gym, and yet Paul still felt that there was something lacking there, some part of his physique that didn't quite stack up. His two-stone weight-advantage looked to be all muscle, but the longer the fight progressed, time would begin to tell the real story. As he contemplated all of this, suddenly McKenzie crashed into him and landed a dozen rapid-fire blows straight into his face.

Paul cursed himself for not anticipating this early strike. He felt his head reeling from the series of powerful hits, the last one connecting with sledgehammer-force into the side of his cheekbone, sending him sprawling to the ground, dazed and dizzy.

McKenzie closed in and let loose with a numbing kick to the stomach. The sound of the impact reverberated in the chill air and triggered a gasp from the bemused onlookers, the momentum of the strike lifting his opponent clear off the stony surface. Suddenly everything was beginning to happen so fast. He lay squirming in the mud, the pain in his abdomen like fire as yet again McKenzie's steel-capped boot crashed into his ribcage. He tumbled across the icy ground, his head spinning as he scrambled in vain to raise himself off the surface, but with the impetus now firmly in his grasp, McKenzie anticipated this reaction with ease. His mind was focused and he sensed that there was an early chance to finish this. He surged forward and buried his boot in the base of his opponent's spine, forcing him face down into the mud.

Paul felt his ribs explode and knew for certain he couldn't sustain another blow like that. His mind seemed to be reacting in slow-motion. In his peripheral vision he saw Rob Morgan make a move in his direction only to be restrained by the powerful grip of Jamie Sinclair. The noise seemed to reach a crescendo, a cascading wall of sound blurring through his brain like a controlled screaming siren. In an instant his mind flashed back through those childhood days at the Grange, growing up with Jamie.

Never close your eyes for one second in a fight, Jamie had taught him. Never look away from your opponent. Don't even blink an eye when the blows come raining down. Never hit back at normal strength. Strike with every nerve and sinew of your body. Delve into the depths of your strength, strength you never even knew you possessed, the hidden strength in your inner core just waiting to be unleashed. Target the vulnerable areas, the shins, the kneecaps, the ankles, the testicles, mouth, nose and eyes. Focus on your opponent to the exclusion of all else. Blank out everyone and everything around you. Breathe deep.

Rob Morgan had felt Jamie's steely grip dragging him back into the chanting crowd.

'He's going to kill him! I've got to do something!'

'No, not yet. He'll never live it down if we intervene now. Be patient. There's a way to go yet!'

McKenzie dug his boot into the back of Paul's neck, bringing his weight to bear crushingly downwards. He felt his nostrils explode with blood as his nose connected with the cold, stony ground. McKenzie stared out triumphantly and raised a hand to the crowd, demanding their silence, commanding their attention, and when the noise slowly faded, he looked down at his opponent.

'Beg me for your life, Bannon, and spare yourself further embarrassment. And if I don't hear you begging, good and loud, for everyone to hear, then I'll surely fucking kill you here today.'

They stood and stared and waited in dumbstruck dread, the silence broken by a lone peal of thunder far in the distance. McKenzie held his boot firm, bearing down mercilessly with all his weight, his gaze shifting defiantly along the line of spectators, smirking at some of the frontline boys peeling away in disgust, the sickening spectacle too nauseating to witness.

Then something happened that nobody quite seemed to comprehend when they relived it again and again during the weeks and months that followed. Suddenly the ground below McKenzie appeared to move, and a fist flew upwards at lightning speed, the body on the ground no longer lying prostrate, but swiveling behind the blow to deliver maximum impact. Drawing on all his reserves of power and concentration, Paul slammed his fist into McKenzie's testicles, then rolled from beyond his reach and scrambled to his feet.

An electric frisson ran through the spectators as they sensed a change in the atmosphere, a mixture of astonishment and disbelief rippling in the air as the enraptured crowd held its collective breath. He blocked all of this out of his mind as he turned to watch McKenzie struggling to absorb the shock. Sure in the knowledge that his blow had been delivered with accuracy and severity, he drew the cold air deep into his lungs and rebalanced his mind and body in preparation for the next inevitable onslaught. He stared at his opponent with undiluted hatred, at the cruel lips drawn tightly over his teeth, the watery eyes, the shocked look on his now-pale face as it wavered between bewilderment and disbelief. Rob Morgan turned and glanced at Jamie, but Jamie's face showed no reaction.

A deafening roar erupted as the fight resumed, the two of them crashing headlong into one another, the blows delivered fast and hard, the pace unrelenting, the contest played out with the deadliest intent. Hovering just under six feet, Paul Bannon towered four inches over the powerfully built McKenzie, but his thin gangly frame should have been no match for the heavier, stockier boy. And yet they stood under the shadow of the Wall for all of seven minutes, delivering blows in an unrelenting, ferocious exchange, until the crowd, anesthetised by the fierce thumping sound of bare-knuckle fist upon flesh, was once again lulled into a gradual, numbing silence.

The thousand boys at the Wall that day watched in muted shock as the two opponents before them, hair caked with mud and faces stained red with blood, fought the longest, most vicious fight ever to be seen under the Wall at Saint John the Baptist.

Never taking his eyes off McKenzie, Paul gradually began to sense the faintest trace of a pattern emerging from the punishing, relentless savagery of the encounter; nothing much to go on but there nonetheless – an imperceptible movement, barely more than an irrational, haphazard, momentary tensing in the instant, before delivering his most damaging strike, a straight left-handed blow followed by a fearsome right uppercut. Was it possible, he wondered, to exploit the weakness in this slight predictability, a vague idiosyncrasy in the fight-pattern of this lethal bully each time he worked his, clearly often-used, much-practised combination? McKenzie didn't appear to be displaying signs of tiring, and yet Paul knew he must. Every bone in his own body was aching and he knew this deadly exchange couldn't last much longer.

He knew also that the plan formulating in his mind could easily spell disaster unless it was executed with split-second precision. He steeled himself for the moment, then waited until he saw it begin to unfold again, and in an instant he drew back and felt the air rush past his face, the punch missing him by a fraction. He saw a fleeting look of surprise in McKenzie's eyes and then the slightest loss of balance. He spun quickly, a full three hundred and sixty degrees, and drove his elbow hard into McKenzie's throat, the weight of his pirouetting body delivering maximum power behind the strike.

The crowd gasped as McKenzie staggered backwards, clasping his neck with both hands, choking and wheezing as he struggled to inhale mouthfuls of the freezing air. He stood there, teetering, his eyes glazed and watering in the aftermath of the strike. Then his legs slowly gave way and he crumbled to the ground, pain and shock etched agonisingly on his face. He seemed to stay that way forever, until gradually, in slow motion, he toppled forward on bruised, outstretched hands, his unfocused, disorientated gaze seeking out his opponent.

The final blow, when it came, lifted McKenzie into the air in front of the astounded gathering, a thumping kick into the crown of his mouth, smashing jawbone, crushing cartilage and sending loosened teeth clattering noisily across the icy surface. The ferocity of the impact whipped his head, and released a blood-splatter across the heaving row of startled onlookers packed onto the front line.

Anthony stood, lost somewhere in the depths of the baying mob, transfixed by the savagery of the scene unfolding before his eyes, a sad, silent spectator to a merciless onslaught played out in an unforgiving arena. He watched in disbelief as the blows rained down relentlessly in this most fearsome, shocking contest.

In all his life he'd never witnessed anything quite like this.

The rain had begun falling heavily now, the great icy droplets running off the fighters in rivulets of red as they mingled with the bloody carnage. Paul stood in a trance-like state, feet apart, chest heaving, arms by his side, unaware of the all-enveloping, surreal silence around him. Then somewhere in the distance he heard the sound of someone clapping, then the same sound from somewhere else, and then a rolling crescendo, a sustained, thunderous wall of applause ringing in the cold evening air.

He gazed distractedly at his audience, their laughing faces staring back with awestruck admiration, then slowly he turned his back on McKenzie and began walking towards the distant lights of the school.

A human passage opened before him and suddenly Rob Morgan was beside him, an arm on his shoulder, steering him through the door of the senior changing rooms, the chanting crowd following in their wake. The senior squad sat on the benches and slow-hand-clapped as their captain led him through to the showers beyond. He flipped the lever to the hottest setting and stared into his battered face.

'You fought the fight of your life out there today. Just listen to them. They've found themselves a new hero.'

He pushed him under the steaming hot water.

'Oh, and by the way, your friend Jamie's gone back to the Grange. He told me to tell you there's nothing more he can teach you.'

3

Held each year in the month of November, the gala hunt ball at Grange Abbey was the most glamorous social event on the hunting calendar, the guest-list comprising a 'Who's Who' of the family's connections throughout Ireland, England, and across the wider continent of Europe. The largest guest representation emanated from the London region, the company's most active and lucrative theatre of operation.

It was in London that the company originated in the immediate post-war era, when James Bannon and his brothers Matthew and Charles set up a small house-building company to capitalise on the reconstruction of homes in the war-damaged suburbs of the city.

Four hundred thousand houses had been destroyed by the Luftwaffe during the London Blitz, and in the midst of this devastation the Bannon brothers carved a swathe through the dust and the rubble, churning out tens of thousands of new dwellings from their relentless production lines. But the brothers quickly realised that the destruction inflicted by the Luftwaffe paled beside the response of Britain's RAF, the ferocity of their nightly bombing raids consigning a staggering two and a half million dwellings in the major German cities to rubble.

Recognising that somebody also had to rebuild these houses, they set about deploying hundreds of construction crews to the war-torn suburbs of Cologne, Dusseldorf, Hamburg and Berlin to capitalise on the rebuilding programmes formulated around those ruined cities.

Meanwhile, in London, the company emerged from humble beginnings and expanded under James's intrepid leadership, forging lucrative working relationships with the various local authorities, including, crucially, the most powerful of them all, the

Greater London Council. This unique relationship was grounded on the brothers' ability to annually deliver vast numbers of newly reconstructed houses in record time. Throughout the mid-fifties, from their power base in London, Bannons expanded across the United Kingdom, seamlessly completing the transition from demolition and reconstruction into the burgeoning new-housing market, where they were soon destined to become a leading national operator.

In the spring of 1959, following its initial listing on the London Stock Exchange, the company was ranked the third largest housebuilder in Great Britain, uniquely among the top-ten national operators retaining eighty percent of its shareholding within family ownership.

Against this background in the weeks leading up to the ball, Dublin's grandest hotels had been block-booked to facilitate the influx of national and international guests. Scheduled to take place on the first Friday of November, activity around the mansion climbed to fever pitch as the big day drew ever closer.

In the preceding weeks, an army of workers and stable hands operating under the watchful eye of estate foreman Jamie Sinclair began the formidable task of transforming the estate into the ultimate party event. The centrepiece of all activity would once again focus on the marquee, a structure four hundred feet square, its twin domes towering into the sky from its setting in the walled gardens to the rear of the mansion.

At all times, in excess of two hundred racehorses stood in the loose-boxes at the Grange, the great cobbled yard with its arched entrance gates the focal point for all the activity. The vast working farm at Grange Abbey was inundated with hundreds of workers swarming through the house and gardens in the build-up to the premier event in the estate's calendar. Frank Bannon flew in on a chartered jet from London early on the Thursday morning to assume his role as master of the hunt. He was accompanied by an entourage of the company's top London executives and their wives. They were met by a fleet of limousines and transported to the Grange to kick-start the festivities with a lunch in the ballroom of the mansion.

Following the completion of his final year at Saint John the

Baptist, Frank enrolled at Magdalen College Oxford to read business studies. Always the avid sportsman, he immersed himself in the game of rugby and went on to captain the Oxford Blues for two successive seasons. At a height of six feet four, with a gregarious personality to complement his film-star looks, his reputation as a ladies' man was even then the stuff of legend, his wealth and seeming insatiable desire for life catapulting him to centre stage at Oxford. Frank's smiling face regularly featured in the society pages of most London newspapers, with invariably a different beautiful woman on his arm each time.

★

Hours later, with lunch still in full flow, Frank slipped away to a rendezvous with Marcus Carruthers, the suave head of the in-house accountancy team at Bannons. Smart, efficient and unafraid to speak his mind, Frank trusted his mild-mannered chief accountant implicitly. They sat in the library by the window on green leather armchairs.

'So, spit it out, Marcus. What couldn't keep until we're back in the office on Monday?'

'May I be blunt?'

'*Sure.*'

Marcus stared at his volatile boss and suppressed a fleeting tinge of doubt.

'Frank, this current expansion programme of yours is causing me sleepless nights.'

'Oh yeah. Why's that?'

'Because what you're proposing is unnecessary, unwarranted, borderline reckless, and certain to play havoc with our loan-to-value covenants. If we continue on this course then it can only be a matter of time before we breach our banking term-sheets, and we really shouldn't contemplate doing that right now, especially when there's patently no need to do so. Switching specifically tailored bank facilities from one entity into another without authorisation breaks every accounting rule in the book; is a flagrant breach of the most basic company law; is downright dangerous and damn well illegal. I urge you to reconsider now

30

before it's too late to undo the damage.'

Frank sat back in his armchair, arched his fingers, and eyeballed his accountant.

'Marcus, I'm aware of your views, so let me be equally blunt. From an accounting perspective and from your own perspective, the strategies upon which I embark simply must be achieved, and whatever that entails, whether legal or illegal, I expect you to ensure that in the end I get what I want, and by implication that this family gets what it wants. Now is precisely the time to expand our UK house-building programme. The market is sluggish and money is scarce, which is good, because a depressed market signifies depressed land values, and that means we need to be out there hoovering up prime land-banks in all the best locations. Right now we've got eighteen thousand housing plots, and if we really want to become market leaders then we're gonna have to double up on those numbers. I expect to see forty thousand plots on our books by the end of the calendar year, and don't try and convince me we don't have the wherewithal to fund all of this. You know me well enough to know I'm not going to be swayed from this strategy, and I'll be looking to you to secure the required funding package to deliver the numbers. Simple as that.'

'If you're suggesting that I should raid current, specifically tailored bank facilities in order to fund this suicidal acquisition programme, then forget it.'

Frank glanced dispassionately at his financial controller.

'That is precisely what I'm suggesting, and don't insult me by describing my programme as suicidal. This industry is not for the faint-hearted, and if we want to get to the top of the heap, we need to have the foresight, the wherewithal, and the balls to seize the opportunities when they present themselves; otherwise we risk being overtaken by events and outsmarted by our competitors. You're a good man, Marcus, and I'm guessing you're smart enough to know I'm never going to allow that to happen. From a personal perspective you need to understand that any attempt to try and dissuade me would be naive, foolhardy, and a fatal error of judgement.'

'Frank, you're asking me to break the law, which clearly I'm not prepared to do.'

'I'm asking you to bend the rules, which is not quite the same thing. As long as this family controls most of the shareholding, then we cannot be construed as strictly a publicly quoted company, and if ever we *do* decide to go private, we simply rein in the issued share capital and delist. Right now if we really were publicly quoted in the true sense, then of course different rules would apply – greater accountability, greater transparency, all that shit. Marcus, we're in a unique position poised close to the top of the chain. This is an opportunity we dare not miss. Let's gear up! Let's fucking do it!'

Marcus Carruthers knew that Frank was blurring the lines between good practice and sharp practice, but he also knew that there was little to be gained from arguing the toss. His driven boss was hell-bent on pursuing a game of russian roulette, and it seemed pretty damn clear that his mind was not for changing.

'How much time do I have to, shall we say, "reorganise" our finances to fund this . . . scenario.'

'None, actually. I signed contracts yesterday for the acquisition of twelve hundred acres of zoned land on the Surrey-Sussex border south of Guildford, with a further thousand acres of mixed-development land near Cheltenham in Gloucestershire. Deposits have been released to the vendors on a non-refundable basis, and that effectively means the process has already begun. All the relevant details are on your desk right now, and I'll be expecting to receive a comprehensive funding strategy no later than close of business Monday. Don't disappoint me, Marcus. You're part of my core team, and I'm anxious for you to remain so, but I'm an ambitious guy. My goals are set in stone and they will be achieved, and that is why I need to know if you're with me on this. If you are – great – and if not, then now's the time to say. There are only two choices. You're either with me or against me. So tell me, which is it to be my friend?'

Marcus stared thoughtfully at Frank wondering why he might ever have believed it would come down to anything other than a black-and-white call. All prior experience should have told him that there were only two colours in Frank Bannon's kaleidoscope. To have ever imagined otherwise would have been bordering on naive.

'Frank, I felt it would be remiss of me not to appraise you as to the possible downsides of the strategy, because knowing you as I do, I believe you'd expect nothing less of me. It is my professional duty to lay these matters out, warts and all, so that all of your decisions are founded on credible advice, and are fully informed to avoid any future eventuality which may have caused you to decide differently. But to answer your question. Yes, Frank – in for a penny, in for a pound. I give you my word. I'm with you on this.'

Frank smiled for the first time, then poured two tumblers of Midleton. They clinked.

'Thanks Marcus. That's what I was hoping you'd say.'

They downed them in one gulp and Frank placed a hand on his shoulder.

'Let's wander back downstairs. In case it has slipped your mind, I *do* have some guests to entertain.'

4

In the early hours of the morning the bar in the marquee gradually began to clear. The highlight of the evening's entertainment had been the arrival on the stage of the Irish folk group the Clancy Brothers, their chart-topping song 'Fine Girl You Are' drawing rapturous applause from the delighted gathering. A lively rendering of 'McAlpine's Fusiliers' raised a chorus of good-humoured groans and wolf whistles from the heaving boisterous crowd, the fabled song depicting the travails of one of Bannons' largest civil-engineering competitors in England and Scotland.

In the pre-dawn semi-darkness of the early morning, a mini-bus carrying the Saint John the Baptist party rolled in through the main gates. The group included the school's headmaster Monsignor Charles Ingram, and rugby coach Steve Bishop, both automatic inclusions on Bannon party lists. The hunt, scheduled to commence at midday, was large by any standard, with one hundred and twenty riders participating over a distance of forty miles spread across various land holdings bordering the Grange Abbey estate.

Originally intended to straddle both sides of the Liffey, whose waters dissected the Grange lands for a distance of five miles, this year the organising committee had been forced to restrict the event to the mansion-side of the river, a decision dictated by the ominous weather conditions which had been steadily worsening all week. From dawn the previous Sunday the rain had begun to fall in earnest, and by mid-afternoon the winds had blown up to storm-force, the precursor to an unbroken four-day torrential downpour. Late on Thursday afternoon the rains finally ceased, but the Liffey's waters had by then reached capacity and were running at full flow, coursing across the estate's western flatlands on a remorseless journey downstream.

The storm had swollen the waters to their highest level since records began, with the river twice bursting its banks south of Straffan village, flooding the countryside for miles. The traditional river crossing, four miles upstream of the mansion on a shallow curve where the banks narrowed into a much favoured fording-point for hunt parties over the years, was now hopelessly flooded, rendering the crossing an impossibility, and forcing the re-routing of the hunt across lands exclusively to the west of the river.

Shortly after seven, Frank sauntered into the marquee and made his way to the Saint John's table.

'Good morning Charles, Stevie. Glad you guys could make it. Mind if I join you for some breakfast?'

Charles Ingram nodded sombrely, barely bothering to look up from his plate. *Still the same cranky old bastard*, Frank mused as he took a seat next to his younger brother. *No standing on fucking ceremony here.*

They ate in silence as was the custom at Saint John's. *Old habits die hard*, Frank reflected as he glanced around the table and smiled quietly.

The marquee began filling gradually, the early arrivals looking disshevelled and weary from the excesses of the night before. Soon the place was in full swing, with teams of chefs firing out breakfasts in short order to the thousand-strong crowd.

By the time the clock on the stable tower struck nine, the cavernous courtyard was already brimming with trucks, jeeps and horseboxes, the brooding presence of Jamie Sinclair calmly overseeing the unfolding operation with barely three hours remaining to the start of the hunt. A demanding boss, an uncompromising perfectionist, hard but fair, Jamie ran the farm detail on the Grange estate with fluid efficiency. The estate labourers, farm-workers, grooms and stable lads all knew that Jamie feared no living man. Those that crossed him did so at their peril and invariably lived to regret the stupidity of so doing. His innate physicality and volatile temper conveyed a veiled message to all who crossed his path that it would be unwise to tread on the dark side of this man's aura. Jamie possessed an almost animal-like earthiness and self-assurance which women found attractive, and an underlying, smouldering aggression which most men thought best to avoid.

By mid-morning the first riders and horses began to assemble on the cobbled sweep fronting the entrance doors to the mansion. Stable lads and grooms made feverish last-minute adjustments, and teams of catering staff moved among the riders carrying trays laden with champagne and whiskey-punch. As noon approached, the warm southerly breeze seemed to cool as it picked up strength. Ominous black storm clouds appeared on the horizon and the first droplets of rain began falling steadily.

Seated on his bay gelding Frank stared into the distance and didn't really like what he saw. Deep down he was beginning to have a bad feeling about the worsening conditions and thought briefly about calling the whole thing off. But then he decided, *to hell with it*. He, Frank Bannon, was master of the hunt, and that meant his guests would be expecting nothing less than business as usual. He suppressed his concerns and blew one shrill blast of his horn to call the hunt to order, then nodded to Jamie, the signal to unleash the side-paddock gate and release a hundred baying bloodhounds out among the riders. Frank kicked his horse smartly, coaxing him expertly up the steps to the front entrance, then turned to face the riders.

'Reverend Fathers, ladies and gentlemen, let us observe a moments silence for Monsignor Charles Ingram to bestow his blessing on this year's event. Monsignor.'

The Monsignor swivelled in his saddle as a distant peal of thunder rumbled across the landscape. He glanced furtively in its direction as he began.

'May God bless this hunt and all who ride these lands today. May he watch over those who participate, and carry each one of us home safely to the bosom of this marvellous house. As we prepare to begin our journey, I ask Almighty God to bestow upon you his solemn blessing.'

The riders bowed their heads as the Monsignor's lips moved in silent prayer, his hand raised high in the air, tracing the sign of the cross over the assembly.

'And so,' Frank bellowed, 'without further ado, let this, the eleventh annual Grange Abbey hunt, commence!'

The riders peeled off in single file and cantered into the spreading gloom, crossing the lower pasture and kicking out towards the distant hills beyond. It would be hours before the first of them reappeared, their quest today rendered infinitely more difficult by the rain, which had once again begun to fall from the low angry sky. The main body of riders cleared the blackthorn hedge on the brow of the hill, the hounds baying hysterically as they sought to home in on the elusive scent. Frank gazed back from the front of the group across the long line of advancing riders strung out behind.

The storm was gathering pace, with peals of thunder breaking vertically overhead and rain falling in vast waves. Against this backdrop of ever-worsening conditions, Frank once again questioned the wisdom of continuing, but with the hunt now in full flow, he opted to let it run its course.

The leading riders cleared an open ditch running high with storm water, and raced across the flatlands towards the mist-shrouded woodlands beyond. A shrill blow of a bugle sounded from far out on the left, signalling confirmation that the lead hounds had picked up on the fox's scent, and now, finally, the chase was on. Horses and riders raced into the woodland, crashing through the thicket of low briars, forcing the pace, eager to stay abreast of the delirious hounds.

Adam Gilbert pulled up abruptly at the next ditch and spun round, almost unseating Rex Chalmers, his riding companion and closest friend.

'What the– 'Rex gasped, pulling desperately on the reins, his body half out of the saddle.

'There he goes!' Adam screamed, gesturing wildly down to the river on their left. Rex turned and stared into the mist just in time to see the fox break cover and race along the riverbank.

'Let's backtrack and head him off on the far side of the Grange bridge before the crafty little bastard eludes us. It's our only chance. Let's go now!'

Sharon Baird had begged Francesca Sinclair to ride with her that morning. They had been best friends forever but during the months since Sharon had started dating Adam Gilbert, the girls had gradually begun to drift apart. Francesca despised Adam for the cruel personality hidden behind his haughty arrogance and had tried in vain to convince Sharon not to become involved.

The previous autumn she had been part of a group of riders following behind Adam in a cross-county horse-trial when his filly hesitated at a stone wall and unseated him. His companions watched in dismay as he grabbed a riding-crop and began whipping the petrified animal.

'Cowardly bastard!' he had screamed. 'I'll teach you to fucking unseat me.'

The pitiable screeching of the animal seemed to provoke his temper further. He lashed out in frenzied rage, oblivious to the other riders who had begun gathering at the scene. Jamie rode in from behind and dismounted quickly.

'Swing that crop one more time and I swear I'll use it on you the same way.'

Adam turned and stared at him coldly.

'You'd do well to mind your own fucking business,' he snarled.

Jamie walked forward and snatched the crop. A fist came flying but he caught it, as if squatting a fly. Adam lost his footing and fell backwards. Jamie stared down at him.

'I've known the filly since she was a foal,' he said quietly. 'Since the day your father bought her from the yard up at the Grange. She's as good as any I've seen, so don't go blaming the filly. You lost your bottle on the approach to the wall, and she sensed it. Simple as that.'

Adam glanced at the group who had gathered, then stared at Jamie with hatred in his eyes. He stood and brushed himself off, his thin lips taut with anger.

'You think you're something special in these parts, Sinclair, but you mean fuck all to me, and you've made a damn fool of me here today.'

'You managed to do that all by yourself.'

He spat on the ground and pointed an accusing finger, his hand mimicking the shape of a gun.

'Someday I'll have my revenge, Sinclair.'

Jamie stared him down.

'Have it now, you fucking weasel.'

But Gilbert made no move and Jamie turned and walked away. Suddenly the crack of a gunshot filled the air and Jamie spun round. Gilbert stood facing him, a pistol dangling from his right hand, his face contorted in a self-satisfied sneer, the filly dead on the ground beside him.

'Go on and say what have you have to say, Sinclair.'

Jamie regarded him with such disgust that Gilbert took an involuntary step backwards.

'To you I've got nothing to say,' Jamie responded. 'But to these others who bear witness to your brutality I say, between your life and the filly's life, the best life is gone.'

Jamie stood and watched silently as Adam Gilbert turned and strode away. His father Colonel Nigel Gilbert, a popular and highly-regarded former English army officer, lived up on the old Priory estate, an Edwardian mansion on six hundred acres of prime stud land. For as far back as anyone could remember, the Colonel, a long-time widower, had lived there with Adam, his only child, upon whom he showered everything a son could ever want. In contrast to his quietly spoken, mild-mannered father, Adam had a menacing, surly disposition, which had brought him to the attention of most police constabularies across the southern counties. The locals regarded him as an unsavory buffoon, to be treated with caution, or best avoided.

Seamus Ellis, a senior course-steward, watched Gilbert in a party of four riders break from the hunt and swing south along the river. He cantered up to Frank's position on the crest of the hill, shouting to make himself heard above the howling wind.

'Mister Bannon, I've just seen Adam Gilbert lead a group of riders along the river. They must know it's off-limits and yet they're already halfway down the slope.'

Frank gazed down angrily and cursed under his breath.

'There's not a lot we can do Seamus. Kick out along the brow and monitor their progress. Wave them back if you get the chance.'

Paul cantered in beside his brother.

'What's the problem, Frank? Why are you guys all backed-up?'

'It's Gilbert's group. They've broken down the slope towards the river, which they were warned not to do.'

Frank turned to the steward.

'OK Seamus, get to it.'

The steward pointed into the distance.

'Sir, I think you should know I spotted that young lass Francesca Sinclair, the foreman's sister, riding with Master Gilbert's party.'

From his position high on the crest of the hill Frank had a clear view all the way to the river. He watched Gilbert and his companions gallop off the slope on a course close to the edge of the bank.

'Crazy bastard,' he muttered. 'What's he thinking!'

Frank's party of riders followed their progress as they cantered in the sticky mud along the water's edge. And as they watched, they saw Gilbert inexplicably fall back from the main body of riders until the gelding carrying Francesca Sinclair, the last horse in the group, drew level. He galloped beside her stride for stride, then suddenly barged into her, forcing her onto the sheer edge of the bank. She struggled desperately to hold her position, but Gilbert raised his crop and struck out at her, causing her to lose her equilibrium and disengage her stirrups. From the hilltop Frank watched in trepidation as Francesca momentarily lost control and clung desperately to the reins. Suddenly Gilbert cut in front of her, blocking her momentum, and lashed out repeatedly at horse and rider, until finally the animal began to topple towards the edge.

'What's the madman doing?' Frank gasped as suddenly the horse collapsed on the muddy slope and catapulted Francesca into the full flow of the current. Gilbert pulled left, then raced from the bank and kicked out in pursuit of his companions, who had ridden ahead and were no longer visible. He snatched a furtive glance over his shoulder, then disappeared into the rainy gloom.

5

Scarcely able to comprehend what they had seen, the twenty riders on the hill, led by Frank, set off down the valley towards the river's edge. Paul kicked his three-year-old horse Ricochet into full gallop, and soon drew neck and neck with his brother, easing past him as the powerful stallion charged across the sodden terrain.

'Go, Ricky, go!' he commanded urgently.

Sensing the alarm in his young master's voice, the stallion raced out fearlessly, covering the treacherous terrain with lightning speed. The Liffey, swollen high from the deluge, thundered through the meadow, its heaving waters coursing relentlessly downstream. Paul galloped on a precarious line close to the edge of the flow, acutely aware that Francesca was somewhere out in those waters, and that each passing minute diminished whatever marginal chance of survival she still might have.

From the back of his charging mount he scanned the water feverishly, straining towards the far bank for the faintest hint of movement. He glanced back to the chasing group and could barely make out their shapes as they advanced through the blizzard.

'Good boy, Ricky, good boy,' he whispered in the stallion's ear when he realised how much ground he had made on this most formidable of all the horses on the Grange Estate. By now word had spread through the hunt that there was someone in the water, and gradually the main body of riders abandoned the pursuit of the fox and turned about, then fanned out across the crest of the hill to witness the dramatic chase unfolding before them.

Paul gradually began to realise that the speed of the current was running at a similar pace to his, making any attempt to outrun the flow impossible. Ahead in the distance he saw the outline of the Grange driveway snaking across the open fields towards the mansion, and then the shape of the lake bridge looming in the mist. He stared ahead at the bridge and the rudiments of a different plan began to formulate in his mind.

Then, in an instant he knew what he needed to do, and he galloped onwards through the storm until the grey ghostly span of the bridge materialised, the swollen waters sluicing through its five arches.

'This way, Ricky! This way, boy!' he commanded, slowing marginally to turn from the riverbank, then clattering loudly onto the Grange bridge. The stallion's hoofs sparked on the sodden cobbles, but he miraculously maintained his footing and raced out into the open fields beyond. The chasing pack pulled up in disarray, bemused as to why Paul had broken for the far bank.

Frank stared across the empty bridge into the darkness beyond, then waved his riders forward, opting instead to continue along the mansion side of the river. Paul stood on the stirrups and felt the stallion's heat rising, the steam billowing off its chest, the froth foaming beneath the saddle. And yet the animal showed no sign of fatigue, no hint of nervousness as he galloped into the pitch-black night.

Earlier he had realised that the only prospect of outrunning the flow was to cut a swathe across the pasture, and rejoin the river as it coursed down the far side on its eventual journey to Dublin bay and the ocean beyond. He sat rigid in the saddle, consigning his trust and his life to the care of the stallion beneath him, until finally, somewhere in the distance, he heard the unmistakable sound of crashing water. He swept across the grassland and then suddenly the stallion hesitated and pulled up yards from the river's edge. He stared into the swirling black water, then jumped from the saddle and scanned the current as it raced downstream, his mind pondering how a life, human or animal, could survive any length of time in these fearful conditions. Throwing his coat to one side, he kicked off his boots and focused on the foaming surface of the river. He stood immobile and watched the water flow muddy and fast as the seconds became minutes and the night became darker. He inhaled long deep gulps of cold air and forced himself to concentrate, conscious deep down that if he didn't stay calm and alert, then all hope of rescuing Francesca Sinclair would be lost.

It was then that he sensed a movement in the upstream flow. He stared out into the heart of the current and in an instant he caught sight of it again, a streak of golden hair trailing through the water, a split-second slash of brightness in the heart of the speeding river.

He sprinted along the bank, forcing his mind to concentrate on what he knew he was about to do next, aware that the timing of this move would need to perfect: there would be no second chance. Running at full stride, his lungs straining for air, he sprang from the river's edge and plunged headlong into the flow.

Nothing could have prepared him for the numbing, deadening shock of the freezing black water. He was somersaulted through its icy depths, the power of the surge forcing mouthfuls of liquid black mud into his lungs. The current hit him sideways, dragging him down through the swirl, then tossed him back onto the surface in the centre of the flow. Up ahead he saw a cascading ribbon of gold disappearing into the depths.

Aware that his own survival, and Francesca's life, depended on what would unfold during the next vital minutes, he held himself in the water and swam with the current, trashing wildly, counting down the seconds until he sensed he was in the zone, beside where she must be if his sighting was correct. Earlier, on the riverbank he had tried to estimate the speed of the flow and concluded that it must be running close to thirty miles an hour. When he first broke the surface he guessed he was several yards behind his target, possibly four minutes in these appalling conditions.

Suddenly there it was, barely in front of him, a golden mane of hair shimmering tantalisingly below the surface. He swam beneath a dark lifeless shape suspended in the water, then surged forward and enveloped her in his arms, enmeshing his fingers in the strands of her hair. He gazed briefly at the cold white face of Francesca, then turned on his back and projected her listless frame in the waters above him.

The current spun him effortlessly, its pace and power defying him to extricate himself from his precarious position. He lay in the water, feeling at once exhilarated, then disconsolate, then drowsy, then when he felt himself slipping beneath the surface, drawing on some inner strength to propel him back to the top. As mile upon mile he fought the river, time became meaningless and distance became impossible to comprehend.

In the end it was the soft brush of leaves that first surprised him, then jolted him out of a numbing, deadening fatigue as he floated into the calmer waters of the river's edge. He swam closer to the side until he felt the thump of wet mud on his shoulders, then in one last exhausting scramble he propelled her to the safety of the bank.

Paul lay her on the grass and placed his ear to her mouth but could detect no sign of life. He pressed her lungs, then held her nose and breathed into her mouth, repeating the process again and again, but she lay there dead to the world. Her skin was white and cold, her lips puckered and devoid of life, and yet he persevered in desperation, straining to breathe life into her lifeless body. The rains tore down remorselessly, drenching them to the bone, and still he pressed his mouth against hers, but Francesca just lay there, still. Finally, hot tears of frustration fell from his eyes, rolling down his cheeks onto her face.

He gazed at her motionless body and screamed, 'Wake up, Francesca! Wake fucking up!'

It was then, when he closed his eyes and tilted his head to the sky, that he imagined he heard the faint sound of a cough. He looked to where she lay before him, wondering could it have been real. His body rigid, his eyes wide, he watched her lips part and spit a mouthful of water. He gazed at her in disbelief.

'Francesca,' he whispered in her ear, 'stay a while longer . . . it's time to go home.'

He gathered her in his arms and walked slowly through the trees away from the river.

6

Simon watched the skies darken and shivered in the pouring rain. He sighed in exasperation and swore under his breath. The elements were mercilessly compounding his sense of bewilderment and abject misery. The search for Francesca Sinclair seemed interminable and beyond futile. Almost three hours had elapsed since her body had been subsumed by the river. Earlier, following a fearsome burst of thunder, his skittish horse had unseated him and raced panic-stricken towards the river, leaving its hapless rider spreadeagled in the sodden terrain. He gagged at the vision of the animal plunging into the swollen waters, his greatest nightmare bar none. The realisation of how precariously close he had come to that very fate had he somehow remained on board, made him spew his guts up.

He sat with his back to a large tree-trunk and massaged his throbbing hip, the left side of his body having taken the brunt of the fall, and yet still, he was here in this place, miserable but alive.

Earlier he had witnessed his chivalrous sibling's daredevil gallop along the riverbank to try and save the life of Francesca. Hours had passed since then, with the two of them still unaccounted for, both most likely swallowed in the depths of the flow. It made him sick in the pit of his stomach to ponder their watery fate. He'd always fancied the cold, unapproachable bitch – fancied breaking her in the way his brother tamed the fieriest horses on the estate.

And yet as he lay there in the rancid smell of his own puke he could hardly believe what he was now seeing. His heart missed a beat. A shard of lightning lit the sky, and he gazed at the trance-like silhouette of his brother clutching a lifeless shape in his outstretched arms. The apparition passed in front of his eyes and seemed suddenly to disappear. He remained rooted to the spot until the skies lit up again, but there was nothing to be seen. The ghostly vision had evaporated in the night.

He rose shakily and glanced wistfully towards the distant lights of the mansion. He had pondered returning there earlier to the luxury and warmth of its fires, and the myriad aromas of hot food filtering up from the kitchens, but hesitated in the end knowing that too early a return would be frowned upon in these tragic circumstances. He pushed through the brambles and stumbled to the place where he had seen the eerie spectacle, then stared in disbelief at his brother's lifeless body, the frozen face of Francesca Sinclair half-hidden in the nape of his arm.

He struggled to make sense of it, not knowing if they were dead or alive, wondering how they could ever have disentangled themselves from the ferocity of the flow. And now all of a sudden his mind was racing.

Could there be an opportunity to capitalise on this fateful circumstance, and demonstrate to the world that it had misconstrued his mettle, and that he, Simon Bannon, was the equal of the rest of them?

He knelt on the grass and painstakingly disentangled her from his brother's embrace, watching for the hint of a movement, but seeing none from either. He eased her slowly away, then lifted her in his arms and walked out of the woodlands.

Only then did he begin to notice the frantic activity: riders with lanterns skirting the riverbank on either side, and up at the mansion the swirling blue strobes of police cars and ambulances parked along the entrance. A Land Rover cruised the driveway in his direction, its twin roof-mounted searchlights scanning the terrain. A beam traced across his face, then disappeared, then swung back instantly, blinding him with its power. He heard the growl of the engine as the vehicle gathered pace and crunched to a halt in front of him. He saw Jamie and his foreman Tim Davies jump onto the driveway and gaze in astonishment at the sight before their eyes.

'Is she alive?' Jamie whispered.

Simon nodded. 'I can't be sure, but if she is, then only just.'

When Simon appeared to falter, Jamie surged forward and

steadied him. He gathered his sister in his huge arms, then turned to him.

'I can never repay you for this.'

'There's nothing to repay,' Simon said quietly. 'All of us would have done the same.'

Jamie stared at him and nodded slowly.

'They still haven't found Paul.'

'Then I must continue the search.'

'Are you crazy!'

He nodded to the foreman.

'Get him in the car. He's done enough.'

★

At midnight a flare lit the sky. An ambulance sped to the spot where Paul's body lay partially hidden in the long wet grass. The news that he was unconscious but still breathing lifted the pall of gloom that had descended on the day. Jamie ran through the long grass and saw Frank climb in the ambulance.

'How is he?' he shouted.

'He's alive but I just can't figure it. The stallion must have thrown him.'

The doors slammed closed and the ambulance accelerated into the night. If Frank had looked back, he might have caught the bewildered expression on Jamie's face.

7

In the dead hours of the morning Simon walked along the corridor to Paul's bedroom and opened the door quietly. He switched on a lamp and made his way silently towards the bed, hearing only the sound of his brother's deep breathing. He sat on the edge of the bed and shook him gently.

'Wake up,' he whispered. 'We need to talk.'

He stirred but lay still in the depths of sleep. Simon shook him again, harder this time.

'Wake up, I must speak with you.'

Earlier Doctor Rupert Kearns, the family physician, concluded that the boy had come through his ordeal relatively unscathed. His temperature had risen sharply and Kearns prescribed a course of penicillin to be repeated every four hours. He left instructions to be contacted in the event of any change in condition.

He turned slowly in the bed, trying to shake off the drug-induced sleep, then stared at his brother.

'What is it?' he asked, speaking in low tones. Beads of perspiration covered his brow and his throat felt like fire. He stared at his brother, a feeling of dread building in the pit of his stomach. Instinctively he began climbing from the bed.

'It's Francesca! Something's happened!'

Simon placed a hand on his shoulder and eased him back on the pillow.

'Relax. This is not about her, or at least not in the way you think. Francesca's fine. Her doctors say she'll make a full recovery.'

Simon stared into his eyes and a wry smile crossed his lips.

'Congratulations, little brother. It seems you saved her life.'

He wiped the sweat from his brow and turned on the pillow. He was beginning to feel feverishly hot.

'Why are you here, Simon?' he whispered, but there was no response.

He struggled to focus in the gloomy light.

'Why are you acting so . . . strangely?'

Simon's smile evaporated. His tone sounded ominous.

'Francesca will never know you saved her.'

He stared mystified at his brother.

'But you're telling me she's fine . . . '

'She's traumatised,' he snapped impatiently, 'but otherwise OK.'

He lay back on the pillow and closed his eyes.

'Francesca will know I saved her . . . '

Simon's face was so close he could smell the alcohol on his breath.

'When Francesca wakes up she'll be told that it was I who saved her. She and those other morons will believe that Simon Bannon dived into that evil fucking river and plucked her from the jaws of death. That's what I came to tell you.'

He struggled to comprehend the words he was hearing. There was a self-satisfied leer on his brother's rheumy face. His foul-smelling breath was beginning to make him nauseous.

'What is it with you and this rambling bullshit. You must be drunk – I can smell it.'

He twisted away but Simon grabbed his shoulder and pinned him to the bed.

'You'd do well to shut up and listen carefully this time. Yeah I've had a few drinks, but I'm a helluva long way from being drunk. Things have moved on since you walked out of the river with Francesca. While you've been sleeping off the effects of your ordeal, I've worked hard to brainwash the rest of these idiots into thinking it was me who saved her.'

Wondering if he was imagining all of this, or hallucinating, he sat up slowly in the bed and tried to focus.

'Tell me what's going on, Simon, because none of this is making sense.'

Simon leaned forward and whispered in his ear, 'It's all quite simple really. I want Francesca to believe that it was me who saved her, because I intend to marry her. Simple as that.'

His words struck like a dagger to the heart. He struggled from the pillow but Simon pushed him down roughly.

'I plan to snare the cocky bitch and there's nothing you can do about it. Everyone is onside. Your participation is an academic, incidental, unimportant piece of the jigsaw.'

Paul stared in bewilderment at his brother.

'Are you out of your mind thinking you'll get away with this . . . madness?'

Simon's anger boiled beneath the surface.

'You just will not listen,' he seethed. 'I'm telling you it's done. There's nothing more to say.'

With a growing sense of dread and disbelief, he struggled to absorb this tissue of lies his brother had seemingly concocted to try and dupe Francesca into marrying him. It sounded preposterous and beyond surreal.

Simon had only recently joined the Irish subsidiary of the family business straight from leaving Saint John the Baptist. Paul had never been able to penetrate the cold shell of his elder brother's brooding exterior. Their four-year age gap didn't fully explain it, because he had always felt closer to Frank, the eldest of them all by five years.

Frank's popularity was contagious, and what he may have lacked in academic achievement paled beside his exploits on the rugby fields of John the Baptist. Simon's dislike of sport had set him apart from the others, and Frank and Paul had invariably gravitated towards one another. Paul idolised his popular elder brother and was determined to emulate his accomplishments on the playing fields of Saint John's.

In truth he had never given much consideration to his relationship with Simon, or the lack of it, and yet now for the first time it was beginning to dawn on him how little he really knew about his aloof, sullen older brother. In reality he now realised he didn't really know him at all. The draining fatigue and light-headedness he was feeling made him wonder if it was all just a bad dream, and yet the more he tried to grapple with the implications of this inexplicable deceit, the more he found himself overcome with a profound sense of disgust and nausea.

'I'll never be a part of this sick charade,' he replied weakly.

'I can't believe you intend to dupe Francesca into marrying you with this nauseating tissue of lies, and think you'll actually get away with it. If you really do want to marry her, then go and ask her straight out. She'll never believe you, and even if the rest of them do, you'll never get Jamie to agree to this.'

Paul saw the same thin smile cross Simon's lips.

'Don't be naive. The dogs on the street know Francesca Sinclair would never accept an offer of marriage from me. Christ, even I know that. But this family is rich, and rich people behave differently. If we want something, we don't ask. We just take it by whatever means at our disposal, and that's all that's going on here. Rich people doing what rich people do best, getting what rich people want. You just need to get used to it. Oh, and by the way, Jamie's already taken care of. Didn't take a lot of persuading in the end. Your old pal Jamie's no different from the rest of them.'

Paul stared at his brother disdainfully.

'It shames me to have you as a brother, you sick bastard.'

Simon's smile disappeared and his mood darkened. He stared down with hatred in his eyes.

'You know I've always despised you,' he said through clenched teeth, his voice raspy and tense. 'Your physicality, your personality, your popularity, your . . . fearlessness. I could quite easily . . . kill you.'

Suddenly he snatched a pillow and covered his brother's face, pressing downwards with all of his fourteen-stone bulk. It was impromptu, it was unexpected, and there was no escape. Simon's weight was so all-encompassing that Paul could scarcely breathe, and found it impossible to disentangle from the suffocating darkness. He lay there convulsing, his system closing down, his senses beginning to black out, until suddenly, unexpectedly, the pillow was lifted and he gulped air into his burning lungs. When he opened his eyes, his brother was staring at him venomously.

'But then why should I kill you? Better to let you live in the knowledge that every night you'll lie in your bed knowing that I'm the one who's fucking her.'

He stood and stared down at his brother, his face half-hidden in the shady gloom.

'Sleep, little brother, and shake off this ordeal, and when you wake, pretend it was just a bad dream where some of the facts got muddled along the way, and in the end it all worked out fine.'

Simon switched off the lamp and walked silently from the room, leaving Paul to grapple with the implications of his brother's strange nocturnal visit.

8

That night Paul's temperature rose to one hundred and four and Doctor Kearns was summoned to the Grange again, where, following a cursory examination, he quickly diagnosed the onset of pneumonia. For nine days and nights the fever racked his body, and a team of nurses from the Kildare county hospital tended to him on a round-the-clock basis. The doctors concluded that the severity of the symptoms were consistent with a prolonged drenching and a weakened immune system resulting from extreme exposure to the elements. At times he lay so still, and his breathing was so shallow that the nurses feared his body would succumb to fever. And yet he held on miraculously through the days and nights in his darkened bedroom, wavering between life and death as all around him the family collectively held its breath and prayed for his survival.

Early on the morning of the tenth day the day-nurse walked in to find the curtains drawn back and the room flooded with light. When he emerged from the bathroom in a dressing gown she stared at him open-mouthed.

'I can't believe it is . . . you,' she whispered.

'Yes it's me,' he smiled. 'I promise.'

'What a shock to find you out of bed. You startled me. I thought I'd seen a ghost!'

He was conscious of her staring at his thin, frail body.

'I looked in the mirror a moment ago and I was *sure* I'd seen a ghost!'.

When news broke of his illness, his parents departed their villa on Cap Ferrat and flew out of Nice to Charles de Gaulle airport, then to London and across to Ireland to be at their son's bedside. They remained at the Grange during the ordeal, and when the fever finally broke they were the first to be summoned to his room. The relief that swept over them was tempered by a sense of shock at how frail he had become in such a short period. His mother hugged him warmly.

'How wonderful to have my little son back,' she sighed. 'My poor, emaciated boy, you must be so weak. At times we thought you'd never make it through those dark, desperate days . . . '

Her voice faltered and she cried openly, the smile of joy on her face mirroring the wave of relief washing over her. His father took him in his arms and embraced him.

'Last week when you were at your lowest, and the parish priest came and administered last rites . . . it was as bad as it gets. I feared we'd reached the end but you kept clinging on to the thread of life, as I always knew you would.'

He stared at his mother and father, mystified.

'I swear to God I never had a clue.'

His mother kissed his cheek and smiled.

'All that matters is, you've come back to us.'

His father stood and appraised him contemplatively.

'Lady Luck was at your side, and let's hope it always stays that way. She's one hell of a fickle lady.'

'Oh would you listen to him,' his mother laughed. 'Your father truly believes there are some who are born lucky, and who knows, perhaps he's right. We're just thrilled you made it through, my darling.'

'It feels like I've been gone for such a long time,' he replied quietly. 'I can barely remember the . . . river.'

His mother reached out and took him by the hand.

'And this the second bit of good fortune in as many days,' she smiled. 'Darling, you couldn't have heard the news about Francesca. While you lay in this darkened room, the poor girl survived her catastrophe in the river and now, this very morning, her doctors have discharged her. Isn't it the best news?'

Paul gazed at his mother and felt a shudder in his bones at the mention of her name. He didn't need anyone to tell him that Francesca had come through her ordeal in the river. He had practically lost his life in the act of saving her. When, moments later, he watched his parents leave the room, his thoughts strayed back to that surreal nocturnal encounter with Simon. He lay back and pondered the possibility that his brother's preposterous ramblings were nothing more or less than the rantings of a drunk or desperate man. But then the door opened and his thoughts were interrupted by a smiling young nurse pushing a breakfast trolley.

'Let me prepare this for you', she offered. 'You must be so hungry.'

9

Of the four thousand construction workers on the payroll of the Bannon Group in England, John Considine was the man the others feared the most. His reputation went all the way back to those early days, when in the aftermath of the Second World War he organised the Bannon labour gangs in London initially, then across the southern counties of England, and then nationwide.

The Bannons regarded him as a fourth brother, an indispensable component in their ruthless drive for national dominance. Those on the inside knew that among the three brothers 'Big John' had always been closest to James, and in the early post-war years the two men were never far from one another's side.

Across all levels of the operation James was recognised as indisputably the boss at Bannons, his majority sixty-percent stockholding conferring on him outright authority over his brothers, Matthew and Charles. They shared the remaining balance of stock in equal measure. Nobody in the Bannon outfit, including the brothers ever doubted who really ran the show. Newcomers joining the company for the first time soon learned that if you wanted to move on and work your way through the ranks, then it was wise to remember that the buck always stopped with James.

On the rare occasion when some ill-informed or naive individual, or maverick competitor, sought to show slight or disrespect to James, the inevitable follow-up visit from Big John seemed always to resolve such matters.

Late one afternoon in the run-up to Christmas on a snowy December day in 1946, John Considine's London-born wife Diane and his two-year-old daughter Judy were killed in a hit-and-run car accident on the Earls Court Road. From that day the giant facilitator chose to remain a single man and channel all his energies into the Bannons' nationwide expansion surge.

Six feet in height and weighing nineteen stone, the hardest men in the hardest industry mostly thought it prudent to give Big John a wide berth, and that suited Big John just fine. He was by any measure a formidable man, his steel grey hair cut tight, his eyes narrow and piercing, his demeanour on the cold side of unfriendly. Known as a man of few words, when he did decide to speak in those deep gravelly Connemara tones, people mostly concluded that the healthier option was to pay careful attention, then follow instructions to the letter.

An eyewitness to the incident came forward and identified a blue or possibly black Ford saloon carrying three male passengers that had sped from the scene on that dark December evening.

The witness, an ex-army officer, was able to provide the Metropolitan Police with the first three digits of the registration number, and commented that the car appeared to be driving erratically. In his sworn statement, he said he believed the driver was either drunk or had been drinking heavily. Four months later the police tracked down the vehicle and apprehended the owner whom they identified as Harold George Whitfield, a small-time criminal and member of a South London gang with underworld connections. The police were surprised to find that he was still driving the same car, with indentations to the front quarter-panel indicative of an impact matching the one witnessed the previous December. No attempt had been made to disguise or repair the damage.

When Whitfield appeared in court the following January, he claimed he hadn't been driving the car that particular night. He stated that the car was regularly used by other associates and members of his group, and he also produced a witness who swore that they were together in a house in Stepney on the night in question, drinking and playing cards.

Under cross-examination the retired army officer who witnessed the incident stated that he couldn't positively identify Whitfield as the person driving the car that evening, owing to the fact that the car had been travelling away from his line of sight. When the judge excused the witness, Whitfield smirked and stared defiantly towards the back of the courtroom, to where John Considine had been sitting quietly during the proceedings.

Despite forensic evidence linking the damage on the car to an impact which would likely have been caused by a collision with two pedestrians, the judge dismissed the case that afternoon based on lack of clear evidence. Whitfield left the court laughing and joking and set off with a group of friends to celebrate in the Britannia, a pub across from the law courts.

Two nights later in the early hours of Sunday morning, Roger Denham, the bar-manager of the Britannia, unbolted the rear door and walked to the dumpster in the far corner with two sacks of rubbish, the remnants of a busy Saturday night. He was the last man on the premises, the rest of his seven bar staff having departed minutes earlier. The day's takings had been locked in the safe. The floors had been swept and washed, and this was the last task remaining before Roger retired to his small flat upstairs for a well-earned rest. He was a strong, fit man and he threw the two heavy sacks across the top of the dumpster effortlessly, then turned back to the bar. It was then that he stumbled in the dark and lost his footing. He pulled himself up along the edge of the dumpster and glanced around to see what had caused the problem.

'Holy fuck!' he gasped, as he stared at the half-hidden body of a man at his feet. He ran to the kitchen and hit the switch, flooding the yard with light, then walked back slowly and gazed down at the lifeless apparition staring up at him.

What he saw made him spin sideways and throw up. He spat on the ground and wiped his mouth on the sleeve of his shirt before taking a second look at the grim spectacle. The man's throat had been slit from ear to ear, leaving the head lolling hideously to one side. Roger stared into startled eyes, taut anguished lips snarled back from the teeth in a final agonised death-grimace. He had seen that same look on the odd occasion during the war, and it made him conclude that he was staring into the face of a man who knew what was about to happen to him. The murderer must have tortured his victim, then kept him sufficiently alive to experience the ultimate savagery of the knife slicing through his windpipe.

Roger ran to the bar, dropped some coins in the public telephone and dialled an unlisted number at Scotland Yard. The telephone answered after one ring.

'Dave Richards.'

'Dave, it's Roger. Am I glad I caught you!'

'The Old Bill never sleeps Roger. They don't pay us enough for such luxury. Still, you're lucky you got me. I was about to call it a day.'

'You ain't going home yet Dave. You need to get over here right away. I just stumbled on a stiff lying outside my back door.'

'Another silly bugger you've been plying with too much drink Roger. Gimme a bell if he's still there in the morning. Otherwise . . . '

'Dave, this guy ain't going nowhere, not now; not ever, and definitely not with a gash across his throat wider than the Suez Canal.'

Dave Richards sighed.

'Roger, if this is a wind-up . . . '

'Dave, please, will you listen. The guy wasn't just killed. He was fucking slaughtered. It's like an abattoir out there. You need to get over here right away.'

The detective picked up on the palpable tension in his friend's voice.

'OK, calm down, I'm on my way right now. Don't leave until we get there.'

Roger replaced the receiver.

'I ain't going nowhere,' he muttered.

An hour later the premises were cordoned off and a forensic team had already begun their initial examination. Roger sat in the downstairs office, drinking coffee with the two detectives. Dave introduced his partner Eddie Jenkins. The two detectives operated in the area, and sometimes frequented the pub for a few drinks before heading for the hills.

'We've identified the guy from his driver's licence,' Eddie said, sliding the photograph towards Roger. 'Name's Harry Whitfield. A local jerk, known to us, petty criminal, nobody important. Ever see him around?'

Roger examined the photograph closely, taking his time before responding.

'I can't say I know the guy. Most definitely not a regular. He's familiar though. I may be mistaken, but I've a feeling this geezer's been mooching around recently, maybe in the last week. I'm almost sure . . . '

Dave Richards was on full alert.

'Roger, this could be important,' he said calmly. 'Take your time. Think carefully.'

He picked up the photograph and examined it, then nodded slowly.

'Dave, I've seen him. After a while you remember everything about this place. We get a lot of once-off punters breezing in from the courthouse down the road.'

'Think, Roger. Think!'

He glanced at the photo one last time, then clicked his finger.

'Dave, I've got it. He was in with a group of three or four others these past few days, last Thursday, mid-afternoon. I'm sure of it. They were noisy bastards, drank a lot, stayed maybe two, three hours, all in high spirits. If you're asking me to best-guess it, I'd say, judging by the time of day, that these guys were celebrating a good result in the courts.'

In the early hours of Monday, Dave Richards and a team of detectives began working the case, knowing that the best chance of a breakthrough would be in the immediate aftermath of the murder. A window of opportunity was likely to extend out over the following thirty-six hours.

After that, based on past experience, solving crimes, especially crimes involving murder, tended to prove infinitely more difficult. Even after a week, Dave and his team knew that the trail got colder, and after a month, in most cases, you could forget it. But things began moving quickly that morning, the first real breakthrough coming just before noon.

At an earlier briefing, Junior Detective Alan Wilkins was assigned the task of visiting the Court Registrar's office to check the listings for the previous Thursday in an effort to establish a link between the victim, Harry Whitfield, and the proceedings in which he had been involved during the three days ending that

Thursday. Dave Richards ordered Detective Wilkins and all the other detectives to report anything of interest directly to him.

'It doesn't matter how insignificant or stupid it may seem to you guys at the time,' he advised them during the briefing. 'I'll be the ultimate arbiter as to whether something is important or not. Now get going, guys. The clock's running.'

At midday Detective Wilkins knocked on his boss's half-open door. Richards was on the telephone but waved him through and pointed to a seat. He finished his call and stared at the eager young detective.

'What have you got, Alan?'

'Sir, a case against Harry Whitfield was dismissed due to lack of evidence last Thursday following a full three-day hearing. Last Christmas a car owned by Whitfield was involved in a hit-and-run on the Earls Court Road. The driver killed two pedestrians, a mother and her three-year-old daughter, and then fled the scene. Several witnesses gave evidence that the car, a blue Ford saloon, mounted the footpath at speed and took off erratically. The two pedestrians never stood a chance. They were confirmed dead on arrival at Fulham Hospital. There were four adults in the car but it was a dark, wet evening, and none of the witnesses could identify Whitfield as the driver. It took a good few months to piece the whole thing together and link the accident back to Whitfield. He was arrested and charged with manslaughter and abandoning the scene of a crime.

'Like I said earlier, sir, the judge dismissed the case last Thursday. Seems he really had no option. Whitfield produced a water-tight alibi, a witness who swore on the Bible that they were together all evening, which, combined with a failure to positively identify the driver, left the judge with little choice but to dismiss. And that's about all I've got sir.'

'Together all evening? Doing exactly what, detective?'

Wilkins checked his notes.

'Drinking and playing cards, sir.'

Whitfield stared at him thoughtfully.

'Did you speak to the investigating officer?'

'Caught up with him an hour ago, sir. A Detective Sergeant Paul Prior, says he knows you.'

'Yeah, I know Paul Prior. He's a good man. So what's he saying?'

'Off the record sir, Detective Prior believes Whitfield is guilty as hell. He maintains that a few of the locals at the Rose and Crown in Hackney actually heard Whitfield boasting on the night of the acquittal about how easy it is to get away with murder these days.'

Dave Richards sat back in his chair and whistled softly.

'Fucking hell, Alan, you've done really well. So where's it all leading?'

'This is where it begins to get interesting sir. Detective Prior says that throughout the proceedings the husband sat in the back of the courtroom, an Irish guy, name of Considine, and just stared Whitfield down during the entire period he was in the witness box.'

'That ain't unusual. I'd expect most guys in his position to do the same.'

'I agree, sir. But Detective Prior says that there was something different about this guy Considine.'

'Alan, the suspense is fucking killing me. In what way different?'

'Detective Prior is of the opinion that Considine didn't seem concerned if Whitfield was proven innocent or guilty. The detective swears the guy had already made his mind up on the verdict.'

Dave stared at the young detective.

'I've always regarded Paul Prior as a first-rate police officer, but a fucking mind-reader. I reckon I'll pass on that one.'

'Sir, I asked him about it and he replied that he'd trust his instincts all day on this one. He also said that sometimes when you look at someone, an inner sense tells you that that person is capable of killing another human being. Detective Prior reckons this Considine guy ticks all the boxes on that score. The detective said he was sure you'd know what he meant by this.'

Dave Richards didn't respond immediately. He put his feet up on the desk, lit a cigarette, threw the packet to Wilkins, blew the smoke skywards and stared thoughtfully into space.

He knew what Paul Prior meant all right. Prior was ex-murder squad, and would have known from years of working homicides that a high proportion of murders are committed by blundering amateurs acting in the heat of the moment. Dave Richards also knew that his street-wise colleague wasn't contemplating your average amateur here. Paul Prior was referring to a different type of killer. The sort of man who could take another man down without breaking a sweat; a man who placed little value on life, and less on the consequences of his actions.

Based on what he was hearing, he was guessing Considine had probably decided to take the law into his own hands, maybe because he lacked faith in the ability of the courts to ensure that justice would be served. Dave turned his attention back to Wilkins, who was sitting quietly.

'Detective, bring Considine in as soon as possible. Arrest him, detain him and charge him. Move now, without delay and don't go half-cocked. Make sure you've got the appropriate backup. No mistakes. That's it. Get going.'

Wilkins stood, but seemed to hesitate.

'Sir?'

'Yeah. What?'

'Sir, the anniversary of his wife and daughter's funeral is tomorrow. Shouldn't we wait until –'

'Alan, go and arrest him now and stop fucking about.'

Two hours later John Considine was detained at his home near Wandsworth Common and taken by car to Shepherd's Bush police station, where he was placed in a holding cell. He offered no resistance when the police arrived at his door, and following the reading of the arrest warrant, he agreed to accompany them voluntarily. He remained in his cell for four hours until finally the door was unlocked and a uniformed officer led him to a windowless interview room on a lower level.

Dave Richards and his partner, Bob Diamond, a senior detective and war-veteran with thirty years' experience in the armed forces and the Metropolitan Police, studied Considine through the observation panel.

'Dave, is this guy on our radar?'

'Not a crumb. No track record in the system. We've searched everywhere.'

Richards turned and stared thoughtfully at Considine.

'What is it about this guy? If you asked me to second-guess him, I'd say he's just another hard case, too tough to be intimidated. Pretty fucking calm for a guy who recently lost his wife and kid and then gets dragged down here on a murder rap. Let's get in there before he falls asleep.'

The detectives entered the interview room and sat on the two vacant chairs on the opposite side of the table to Considine. Considine remained motionless, fingers entwined, hands resting on the table. Dave Richards introduced himself and Bob Diamond.

'Please confirm your name,' Dave Richards said brusquely.

Considine slowly raised his eyes from the desk and stared at the detective.

'You already know my name detective,' he said in a calm, unmistakably Irish brogue, 'but for the record, it's John Joseph Considine.'

'Mr Considine, have you anything to say about the charges against you?'

Considine stared at the detective in a languid, vaguely uninterested way.

'I've given you my name detective. That's all I'm obliged to do, as I'm sure you well know.'

Just then there was a knock on the door and a police constable stuck his head in and nodded to Dave Richards.

'Sir, the duty-sergeant needs a word. Urgently.'

Richards knew that an interrogation in motion, especially one involving a murder suspect, would never be interrupted unless it was a matter of considerable importance. He walked out of the room and pulled the door behind him. He nodded to the duty officer.

'This better be fucking good, Bill.'

'Really sorry to interrupt sir, but we've got two legal eagles down the hall making a hullabaloo about your prisoner. They're insisting they get to speak with the arresting officer, or otherwise they're off to the High Court to secure an injunction. I thought it best to inform you.'

'Yeah, you did the right thing sarge.'

'Oh, and they asked me to give you this sir,' he said, handing him a business card.

Richards stared at the name. Louis J. Goldberg and Partners.

'Sarge, Goldbergs are one of the biggest law firms in the City, and this says it belongs to the man at the top. Are you telling me it's Louis fucking Goldberg that's out there?'

'I believe it is sir.'

Richards nodded to Bob Diamond and they followed the sergeant down the corridor, through the public waiting area to a small room on the far side. Two men dressed in dark tailored business suits stood staring out the window. When the door opened they both turned. Richards immediately recognised the distinguished-looking, slightly stooped older man in his late fifties from newspaper photographs as the famous City lawyer Louis Goldberg.

'Thank you for seeing us without prior appointment Detective,' Goldberg smiled as he stepped forward, 'but in the circumstances, I'm sure you'll understand the necessity for us to act quickly. As soon as we learned that our esteemed client John Considine had been arrested and detained against his will . . . '

Richards stared at the smooth Old Etonian lawyer with interest, curious to know why he hadn't delegated this to one of his four hundred or so minions.

'Detective Richards, perhaps you'd kindly explain why you've chosen to pursue this inexplicable course of action.'

Goldberg's blue eyes stared at him sharp and unblinking, his words articulated in a suave, plummy accent; cool, confident, straight to the point, the hint of a smile on his lips – a smile that was, Richards noted, devoid of any warmth. He pulled the business card from his pocket and glanced at it casually.

'Mister . . . Goldberg, we arrested your client this afternoon on suspicion of committing a murder four nights ago in south London. The victim was tortured and had his throat slit from ear to ear. Our investigation revealed that a case was brought recently by the Metropolitan Police against the victim, Harry Whitfield, for manslaughter, arising from a hit-and-run accident resulting in the deaths of your client's wife and daughter. It was dismissed four days ago. I'm sure you're aware of the circumstances surrounding that particular case Mister Goldberg, as I've no doubt that the timing of both these events and their obvious potential connection will not have been lost on you. We're satisfied that your client had sufficient motive and capability to carry out this heinous act, and that is why we're treating him as our prime suspect. We are entirely within our rights to arrest this man and interrogate him, which is precisely what we intend to do.'

Goldberg blandly stared at Richards, showing no hint of a reaction.

'And you say that this murder of which my client is accused took place four nights ago, which, if I'm calculating correctly, was sometime on Thursday evening last. Is that correct?'

Richards was beginning to get the feeling that it was he who was being interrogated, but, still curious to know where this might all be leading, he chose to answer anyway.

'Yes, that is correct. The coroner estimates the precise time of the murder to be one o'clock Friday morning.'

Goldberg's companion whispered in his ear and the lawyer nodded imperceptibly.

'Detective, please excuse us for a moment. I shall not waste a moment of your time.'

They drew aside and consulted briefly in low tones, then Goldberg turned to the detective and spoke calmly.

'Detective, I must ask that you release my client immediately. You have no basis for holding him, and no basis whatsoever for arresting him in the first place.'

Richards was taken aback, but he struggled not to show it.

'You're entitled to your opinion, Mister Goldberg, but I happen to disagree. We are within our rights to detain your client for a period of up to twenty-four hours, or longer if we procure a court order. We have reason to suspect that he is guilty of this crime, but if this turns out not to be the case, he will of course be released without charge.

'If, as we suspect occurred in this instance, an individual decides to take the law into his own hands, and we allow this to become the norm, I imagine that we as a police force will very quickly become superfluous, and society will end up in chaos. And now gentlemen, if you'll excuse us, we have a busy night ahead of us.'

Richards nodded to Bob Diamond and they turned to leave.

'Detective, before you waste your valuable time attempting to pin this charge on an innocent man, I should advise you that Mr Considine has a watertight alibi in respect of his whereabouts at the time the murder was committed. If you insist on pursuing this unwise course of action, I must respectfully inform you that you'll end up with egg on your face, not to mention the effect that the resultant collateral damage will have on what I understand so far to be a very promising career.'

Richards turned and stared at the lawyer.

'Don't threaten me, Mr Goldberg, or you might find yourself grappling with the implications of attempting to pervert the course of justice.'

Goldberg remained unflappable, the smile faintly condescending, the voice a clipped deep tone of impeccable restraint.

'I wouldn't dream of threatening you, detective. I'm a man who deals in facts, and in this case the facts speak for themselves. My client has an alibi, which will withstand the most forensic scrutiny, and I am merely pointing out that pursuing this course of action is a pointless and wasteful exercise. If you insist on detaining my client, there will undoubtedly be serious repercussions, with consequent negative impact on your career. It's as simple as that.'

Richards stared hard at this unflappable lawyer who had coldly, blatantly, nonchalantly repeated a threat to his career in the presence of witnesses. The message seemed abundantly clear: back off or expect a declaration of war. He somehow doubted Louis Goldberg indulged in idle threats.

'This alibi you speak of,' Richards responded curtly. 'Care to elaborate?'

'But of course detective. There is a witness who will swear that he was with Mr Considine at all times during the day preceding Mister Whitfield's murder, during the entire night in question, and for most of the following day. I have in my possession a sworn affidavit confirming this to be the position precisely and unequivocally. I am advised that the statement, a copy of which I am more than happy to convey to you tonight, will be sufficient to establish my client's innocence beyond doubt in any court of law.'

He opened his attaché case and handed the detective what

appeared to be a relatively thin three-or-four-page sealed document.'

Richards glanced at it briefly.

'This witness you speak of; we'll obviously need to interview him.'

'I assumed as much detective, which is why I requested him to accompany me here tonight.'

The detective struggled to rationalise the implications of what he was hearing. If an alibi did exist such as had been described, then he already knew that they were wasting their time, notwithstanding the fact that all of his instincts told him that the man who murdered Harry Whitfield was sitting in the interrogation room downstairs. Richards glanced at Bob Diamond. Then he turned to the second man, as if noticing him for the first time. He was a handsome, well-built, stocky type of guy, probably mid-forties, six three or four in height, with dark wavy hair and an air of confidence or boredom, Richards couldn't quite figure out which.

'And you are?'

'The name's James Bannon.'

'May I inquire as to what you and Mr Considine were doing during all this time together?'

The stare was steady, unblinking, icy, disconcerting. The reply, when it came, was delivered in a gravelly unflinching drawl, the coldness of which lingered in Richard's mind long into the months that followed.

'Drinking and playing cards, detective.'

Still contemplating the irony of those words, Dave Richards and Bob Diamond gazed down from the station canteen on the second floor as Louis Goldberg and James Bannon accompanied John Considine to a waiting black Mercedes Benz saloon. They watched the car speed towards the West End and disappear into the night. Richards continued staring out the window for a long time afterwards.

'Who the hell once tried to convince us you can't get away with murder?' he muttered ruefully. 'Most likely one of those idiots in training college.'

Bob Diamond lit a cigarette and inhaled deeply.

'C'mon Dave, let's go and get a drink. I reckon we need one.'

10

In the weeks following his ordeal in the river, almost out of nowhere the remnants of the fever hit him face-on, full blow. An icy wind blew in from the east and sprayed the land with sleet and snow during the whole month of November. The thousand head of charolais out on the north pasture were herded in and fed on the fodder collected from the previous summer's bumper crop. In the wake of the fever breaking, Paul crashed out, sleeping late in the days that followed, and then as the snows melted and the winds eased, his physical strength slowly began to stabilise.

On this sunny Saturday morning at Grange Abbey, he sauntered along the lower corridor and ate breakfast in the staff canteen. In two days' time he would make the return journey to Saint John the Baptist and once again bid farewell to these people who had always treated him as one of their own.

'How are you this morning, Mags?'

'The better for seeing you Master Paul.'

Maggie Pritchard had run the kitchens at Grange Abbey for as far back as he could remember. Paul loved Maggie, but Maggie Pritchard surely loved Paul Bannon like a son. For as long as she could recall, he was the only Bannon who ate with the staff, mixed with the staff, and mostly, during his parents' long absences, lived out his days with the staff.

Nobody paid particular attention when he sat alone in a corner by the window. The days had turned warm and languid, and all week the Grange had been bathed in hazy late-autumn sunshine. He gazed absentmindedly into the orchard, to the fruit trees lining the ivy-covered stone wall, blissfully unaware that someone had slipped quietly into the seat opposite.

'A penny for your thoughts.'

It was a voice he had known forever. He turned from the window and gazed into Francesca's smiling face. This girl he had known since they were children had lately begun to occupy his every waking thought. The child was no longer a child, but instead had blossomed into a smouldering beauty, so gorgeous he knew of no one else who even came remotely close. He stared into the deep green pools of her eyes.

'My thoughts?' he replied. 'Oh, nothing mysterious. You know I hate leaving this place.'

She took his hand gently in hers. Maggie Pritchard glanced across from the far side and smiled to herself.

'You'll be back again soon.'

He smiled wistfully.

'Yes, but still, I think you know what I mean.'

They sat back when Maggie came and cleared the table, staying silent until she was gone.

'It's so lovely to see you. What a surprise! I hadn't expected that.'

'I needed to meet with you. There's something I have to say.'

He felt her long cool fingers tighten, and when he looked in her eyes she averted her gaze.

'Francesca,' he whispered. 'You are so utterly . . . beautiful.'

She smiled but there was a sadness about her, a tentative, troubled look, and when she spoke, her words were like a hammer-blow to his heart.

'I'm sure you've heard that Simon saved my life.'

'Francesca – '

'Simon, the one who always seemed so fearful of the river.'

'Francesca –'

'What's happened these past few days seems . . . incomprehensible! Beyond belief!'

She looked up at him.

'He's asked me to marry him. Can you imagine? Simon Bannon and Francesca Sinclair. Who'd ever have thought?'

He stared at her, stunned by the words he was hearing. He had already decided to treat the weird encounter with his brother on that fateful night as an aberration, a figment of his own crazed imagination. He leaned towards her and spoke quietly.

'Francesca, what is this madness you're telling me? In a million years how could he ever think you'd agree to this.'

She sat for an age before replying, utterly still and silent.

'His courage is all that's being spoken of. You saw the river that day . . . '

He was staring at her with such intensity she hesitated in mid-sentence, and then, when she spoke, her words had an eerie ring.

'I accepted his proposal. I came to you hoping that you, my closest friend, would wish only the best for me. I came to you to seek your blessing.'

A feeling of dread crept over him.

'Francesca, it's a mistake – you must tell him, or let me do it for you . . . '

She drew her hand away and stared into his eyes.

'I came looking for approval and all I'm sensing is annoyance. Yes, that's it. You're annoyed with me and jealous of your brother.'

He looked at her pleadingly.

'And how could I be any other way? What do you expect of me!'

He held her hand and squeezed it, and his words came out softly.

'Do you remember the promise we made to one another when we were children? We swore we'd be together all the days of our lives, that you would wait for me and I would wait for you.'

He lifted her hand to his cheek and kissed it gently.

'Francesca, you owe Simon nothing. All of us tried to save you because we love you, not to ensnare you in a marriage contract. I swear to you I went out that night because I . . . love you.'

He sat there forlorn, searching for the words to make this nightmare disappear.

'My brother didn't save you,' he whispered. 'They're lying to you, all of them. I swear it on my life. So don't ask me for my approval. You'll never receive it.'

'Don't do this to me!' she responded angrily.

He was taken aback by her intensity, and she could see that he was distraught. He stared at her with utter sadness, not knowing what to say.

'Francesca, believe what I'm telling you . . . '

'Why should I believe you when I know what I know!'

They sat in unbearable silence, the weight of their words resting heavily on each of them.

'You mustn't allow this jealousy to consume you,' she said quietly. 'It ill behoves you. Jamie swore it happened, the others too. They saw him carry me up from the river. All of them!'

Her voice faltered.

'And yet . . . '

She hesitated as if lost to some faraway thought. He stared into her eyes, barely daring to breathe. She seemed preoccupied, troubled, unfocused, trancelike, and when her lips moved, she spoke so quietly he strained to hear.

'And yet when I lay unconscious on that fearful night, in the darkest of places, in the depths of oblivion, I imagined that somewhere out there beyond the boundaries of my subconscious I heard someone call my name, over and over.' She hesitated, and then looked into his eyes.

'I imagined it was you, Paul. I must have been hallucinating, perhaps mistakenly longing for the one voice I yearned to hear the most.'

When she pushed her chair aside there were tears in her eyes. She stood, and ran out the door.

11

He whistled and his dogs came running across the frost-covered fields at the back of the mansion. It was early dawn, and the house was silent on this chill Sunday, its rear walls dark and shadowy where the sun's rays had yet to penetrate. On this, his last morning at the Grange, he climbed the wrought-iron gate that led into the grazing fields, his two retrievers racing out ahead.

'They told me you sometimes come this way.'

He spun round and was surprised to see Jamie lounging on a moss-covered bench.

'Are you waiting for *me*, Jamie?'

He nodded. 'We need to talk a while.'

'Well, come along then; we can talk while we walk.'

'I'll say what I have to say, and I'd sooner say it here.'

Jamie's tone betrayed a hint of urgency. He pointed to the seat beside him.

'Please . . . it shouldn't take long.'

He sat and strung an arm around Jamie's shoulder.

'So tell me what's so urgent it can't wait a while,' he said, thinking that this must involve Francesca. There was a tenseness about Jamie, a silent preoccupation you didn't often see. He gazed out across the shadowy field.

'You and I have known each other a lifetime,' he began wistfully. 'Nothing's ever come between us. How I wish it could always stay that way.'

Paul glanced at him and shrugged.

'Why should anything come between us? Nothing ever will. Nothing ever should.'

'Except that what I'm about to tell you has the potential to destroy all of that.'

There was a desperation, a coiled tension in his demeanour.

'Jamie, you're my greatest friend. You're my brother. I've known you all my life, so let's do what we've always done and get this over with. Say what you've got to say and let me get walking with my two fucking dogs before the sun goes down.'

Jamie smiled at that, briefly.

'Then I guess it's best coming from me. You'll get to hear it soon enough.'

'Hear what, Jamie?'

Jamie stared into the distance.

'Simon asked Francesca to marry him.'

Jamie felt Paul's eyes upon him, but there was no warmth in the stare.

'I already know this. She told me yesterday.'

'Francesca . . . told you!'

He nodded. Jamie stood and shuffled from foot to foot.

'Did she also tell you she accepted his proposal?'

'Yes she did.'

Jamie regarded him with uncertainty.

'I'd swear she feels indebted since he rescued her from the river. It's the reason she accepted. I'm sure of it.'

'Oh really.' Paul responded bitterly. 'You ought to think about what you're saying, Jamie, because none of it is making sense.'

Jamie seemed perplexed.

'What do you mean?'

'You and the rest of them have it all wrong.'

'Wrong in what way?'

'I was the one who rescued your sister that fateful fucking night, and now I'm placing my trust in you to set the record straight, which is what I thought this was all about. I don't remember a great deal about that night, but I do remember walking away from the river carrying your sister in my arms, and after that not much else. The lights went out.'

Jamie's expression was one of bewilderment.

'This just doesn't make sense. You're telling me you saved her, and yet I saw Simon carry her up from the river – saw it with my own eyes. It's what we all saw.'

Paul stood and placed a hand on his shoulder.

'Look me in the eye, Jamie. Do you honestly believe I'd lie

about this, about your sister, to you of all people, my closest friend? Did you ever once have reason to question my integrity?'

Jamie looked disconsolate under Paul's steely stare.

'It is not what I saw, is all I'm saying.'

'And this is what you've concluded, even if I tell you it's a lie. When even the dogs on the street know Simon's scared of the water in his own bathtub. I'm asking you to set the record straight Jamie. You have to do this for me.'

Jamie looked exasperated.

'It's too late to set the record straight dammit. Your brother wasted no time on this. It was done and dusted while you lay in your bed fighting the fever'.

Paul regarded him dispassionately.

'So you allowed this thing to happen while I lay in my sick-bed wavering between life and death, and now you're saying you can't deal with it when you and I both know it's never too late to set the record straight.'

'Only this time the record is saying something different. You tell me you saved her, and Simon swears it was him, so who are we to believe? It simply has to be Simon because it's what we all saw.'

'All . . . including you, Jamie?'

'You were out of your mind that night . . . delirious.'

Paul stared silently at his lifelong friend, flabbergasted at what he was hearing. He felt nauseated by the evil manipulation his brother had so cleverly constructed, the blatant exploitation of a near-tragic set of circumstances designed to dupe the world into believing he was the one who had saved Francesca's life.

'Jamie, we must act, or we'll both of us be tainted forever by this deception. We simply have find a way to stop him.'

'Don't be naive,' Jamie replied, his tone suddenly cynical. 'Your brother seized the initiative and you haven't even reached the starting block. Frank's gifted him the Irish operation and the wherewithal to do as he pleases, at least as far as we his employees are concerned. Who am I to question the word of a man who holds sway over my future well-being? This is one dirty little mess you're just going to have to sort out yourself. The Bannons are a powerful family, and you're a part of that family, so don't try and suck in the rest of us. Sort it out between you and that nasty piece of work you call a brother.'

Paul glared angrily at Jamie.

'I resent the insinuation lurking beneath those words, Jamie. So you've decided it's a "them against us" situation, and you're aligning me and the rest of my family with Simon in this treachery. You disappoint me. I'm entitled to expect better from you. You can't just walk away from this. We have to establish the truth while we've still got time – '

'There *is* no time. The die is cast. It's already out there in the public domain. He asked her to marry him. She accepted his proposal. Simon figured it all out and he's the one calling the shots.'

He listened to Jamie's words with trepidation.

'This appointment you speak of. I can talk to Frank – '

'Don't waste your breath. Frank's yacht sailed out of Cannes ten days ago. He and his buddies are probably half-way down the Italian coast by now. God only knows where the hell they are!'

Paul was brimming with anger.

'So the die is cast, you say, I imagine mostly put in place while I lay unconscious in a darkened room, never knowing if I'd see the light of day again. You really do surprise me, Jamie, with your acute sense of self-preservation and all of that. Why don't you just admit you don't have the balls to act against Simon and do the right thing? Have you at any stage given a moment's thought as to the effect that this deception, this . . . charade may have on your sister, or is she a mere pawn in the whole dirty little business?'

'Oh no need to worry on that count,' Jamie replied, hardly bothering to conceal his annoyance. 'She could do worse you know. After all, she's marrying a Bannon. Life doesn't get much better!'

Paul could hardly believe what his greatest friend was saying.

'Your cynicism ill-becomes you, Jamie. She's marrying Simon for one reason only, because she's under the misapprehension that he saved her life, because that is what you and the rest of them have misled her into believing. Francesca's an innocent pawn at the ugly heart of this despicable game. However this eventually plays out, and I have a bad feeling about it already, every instinct tells me you'll regret this decision for ever more.'

Jamie stared coldly at his friend.

'Now I'm beginning to wonder if this has more to do with you than I originally imagined. Are you not just a little aggrieved that Simon has stolen the show and robbed you of your moment of glory? Simon Bannon, hero of the hour, lands the glittering prize. The girl whose life he saves, the most sought-after girl in the county, accepts his proposal of marriage while little brother watches helplessly in the wings. Christ, it must be upsetting for you, the one who always thought Francesca would be yours and yours alone. The best-laid plans and all of that. Ironic how deluded we can all sometimes be.'

Paul walked over and struck Jamie on the chin with a blow of such force that he shivered from the shock of the impact. He teetered a while, then fell backwards on the grass, dazed from the impact. He raised himself gingerly on one elbow and rubbed his chin with his free hand, but made no effort to rise to his feet.

'Fuck me but I surely felt that one. I taught you too well, my friend.'

Paul stared down at him, his eyes cold as ice, and when he spoke, his voice was devoid of warmth.

'Don't *ever* call me your friend. I'm no longer your friend. You're no longer my brother. You branded me a liar, and from this day on you will never be a part of my life.'

He turned and walked through the meadow gate, silhouetted in the sun's early rays, his two dogs ambling out ahead of him. Jamie lay on the dewy grass and watched his lifelong friend disappear in the misty morning light, the chill realisation dawning on him that a door had been slammed shut on a world he had known forever, and that life would never be quite the same again.

12

There was a stormy sky over the Grange that night, a noisy force-seven blow. The wind hovered around the old place, sending shivers through the roof timbers and swirling summer winds down the endless corridors. The old creaking staircase resonated its almost sad groans through the cavernous spaces of the shadowy mansion. The great chandelier hanging from the central dome seemed to strain under the weight of its decadent magnificence.

She slipped through a side-entrance down in the old south annexe, a complex maze of rooms spanning the lower mezzanine level of the mansion. The doors were never locked in this house. No strangers ever entered these idyllic grounds. Rarely did a passer-by think to cross the endless walls guarding this hidden domain.

Silently, barefooted, she ran through the kitchens and skipped along the backstairs leading to the great hallway, pausing nervously, listening for any sound, and hearing none, moving swiftly, soundlessly onwards. She bounded through the gloomy spaces, then climbed the stairs to the upper floors. She stood and listened, her heart beating, her body trembling, then ran through the shadows until she knew she had arrived at her destination.

She pushed open the door and closed it carefully, then let her shift fall to the floor and tiptoed towards the bed. The early-dawn chorus of the first birds carried on the rays of sunlight filtering through the heavy satin drapes. She slipped smoothly beneath the sheets and slid close to him, not knowing if he was awake or asleep.

'My darling,' she whispered in his ear. 'Take me in your arms and love me, my darling.'

He turned and gazed into her eyes.

'Francesca – '

She put a finger gently to his lips.

'Hush my love,' she whispered, cupping his face in her long cool fingers, her shimmering sighs like sweet music in the stillness of the morning. She kissed his face lightly, leaning so close he could feel the heat of her breath engulfing him as he lay there.

Then, suddenly, she kissed him with a passion that sent shockwaves coursing through him, a searing overwhelming kiss brimming with a lifetime of supercharged desire. He pulled her so close he could feel the thump of her beating heart, her succulent lips, her panting breath, her intoxicating nakedness, her aroma. He felt the alluring heat of her body pressing against every part of him as he turned her beneath him and moved effortlessly above her. They enveloped one another breathlessly, the seismic thrill of their emotions crashing through them in a tidal wave of rampant passion. He wrapped his arms and legs around her as if fearing she might evaporate in his grasp. He gazed down at her face, her long golden hair in tangled disarray on the pillows around her, his heart bursting inside him as never before, with the sheer intensity of a love he had never known before. He felt the mesmerising rise and fall of her breasts against him as he stared into the depths of her coral green eyes.

'Love me Paul,' she whispered breathlessly. 'Love me, my darling.'

He kissed her with such desire she almost fainted in anticipation of what was to come. Her thighs moved beneath him, her hot breath caressed him, her lips enveloped him with a thousand kisses.

'Love me, my darling. I cannot wait . . . '

She gasped as she felt him powerfully inside her.

'My darling, oh my darling, I love you with every beat of my heart . . . '

Their orgasm coursed through them in heart-stopping waves of explosive desire. Afterwards, they clung to one another in an embrace of blinding love, a passion that transcended all the days of their lives, entwined in each other's arms as the early-morning dawn rolled slowly out.

He couldn't quite recall the moment when eventually they slept. He remembered telling her how much he loved her. He remembered telling her she was the most beautiful girl in the world. He remembered telling her that without her, his life would be worthless and unimaginably empty. Yes, he clearly remembered all of that. What he couldn't quite remember was the moment she slipped away from his embrace and crept silently from the room.

It was the incessant drumming that eventually woke him from his dreamy reverie, a distant sound growing ever closer, ever louder. He turned in the bed and realised that someone was knocking on his door.

'Wake up, Master Paul! Wake up!'

He recognised the voice of Martha the housekeeper.

'What is it, Martha?' he called, still dazed and disorientated.

'It's time to leave for college. Remember, we arranged all of this yesterday. Patrick is waiting.'

'Oh yes, Martha, I'll be with you shortly.'

His gaze panned slowly around the room as the memories of the night came flooding back. He stared at the empty pillows and the empty space beside him. He tore back the covers as if expecting to find her lying there, still asleep beside him. He walked to the window and pulled the drapes, allowing the sun's morning rays to flood the room. He turned and gazed back at the empty bed, stunned, dejected and devastated, as he finally began to realise that she really was gone.

It was the first day of December, the winter of 1966, the year of the flower children on Brighton beach, the Mods and the Rockers, the Rolling Stones, the Beatles, the Beach Boys, Bob Dylan, Joan Baez, the blustery end to another year of mixed weather and mixed memories. He sat in the front passenger seat and stared into the distance as the Mercedes sped down the driveway. He gazed wistfully at the majestic oak trees casting their shadows on the grasslands in the sun's early rays.

Seventeen years would pass before he would lay eyes on Francesca Sinclair again.

13

The immediate post-war years were frenetic times for the Bannons as the construction industry across England began quickly to gather pace. England had fought a war and won a war that needed to be won. Forty-five thousand RAF pilots and crew had lost their lives for a cause in which they fervently believed, defending England's shores against the hugely powerful and incredibly well-equipped German Luftwaffe.

When the war finally ended, the victorious forces returned to a tumultuous welcome from a nation devastated by the war effort. The rapturous homecoming that greeted the returning troops soon became a distant memory in the months that followed, as the country struggled to find its feet, and England's war veterans were forced to embrace the reality of austerity and unemployment.

In this fraught atmosphere the Bannon brothers opened their doors to the returning forces and welcomed them into the fold, harnessing their skills, their temperament and their work ethic. Many were trained engineers, mechanics, road-builders and bridge-builders, all of them men who had been willing to place their lives on the line, the quality most highly prized by James, who believed that this, more than anything else, gauged the true mettle of a man's character.

And so, as the economy gradually gained momentum on the back of the powerful construction industry, Bannons began steadily increasing their workforce, expanding their turnover, and inexorably morphing from a fledgling contractor operating on the peripheries, to become the largest reconstruction company in the Greater London area. The relentless expansion programme that catapulted the company into the forefront of the construction cauldron that was then the City of London, was widely perceived to be a cumulative effort on the part of the three brothers. But despite this cumulative effort, no one was under any illusion that the phenomenon the brothers created was ultimately fuelled by the insatiable drive and energy of James Bannon.

Bannon construction sites operated from six in the morning until ten at night, seven days a week, all the days of the year. James adopted a routine of visiting his sites often and when he was least expected. The management teams never knew when their demanding boss might appear in the trenches or out on the construction platforms. Sometimes a contracts manager would walk in to find James sweeping the floors alongside a jobbing labourer, or in a trench, sleeves rolled up, shovelling concrete in a team of ground-workers. A powerful message began to permeate the ranks of the Bannon labour gangs. There was nothing their driven boss would ask a man to do that he wasn't willing to do himself.

14

The service she provided was tailored to the needs of an elite, high-end, high-net-worth clientele scattered across the globe. Access was impossible other than by referral, and only then following exhaustive research into the credentials and financial substance of the intending mark. Repeat business accounted for the bulk of the activity. The minimum fee was fifty thousand, the average fee one hundred thousand, specific 'bespoke' fees, including unorthodox requirements, subject to negotiation; travel and associated expenses extra; payment strictly in advance to a numbered account in the Bahnhofstrasse branch of Credit Suisse in Zurich. The first encounter was generally sufficient to cauterise the pain from the monetary side and instill an appetite for a repeat session. Her pseudonym was Aurora.

She sat sipping a glass of ice-cold Dom Perignon in the semi-darkness of her Eaton Square penthouse, the captivating voice of Maria Callas playing low in the background, the only light in the room the reflected glow from the street-lamps below. In the background she saw the monitor in the office light up. She walked to her desk and glanced at her watch. It was four in the morning. The introduction had been referenced through an existing Middle Eastern mark, but the name was unfamiliar. She keyed in the access-codes to her account and received confirmation that a one hundred thousand transfer had been completed minutes earlier. She typed in verification of the rendezvous time, ten the following evening, noted the address, a house in Kensington Park Gardens, then stared thoughtfully at the screen. Of course she knew this street well. She'd been there many times at various locations, although never at this address. She emailed Nick and gave him the details, then switched off the computer.

Nick Penn had worked for her in an exclusive capacity for four years, on a strictly business basis, because that's how it needed to be. She trusted him with her life. She knew she could safely do so because of prior experience in situations which, but for his intervention, would most likely have proven fatal.

An ex-Captain in the Special Air Service, Nick was a rugged, six foot one, thirty-nine-year-old Londoner, unmarried, and as far as she was aware, unattached. His SAS experience spanned a number of Middle Eastern locations including Beirut and Damascus, and more recently in Iraq inflicting irreparable damage in terms of destabilising activity and multiple-target reconnaissance. Nick liked to believe that he and his group were the ones most responsible for 'softening up' the war-zone ahead of any invasion, thus making the eventual outcome infinitely more predictable. But that was then, and now he was content to consign the rights and wrongs of strategy to others, and leave the bigger picture for the historians to ponder.

These days his job was to look after one client only, Aurora – not her real name of course – but he wasn't concerned with such detail. It was none of his business. His job was to look after her, not analyse her. It was a job he carried out with singular efficiency, a specialised, uniquely tailored service for which he was extremely well paid. This lady operated in a war zone all of her own, where interaction with people for whom life held little value seemed to occur with alarming regularity.

Although in his travels he had encountered a myriad of truly stunning girls, she was beyond doubt the most beautiful woman he had ever laid eyes on, her allure so powerful and magnetic it caused an electric frisson whenever and wherever she appeared. Those qualities had catapulted her into a world where opulence, wealth and extreme danger ran side by side in an explosive, high-octane mix that contrived to make her the most highly paid, most eagerly sought call-girl on the planet.

Her hair was naturally blonde, sleek, cut below her shoulder, parted to one side Lauren Bacall style, her eyes liquid pools of coral green, her lips full-on sensual, vaguely stand-offish, her make-up understated, her skin pale as milk. She stood six feet tall with long, perfectly shaped legs, her breasts borderline heavy, her hips rounded and firm, her stomach flat and toned. When she walked into a room in thousand-dollar heels and a cocktail dress that accentuated every curve, men and women unfailingly turned to steal a second glance. She moved with an air of feline confidence that complemented her sexuality and ignited a primed supercharge into the atmosphere surrounding her. Nick had seen this gorgeous woman reduce a room full of people to putty in her hands, her breathtaking looks and intoxicating appeal contriving to place her at the pinnacle of the international theatre in which she operated.

He jogged along the private road that ran from Kensington High Street to Notting Hill on the western edge of Hyde Park. This was part of the job, the preparatory work, checking locations, checking the mark, checking anything out of the ordinary or anything that didn't feel quite right. He was dressed in a regulation black tracksuit, black sneakers, black woollen hat, no labels. A hundred yards from the house he slowed to a walk and crossed to the opposite side of the road. The property was a large square three-storey-over-basement stucco mansion, partially hidden behind trees, set back from the public footpath behind high railings and electrified steel gates. Located on the middle section of the street, it was not dissimilar to the other dwellings on this most exclusive of roads. Although not quite derelict, it had a curiously vacant, unlived-in, empty aspect. The basement windows were security-enhanced with heavy steel bars, and all windows on the front facade, including these, had their shutters firmly closed. There were no visible signs of activity, no cars in the driveway.

Nick knew that the appointment had been scheduled for ten the following evening. It was feasible that the owners lived abroad and maintained this property as their London base. He took out a camera and snapped half a dozen photographs in rapid succession. Then he jogged into Notting Hill and doubled back along the rear boundary. From this vantage point he could see that the windows on the top two storeys, the only ones visible above the rear boundary wall, also had their shutters firmly closed.

Later, back in his apartment on the Fulham Road, he ran a property search on number forty-four Kensington Park Gardens and drew a blank; no ownership listed or leasehold history available. This didn't unduly surprise him; he knew the area was embassy belt, with the majority of the properties on the road constituting residences held in foreign diplomatic portfolios. Still, something nagged him about this place, and he decided to stake it out.

Arguably the most important part of his brief was to run multiple checks on Aurora's marks, particularly the 'cold' ones, the first-timers not previously registered in the system. He and she both knew that straying into the realms of the unknown was a risk too far in this game, and whilst it might be impossible to guarantee certainty in all cases, it was imperative to take whatever steps were necessary to minimise risk. Aurora was the consummate professional, a lady with highly developed antennae, her all-round fitness honed to absolute perfection from a daily regime devised and supervised by her personal trainer Mickey Jordan. Nick had never met Mickey Jordan but knew he was ex-SAS too. He operated in another facet of Aurora's highly compartmentalised life. Jordan dealt exclusively with a small group of extremely wealthy private clients and was singularly responsible for Aurora achieving black-belt karate status.

Surveillance was never going to be easy on a street with manned security barriers at either end, restricted traffic movement, regular police patrols and heightened activity resulting from its proximity to Kensington Palace. The location he settled on was the garden of an unoccupied residence on the far side of the road, fifty yards closer to Kensington High Street.

He lay an all-weather blanket behind a hedgerow close to the front railings, set his night-vision binoculars on a titanium tripod, adjusted his canvas chair, then sat and waited for however long it would take.

A glance at his watch confirmed that it was approaching five on a cold afternoon in late October. He was certain nobody had entered the house during the two hours it had taken him to leave, return and set up surveillance. Now all he had to do was sit and wait.

Apart from the usual activity of residents toing and froing, maintenance men, delivery trucks and domestic staff commencing and finishing shifts, he saw little of interest throughout the night and into the afternoon of the following day. Then, just after two o'clock, almost nineteen hours into the shift, he focused on a black Mercedes sedan moving slowly up the road from the Kensington side. He registered the diplomatic plates and raised his binoculars, adjusting the mechanism to deliver maximum clarity, his instincts telling him that this had to be it.

The two front passengers were clearly Middle Eastern types; young, possibly early thirties, dark suits, white shirts, short cropped dark hair, manicured beards, dark glasses, stereotypical. It was difficult to identify the two passengers seated in the rear until the car drew level, but as it slowed momentarily he caught a brief glimpse of a thin, greying man in his early forties and a heavier older man, possibly mid-sixties. These guys were all Middle Eastern, Saudi, Kuwaiti, Emirates; difficult to say for sure.

He watched the gates roll back and tracked the vehicle as it cruised the driveway and drew to a halt in front of the main entrance. It was impossible to get a clear view of the passengers as they alighted and disappeared inside. The car moved around the side of the house and never reappeared. Nick assumed that the driver parked and then gained entry elsewhere. He waited an hour for any sign of further activity, possible backup security or catering staff, but nothing materialised. Satisfied that there was little else to be achieved, and with less than six hours remaining to the rendezvous, he slipped away silently, leaving no trace of his presence behind.

He called her on one of several unlisted numbers he retained for her.

'I was expecting to hear from you before now.'

'It took longer than I thought.'

Always the same format. No names. Minimal discussion.

'So, what have you got?'

'Four males. Arab. In situ ninety minutes ago; three younger guys, thirties, forties, one older, possibly mid-sixties. The place looks unoccupied; shutters down, et cetera.'

A pause at the other end.

'So, it's still on?'

The big question. Always the big unavoidable question

posed by a woman who trusted him with her life. There were no guarantees, no certainty. She knew it. He knew it. Evaluate the downside, minimise the risk, and then call it. Either press the button or abort.

'They came in on client recommendation, which is good, but something doesn't feel quite right, so we play this one tight. After the drop-off, follow the usual procedure with split-second precision. I'll be fully equipped on this. Miss a deadline and it's all systems go'.

She knew all about split-second precision, the format they adopted for a journey into the unknown, a situation with the potential to go red-alert. An MI6 IT geek had devised a simple but effective early-warning system, a super-sensitive in-built mechanism embedded in a sapphire solitaire ring, the stone set in eighteen-carat gold, mounted on a micro-spring floating above a tiny sensor hidden in the gold base. The gentlest depression of the stone relayed a signal to a monitor within a five-mile radius, a single blip delivered five minutes after entry onto the mark's property to confirm no surprises. A second single blip delivered precisely five minutes later reaffirmed that everything was still OK. Two depressions emitted at any stage in rapid succession indicated 'situation out-of-control – abort immediately'.

She ponders this briefly.

'Understood,' she replied, abruptly ending the conversation.

At a minute before ten, Nick drew up beside the entrance, walked around the car, opened the rear door and stood back to let her out. He closed the door and watched as she depressed the intercom. A light came on immediately, the gates slid open and she walked through. He eased the car away from the curb, glanced in the rearview mirror and saw the gates close smoothly behind her. She climbed the stone steps to the entrance, pressed the bell. The door was opened by, she guessed, one of the younger men Nick had identified earlier. She stared at him, unsmiling.

'My name is Aurora. I'm expected.'

'This way,' he responded curtly, standing back to let her pass. 'Please follow me.'

He walked ahead of her along a dimly lit hallway to a stairs leading to a lower level, then hesitated by the stairs, his back to her. The sound of her heels on the marble echoed through the house. She stopped behind him.

'Is anything the matter?' she inquired.

Suddenly, unexpectedly, he spun round and swiftly punched her in the stomach. She buckled from the impact and gasped as the air was sucked out of her lungs. It was a professional strike delivered with precision, and the momentum crashed her backwards on the floor, dazed and disorientated. Still reeling from the shock, she felt herself being grabbed by her hair and dragged down some stairs, along a darkened corridor on a lower level, through a door into a brightly lit room.

She heard the distinctive sound of the door closing, the smooth tell-tale swish of an air-sealed unit indicating that she was in a sound-proofed environment. Realizing that this might be her only opportunity, she pressed down on the sensor but she instantly knew something didn't feel quite right. With growing trepidation she realised that the stone and the trigger-mechanism must have been dislodged when she stumbled in the hallway. Now she was beginning to feel helpless and panic-stricken.

All of a sudden she felt herself being lifted roughly onto a mattress, her arms pulled sideways and secured with leather straps. Her dress and underwear were smoothly cut away leaving her bound and naked. She felt the jab of a needle in her arm and the cold sensation of fluid dispersing beneath the surface of her skin. Her body was on fire from where he had struck her, and a thumping pain from the impact of her head on the floor was making her vision blur. She struggled to focus and squinted to shut out the intensity of a halogen light which was suddenly switched on.

She tried to stay calm and focused but everything was happening in a drug-infused blur. She could feel her heart racing from whatever substance they had injected into her, the immediate shock and turmoil of the past few moments rendering all efforts to concentrate hopeless. She guessed from the light that they intended to film what was about to occur. She lay there shocked and terrified and gradually began to realise that everything had become eerily quiet. Unable to focus in the dazzle of light she began wondering if they were still in the room, but then she heard his voice, rasping and cold.

'Open your legs, bitch.'

She squinted at the black silhouette of the grey-haired man Nick had earlier described as in his forties, standing above her, naked, erect. She turned her head to momentarily shield her eyes from the intensity of the lamp.

The blow to the side of her face was massive and unexpected; she felt her senses exploding, her neck muscles wrenching, her ear rupturing, her teeth loosening.

'Open your legs, bitch.'

She struggled desperately to focus but it was impossible. Her body shivered in waves of intermittent shock.

'I promise you, you will not want me to ask again.'

Slowly she spread her thighs and waited for her hell to begin.

'Wider, bitch . . . '

He wedged her thighs apart and rammed into her. She screamed a silent scream, and prayed a silent prayer, but in the end it didn't matter. He pummelled her like a wild animal out-of-control, thrust after thrust, grunt after grunt, until at last she heard the low guttural gasp of his orgasm. When he withdrew, he leaned down and whispered in her ear.

'Don't make me ask twice next time, bitch.'

But even as he spoke these words he could gauge no reaction from her. Her eyes were closed. And then to his surprise, suddenly, unexpectedly they flickered open. She stared up at him, then spat at him a mix of bile and blood that struck him squarely in the eyes. He recoiled, then shook his head and clawed at his face wildly. In his eyes she could see his incomprehension turn to rage, and then she smiled. He spun round and reached for the nearest knife but a powerful hand restrained him.

'No, not now,' a voice said. 'Be patient Sadiq, we're not finished with her yet!'

When he slid away she squinted up at the silhouetted figure of a second man bathed in the light above her.

'Open your legs, bitch.'

15

When Nick didn't receive the vital first contact he immediately concluded she was in mortal danger. There could be no other explanation. It was a situation that occurred only on rare occasions, but when it did occur it presented a deadly scenario necessitating instant response. She was either incapacitated, or they were utilising a blocking mechanism to scramble the signal, or most likely both.

He scaled the rear boundary effortlessly, dropping into the garden and crossing it in seconds until he stood motionless between two windows on the rear façade. It was a dark, cloudy, moonless October evening. He slid a set of headphones into position – he had earlier connected them to a small but powerful noise-detection mechanism pinned to the pocket of his jacket. He glanced upwards towards the higher storeys knowing that the mechanism would be wasted up there – only ground-floor and basement levels were feasible. He descended a concrete stair to the basement and ran the device across the first two windows, but it registered nothing. He was pretty certain those rooms were empty. He moved swiftly onwards to the third window. These were triple-glazed plate-glass units, but he knew that the technology had the capability of penetrating the sealed vacuums separating the glass panels.

He was about to move again when he heard it, a piercing scream followed by a succession of low thumping sounds. Based on previous experience dealing with this lady he immediately concluded that she was being tortured and beaten.

A part of the service? On this occasion he doubted it. Whatever weird and wonderful treats Aurora provided to her tattlers' parade of kooky clients, the treatment she was being subjected to on the other side of the wall was unlikely to be included on the standard weirdo wish-list.

With little time to waste, and on the assumption that at least one of the four guys was stationed on site, not to participate, but to deal with uninvited guests or anything that might spoil the fun, he quickly made his way to the front gate and pressed the intercom. Seconds later a light came on, followed by a click which told him there was someone on the other end, but no voice, only silence.

'Sir, I'm a detective from the Kensington Metropolitan Division and I'm responding to a report of a trespass at this property. Please confirm that everything is in order.'

Still nothing.

'Sir, unless I receive a satisfactory response, you leave me no option but to call for immediate backup assistance. Are you hearing me, sir?'

He guessed the guy was probably staring at the monitor trying to figure out what to do next.

'We have no break-in.'

Tell me something I don't already know, Nick thought.

'Please open the gate sir. Standard protocol requires me to identify you as the legal occupant of this premises.'

No immediate response, but he was still on the line. In the end, maintaining contact could prove vital.

'Detective, this is a diplomatic property, with consequent entitlement to full diplomatic-immunity status. I trust you are aware that the government of the United Kingdom has no jurisdiction within these grounds.'

Not bad, Nick thought, but he needed to think fast. This asshole had it right, but when did *that* ever matter.

'I'm afraid that is not strictly correct, sir. The law governing diplomatic immunity applies exclusively to the living space within the dwelling, and if there is reason to suspect that a crime or misdemeanour has been perpetrated on the property, then our law-enforcement agencies are empowered to enter the grounds. Sir, unless you are willing to co-operate, I am obliged to request immediate backup assistance and procure a search warrant if necessary. I assure you that a little co-operation now will cause minimal disruption. I reiterate that I am authorised to enter the grounds only, not the premises. Please allow me to do my job sir, and I can be on my way in a matter of minutes.'

Judging by the amount of time he took to respond, the guy appeared to be weighing the options.

'Show some identification.'

Nick extracted a fake Metropolitan Police identity card and held it up to the camera. A lengthy pause followed, but he knew the guy was still there.

'This is a most annoying and unnecessary intrusion into the jurisdiction of a sovereign state. I shall be making a formal complaint to the appropriate authorities, but if you insist detective, please come through and I will meet you at the door. You will not be permitted to enter this dwelling.'

The gates slid open and Nick walked the gravel driveway, climbed the front steps and waited.

Minutes elapsed before he heard the bolt slide backwards. The door opened a fraction.

'Detective – '

Nick raised the silenced Beretta and shot him in the left eye. He saw the surprise register briefly and then his legs began to buckle. He grabbed him under the arms and manoeuvred him down gently to minimise the noise, then stepped inside, propped the body against the wall and silently closed the door. He stood and listened, then walked soundlessly down the hall and descended the stairs to the lower level. All the doors on the corridor were open except for the very last one. This room appeared to align more or less with his position earlier on the outer perimeter, but he couldn't detect even the faintest sound, which led him to conclude that the room had to be soundproofed.

Not knowing what to expect, but confident that he still had the element of surprise, he depressed the handle and eased the door open. In the instant it took for his eyes to adjust to the glaring brightness, he struggled to make sense of the scene before him.

Aurora lay shackled to a mattress in the centre of the floor. A naked man sitting astride of her had his head bent close to her as if talking to her. Nick shot him through the back of the head. His body spun in the air, spraying blood and tissue across Aurora's upper body and face. An older, forty-something man, sitting naked in a black leather armchair, stared in disbelief as Nick raised the gun and shot him between the eyes. The chair flew backwards; his brain splattered the wall; he lurched sideways and tumbled across the floor.

In his peripheral vision he sensed a movement to his left. He raised the gun and levelled it at a heavy-set man in his mid to late sixties moving towards him with surprising speed. Dressed in a white kaftan and brandishing a small curved knife, he stopped and stared at the gun, then at Nick.

'You are trespassing on sovereign property. I am the owner of this house and I claim the sovereign protection of diplomatic immunity. This woman is a whore, bought and paid for to provide for my amusement. You have no jurisdiction here. You will pay dearly for this intrusion.'

Nick shot him in the heart and watched him go down, then released another into the crown of his head for good measure. Then he turned his attention to Aurora. He knelt beside her and unbuckled the two straps securing her arms, and quickly checked for a pulse. It was weak, which didn't surprise him in light of the trauma she had endured, and judging by her advanced pupil dilation he concluded that she'd been pumped up with some kind of incapacitating drug.

But it was the heightened level of violence she'd been subjected to that astounded him. These savages had beaten her black and blue. From a cursory inspection he concluded that her right arm had been dislocated, and the index finger on her left hand had been fractured so badly it hung by the skin. He glanced around the room and ripped a curtain onto the floor beside her, then lifted her from the mattress and wrapped it around her.

He walked to the camera and ejected the cassette, only then noticing the array of knives laid out neatly on a silver tray by the edge of a small side-cupboard. It gradually dawned on him that this had all the hallmarks of a sophisticated, well-organised 'snuff' op. They were never going to let her see the light of day.

He knelt beside her and saw that both eyes were closed, her head now moving rhythmically from side to side, mirroring the onset of trauma – hardly surprising. He ran upstairs and found the keys of the Mercedes in the first guy's pockets. Then he carried her out through the rear basement door and laid her across the back seat. He made one final visit to the room, took one last look around, then sprayed the mattress with lighter fuel and ignited it. He watched the flames spread instantly along the carpet, hopefully obliterating any trace of a physical connection to Aurora.

He exited through the Kensington barrier, guessing correctly that it would raise automatically, and drove swiftly out onto the M4. An hour later he arrived at Brookhaven, an exclusive sanatorium on the outskirts of Horsham in Sussex, an occasional destination for Aurora whenever she felt the need to de-stress, chill out, or recoup from the physical and mental effects of a demanding assignment.

At the entrance hall he could see two male orderlies wheeling a gurney, accompanied by two female nurses and a doctor. He had telephoned from a public kiosk on the Ealing Broadway to warn them what to expect, describing in general terms the physical damage, and advising that they should make arrangements commensurate with dealing with a victim of a gang rape.

16

Simon Bannon married Francesca Sinclair on the first Sunday of April 1967, two days after her seventeenth birthday, and barely six months after her dramatic rescue from the river at Grange Abbey. The wedding party flew to Rome, then drove to the Amalfi coast to the small but intimate Sirenuse Hotel high on the hills above the bay at Positano. Simon had asked Frank to be his best man, and when the wedding party arrived in the town, Frank's seventy-seven-foot yacht 'Hurricane' was already moored out in the bay.

Francesca had during those few months been swept away by the frenetic sequence of events surrounding the preparations for the wedding. The early date for the festivities had been at Simon's behest and reflected his anxiety to have the ceremony concluded prior to his assuming the role as chief executive of the company's Irish interests.

They married in the old church on the square in Positano on a glorious Sunday morning, and afterwards they walked through narrow streets teeming with tourists and cheering well-wishers, back to the Syrenuse. On a terrace overlooking the ocean a quartet of musicians entertained the wedding party with a medley of Italian operatic arias, while far below, the glistening blue waters of the Mediterranean stretched to the distant horizon.

Francesca looked breathtaking in a simple dress of white satin, her golden waist-length hair held in a ribbon of the palest pink to match the dress of Sharon Baird, her bridesmaid. The two girls stood and gazed from the terrace across the ancient roofs of the town to the shimmering waters of the bay. Sharon sighed.

'A nightmare to a fairytale, it's like a dream come true.'

Francesca stared unsmiling at her friend. In six short months her life had been turned upside down.

'Have you spoken with Adam?' she inquired absent-mindedly.

'Only to tell him it's finished, and that everyone knows what he did to you.'

Her thoughts seemed to be elsewhere.

'He never came you know . . . Paul . . . he never came.'

Sharon glanced at her but Francesca appeared detached, transfixed in time, unapproachable.

'There is a rumour,' she whispered, 'about the night in the river. People are saying strange things.'

'I've no interest in rumours.'

'But . . . '

'Sharon, please don't tell me. I've no desire to hear it.'

'That may be so,' came a voice from behind. 'But you can tell me. I always love rumours!'

They turned to see Catherine Bannon standing beside them. She embraced them and whispered conspiratorially, 'Fill me in, Sharon. I'm all ears!'

'No Sharon, you mustn't . . . '

Sharon looked at her friend and smiled, then stared thoughtfully at the two of them.

'Perhaps it's best I leave you girls to chat a while.'

She placed a reassuring hand on Francesca's arm.

'Don't worry,' she whispered. 'It's just a rumour.'

They watched Sharon melt into the crowd, and when she was gone Catherine took Francesca's hands in hers.

'My darling, you look radiant this morning. My son's a lucky man.'

She smiled wistfully.

'I'm so happy to be a part of this family.'

They linked arms and strolled slowly along the veranda.

'We've always regarded you as part of our family. It's just that now it is official. Such a thrill for all of us, although for me I have to say . . . something of a surprise.'

'A surprise?'

Catherine turned to her and smiled thoughtfully.

'Only because it's Simon, of all my sons, who ends up winning the hand of this ravishing bride. I wasn't expecting that. Who'd ever have thought?'

Francesca averted her gaze.

'Catherine, Simon saved my life,' she responded quietly. 'None of this would be happening but for him.'

'I know you say that, my dear, and yet it seems so out of character. Simon, always the timid one, always so fearful of the water . . . '

She leaned towards her, squeezed her hand and kissed her cheek.

'I always believed it would be you and Paul,' she whispered. 'You two were so . . . inseparable.'

The day meandered on, an idyllic occasion marred only by Simon's heavy drinking. Early in the evening he collapsed in the bar and needed to be escorted to his bedroom. Hours later, with the party in full swing, he reappeared among the boisterous, noisy crew from Frank's yacht, all of them clearly revelling in the festivities. He paid little heed to them but stared instead at Francesca, as she waltzed across the floor smiling and laughing in Frank's arms. Then when she caught his eye, he turned away and strode to the bar.

'Scotch on the rocks, barman,' he barked. 'And this time make it a large one.'

She walked up to where he stood and draped an arm around his shoulder.

'Darling, come and dance with me,' she whispered.

He pondered her coldly.

'It seems there's no shortage of volunteers to accommodate you on that score. I'll decline thank you.'

He leaned across the bar and grabbed the bottle of Scotch, then pushed her aside.

'Simon, why are you leaving?'

He stopped and stared at her.

'Isn't it obvious. I'm leaving because you embarrass me.'

He pushed past her and left her standing, self-consciously disconcerted for all to see. She saw people avert their eyes and thought, *surely it isn't meant to be like this.* In the end it was James who took her by the hand and whisked her to the centre of the dancefloor.

'I've been biding my time.'

'You *have!*' she laughed.

He winked conspiratorially.

'Let's show 'em how it's done.'

The orchestra struck up and he spun her around the floor with the confidence of a born dancer.

'I never knew you could waltz like this! Where on earth did you learn?'

'On the dance floors of London town, my darlin', but mostly in the Galtymore, the ballroom of a thousand romances, mine included.'

They waltzed with the floor to themselves, to the delight of the enraptured guests. The crowd clapped and cheered as he held her, led her, and turned her with split-second precision.

'This is so wonderful, James, but should not my husband be the one leading me around the room on this night?'

He gave a dismissive shrug.

'If your husband's too dumb to appreciate what he's missing, then, I say, to hell with him.'

He leaned close to her and whispered in her ear, 'Francesca, whatever the future holds for you, this family will always be there for you. That is my solemn pledge to you this day.'

When hours later she crept silently into bed, her husband's snores resonating through the room, her thoughts kept returning again and again to James's words, and their significance, if any, apparent or hidden, she couldn't quite decide. She thought back to the whirlwind of events that had played out over the past seventeen weeks, culminating in this unforgettable night on this idyllic coastline high above the blue Mediterranean. She contemplated her husband's beautiful mother Catherine, his charismatic father James, the larger-than-life personality of Frank, and his fun-loving crazy group of friends.

And then her thoughts turned to the one person who had remained absent from the day's celebration, and the emptiness that attached to it; a bitter-sweet cocktail of sadness, longing and yearning for a dream she once had; an angst-filled dream that lay forever beyond her reach.

17

Mid-morning on a blustery Saturday, the first day of November, the start of the shooting season, nine men are seated in the library at the Grange, smoking cigars and sipping tumblers of malt whiskey. The short journey on the chartered Lear out of Luton five hours earlier had been turbulent to say the least but now at last they're beginning to chill out. There's a palpable air of excitement about the place: John Considine and his buddies have arrived on the estate for four days of shooting, partying, late nights and early mornings. Seven months have elapsed since the wedding and there's an issue to be resolved, a frustrating little detail that's been nagging away at the big man these past months. It's a detail he's determined to get to the bottom of on this trip to Ireland. Earlier he summoned Liam Littlewood, an apprentice chef from the kitchen, and dropped a whopping fifty-pound note into his trembling fist.

'Go fetch Jamie up to the house, Liam.'

The young trainee sprinted the half-mile to the plant yard, to where he knew he'd most likely find Mister Sinclair. He ran breathlessly into the work shed and saw Jamie standing beneath a raised tractor, staring into the camshaft.

'Mister Sinclair!' he shouted. 'I've been sent to fetch you up to the house!'

Jamie barely glanced at the young, red-faced, ruffle-haired kitchen hand.

'Why all the fuss, Liam?'

'No idea sir,' he responded breathlessly.

Jamie seemed distracted.

'Can't you see I'm busy right now. Go tell them I'll call by later.'

But Liam wasn't about to move. He stood his ground.

'Sir – '

'You heard me, Liam,' Jamie muttered absentmindedly. 'I've got a busted engine to deal with. Now scoot!'

The young chef hesitated, then ran towards the door.

'OK, sir, I'll go tell Mister Considine.'

Jamie ducked his head out from underneath the tractor.

'Liam!'

'Sir?'

'Did I hear you say Considine?'

'Yes sir. Mister Considine sent me to fetch you and I think he means right now. Beggin' your pardon sir.'

Jamie wiped his hands on a cloth.

'You might have said as much you little rascal. Wait a while. I'll walk with you.'

On the approach to the house they passed three Land Rovers parked by the main front entrance, their signature green metal shining as the sun's pale rays shimmered through a rare gap in the clouds. There were five, maybe six men working the cars, loading and strapping down equipment, preparing to move out. Up close Jamie recognised the glisten of shotgun metal and counted six twin-barrelled weapons laid out military-style on the roof racks of each vehicle, together with ammunition boxes strapped down and secured with leather bindings. Considine and his shooting buddies inside, he surmised, with the backup team outside, fully equipped, locked down, ready to roll. This platoon looked like it meant business. These guys were all tooled up, and that meant that Big John was back in town.

He walked the south-wing corridor, past the oak-panelled dining room, the sun room and the cocktail bar to the open door of the library at the far end. He heard muted conversation and caught the waft of cigar smoke heavy in the air as he entered the room. Most of the men were sprawled on leather couches around the vast fireplace, the flames licking and crackling noisily up the chimney. Considine waved to him from a seat by the window.

'Mornin', Jamie. Come and say hello to the lads.'

Jamie glanced at them. A few raised their glasses and nodded, but most said nothing. He guessed they were from the UK side, a mix of Irish and English, high-ranking, surly, rough-and-ready types. You just never really knew where you stood with these guys.

Considine nodded and the waiter rattled some ice cubes into a crystal tumbler, poured a measure of Midleton and handed the glass to Jamie.

'They tell me you're doing a fine job up on the farm Jamie. I drink to your good health!'

They clinked.

'If there's anything I can do for you and your buddies, just say the word.'

'Sure Jamie, sure, but you know what. I reckon we've got pretty much everything sorted. Thanks anyway.'

He eased his nineteen-stone frame out of the leather chair, drained his whiskey and set the glass down.

'Now if you gentlemen will excuse us, young Jamie and me have a little business to discuss.'

He placed a hand on Jamie's shoulder and steered him along the corridor to the front entrance. The driver of the first Land Rover hopped to attention.

'Where to boss?'

'Cissie Brennan's on the Dunboyne Road.'

'Sure thing boss.'

The vehicle turned sharply around the back of the mansion and sped along a dirt track to a remote entrance, then drove for a mile before turning into the forecourt of the isolated tavern. Even at that time of the morning the place was buzzing. Probably down to Cissie herself, Jamie thought. The attractive forty-something proprietress had buried her second husband three months previously.

'Two pints, Ciss,' Considine grunted.

She smiled from behind the counter.

'Well pinch me if it isn't Big John himself. Take a seat and I'll deliver 'em.'

They walked to a bench by the window.

'What a place this is,' Considine said absentmindedly as they sat. 'And these fine people. Ain't they the salt of the earth!'

Jamie sipped his drink and wondered where all of this was

headed. Considine pulled on his cigar and stared reflectively through the smoke.

'I brought you here for a reason, Jamie, and the reason is I need you to tell me what really happened on the day that poor little girl was plucked from out of the river.'

Jamie felt his gut tightening. He glanced at the big man, but Considine hardly seemed to notice. He continued talking in a calm, quiet, matter-of-fact tone.

'I was on the estate for a while that day you know, mixing business with pleasure. Had a meeting with James early on, a couple of drinks, then a bit of socializing; hanging with the boys, shooting the breeze, that kind of a day. I'm no huntsman Jamie, and horse-riding was never my forte, but like I said, I drifted around, did a little bit of this, a little bit of that, soaked in the atmosphere, that sorta shit. And yet the one thing I recall most of all about that day was the river. I remember looking down there and seeing it coursing through the meadowlands out of control, a fearsome sight to behold. No living creature could have survived in that water, and yet, inexplicably it seems that two people somehow did.'

He stood and gazed out the window, then turned, hands in pockets and stared at him thoughtfully.

'I've been around men a long time, Jamie. I've met pretty much every sort there is: brave men, cowardly men, smart ones and stupid ones. But I've rarely met the kind of man with the nerve and stupidity to plunge into that swollen river and pluck a little girl out of there alive, and live to tell the tale. The man that did this is a man of rare courage, and I'm talking about the sort of courage most men simply do not have.

'It's a racing certainty that Simon Bannon was not the man who went into the river that night. And yet this version seems to be the one that's doing the rounds. Except that you and I both know it didn't happen like that. In all truth it insults my intelligence when I have to listen to this shit. And that's why I'm asking you to tell me what really happened, because I know you know the real story, and you also know I'm going to find out eventually, so I may as well hear it from you. So let's start at the start, and a word of caution before you begin. I don't take kindly to bullshit from anyone, and that includes you.'

He stared at this huge man standing by the window, indisputably a part of James Bannon's tight inner circle; the family's troubleshooter, enforcer and lifetime confidante of the old man, with the freedom to do and act in the family's interest in all areas and at all levels of the sprawling conglomerate. His heart thumped and his mind raced as he weighed the options. In the days following his ill-fated encounter with Paul, he had thought long and hard about their heated discussion, and in the end concluded that his lifelong friend's version of events had a deadly ring of truth.

Sometime afterwards he revisited the site where Paul had been found unconscious in the long grass, and had a few quiet words with Tommy Hopkins, the farmworker who first discovered him.

'He was laying right there, Mister Sinclair,' Tommy had told him, 'like a drowned rat, dead to the world.'

Jamie stared for an age at the vaguely flattened grass upon which a film of caked mud still lingered, and just when he was about to turn away something caught his eye. He knelt down and carefully parted the long reedy sheaves and picked up what appeared at first glance to be a black mud-encrusted coil. He walked to the river's edge and held it in the flow, then plucked it from the water and stared mesmerised at a long golden tress of his sister's hair.

'What have I done!' he gasped, knowing that the wheels of time had consorted to ensnare him in a lie that could not now be unravelled; a lie that had cost him the loss of his greatest friend, and consigned his sister to an uncharted future with a man she would never otherwise have chosen.

He pondered the consequences for all those involved if the truth of what transpired that night ever became public knowledge. As if reading his thoughts, Considine fixed him with a cold stare.

'You've got no wriggle-room on this, Jamie, so let's hear it. I've a hunting party waiting for me back at the Grange.'

Jamie, smart enough to realise he'd run out of options, took a deep breath to steady his nerves.

'Although I didn't know it at the time, Mister Considine, I now realise that Simon Bannon wasn't within an ass's roar of the river that night. But it still didn't prevent him from claiming the ultimate credit for rescuing my sister. Amid all the confusion that seemed to define that whole day, Simon appeared out of the darkness carrying my sister's lifeless body. He told us he rescued her from the river, and we were all so relieved that she'd made it out of there alive I guess we were happy to accept any explanation. She was alive, Mister Considine, and no one thought to question Simon's version of events, preposterous as this might now seem.'

Considine listened quietly, his eyes hard and cold, his face an unreadable mask.

'And you were one of the witnesses to this.'

'Yes I was.'

If he was having difficulty absorbing the ramifications of the unfolding story, he didn't show it. Jamie felt the big man's steely stare slice right through him.

'You obviously ended up having second thoughts. Explain a little bit about that.'

Jamie averted his eyes.

'Afterwards I met with Paul and filled him in on all that had taken place, and during that conversation he swore to me it had never happened like that. He swore that it was he, and not his brother, who had saved my sister. At that stage I couldn't piece it together Mister Considine. With my own eyes I'd seen Simon emerging from the river meadow with my sister in his arms. Then afterwards the news of Simon's bravery and his forthcoming marriage to Francesca was all that was being talked about. Simon moved real fast and made damn sure that the whole farce couldn't possibly unravel.'

'You actually allowed that cowardly piece of shit to manipulate all of you like this. You, more than the rest of them, Jamie, a man this family respects and trusts to always do the right thing.'

Jamie's eyes were cast down.

'Yes I did sir,' he replied.

'Then there's no other way for me to say this, Jamie, so I'll say it anyway. You're a fucking disgrace.'

Jamie bowed his head in mortified silence. Those words, articulated from the mouth of this powerful man, amounted to a stinging indictment of his character, arguably, for Jamie, the greatest criticism imaginable.

When he spoke, it was in quiet tones. 'I'm ashamed of myself, Mister Considine. Simon threatened us and I feared what he might do to us with the power he now had. We all did. He was way too clever for us. He seized the opportunity the minute it landed in his lap.'

Considine turned from the window and sat heavily, pondering all that he had heard. He finished his drink and fixed Jamie with a withering stare.

'Simon fucked you and that's the fucking truth.'

Jamie hung his head in shame.

'If you say so, Mister Considine.'

Two more pints materialised in front of them.

'So, how did you eventually conclude that Simon duped you along with all those other morons?'

Jamie sat back and stared out the window.

'When the dust had settled and everyone had gone their separate ways, I went back to the place where he'd been found – Paul that is – and it was there that I finally unlocked the truth of what happened that night.'

'Oh yeah?'

He pulled an envelope from his pocket and spilled the contents on the table.

'I found this buried in the mud.'

Considine stared at the strand of golden hair and gradually it began to dawn on him.

'She was there,' he whispered. 'She was with him where he lay.'

'Yes sir,' Jamie replied quietly. 'There's no other explanation.'

They gazed at it for an age, pondering the implications.

'It was bravery beyond belief. No two ways about it. I'd lie if I said I wasn't impressed by what you've told me, and yet still the truth didn't come out.'

'Circumstances conspired to facilitate the whole sorry mess, Mister Considine. In the aftermath of the rescue, Paul contracted a fever from the river that practically killed him. There were times when we all thought he was gone, but he fought it day after day, night after night, and against all the odds he survived it in the end, but by then it was too late. The whole thing had been done and dusted. Before he left for boarding school, I filled him in on the detail, and I'm guessing he must have decided that there was little point in revisiting the whole sorry saga. Who would ever believe his version of events? No one, probably. Not even my sister, the only person in the world who really mattered.'

Considine listened, nodded, then walked to the bar and dropped a fifty on the counter.

'Anything else you'd care to tell me?' he asked.

Jamie smiled briefly.

'That time when I met him, we'd an argument about my sister. I said some things I regret, and he landed one on me pretty much out of nowhere. I guess I had it coming.'

The big man stood and walked to the door, then turned.

'You got away lightly. He should have beaten the shit out of you. C'mon, we're outa here.'

Cissie crossed from the bar and held out the fifty.

'No way I can change a note this big so early in the day. Those drinks are on me.'

Considine stared at the note and shrugged.

'I don't recall asking for change, Ciss.'

She smiled, then walked ahead of them and held the door.

'You can rest your head on my pillow anytime, Big John.'

She placed her hands on her ample bosoms and held them up to him.

'It's a while since they've been suckled.'

18

Paul's late return to Saint John the Baptist in the month of December superseded the chaotic annual student exodus to new classrooms and new dormitories. By now there was a calmness about the place, the stillness of practised, year-on-year routine. The time had come to bid farewell to the junior house and cross the quadrangle to the ivy-clad walls of the upper house, where he would complete his final two years at the famous school.

Every hour of every day his thoughts turned to Francesca. He wondered if her thoughts ever turned to him in the midst of the swish new life she had chosen. It affected him to the detriment of everything that mattered to him, so much so that as the days turned to weeks he became ever more sullen and withdrawn. His sense of loss at losing her was exacerbated by the injustice surrounding the act of losing her.

Even the scramble for representative team places held little interest for him, despite seeming paramount to those around him. Jostling for places and positions was openly encouraged in this most competitive of schools.

The team coaches had begun focusing on individual players, a previously hidden talent, a boy whose potential may not have been apparent but was now displaying the critical attributes necessary to warrant selection for the school's two cup teams.

The upshot of Paul's brooding lack of commitment was a rebuffing by the senior selection committee and a demotion to the second team squad. In the end his form was so erratic he barely made it onto the second team substitutes' bench.

Then one Saturday late in the season a flu-epidemic swept through the senior team, and Steve Bishop reluctantly elevated him to the position of fly half on the senior squad for an away game against Clongowes Wood College, which they didn't expect to win.

Steve watched him deliver a mesmerizing performance in difficult conditions on a rain-soaked pitch, crossing the line twice late in the game to score the only two tries of the match. He immediately elevated him to the senior squad panel.

But Steve was a tough taskmaster, and warned him privately that nothing but his best would do – otherwise he was gone. Following dinner later that evening the coach stood to address the squad.

'You guys won a game you should never have won today, and I guess you deserve a little bit of credit for that. But if I tell you that no team in the history of this school has ever won anything by simply playing well, then maybe you'll begin to appreciate precisely what you're up against. Playing well means it's only a matter of time before you get the crap beaten out of you by a team that's playing out of its skin. You have to stop behaving like a bunch of schoolgirls, and ratchet up through those extra gears you clowns don't even know you possess.'

Steve stared at them dispassionately.

'Based on today's performance it'll be a struggle to make it through to the second round against the competition that's out there, because this year's competition is the toughest I've seen. Those other teams are gonna blow you away, especially teams that have won this trophy in the past. Teams with the tradition and the self-belief to go out there and win it one more time. Winning isn't just about playing better than all the rest. You have to want it so badly you'll allow nothing to stand in your way.'

Carl Jones, the team captain, raised a hand.

'Yeah, Carl.'

'Steve, if you're telling us we're not good enough, then what's the point in breaking our balls for the next three months. The school's won zilch in the past four years, and this year it's beginning to look like more of the same. And Steve – '

'Yeah, Carl.'

'I'm outa here.'

Steve pondered him dispassionately.

'You're outa here when I *say* you're outa here.'

'Aw, c'mon Steve, exactly how long do we have to sit listening to you telling us how shit we are? It's Saturday night in case you hadn't noticed, and that means disco night in Laurel Hill. It's where everyone's headed.'

Steve sighed wearily.

'Have you actually listened to anything I've said?'

'Yeah *sure*. I have. In fact I'm pretty sure we've all got the message.'

'I'm not talking about the others. I'm talking about you Carl. You're the captain and I expect you to lead by example.'

'Steve, I'll give you all the leadership commitment you want at the practice ground on Monday, and that's a promise, but if we don't shift our asses and get outa here right now, then the good-looking chicks will be gone by the time we get there.'

'And you reckon you're in with a chance, Casanova?'

Carl shrugged.

'How the fuck do I know?'

The other guys laughed but Steve wasn't amused. Carl Jones was team captain, tough, popular and lethal on the pitch. But sometimes he was a pain-in-the-ass joker and needed to be controlled.

'Carl.'

'Yeah Steve.'

'Do me a favour?'

'Sure Steve.'

'Sit fucking down and shut your trap, you idiot, and maybe we can all be outa here.'

There were a few grunts of approval and a few sneering guffaws. Steve waited until he had their full attention.

'Listen, you morons, I wouldn't be wasting my breath if I didn't believe deep down that you guys have the ability to take down the other teams in this competition, shrug off everything they throw at you, and conquer all before you. Nothing's cast in stone, but with absolute commitment and total focus right through to the conclusion of this campaign, in the end I actually believe you guys might just do it. I'll leave you to ponder this, but be under no illusions that any player who fails to demonstrate absolute commitment from this day forward will be summarily dumped from the squad. You have to think of this as a military campaign where the battle lines are drawn, and the next game is another skirmish which simply has to be won, or else we risk losing the war; and then . . . '

He regarded them pensively.

'And then we just might do it. Now do me a favour and get lost, you bunch of idiots.'

19

The lights were low and the music loud as they pushed through the doors and moved across the disco floor, edging their way through bodies swaying to the sound of the Beach Boys smash hit 'California Girls'. The Saturday night dance in the concert hall of the exclusive Laurel Hill girls boarding school was the favoured destination for all students within a ten-mile radius. It was a chilly December evening, and with barely a week to the Christmas break there was a buzz of excitement in the air. The Saint John's boys moved across the floor, spreading along the bar, stirring Bacardi from hidden bottles into innocuous glasses of Coke, smiling and laughing with the guys from the other schools.

Paul gazed at the stunning girls gathered in groups, chatting, smiling, giggling, flirting; a heady cocktail of long legs and short skirts sending an electric charge through the atmosphere. Mostly his thoughts still lingered on Francesca and where she might be right now, and with whom. He wondered could she ever have imagined the desolation, the isolation, the crushing emptiness her incomprehensible naivety had inflicted.

He barely paid attention to Mickey Shinners, the self-proclaimed Saint John's sexpert who nobody really believed, ranting on in the middle of the group as usual.

'You silly bastards haven't got a clue,' he bawled at the top of his foghorn voice. 'I already shagged her a dozen times in the bicycle shed, and guess what – her little sister's even hotter!'

'Shinners, you're a wanker,' Carl Jones yawned.

'On my mother's life it's the truth.'

'Go fuck your mother. It's the only fuck you'll get.'

'It's true Carl, I swear – '

'You'd swear black is white – you fat fuck.'

They laughed and drank and cruised the floor. The drinks flowed. The girls flirted.

'Next set's a ladies' choice,' the disc jockey announced, 'so let's get the show on the road with Bob Dylan's "Positively 4th Street", and . . . here . . . we . . . go!'

Ladies' choice always held a certain cache, an allure attached to the one dance in the night where roles were reversed and it was the girls' turn to ask the guys to dance. A teaser guaranteed to excite, ladies' choice offered a heady shot of adrenalin-laced anticipation for what might lie ahead – the disappointment of being overlooked, or the possibility that this could be your lucky night. Suddenly the girls were moving in all directions, adding a thrill to the atmosphere driven by the synergy of raw girl-power. The room pulsated to the mesmerising sound of Bob Dylan's gravelly voice, the cynical words of his love-hate song reverberating, at full volume, across the hall, ramping up the mood, fuelling the onslaught to the senses.

In keeping with age-old tradition handed down from father to son, the sixth-year students invariably socialised together to the exclusion of all others, but particularly their nearest rivals, the fifth-year boys. The sixth-formers had arrived, and were eager to embrace their brash new role as self-assured, condescending participants in the ultimate clique. They exuded an air of practised superiority as they swaggered through the halls and corridors, cocky and confident, masters of all they surveyed.

In the weeks following his inclusion on the senior-team panel, Paul's friendship with team captain Carl Jones inadvertently opened a door into the rarified world of the haughty sixth-formers. If some considered it an indefensible break with tradition, then few were prepared to contradict the wishes of their popular team captain, or face the possible added complication of having to contend with Frank Brilly, a prospect considered too unpalatable to warrant the effort.

It seemed as though the Brilly family had been associated with the Bannons forever, the London-based contracting firm of Frank Brilly and Son, having as far back as anyone could remember exclusively supplied concrete gangs to fuel the

Bannons' insatiable appetite for supremacy. Old man Brilly was known to be a fearsome operator with a no-nonsense reputation based on performance and reliability, qualities the Bannons held in high regard. Testament that Frank Junior had inherited those qualities was encapsulated in his singular two-year domination of the ferociously contested hooker position in the centre of the senior team's front row.

The school's head prefect, Tommy Masterson, sauntered along the bar to the stool where Carl sat nonchalantly surveying the room. Masterson, a consummate snob, his future already mapped out by a certainty which dictated that he would follow in the footsteps of his renowned gynaecologist father and grandfather, masters of the famed Rotunda Hospital in Dublin, regarded Carl with withering disdain.

'What is it with you these days, Jones? The word is you've gone and admitted Bannon, a fifth-former, into the group. Is this correct?'

Carl glanced at him and yawned.

'Completely correct, Tommy. Got a problem with that?'

'Yes I bloody well do, you arrogant asshole. You've just gone and broken one of our oldest traditions, and as head prefect of this college I'm demanding you reverse it.'

'Oh really'.

'Yeah really.'

'Ain't gonna happen, Tommy, so tough titty.'

'I'll take it to a vote if I have to. I'm entitled to do that.'

Carl took a swig of his drink and belched.

'A word of advice Tommy?'

'From you, not particularly.'

'If it's upsetting you this much then go have a word with Brilly.'

'Why Brilly?'

'Brilly wants Bannon in, so go tell him how you feel.'

Masterson glared at him.

'Nobody mentioned anything about Brilly . . . '

Carl pondered him disdainfully.

'Somethin' the matter Tommy? All of a sudden you're looking kinda peaky.'

'All I'm saying is that if Brilly wants him in then at least it's a consensus . . . '

Carl belched. Masterson recoiled.

'And all I'm saying to you is, go and fuck yourself, you supercilious prat.'

Paul excelled in the rarified atmosphere of Saint John the Baptist, his privileged upbringing seeming to matter more to others than it did to him. His two elder brothers had long since departed but their legacies lived on in differing ways. If Frank's success derived from his achievements on the rugby fields of Saint John's, then his brother Simon had proven to be the polar opposite, the school's governing body conferring on him the title of Head Boy in his final year, a decision widely interpreted as a perfunctory nod to one of the school's most illustrious families. In contrast to Simon's introverted, sullen persona and Frank's brash, larger-than-life personality, Paul exuded an air of quiet confidence, and nothing seemed to faze him.

The Bannon family had in the years since the war accumulated unimaginable wealth, their property and construction empire outperforming all but the largest international publicly quoted firms. Paul's speed and awareness on the rugby pitch was remarked upon more and more as the season rolled on, but down all the years, and across all the houses, it was the infamous fight at the Wall with the school's most hated bully that others still remarked upon the most.

Carl Jones waved him to a seat by the bar and they casually scanned the floor. The strobe-lights shone low across the smoke-filled room and the pulsating sound of the Rolling Stones 'Let's Spend the Night Together' reverberated in the air.

Just then Anthony Selwyn materialised carrying glasses.

'Coca-Cola with just a touch of embellishment,' he smiled. They clinked.

'Mmm, this jungle juice tastes good,' Carl spluttered, demolishing the contents in one gulp.

Life for Anthony had changed in the years since the fight with the 'Bunter'. McKenzie's abrupt deposition had largely heralded the demise of the Westies and the remnants of what had once existed no longer constituted a meaningful threat.

Since those early days Anthony had gained almost a foot in height, his new-found confidence, patrician looks and suave elegance in some way explaining his remarkable success with the ladies. Carl tapped them both on the shoulder and pointed to the stunning brunette heading in their direction.

'Check out the hors d'oeuvres,' he smirked.

Paul turned and watched the girl approach, her hair swishing, her hips swaying slow, self-assured and predatory. She was slinky and gorgeous, her legs long and brown, her silver dress shimmering in the light. She threaded a hand through her dark shining hair and swept it casually away from her face, then smiled at Anthony, glanced briefly at Carl and sashayed past to the place where Paul sat.

'Like to dance?'

'Of course,' he replied, slipping down from the stool. She took him by the hand and led him onto the floor.

'Forget the hors d'oeuvres,' Carl muttered as he passed. 'Go straight for dessert.'

The lights dimmed low and the haunting sound of Procul Harem's 'A Whiter Shade of Pale' filled the room. She moved in close, her arms resting on his shoulders, her face touching his. They swayed slowly.

'Your friend back there. What did he whisper?'

'I'm not quite sure . . . something about hors d'oeuvres and dessert all rolled into one.'

She smiled.

'I'm Natalie.'

'And I'm Paul. So nice to meet you.'

'Nice meeting you too.'

This one was a real beauty and he was having difficulty stringing the words together.

'I saw you smile at Anthony. Do you two know one another?'

'Yes we do,' she whispered. 'You can ask him later.'

He felt the heat of her body as she drew him closer, the smell of her perfumed hair, her breath on his skin, and he was instantly aroused. He tried pulling away but he could feel her arms tightening.

'Don't,' she smiled, drawing him back in. 'I like the feel.'

They swayed to the music in the swirl of the crowd, wrapped in each other's arms.

'You're so . . . beautiful,' he whispered in her ear.

'Thank you,' she whispered, then she leaned up to him and kissed his lips full on as they swayed to the music in the dim glow of the light.

'You're so . . . sweet,' she sighed, and then she kissed him again, deep and warm and lingering slow. They lurched to the sound of the Marianne Faithful hit 'As Tears Go By', then 'Je t'aime', and then the stunning Cilla Black number 'You're My World'. And then suddenly the dance ended. She stood and gazed at him.

'I know I'll see you again,' she said matter-of-factly. 'It's written in the stars.'

She kissed him one last time, then moved slowly away, glancing back before melting in the crowd. He stood staring at the space where she no longer was.

'She came to visit me along with some of her friends.'

He turned to find Anthony beside him, hands in pockets, staring thoughtfully in the same direction.

'She came to visit . . . you?'

'Yes she did,' he replied flippantly before making his way back to the bar. Paul pulled a stool up beside him.

'Anthony, quit being evasive and tell me who she is.'

Anthony turned and smiled.

'I thought you'd have guessed by now,' he replied. 'She's my sister, of course!'

20

She sat in the shadows of the late afternoon; young, gorgeous, apprehensive, anticipating the sounds she had grown to hate, the key in the lock, the door opening and closing, the scrape of footsteps in the hall, the whiff of alcohol as he entered the room, his blotchy red complexion, his rheumy eyes, the terse set of his mouth.

His insecurities had begun to manifest themselves early into their marriage and had magnified with the years. From the outset, sex seemed incidental, a rare occurrence, never a priority with him, and seldom successful in the alcohol-fuelled haze in which he lived his life pretty much permanently these days. She had long-since grown to hate his touch. She found his presence repulsive, the endless stream of verbal abuse debilitating, the mental torture deflating, the public humiliations degrading, and now in these past few months the accelerated physical violence frightening beyond belief.

At first it had been innocuous, an arm raised in threat, the odd stinging slap across the face. But now during these past few months she was being punched, kicked and spat upon, the punishments more frequent, the violence more prolonged, as lately his dreaded mood-swings occurred with alarming regularity. Initially she tried to engage with him, attributing the escalating violence to the tensions she knew he was experiencing within the company, but despite all her efforts he showed little appetite to discuss these matters with her.

Instead he almost seemed to sense that she despised him, and yet the look of fear in her eyes since the beatings had begun appeared to empower him like never before. Lately she noticed guests declining dinner invitations. These days only directors or employees of the company attended, reluctantly she guessed, suspecting that they had little option. She dreaded those nights, the pretence, the alcohol, the inevitable scenes of humiliation invariably at her expense, which he relished more and more. He stared at her disdainfully.

'What exactly do you think you're doing?'

The tone was threatening, dismissive. She didn't dare look him in the eye.

'I've been feeling unwell all day. I needed to sit.'

He paced the room slowly and stood above her.

'Do you realise what time it is?'

'Yes I know it's late, but – '

'But nothing!'

'I . . . I feel awful . . . '

When he leaned down she gagged at the smell of his rancid breath.

'Go and get fucking ready now! Our guests are due in an hour.'

She raised her eyes and clasped her hands together tightly.

'I don't feel well. I need to go to bed. Otherwise I'll collapse.'

'Out of the question,' he responded icily.

'I've prepared everything, the food, the drinks, the music, the catering staff . . . '

He grasped her chin painfully and lifted her from the chair.

'Ouch – '

'Francesca, you're being disobedient.'

His grip tightened on her chin.

'And what happens when you're disobedient?'

'I . . . '

He stared into her eyes.

'Answer me!'

'I make you angry.'

'And what happens when you make me angry?'

'I . . . '

'Answer me!'

'I . . . get punished.'

He released his grip and she sank back in the chair. Slowly she stood and walked from the room, hearing as she climbed the stairs the familiar clinking of ice on crystal.

★

This was the time of the night she had begun to dread the most, when the last guests bade their farewells and the door closed behind them. It was the autumn of 1971 and the English property market was already beginning to display the classic signs of overheating, so much so that the cost of development land had ridden to record heights on the back of the cut-throat bidding policies adopted by the major national players, including the Bannons themselves. The result of this soaring recklessness was that many leading developers found their debt-equity ratios hovering at levels which were no longer sustainable. The underlying trends were ominous, and amid dire warnings from leading economists, the market quickly reached boiling-point and spiralled out of control, the precursor to economic meltdown and freefall in the property market.

For much of the evening the subject had monopolised the conversation.

'Frank is adamant that our UK acquisition strategy is sustainable,' Simon confidently informed his guests.

'Our current foray into the market will continue until our land banks have expanded by at least ten percentage points. My brother can sometimes be a pain-in-the-ass hot-head, but I happen to agree with him on this, if only because caution has never served this company well. Opportunities are bound to emerge from the indecisiveness of our competitors, and that is why I tell you that during these times of economic crisis this company will not be found wanting. I assure you that those same strategies which have served us in the past, will continue to sustain us in the difficult times ahead.'

He sat back and gulped his wine, seeming pleased with the positivity of his delivery. The waiter refilled his glass immediately. With a mischievous twinkle in his eye he surveyed the table, glancing at each of his eight guests before finally fixing on Francesca, seated at the far end.

'Darling, I imagine our guests would be interested in hearing your views on these crisis-driven policies. Have we got it about right do you think, or would you perhaps favour an alternative approach? Come dear and let us hear what you have to say on this.'

She sat quietly, her hands clasped on her lap, eyes down; tense; nervous; conscious that he was baiting her. She knew that whatever response she gave would be the wrong one as far as her husband was concerned. He wasn't interested in her opinion on matters of business, or on any other subject. This was just the beginning of his fun-time. She was now the focus of his amusement. His plaything. Sensing the tension in the room from these people, who had so often witnessed the same embarrassing scenes, she tried to gather her thoughts, but in the end it was contracts-manager Tom Cassidy's Yorkshire-born wife Laura who sought to diffuse the situation. She stared at Simon, making little effort to disguise her distaste.

'None of us has the slightest interest in hearing what Francesca's got to say on this. We women are happy to consign decisions of policy to our savvy, well-informed, perceptive husbands, because we trust their judgement. Let's face it, Simon, how can those of us who do not participate in the day-to-day formulation of company strategy be expected to make meaningful comment on such fraught matters. It's ridiculous.'

He fixed her with a cold stare.

'I hear what you say, Laura, but I'm curious nonetheless to hear my wife's opinion. There is absolutely no need for you to intervene on her behalf. Francesca's perfectly capable of answering for herself.'

He glanced tersely down the table.

'Isn't that right, dear? Come now, don't be shy. Indulge us.'

The palpable silence in the room said it all.

'My opinions on matters of a commercial nature are not well informed,' she began quietly, 'and that is why it is impossible for me to be definitive. But if I'm forced to give an opinion, then, in the realms of borrowing, I would always advise caution of course, particularly in these turbulent times. Real wealth isn't easy to accumulate, so why give it away too easily? I'm of the view that we could do worse than learn the lessons of history, and if we study the patterns of past decades, we quickly realise that sustained economic booms tend to be followed by debilitating depressions. It's the age-old pattern, and in the end I suspect it all comes down to good timing. Those with the foresight to make the right decisions at the right time will be the ones who survive and come out the other end in reasonable shape.'

Everyone seemed impressed by the wisdom of her words. They nodded approvingly.

'Sounds like a wise, well-informed analysis, Francesca,' Ian French, the company's residential sales director responded. 'Land prices are rising at such a rate that many buyers are currently paying far beyond what the market can sustain today, on the expectation that inflation will correct the overspend and make it all work in the end. Fine, if the market keeps rising; disastrous if the market grinds to a halt; and either way a helluva high-risk strategy. As you say, in the end it all comes down to timing, and in the absence of a crystal ball, let's hope that whoever's doing the guessing ends up making the correct call.'

Somewhere upstairs in one of the bedrooms they heard the distant sound of a child crying. Francesca stood and smiled.

'Please excuse me, ladies and gentlemen. James must be having another of his nightmares, and besides it's getting rather late.' She smiled. 'Goodnight to you all. I need to check on my son.'

'Darling, we're all about to leave anyway,' Laura responded, immediately standing up. 'Tom's in the airport for six in the morning. I'll call you in a few days.'

James, their little son had been sleeping erratically these past few months. She knew that the tension in the house had to be a contributing factor to his recurring nightmares. She remained with him for fifteen minutes until his breathing became regular and he finally seemed to settle. She could hear laughter and conversation from downstairs as she walked to her bedroom, separate these days from Simon's; they hadn't slept together for years. When she lay her head on the pillow she felt overwhelmed with tiredness, the aftermath of another tense, strained evening, and she was soon in a deep, dreamless sleep.

He quietly opened the door and switched on the light. She lay in the bed silently, breathing deeply, oblivious to his presence. He moved across the room and stared down at her but she heard nothing. Slowly, methodically, he wrapped a hand around her long golden hair, careful not to wake her until his grip was tight. He stared at her for a time, then braced himself, and in one swift movement dragged her violently from the bed. She fell heavily to the floor, still groggy and disorientated, and groaned softly. When she turned to look up at him, he drew back a foot and kicked her in the stomach. She gasped as the air was sucked out of her, the momentum of the kick catapulting her across the carpet and crashing her against the wall. She stared silently at him standing above her.

'How fucking dare you embarrass me,' he snarled. 'How dare you walk out on me when that bastard son of yours starts to whimper. I've warned you to ignore him. And yet again you've chosen to disobey me. Now you'll pay for your insolence.'

He walked to the bedroom door and turned the key in the lock. She scrambled to the far side of the bed but he paid scant attention. He was in no hurry. Slowly, deliberately, he removed his jacket and rolled up his shirt-sleeves. She began sobbing. He moved towards her until he stood above where she knelt by the bedside clutching a pillow for protection. She gazed up at him beseechingly.

'Please don't hurt me Simon. I promise I'll be a good girl, I promise. Don't hurt me. Please, please . . . '

He grabbed her shoulders, then lifted her up and stared into her eyes, pleased with what he saw.

'You must learn not to disobey me . . . always to respect me.'

'Yes, yes . . . I do . . . I will . . . '

The first blow smashed broadside into her face, the pain so intense that she knew instantly her jaw had been fractured. She cried silently, her face contorted, her body trembling as she waited in desperation for what was to come next. The second blow caught her below the waist, forcing her to double up in agony and hit the wall violently. He straightened her up and pummelled his fist repeatedly into her face, crushing her nose and dislodging her upper front teeth. She felt them floating in a pool of blood inside her mouth.

Outside the door she heard the soft sound of whimpering.

'Daddy, Daddy, please don't hurt Mummy. Please don't make her cry, Daddy.'

The sound of the child seemed to fuel his rage further.

'Mummy must learn a lesson; isn't . . . that . . . correct . . . Mummy,' he snarled through gritted teeth, then punched her again and again, first one side then the other, the serrated gold of his wedding band tearing the skin from her cheeks. Her body contorted in shock and she shivered uncontrollably, spitting blood and teeth onto the floor. But he barely seemed to notice. He kept pounding her, blow after blow, until finally something made him hesitate: he stared at her in bewilderment as if seeing her for the very first time.

He contemplated uncertainly his blood-spattered fists amid the growing realisation that this time he may have gone too far. The gravity of what he had just done slowly began to dawn on him as he watched her cough up blood and saliva, and choke at his feet. The rancid odour of her vomit-splattered nightdress filled the air. He released his grip and let her crumble to the floor, then ran from the room, pushing his hysterical son roughly to one side.

★

She walked the two miles from their gated mansion on Ailesbury Road to the women's refuge on Rutland Street, holding her son's hand tightly. It was five in the morning and the frozen, windswept streets were deserted. The icy rain blowing in off the ocean had been falling non-stop for days and showed little sign of abating, drenching the abandoned pathways, rendering the city streets miserable and forlorn. Hardly a soul ventured out that night as the wind rose to force nine across the churning waters of the bay. So fierce was the storm that the Dublin Bay Authority had earlier placed an emergency restriction on all movements in and out of the harbour. A flotilla of cargo ships lay south of Lambay Island anchored in calmer waters, temporarily sheltered from the worst excesses of the blast. Nothing much moved out on the streets, the inhabitants of the city opting to remain indoors as the storm rolled over their roofs.

That evening the nurses manning the women's refuge were guessing and hoping it would be a quiet night, but these days you never really knew, and tonight would prove no different. When the doorbell rang, the night-nurse, accustomed to witnessing the worst excesses of domestic violence in this city, was taken aback by the faceless apparition standing before her, features indistinguishable beneath a bloody, pummelled mass.

They ushered her inside and immediately summoned Tony Taylor, the resident doctor, a recently qualified general practitioner who stared at her, silently struggling with his composure, aware that the look of shock and revulsion etched on his young face must be glaringly evident to this tortured, broken woman.

'Who did this to you?' he whispered rhetorically, certain that she was unable to open her distorted mouth to offer even the briefest reply. In the silence that followed, it was a voice from behind that startled him.

'My Daddy broke my Mummy's face. My Daddy is a bad daddy. He hurts my Mummy.'

He stared at the boy who had spoken in a calm, matter-of-fact tone, and realised he needed to take immediate control of the situation.

'Why, thank you so much . . . '

He knelt in front of him and held his hands.

'You really are the bravest little fellow, but now I have to make your mummy better, and you must trust me to look after your mummy and go with nurse Eileen now. I promise to come and see you later.'

The boy glanced at his mother, then nodded silently. The nurse took his hand and led him out the door.

21

They pushed through the doors of Bannons' Stephen's Green headquarters, Jamie walking beside her as they entered the crowded, bustling office, the staff busy with their morning's work, conversing on telephones, dealing with the business of the day, oblivious to their presence.

Five days after the incident her face was grotesquely blown out, so swollen and distorted that the doctors decided to forego surgery indefinitely before attempting to begin repairing the damage. One by one people began to turn and stare, the buzz of conversation diminishing, the crowded spacious rooms growing quieter, until there was silence. People watched with shocked expressions the macabre scene unfolding before them. Of course rumours had been rife around the office for years that their sullen boss Simon Bannon was a wife-beater, and many suspected that life at home for Francesca and their child constituted little more than a living hell. And yet nobody interfered, and in a way how could they? Such things happened behind the closed doors of many houses in this city and out there in the big bad world beyond. But whatever doubts and suspicions they may have previously harboured regarding the health or otherwise of the Bannon marriage, the grim evidence before them on this morning was laid out starkly for all to see.

The woman's face was a kaleidoscope of interwoven colour; black, dark blue and yellow; a mass of angry tissue swollen beyond recognition. Her jawbone had been gut-wrenchingly displaced, so gruesomely out of sync with the natural contour of her face that many were forced to look away. Her mouth hung open to reveal a black, congealed space where her teeth should have been. She hobbled painfully down the centre aisle of the office, her left eye closed, her right eye barely open, her once beautiful hair hanging limp and matted around her broken face.

They slowly made their way past his secretary's desk at the far end, ignoring the girl's futile attempt to block their path.

'You cannot go in there without prior arrangement,' she announced in a crisp, businesslike tone. 'Mister Bannon is busy with appointments all day.'

They kept on walking, Jamie leading his sister gently by the arm through to the cavernous inner office. Simon sat engrossed in a telephone conversation and didn't appear to notice their presence. His chair was swivelled in the opposite direction towards a large window overlooking the square. Jamie walked across the room and snatched the receiver from his hand, ripped the telephone from the desk and flung it onto the floor. Simon spun in his chair and gaped at the two of them, struggling to make sense of the scene before him, but in the end seeming to gather his composure quickly.

'I half expected you to orchestrate something like this, Sinclair, except that I wasn't quite sure who she'd go running to. And I'm presuming you've got the brains to realise you'll never work another day for this organisation. Take my advice and get out of here right now before I have you both dumped onto the street.'

But even as he said them, his words had a meaningless ring. Jamie stared at him with such hatred that he recoiled into the depths of his chair as if it might somehow afford him a semblance of protection. Suddenly he felt himself being dragged bodily into the air and propelled across the desk onto the floor in front of Francesca. He stared up in disbelief, then scurried across the room and scrambled to his feet, but Jamie's huge fist caught him in the throat and spun him like a rag-doll. The blow sent him reeling; he lost his balance and hit the floor, his head cracking noisily on the hardwood surface.

Francesca stood in a state of motionless detachment as her husband's high-pitched wailing reverberated in the stunned silence of the outer office. He screeched like a pig, then raced forward on hands and knees through to the main concourse, but he found scant respite there. Jamie followed right behind, mercilessly kicking him and punching him with clenched fists as he struggled in vain to roll away. Jamie Sinclair was a powerfully-built man, but that morning in front of the astounded head-office staff he beat Simon Bannon with such ferocity that they could do little but stand and stare in shocked disbelief. One or two male employees made a half-hearted attempt to intervene, but the expression on Jamie's face was sufficient to make them rethink their hastily constructed strategy.

Simon collapsed on the floor, his expression pleading, his tear-stained face a mixture of confusion and terror, but he saw little comfort in Jamie's icy stare. The staff stood paralysed as the kicks reigned down relentlessly on their aloof, cold-hearted boss, until finally Jamie brought an end to it and regarded him with disgust.

'Now listen to what I say, you despicable cunt, because I'm only going to say this once.' His tone was menacing, and rang clear in the silence of the room.

'You've beaten my sister for the last time, you scumbag.'

He spat the words with venom, then tore a sheaf of photographs from an envelope and spewed them across the floor.

'Evidence of your handiwork preserved in celluloid for the world to see,' he continued, glancing briefly into the faces of the staff who were staring horrified at the images scattered before them. He extracted a dossier from an envelope and discarded it dismissively on top of Simon.

'A verified copy of the medical report detailing the litany of damage you inflicted on my sister – the collapsed lung; the fractured jaw; multiple injuries to body and facial tissue; dental damage; bruising; internal bleeding. All meticulously collated by two independent medical practitioners, countersigned by two reputable law firms and copied to the relevant authorities. The cops are waiting in the entrance-hall right now, hoping for my sister to press the button that's guaranteed to put you behind bars for the rest of your miserable fucking life.'

He stared into the scared, whimpering face of Simon.

'But of course you can avoid all of this by signing the legal document that's sitting on your desk right now. There are no surprises – it's exactly as you'd expect. Marriage annulled from this day forward. All visitation and custodial rights to your son relinquished. Compensation in the amount of fifty thousand pounds, the bulk of which will be used to repair my sister's broken body. Nothing in this is negotiable except for the freedom your money can buy you, you revolting piece of shit.'

Simon sniffed, groaned and whimpered, the depth of his public humiliation and discomfort etched on his bloated face for all to see. He eased himself off the floor, hobbled slowly to his desk and signed each page of the document without bothering to read. He wrote a cheque for fifty thousand pounds and pushed it towards Jamie.

Jamie studied the document, leafing rapidly through the pages to check the veracity of the signatures, then turned on his heel and led his sister out the door. He heard Simon's high-pitched whine resonating behind him.

'You're finished with this family, Sinclair, but then I'm guessing you already know that.'

Jamie turned and stared at him.

'That may be, but I'm sure as hell not finished with you, you evil fuck. Your signature on this cheque may be enough to keep you out of jail, but it'll never be enough to save you from the punishment you truly deserve. And someday, when you're least expecting it, I'll exact my revenge.'

★

Francesca and her five-year-old son James left Ireland on the eight o'clock ferry to Holyhead later that evening. She told Jamie she wanted to leave the nightmare of the past six years behind her for ever, but she also needed to avail of the best reconstructive surgery in Europe, universally recognised then, and still to this day, to be found behind the sedate doors of London's Harley Street.

Acutely aware of his sister's vulnerable physical and mental state, Jamie insisted on travelling with them on their journey across the Irish Sea. During the previous few days he had finalised arrangements to place her under the protection of the one man he knew would look after his sister's future well-being. When the ferry docked at Holyhead, Francesca glanced nervously at two men moving purposefully through the teeming crowds in their direction. They were rough, unsmiling types, and she held her son's hand tightly as they lifted her suitcases and led her to a black saloon car parked along the jetty. Although she'd never met the third man standing by the car, she recognised him immediately. She'd seen him many times with the Bannons at Grange Abbey.

'No need to worry any more. You're in safe hands now, darlin'.'

This giant of a man, whom she knew most men feared, had spoken to her in the gentlest of tones, and so when John Considine held open the door of the waiting Mercedes, her battered instincts told her there was no need to be concerned. She put a reassuring arm around her son's shoulder and nodded to him without hesitation. Jamie stood by the gangway and watched the car move smoothly off the pier, gather speed and disappear into the night.

22

James Patrick Bannon, a tax-exile for fourteen years, gazed out from the veranda of his villa on the Saint Jean side of Cap Ferrat towards the hazy outline of the distant Italian coast. His nine-thousand-square-foot Villa Genevieve, once home to a world-renowned English writer, stood three storeys high, a classic cream stucco mansion set in eleven acres of walled gardens, commanding breathtaking views across the Mediterranean Sea to the Riviera coastline. The villa towered above a hidden private beach in a semicircular deep-water cove accessible by sea, and by land down seventy steps cut into the sheer granite cliff. The previous owners had carved a cocktail bar and party venue into the cliff-face above the small sandy beach. A purpose-built floating jetty, which James had later added to accommodate the Bannons' two-hundred-foot ocean-going cruiser *Scalawag*, stretched out into the sparkling blue water.

A battered Panama hat shading the sun from his face, he leaned on the terrace wall deep in thought, unaware that his wife Catherine was silently staring down at him from the salon two floors above. She knew it took a hell of a lot more than it took most men to fray her husband's steely nerve, but she still sensed that he had been more than usually preoccupied these past few months as the property market skewed out of control and the crisis in the company's British operations worsened by the day. She knew that the situation was deadly serious, and had the potential, unthinkable even a year ago, to bring the whole house of cards crashing down.

Catherine Bannon had idolised her husband since the day they had met and become teenage sweethearts. When she first laid eyes on him as a fourteen-year-old girl, she knew then she wanted to be with no other man. It seemed like she'd been by his side

131

forever, always there for him, never questioning his judgement, always trusting his instincts, giving her unequivocal support to this hugely ambitious, fearless man as he systematically drove his company to the top of the pile.

Her thoughts strayed back to a time years earlier, when her husband made the inspired decision that changed their lives beyond recognition and catapulted them into a stratosphere of unimaginable wealth. Most men might have been content to live out their lives and reap the profits churned out annually by the housebuilding phenomenon he had created, but her husband wasn't like most other men. She gazed down from high on the terrace at his stooped, still frame, and couldn't help but ponder the courage and foresight that had enabled him to see beyond all of that, and operate a million miles ahead of his smartest competitors.

It was the spring of 1950 and even while Bannon bulldozers demolished the bombed-out remnants of the suburbs of London, Coventry, Berlin and Dusseldorf, James found his thought-process inexorably drawn towards what for him was the pivotal prime patch, the devastated wasteland that once comprised the thriving commercial square-mile hub of London, an area stretching from the West End to what is now known as the City. During the early war years, wave after wave of Luftwaffe air raids destroyed vast swathes of inner London, raining down destruction and mayhem on the historic fabric of the city's heartland. Each evening its beleaguered inhabitants braced themselves as the air-raid sirens filled the night and the incessant whine of the engines grew louder and louder. As anti-aircraft fire traced the skies, Londoners may well have gleaned some comfort from the knowledge that the Lancasters and Spitfires of the Royal Air Force were simultaneously inflicting even greater damage in the skies over Hitler's Germany.

But now, as James walked through what had once constituted the financial and business beating heart of the City, he contemplated the physical and monetary implications that this bombed-out legacy must inevitably throw up.

Latest figures from the Home Office confirmed that a staggering ten million square feet of prime London office space had been obliterated during the Blitz, equating to almost fifteen percent of the city's pre-war total of ninety million square feet of lettable space. These mind-boggling statistics intrigued James, as did the unfolding conundrum that this unique set of circumstances must inevitably throw up. But in order to capitalise on the nucleus of the plan forming in his mind, he needed to divest himself of current day-to-day responsibility.

James flew to Ireland in the spring of 1950, having the previous autumn finalised the purchase of a rambling mansion on a vast estate in the heart of Kildare. His bid of three hundred thousand pounds ultimately proved successful, being both marginally above the quoted reserve and the only substantive bid submitted on the day. On this occasion he was accompanied by his brothers Matthew and Charles, and as they drove along the meandering two-mile driveway, James stopped the car on the brow of a hill and watched the glistening white-walled mansion materialise in the hills above the lake.

'The Bannon family residence,' he announced proudly. 'Home to the Earls of Kildare for a thousand years. Welcome to Grange Abbey, boys!'

They stood on the driveway and gazed across the valley towards the distant magical place, and after dinner that evening James sat on the veranda and appraised his two brothers of the strategy that had recently been occupying his every waking hour. They listened intently, and in the end, Matthew, always the cautious one, was predictably the least enthusiastic.

'We three have built the greatest housebuilding dynasty England has ever seen, and right now we're at the cutting edge of a boom that seems destined to run and run. Our companies earn revenue beyond our wildest dreams, delivering profits we could never have hoped to achieve, let alone spend in three lifetimes. And now you propose switching from our core business into commercial redevelopment, thereby committing vast sums of money for infinitely longer periods before ever capitalising on our investment – assuming we ever actually get to do that.

'James, we're housebuilders, not speculators, not gamblers, and hopefully not fools. I say let's stick to what we know and continue exactly as before. Let us at least be honest with ourselves and admit that all we really know how to do properly is build houses!'

James smiled.

'Mattie, always the predictable one, but you know what, I actually happen to agree with the cautious bit, which is why I'm suggesting we allocate half our future profits only to this. And because I'm really keen for both of you to come on board, I'm willing to guarantee that all retained profits shall remain sacrosanct beyond the remit of this proposal. And if you still feel it isn't right for you, then I promise not to pressurise you further. Continue as before if that's your preference, but you, my brothers, know better than most the kind of man I am. I'll go with my instincts and speculate my sixty percent, because I cannot allow this opportunity to slide. All I'm asking is the time to enable me to give it my best shot. Come with me on this and we continue exactly as before, on a sixty-twenty-twenty split. The stakes are high, the risks are high, the rewards are high, and that is why you must consider carefully before you commit to anything. No need to give me your answer now boys – sleep on it. Either way you have my word there'll be no hard feelings.'

And so, after a few more brandies, they bade each other goodnight and went their separate ways, and in the morning when they met again for breakfast it was Charles, the youngest of the three, who opened the discussion.

'James, Mattie and I have given careful consideration to your proposal, and for sure it's a mighty big call, but last night we stayed up a while, and in the end we both decided to stand together with you on this. Your wisdom and leadership has brought us unimaginable wealth, and we're both agreed that whatever the outcome turns out to be, there'll be no recrimination between us three. Although, with stakes as high as this, it'll be kinda fucking helpful if it works out.'

James embraced his two brothers.

'Thank you, Charlie. Thank you, Mattie. Thank you for your belief in me. This is truly what I was hoping to hear.'

They spent the rest of the week in conference with their advisors, reassessing the current management structure, analysing work-in-progress projections, stress-testing the strength of existing land banks, liaising with accountants, lawyers and tax specialists. In the end a workable plan began to emerge.

For the next five years James would step back from day-to-day management of the housebuilding operation but still retain the title of chief executive, with a golden share bestowing on him the power to approve or veto all board decisions. Charlie would assume sole responsibility for the administration of the company's vital British interests, with everything else, including Germany and Ireland, falling under Mattie's remit, both appointments to have immediate effect.

23

When James flew to England on the Monday morning he decided to waste no time. Some months earlier he had signed a five-year lease on a small office suite at the Bond Street end of Maddox Street, close to the heartland of the old, established estate agencies. He immediately hired a war-widowed secretary named Silvia Kendall to administer the paperwork, and a young London chartered surveyor named Garry Patterson, who quickly grasped the thrust of his new boss's motivation. It took Garry a little longer to discover that his discreet new employer was the most famous private housebuilder in the south of England.

One morning James summoned Silvia and Garry into his office and announced that he was doubling their salaries. They stared at one another with a mixture of surprise and disbelief.

'But we surely can't deserve this,' Garry responded, 'it's been less than two months – '

'I disagree,' James replied, staring pragmatically at his bewildered employees. 'On the contrary, I believe you both deserve it, because I'm now satisfied I hired the right people. We face an uncertain future, and it is imperative that we work together as a tightly knit unit, outsourcing pretty much everything else we need. Our priority must be to identify a corporate vehicle tailored to our requirements, a shell company with a low-key listing, small enough to attract the minimum amount of scrutiny, at least in the early stages. And when we do find what we're looking for, I'll be including both of you as share participants.'

The generous salary adjustments, the promise of share participation, and the sheer magnetism that James exuded would guarantee the loyalty and discretion of his two staff in the critical weeks and months that followed. Garry gradually began to construct a network of contacts in the key agencies and among the myriad professions, including surveyors, architects, engineers, planning consultants and anyone else who might prove useful during the formative months of this fledgling operation. For now, James was satisfied that this nucleus of three would serve his immediate needs, and the inevitability of what he had long suspected, that demand for prime central London office space would someday begin to strengthen, slowly crystallised into reality.

The dynamics of the marketplace pointed tentatively towards the alluring prospect of greatly increased demand, with recent newspaper articles already beginning to speculate on the prospect of future occupancy levels outstripping the previous requirement by as much as ten percentage points. James had long concluded that these estimates were erring on the low side, but he could still feel his adrenalin rising despite the fact that activity in the market continued to remain frustratingly static, either through scarcity of suitable product, or the lethargic after-effect of the post-war hangover, or perhaps both. It was impossible to tell.

Others in the marketplace were slowly reaching the same conclusion, endorsed, adopted and about to be acted upon by James during those winter months of 1950, the certainty that if future demand outstripped previous demand by a factor of ten percent, then this must surely lead to an urgent medium-term requirement for a vast amount of prime new London office space.

James had already decided that this unrealised, pent-up, demand could conceivably be in excess of twenty-five percent of existing stock, equating to a staggering twenty million square feet of new floor space. The bulk of existing London office space comprised a sizable residue from the fifty years prior to World War One. All space dating back to the turn of the century was old, jaded, and in urgent need of renovation. The city had a certain run-down feel, and James felt sure that demand, when it materialised, would be for bright, modern, serviced space, once London finally decided to face down international competition and resume business with the rest of the world.

With the passing of each month he became convinced that the stranglehold of stagnation in the marketplace could only be the calm before an approaching storm, and acting on little more than gut-feel he set about constructing a powerful commercial position right in the beating heart of London.

Already the first tranches of funds from his housebuilding operations had begun filtering into a special purpose vehicle to which he had given the enigmatic title of Centrefold Securities. Ever anxious to remain below the radar, he confided in the smallest group of people, adding new contacts and introducing new players on a strictly need-to-know basis. The funds were transferred into three newly formed deposit accounts in the Bank of Westminster, Barclays, and Standard Equity, then Europe's largest international pension fund.

All three institutions agreed to participate in a funding structure which would provide James with the level of liquidity he believed he needed. A simple formula was devised whereby the banks would lend fifty percent of the initial land purchase price, increasing to two-thirds on receipt of planning permission, topped up by a final capital injection to facilitate the cost of construction.

From the outset, Standard Equity flagged a willingness to participate in the wholesale acquisition of the finished product. Buoyed by this positivity, James decided to intensify his search for a suitable shell, to either amalgamate with Centrefold, or instigate a reverse takeover of the 'NewCo' shell.

With a million pounds of housebuilding profit deposited in each of his three bank accounts, James's funding vehicle now equated to a combined immediate war chest of six million pounds. It was time to move to the next phase.

Aware that the old, established agencies who had survived the war unscathed still held the key to unravelling the hidden potential of London's commercial landscape, he set about forging relationships with the most influential of these, targeting key personnel and introducing them to hitherto-untried mechanisms of equity participation linked to successfully negotiated projects. James's preference was always to reward the individual dealer rather than the parent firm, fastidiously imposing secrecy on these personalised arrangements.

In the summer of 1952 James completed the two million pound purchase of a vast swathe of commercially zoned land on a bomb-damaged site stretching from Piccadilly to Oxford Street. Less than a month later an unexpected change in planning legislation would effectively double the value of his acquisition overnight.

The Conservatives had recently swept to power on the back of an anti-austerity manifesto which would hand them the reins of government for thirteen unbroken years. Their determination to kick-start the economy was demonstrated early on, when in a clear show of intent, the new Minister of Housing Harold MacMillan immediately abolished all development charges legislated during the term of the previous Labour administration. James was under no illusions that the thrust of this legislative tweaking was to instil a sense of pragmatic urgency into the current non-existent level of commercial market activity.

With the ink hardly dry on the legislation, a million square feet of commercially zoned land on a dilapidated site straddling Tottenham Court Road and Oxford Street was rushed onto the market. Although the land was strategically located, the issue was complicated in that London County Council had earmarked an indeterminate portion to be frozen to facilitate future road-widening.

Speculation was rife that the 'earmarked' portion could amount to as much as half the entire site area. James telephoned Andrew Gold, managing partner at Maitlands, the marketing agent, to broach the possibility of a purchase prior to tender. He received a definitive rebuff.

'James, I regret that I cannot be of assistance. My vendors are adamant that a sale by tender will deliver a stronger price in an accelerating market, a view that concurs with the advice we've already given them. Interest from one or two of the major players has obviously helped shape our thinking on this.'

'I am sorry to hear it, Andrew,' James replied smoothly. 'It's a problematic piece of real estate, and unless we can deal off market, I'm afraid I shall not be bidding on this. I honestly doubt you'll achieve the six hundred thousand reserve you're seeking.'

'We'll just have to wait and see about that,' Andrew Gold responded tersely.

'Of *course* – it's your call.'

'One I'm happy to make.'

'I on the other hand, am prepared to pay a non-refundable deposit of ten percent, sign a contract tomorrow for eight hundred thousand, and complete in four weeks' time. I'm happy to retain Maitlands as joint letting agent and I'll separately pay a hundred grand for associated professional advice to either you or your agency. I suggest you have another word with your vendors, Andrew, but please make it clear that in the absence of agreement, I'm out.'

Later he received a call from Andrew Gold.

'James, it's an extremely generous offer, but my vendors are still in the mood to wait and see. If you really want to take a shot at this, I strongly advise you to carefully reconsider your position.'

'And you say there are others – '

'As of now there are two other serious bidders.'

'Then I wish you well. If you decide to reconsider . . . '

'I think I've made my position abundantly clear. Good day to you.'

24

Sir Jeremy Wilkins strolled down the hallway of his club in Pall Mall and motioned the porter to fetch him a cab. Dinner at Blake's had been impeccable as always, and the meeting had gone exactly as planned. He'd known Crispin Templeton since their days at Eton and they trusted one another implicitly. The grouse had been cooked to perfection and the '47 Chateau Lafite Rothschild a sheer delight.

It hadn't taken long to broker the deal between their two giant conglomerates. They'd done so on many occasions in the past, except that on this occasion the stakes were mouthwateringly high.

Andrew Gold had warned him about the maverick Irishman with incredibly deep pockets when they met in the club for breakfast that morning. Andrew relished the sedate splendour of London's most prestigious club, even if he knew in his heart that a person of the Jewish persuasion would never be truly welcome within these oak-panelled environs.

This place prided itself on a tradition of haughty sophistication, where camaraderie and class prevailed above all else.

'You've met this . . . Bannon chap?' Sir Jeremy inquired.

'Never. We've spoken by telephone twice, perhaps three times.'

'And . . . '

'He insists on dealing off-market. Otherwise he's threatening to pull out.'

'Then we've nothing to worry about.'

'I beg to disagree.'

'I'm not quite sure I follow . . . '

'Sir Jeremy an eleventh-hour bid has the potential to scupper the entire process. Can you really afford to take such a risk?'

'What exactly are you saying?'

'I'm saying you'll need to put in a strong bid in order to see this . . . Irishman off. I can influence matters prior to the bids being opened, but afterwards . . . '

'I understand, of course.'

The deal with Crispin Templeton had been straightforward in its simplicity. Each company would submit an individual bid, one, ten percent above the reserve, the other, thirty percent higher, pretty much covering all the options. If it emerged that no independent bid had exceeded the lower of the two bids, then the higher bid would subsequently be withdrawn. Otherwise, following the inevitable approval of the higher bid, the spoils would be split evenly based on the average of the two bids, a tried-and-trusted formula that hadn't failed them yet. The cab pulled up and the doorman held the door.

'Eleven Cavendish Place, cabby.'

The driver nodded and did a U-turn. Only then did Sir Jeremy become aware of a second man, who must have slipped in unnoticed behind him. The night was dark, and he'd a few drinks on board, but how could he not have seen it? The cab was speeding away from the West End in a northerly direction towards Camden Town. He glanced from the driver to the man beside him.

'What's going on, cabby!' he shouted. 'Stop this car immediately!'

Neither paid any attention. He checked the door but it was locked, then stared out the window and saw that they were hurtling through a maze of deserted side-streets. Sir Jeremy was beginning to feel strangely disorientated. He sat back and breathed a sigh.

'Who are you gentlemen? What do you want with me?'

The cab turned into a laneway behind a line of derelict terraced houses. The driver slowed to a halt and switched off the engine.

'What precisely do you want with me?' he repeated in his calmest voice. During the war he had commanded a Royal Navy frigate, and nothing gave him much cause for concern.

'We mean you no harm,' the man seated beside him said quietly. Sir Crispin stared at him but could only see the outline of his silhouette in the darkness. He was of slight build, with a distinctly Irish accent, thinning grey hair, casually dressed, mid-thirties, otherwise nondescript.

'Then perhaps you'd care to tell me why you have brought me here?'

'Like I said earlier, we mean you no harm,' the man beside him repeated with a casualness bordering on boredom.

'If this is a robbery I've a little money. You're welcome to take it – '

The man seated in front slid open the glass divider.

'Your company is submitting a bid for land in two days' time. Correct?'

'Yes! But how on earth – '

'In the interests of your continued good health, and the good health of your family, I respectfully advise that you do not submit that bid. If you are willing to take that advice, then you'll have nothing to fear.'

'My family! What on earth do you mean my fam– '

'You have a son in Cambridge, reading politics.'

'Sebastian. Is he in some kind of danger?'

'Brilliant rugby player. Might conceivably play for his country some day.'

'Is my son in some kind of danger! Please answer me!'

'Your son is in danger only if you choose to put him in harm's way. The decision is entirely up to you.'

'This is outrageous! How dare you people threaten me . . . '

The stranger stared at him coldly.

'This is no threat, Sir Jeremy. Submit that bid and your son will never play rugby for England because he'll have no knee-caps. Now get out of the fucking car.'

25

The call came early on the morning of the tender.

'James, despite earlier misgivings, I've had another chat with my clients, and I'm given to believe that we can broker an agreement on the following basis, which I stress is non-negotiable.'

'I'm listening.'

'Nine hundred thousand for the contract, a consultancy fee of one hundred thousand payable to Maitlands in advance, and because I'm assuming you're aware that Maitlands don't do joint agency, we'll be insisting on agent exclusivity.'

James delayed his response sufficiently to bestow a befitting level of gravitas.

'Have the contract on my lawyer's desk by close of business.'

He replaced the receiver and breathed a sigh of relief. Still, under the circumstances, and in light of Andrew Gold's previous intransigence, he was astounded to receive the call. What sort of a tactical game was this?

He was less than surprised that Andrew Gold had sought to tweak the terms. One could have expected nothing less. The Jewish community in London was a formidable and highly respected player in the commercial property arena, and Andrew was considered one of their toughest proponents. The Jews looked out for one another and traded to the non-Jewish sector only those opportunities which were of no interest to those within the community.

James suspected that the vendors were most likely Maitlands themselves, either outright or in part, a common though ethically questionable practice rife among the established agencies. He was aware that agents often introduced a phantom purchaser willing to surpass a delighted vendor's monetary expectation, before subsequently conveying the property to a new purchaser eagerly waiting in the wings, at a profit vastly in excess of what the hapless original vendor had been prepared to accept days earlier. The key to the success of the process was to 'manage' the purchaser's expectation.

What James didn't divulge to Andrew Gold was his intention in the event that no agreement was reached, to participate in the tender process by submitting an eleventh-hour bid substantially in excess of one million pounds. He pondered the agent's surprising about-turn, and in the end put it down to an unexpected stroke of good fortune.

Once again James's impeccable timing was rewarded when the Conservative Minister of Works Nigel Birch announced soon afterwards in the House of Commons that building licences were to be abolished in their entirety. When he flew to Ireland on that bank holiday weekend, little did he realise that those two pieces of legislation, enacted in close proximity to one another, would open the floodgates and usher in the greatest property boom ever witnessed in Europe's largest city.

26

Meanwhile, back in London the following Tuesday, he was surprised to find Garry waiting for him in his office. He pondered him curiously.

'Aren't you supposed to be in Cornwall with your wife and daughters? I wasn't expecting you so soon.'

'They're still there. I came back early.'

'So it seems,' James replied. He rounded his desk and sat in his chair. 'The girls must be having a ball with all that sunshine.'

Garry glanced at him and nodded.

'James, let's park the bullshit. We need to talk – it's the reason I'm bloody well here.'

James raised his eyebrows and smiled. His shy young surveyor was beginning to grow in confidence, perhaps picking up some of that Bannon attitude. Already James surmised, a force to be reckoned with.

'So, what's on your mind?'

'Look, I know you believe you can conquer the world all on your own, and someday perhaps you will, but I don't think we ought to wait that long, and that's the reason we need to have this little discussion. The market's heating up so fast you can feel it in the air, and now is exactly the right time to align ourselves with one or two of the key players. Yes, we've succeeded in getting the basics right, but we must also recognise that we just don't have the wherewithal connections wise to do this on our own. We need to take some short-cuts, and we need to act swiftly and decisively, and get the show on the road.'

James looked at him quizzically.

'Correct me if I'm wrong, but I thought that this was precisely what we were doing.'

'To some degree, yeah, but with all that's going on out there we run a real risk of being overtaken by events.'

James nodded slowly.

'Keep talking. I'm listening.'

'There's a guy called Henry Hyland who's already a legend out on the street, and I'm pretty certain he's your type of guy. In my view, if James Bannon and Henry Hyland hit it off and form an alliance, then the sky's the limit.'

'I've heard the name,' James replied. 'You obviously know him.'

'I first met him a couple of years ago, and even back then he was thinking outside the box, hanging out with one or two pretty powerful people. Henry's aiming for the bullseye and nothing's going to get in his way. When you asked me to chase down a shell listing, I suspect that Henry got to hear about it, because when I met him and explained my connection to you, he asked if I could arrange a meeting.'

James thought quickly.

'OK, I agree. Let's do it.'

'It's already done. He'll be here at four.'

★

Henry Hyland sported a Van-Dyke beard and had a vaguely reddish complexion, whether from heredity or exertion James couldn't quite decide.

'Your housebuilding empire rules the land,' he smiled pleasantly. 'I suspect a similar fate awaits those of us in the commercial world. How impressive!'

The tall, polished young agent had a relaxed, affable personality to which James warmed immediately. His eyes were bright, and so also, James quickly concluded, the brain that functioned behind those eyes.

'The commercial world presents a different set of challenges,' James replied.

'You appear to be adjusting pretty well,' Henry nodded conspiratorially. 'The Maitlands land sale is all that's being spoken about. Rumour has it that sinister forces put the frighteners on some of the rival bidders. I'm assuming you know nothing about that.'

'No, I don't,' James responded tersely.

'I didn't mean to suggest – '

James gave a dismissive shrug.

'If we're going to get off on the right foot, then we ought to focus on how we can be of assistance to one another.'

'It's the reason I'm here. You've managed to singlehandedly create a formidable position in a relatively short period of time. And as I was saying, the "audacity" of your recent purchase really *is* the talk of the town.'

This guy didn't back down. James smiled, then winked at Henry and whispered, 'Let's proceed as discreetly as possible.'

Silvia placed a tray with coffee and biscuits beside them. James poured.

'So what precisely are you aiming to do James?'

James took a sip of his coffee and stared thoughtfully at the legendary trader.

'The government is intent on creating vastly increased activity in the property market. It believes that increased activity will lead to increased employment, increased tax revenue, and a positive long-term ripple-effect across the wider manufacturing sector. We're already seeing signs of extra-curricular interest, and it's only a matter of time before the situation reaches boiling point, and when that happens it's time to get out. There's a narrow window of opportunity, and whatever we hope to achieve has to happen within a pretty tight timeframe. When the shit hits the fan I intend to be long gone, and I suggest you should do the same.'

'It sort of explains the urgency of this shell you're seeking.'

'I'm anxious to formulate a tailored exit-strategy as soon as is practicable. Property has many positives, but it differs from stocks and shares in one fundamental respect – it's an inflexible commodity. Shares, on the other hand, can be traded overnight and that is why they represent the ideal substitute for currency. They can be massaged, manipulated, split, reclassified, reconstituted, reissued, falsified if necessary, and crucially they provide a cash-free mechanism to accumulate shares in other companies or even to purchase those companies outright, lock, stock and barrel. They offer the ultimate flexibility in the inflexible world of property.'

Henry sat back and stared at James.

'Good Lord,' he said. 'I'm flummoxed!'

Garry smiled. 'I did try and warn you what to expect.'

Henry nodded but his gaze remained fixed on James.

'Barely out of the starting blocks and already devising an exit-strategy – Frankly I know of no one who's thinking that far ahead. It's a fascinating concept.'

'Then perhaps we can make it work for both of us.'

Henry stared thoughtfully at the ceiling, his mind racing.

'I've been tossing an idea about for some time, predicated on creating a partnership arrangement with one of the larger contracting PLCs, grounded on the premise that our interests are so closely aligned.'

'And how might that work?'

'It's pretty damn simple. I source the investment, and manoeuvre it into a quoted shell within which my PLC partner and I both participate. My PLC partner constructs the project. We agree to either hold it, let it, or move the fully completed, fully tenanted package on to a receptive pension fund. And then we share the profit.'

James stared at him thoughtfully.

'You've succeeded in sourcing the shell?'

'Yes I have.'

'And what percentage do you and your prospective PLC partner propose retaining?'

'Twenty percent each, with the remaining sixty percent floated out to the market.'

James sat back and pondered the options, then turned to the young estate agent.

'Henry, let's park your PLC partner temporarily to one side. Sounds like a good idea, and *is* a good idea, except for the fact that large PLCs are constrained in their ability to respond quickly by myriad pain-in-the-ass requirements, including duty to shareholders, necessity to obtain board approval, stock-market compliance, stock-exchange notification, due diligence – you name it.

'Their very size dictates that they move at a pace that doesn't always suit specific requirement, whereas with me it's different. I'm the ultimate decision-maker, answerable to no agenda, answerable to no board. When time is of the essence, as it invariably is, I can deliver instant approval. I have the contacts, the skills and the strength to construct any building, any size, in any location, and I can deliver a thousand men into this city at less than a week's notice. Your best option has to be to align yourself with me, but that's ultimately for you to decide – although having said that, you're going to need to make your mind up fast.'

'Like I said earlier, it's the reason I'm sitting here today.'

'Then let's consider how we might do this together, because let's face it, your intimate knowledge of the market provides the perfect mechanism for channelling product out of the market before it ever gets to tender. It gives us the edge. It provides an unassailable lead over the rest of the competition. Obviously we'll need to revisit this shell of yours and fine-tune those percentages you referred to earlier. I suggest we retain forty percent each and float the remaining twenty to the market.'

Henry stared at him in disbelief.

'You're proposing we retain eighty percent!'

'You seem surprised.'

'Naturally, since what you're proposing couldn't possibly be sustainable in terms of the level of activity you appear to be contemplating.'

James stared at him with disconcerting coolness.

'I'm not so sure about that, Henry, but let's take it one step at a time. First we need to focus on this shell of yours and ascertain how many shares are currently in play. Let's move swiftly and grab what we can before the market figures out what the hell we're up to.'

James Bannon and Henry Hyland signed a partnership agreement bestowing on each of them forty percent of the share capital of Newhampton Estates, a listed 'shell' company with a small portfolio of dilapidated suburban property scattered across the north of England. During the following ten trading days, when ninety percent of the shares in Newhampton had been hoovered up for an outlay of less than fifty thousand pounds, James triggered a reverse takeover by Newhampton of the assets of Centrefold, valued at three and a half million pounds, and a simultaneous exercise across Henry's various assets, independently valued at two and a half million. A formula was devised for dealing with Henry's million pound shortfall predicated on adjusted future profit-share across a five-year period.

And so the scene was set whereby an unknown, valueless shell company on the brink of delisting, overnight became the owner of a multi-million portfolio of prime London West End commercial-development land. From its humble beginnings, Newhampton would become the most powerful property company ever to trade on the London Stock Exchange, and the richest in all of Europe.

27

Following the successful completion of a restructuring process culminating in the transfer of two hundred and fifty million pounds to sterling numbered deposit accounts in Liechtenstein-registered banks, the Bannon brothers departed London in the spring of 1965. The running of the company was entrusted to the willing if inexperienced hands of James's eldest son Frank, a less-than-popular decision that gave rise to murmurings of dissent across all levels of management, right through to the boardroom. James's brothers Matthew and Charles conveyed their misgivings to him privately.

'Frank's a good boy but he's thinking with his dick right now,' Matt counselled him, 'so why not let him live the life for a few more years. Every time I open a newspaper, there he is again with a different squeeze staring at him doe-eyed. One of these days he'll come down off the merry-go-round, but he needs more time to exercise that cock of his.'

'I agree with Matt,' Charlie added. 'The job's got Frank's name written all over it, but now's not the time. Let him fuck his way around London a while longer.'

James smiled.

'I respect your opinions, boys, and I know there are others who feel the same way, but the opinions of those people don't matter much to me. I sometimes wonder is there ever a right time for something like this. Frank's a loose cannon for sure, but he needs to be blooded, and I reckon now's as good a time as any. He'll make a few mistakes, so let him – which of us didn't? My mind's made up boys. Time to make way for the next generation.'

The decision elicited a cool reception from the markets when it was officially announced in April that year, but Frank

Bannon showed scant concern. The company's share price dipped nineteen points in the weeks that followed, but the new chief executive shrugged this aside, arguing that the adjustment was small beer in terms of the mammoth scale of the recently completed restructuring. Frank now had something to prove to the world and he intended to let the whole world know that his father had made the right choice. He knew that his appointment was far from popular, but so fucking what. Frank Bannon had never tried to be all things to all men, a fool's pursuit, and he wasn't about to change the rules of engagement.

The day following his appointment, Frank convened a board meeting which began at seven and ran right through to ten that evening. An exhaustive review of the company's operations took place during all of that day. The directors sat around the boardroom table and listened to detailed back-to-back assessments from teams of accountants, auditors, construction managers, salesmen, surveyors, engineers, architects, land-acquisition specialists, corporate bank advisors and company strategists.

At the end of a very long day, few if any still harboured misgivings as to the wisdom and merit of Frank's appointment. In his closing address he laid down a marker which would define the no-nonsense, blunt style of leadership his co-directors ought now to expect.

'I thank all of you for your participation,' he began, casually glancing around the table, shirt-sleeves rolled up, tie pulled loose. If the day had been long, exhausting, and mentally draining, Frank Bannon was showing none of it.

'But I still need to be sure I can rely on your collective support as we face into an uncertain future. I value your knowledge and I acknowledge your talent, but I also understand that there may be some of you who dislike me, dislike my style, and may not necessarily endorse my approach. Let's face it gentlemen, these things I can readily understand. I even find it hard to like myself most of the time. Basically I'm a prick, and that's because when I need to be a prick, I can be the biggest prick in this town.'

He stopped and stared around the table taking a moment to gather his thoughts.

'What I'm really saying is, if anyone wants out, then now's the time to walk, because I need to be sure I've got absolute commitment from my core team. Any man who leaves this room will do so with his respect intact, but those of you who choose to remain must understand that nothing less than absolute loyalty will be acceptable from this day forward. The Bannon family places a high value on loyalty. It's non-negotiable, but when we receive it, we return it with interest. Those wishing to depart should do so now, but those who stay should do so only if your loyalty stays with you. My name is Bannon, gentlemen, and for me the word loyalty is sacrosanct. It transcends all the other attributes you guys bring to the party.'

He sat down and sipped his water, knowing deep down that he had meant every word, yet hiding his apprehension nonetheless. Frank was in awe of no man and had dealt it straight up to the board, the only way he knew how. In his world there were but two choices, no middle ground, no fucking about. Frank was the consummate team player, a born leader who led from the front because he genuinely didn't know any other way. In choosing him to be his successor, he wondered if his old man had identified some characteristic, some hidden quality others might have missed. He didn't expect to receive the unanimous support of these twelve men, but at the end of the day that's exactly what he got, the unequivocal endorsement of a disparate group of diverse, multi-talented individuals, most of whom he barely knew, and one or two, like John Considine, he'd known forever.

He stood again, momentarily lost for words, but when he found those words there was no mistaking his intent.

'In these testing times, the challenges are awesome, the possibilities immense, the rewards incalculable, the risks beyond comprehension. And that is why your support means so much, because for me the challenge has always been clear. I intend to prove to all of you, that you've made the right decision, and those of you whose paths have crossed with mine must surely know that in the end I'll never let you down.'

Frank earned a round of applause for this. He walked the table and shook hands with all of them, and then began his closing address.

'Gentlemen, before we break for refreshments, let me summarise our predicament. We currently have five thousand dwellings under construction across England and Scotland, with a further two thousand in the Greater London area. Seventeen thousand plots are in the planning process, and eighteen thousand more are at contract-purchase stage. Sounds good and is good, if we're content to remain in position three or four on the national chart. We may not be the biggest, and until we become the biggest then let's settle for being the most profitable, because if I'm reading these cashflows correctly, we're on target to realise a fifty-six million gross profit to year-end December. I believe we can out-perform this figure, so let's chase it down, gentlemen, and I assure you your efforts will be generously rewarded.'

He looked around the table and beamed.

'And that's about it, boys!'

True to his word Frank would breach the target he set that night, and as the weeks rolled into months his confidence steadily grew. Long hours spent at his desk, and long days on the road travelling from site to site, ultimately impressed even the most cynical of his detractors. His buccaneering style and gregarious personality finally began to count where it mattered most in the cut-throat cauldron of construction – out on the building sites. The construction crews, the navvies, gangers, charge-hands, section foremen, general foremen, site-agents and contract managers had found themselves a new leader with whom they could readily identify. For the guys that made it happen on the ground, Frank Bannon became their brash new hero, especially among the ranks of the two thousand construction workers based in the company's traditional stamping ground – the home counties and the nation's capital, London.

In the City, Frank became the recipient of growing admiration from high street bankers, merchant bankers, fund managers and financial commentators, their earlier reticence dissipating under the weight of his ice-cool delivery. The company began receiving overtures from prestigious banking conglomerates and lending houses who had hitherto shown little interest, and doors which had previously been closed gradually began to open. In the spring of 1966 the gross UK profits for the year topped sixty-one million, triggering a jump of fifteen points in the company's share price by close of business.

The following day The *Financial Times* published a photograph of Frank on its front page, officiating at the topping-out ceremony of a recently completed, pre-let, twenty-storey office building behind Saint Paul's Cathedral in the heart of the City.

The photograph showed a smiling Frank standing on the rooftop among a group of construction workers under a headline which read, 'Chip Off the Old Block. City Golden Boy Smashes Profit Forecast at Bannons.'

28

In the last quarter of his second year in office, Frank's roller-coaster ride at the top of Bannons was temporarily derailed by the repercussions of a decision which proved surprisingly controversial and in the end taught him a lesson he'd never forget.

His controversial, out-of-the-blue elevation of his brother Simon to head up the Bannon operation in Ireland went down like a lead balloon. In the scheme of things, it might almost have gone unnoticed had his brother not succeeded in rubbing an awful lot of people up the wrong way. Aside from a glaring lack of business acumen, Simon's brooding, cynical persona left most people with a sense of discomfiting ambivalence, so much so that when the matter was raised on the agenda, it triggered a fraught, lengthy debate that split the board fifty-fifty. Frank's deciding vote eventually nailed it, but he was taken aback by the acrimony his decision generated, and afterwards he sensed a real feeling of resentment in the air.

In all areas of activity, the board invariably gave their, at times, qualified support to their charismatic chief executive, but on this occasion even Frank's closest friend Steve Richie postulated why a sibling, and in this instance a patently unsuitable sibling, should be catapulted into a position nobody believed he deserved. The accusations of blatant nepotism hurt him the most of all, but he resolutely stuck to his guns rather than back down on an issue involving an immediate family member.

When, months later, he raised the matter during one of his father's rare visits to London, James counselled him to never leave himself vulnerable to the outcome of a controversial item on a board agenda.

'*Always* canvas individual board members ahead of a critical vote, and *always* gauge the prevailing level of support, or you'll be left twisting in the wind. These guys can *always* be persuaded by argument, *always* flattered by a one-to-one approach, and *always* influenced by the promise of future inducement.'

'*Always?*'

'You've got it, smart-ass.'

Frank grinned.

'I wish you were still around from time to time, if only to steer me in the right direction.'

His father shrugged.

'You don't need me or anyone else to show you the way, although, having said that, it was a peculiar decision handing that level of responsibility to Simon. By all means acknowledge the blood that flows in your veins, but never let it guarantee entitlement. Try and remember you're running a business, not a charitable trust.'

'Logic you chose to ignore when you decided to promote me – not the most popular choice, if my memory serves me well.'

His father glanced at him.

'I don't hear too many dissenting voices.'

If at the time he lacked the benefit of his father's wisdom, Frank was still determined to demonstrate that he had at least inherited the old man's steely grit, and amid a chorus of disapproval he resolutely stuck to his guns. When they eventually voted with the traditional showing of hands, most were taken aback to see John Considine ranged among the dissenters, none more so than Frank, who always felt he could rely on the big man to come down on his side. In the end he had his way, but he felt disconcerted, and exited the room in a hurry.

If anyone chose to interpret this as a weakness in his resolve, then they were sorely mistaken. Frank breathlessly proceeded to push the company forward on the back of an aggressive expansion programme which permeated every facet of the organisation. His infectious enthusiasm filtered down into the farthest reaches of the organisation, and nobody seemed unduly surprised when the company reported a whopping seventy million pre-tax profit at the end of the following year.

For the young City traders who had adopted him as their

poster boy, Frank exuded style, panache and coolness under pressure, displaying flair and determination in the boardroom, and garnering widespread recognition as a savvy, street-wise decision-maker. Suave, flamboyant and charismatic in personality, his swashbuckling style and rugged good looks copper-fastened his seamless entry into inner circles of London Society. Ever conscious of his limitations, he instinctively knew when to source the particular type of expertise that he and his managers lacked and was never afraid to acknowledge his shortcomings by asking the stupid question at a meeting.

'If I sound like an idiot I make no apologies,' he once announced to a room full of bemused auditors. 'Maybe I'm a fool, but if I don't know how to do it, at least I know when to wheel in the guys that *do* know how to do it.'

This almost gullible honesty endeared Frank to a host of high-powered professional advisors, and if their astronomical fees raised a few eyebrows, Frank invariably brushed it aside.

'If those guys save me a million in tax,they're entitled to charge ten fucking percent. No question – they've earned it.'

If it was difficult to argue the logic, it was impossible not to be swayed by the enthusiasm. As the company's fortunes ran the gamut from the spectre of paralysis following the restructuring to becoming the toast of the markets, Frank's photograph appeared less often in the society pages and more often on the business pages. Forever the consummate party boy and dedicated ladies' man, he still popped up, albeit less frequently, in the Fleet Street gossip columns. His broad shoulders, smiling face, engaging personality, and endless stream of beautiful girlfriends consituted a heady mix guaranteed to make him the darling of the City.

On the day his father casually informed him that a whopping two hundred and fifty million had been surgically removed from the balance sheet, Frank unequivocally concluded that he could have no quibble with the arrangement. He knew the strain that this would inevitably place on the company's ability to perform, but to hell with all of that – the old man was entitled to cash in his chips.

With rumours abounding in the City of a massive stripping down of the asset base, the sheer audacity of Frank's in-your-face leadership helped stem the jitters following the initial haemorrhaging of the share price. Frank wasn't about to cry into his drink. It was up to him to make the whole thing work, and that's exactly what he intended to do.

★

'The primary focus of a business is to make money, and don't you ever forget it.'

The day after the board meeting they sat sipping Jack Daniels in the American Bar at the Savoy. The old man called for two more drinks.

'*Sure* there are other reasons to be in business: excitement, prestige, loyalty to the workforce or whatever turns you on, but all of these rank way behind the ultimate goal of accumulating profit and converting it into cash. Timing is the critical factor, and the best time to realise a cash dividend is when the company is strong and profitable and can afford to pay it. This latest raid is a pretty massive call, and the company will inevitably suffer as a result. How much pain it suffers is almost irrelevant, because this is precisely the time to do it, and that's the only thing that matters. Remember, it's all about timing, and all about utilising the offshore tentacles of the greatest tax-haven on the planet, the City of London, which basically means we don't pay a cent in tax!'

Everything his father told him that night in the American Bar Frank accepted in good faith, sure in the belief that his moment had finally arrived. He was being handed the baton. It was neither perfect nor a poisoned chalice, but this was his opportunity to excel and prove to the world that his father had indeed made the correct call in choosing his eldest son to be his successor. This was his moment, and he wasn't about to squander the opportunity.

Under Frank Bannon's mercurial leadership, the next seven glorious years would make Bannons a household name across the entire continent of Europe.

29

She walked into the cocktail bar and glanced towards the far corner table where he was seated as usual. It was an early evening Monday in January and the place was quiet. She kissed him on the cheek and sat opposite.

'You didn't see me arrive,' she smiled. 'You seem . . . preoccupied.'

He glanced at her, then lit a cigar and blew the smoke towards the ceiling.

'I saw you the moment you walked in the door. I'm a man like any other man – a little older maybe, but still a man.'

She smiled.

'Something you'd like to share . . . '

He took another pull on his cigar and gave her a cynical glance.

'Not particularly.'

'Mmmm.'

He pondered her briefly, then gave her a 'what the hell why not' look.

'There's not a lot to tell. I was recalling a conversation I had yesterday with a bunch of guys over a few beers. They were talking the usual bullshit: soccer, rugby, women, work and booze. Then somebody asked what was the greatest insult one man can pay another. It was that kinda night.'

'And . . . '

'And as you might expect, there were differing opinions.'

'Such as . . . '

'Such as telling the guy you despise him, you despise his kids, you're screwing his wife, his daughter, his dog. He's a coward, he's a faggot – you name it.'

She smiled.

'Intriguing, and your response was?'

'That's a no-brainer – for me it has always been about respect.'

'What do you mean . . . respect?'

He sucked on his cigar and sighed.

'I believe that the worst insult you can pay another human being is to tell them you've got no respect for them. In my book that's as bad as it gets.'

She sat for a while, silently contemplating this.

'Do you respect . . . anyone?' she asked quietly.

He contemplated this breathtaking woman as she sat across from him in the dark, dim, low light of the Library Bar in the Lanesborough. Earlier he noticed most of the dozen or so customers scattered around the room turn to steal a glance when she walked in – it was always the same. The waiter served Dom Perignon from the ice-bucket beside her, and placed a Heineken into a silver container beside him. The velvet-soft tingling of the piano filtered through the room. Her question had taken him by surprise. He took his time replying.

'Darlin', there are people in this world I genuinely respect, and you happen to be one of those people. But, besides you and James . . . '

'That's it!'

He stared at her through a cloud of cigar smoke.

'There *is* one other.'

She watched him tip the ash and sip his drink.

'This other one I speak of . . . I'd trust him with my life.'

It was her turn to be surprised. She stared into the weather-lined face of this powerful man she knew stood in awe of no other man; a man with the most fearsome reputation in the toughest industry in the world, articulating the parameters of his respect in a way he'd never done before. It sounded incongruous; she wasn't quite sure why, except that it just did. She was flattered at his reference to her, of course, and aware, like anyone who knew anything, of the mutual lifelong respect that existed between John Considine and James Bannon. She raised the champagne flute to her lips and gazed at him, her liquid green eyes reflected like molten lava in the flickering candlelight.

'And who might this mystery man be?' she inquired, her

voice barely audible, her tone, he thought, vaguely cynical, 'this other one you hold in such esteem.'

He pondered her for a time, the faint hint of a smile on his face seeming to say, 'What kind of game is this you're playing with old Johnny Considine'. But she was a hard one to read. He let the moment pass. The maître d' refilled her glass.

'You know this person.'

'I do?'

'*Sure* you do. He rescued you from the river all those years ago.'

At first she didn't appear to grasp the implication of what he had just said, her expression skewing between surprise and disbelief. And when she *did* regain her composure, which didn't take long, her voice was controlled and steady.

'You'll always have a special place in my heart, John Considine, and I'll be forever in your debt, but this person you speak of is the least worthy of your respect. Hearing it disappoints me bitterly, if you must know. My one regret is that he didn't leave me to drown in those waters on that evil night.'

She stood and walked briskly towards the door. He hadn't expected that, but when he thought about it he guessed it made sense. He glanced at the piano player who gave an imperceptible *'c'est la vie'* shrug of the shoulder, and then began playing 'Bewitched, Bothered and Bewildered'.

He eased himself out his chair and followed her to the entrance just as the Corniche pulled alongside. Damien the doorman held the door and she stepped in quickly. He nodded to Damien. Damien signalled to the driver. The engine purred. The driver waited. He tapped on the window. The car wasn't moving. He could see she was angry. He waited. The rear window slid down silently. She sat there and said nothing, staring straight ahead.

'Don't leave now. We have unfinished business.'

Still she ignored him. He took a deep breath.

'Francesca, come on back inside.'

Still no reaction. He glanced at Damien, then sighed.

'Please . . . '

She gave him a steely stare, then nodded to Damien. Damien

opened the door and she stepped out. She stared at him straight, angry, fiery, definitely pissed off.

'Make it quick. I'm a busy girl.'

He stared back at her, thinking how mesmerisingly beautiful she looked even when angry. He waited until Damien was out of earshot.

'You jumped to the wrong conclusion earlier, and you didn't let me finish. And yeah I know you're busy – we're all busy – but someone needs to set the record straight on the charade they played with your life all those years ago. And I'm that someone, and now's as good a time as any.'

Even as she held his gaze, he thought he detected the faintest hint of uncertainty in her eyes, but with this one you could never tell for sure. He stood back to let her pass, then glanced at Damien.

'Keep the car available.'

'Sir, it's at your service for the evening.'

He escorted her inside and they sat at the same table. The waiter replaced their drinks and slipped away discreetly.

'You OK?'

She glanced at him briefly, then nodded imperceptibly.

'Say what you have to say, John.'

If her icy stare unnerved him he didn't let it show. He took his time unwrapping a Montecristo, smelling it, lighting it, inhaling it, and blowing smoothly into the air. He held it between his thumb and forefinger and stared at her nonchalantly.

'Despite everything that you've been told, Simon Bannon never rescued you from the river that night, and that's the truth, as God in heaven is my judge.'

He studied her intently, never taking his eyes off her; he saw her lips tighten; she stared back at him. Their eyes locked, and then a strange thing happened. A single tear rolled down her cheek, and when she spoke, her voice was barely audible above the soft tinkle of the piano. She spoke so quietly, he strained to hear.

'And if not Simon, then . . . who?'

He was taken aback by the crushing vulnerability of this most unflappable of women, so much so that he realised his words must be shaking her to the core. Whatever the emotional ramifications of this discussion turned out to be, John Considine had decided that she was entitled to know the truth of what had really happened on that fateful night. He spoke quietly, and in the dim light of the cocktail bar he held her troubled gaze.

'Paul Bannon saved you.'

She lowered her eyes and sat motionless for an age. He nodded to the barman and he replenished her glass immediately. She held it with a trembling hand and raised it to her lips.

'He tried to tell me once,' she whispered, 'but back then I didn't want to hear it. I was a stupid . . . naive . . . silly young girl.'

'You cannot blame yourself, Francesca. There were others more complicit. They used you. Simple as that.'

'He . . . tried to tell me.'

She sat in a state of dream-like paralysis, her skin pale as snow. But he knew he needed to finish this. He pulled on his cigar and settled his big frame into the chair.

'It was early afternoon, and the hunt was in full flow, scattered far and wide across the landscape. Paul was in a group of riders up on the meadow hill when they saw your horse being driven into the water. They raced off the slope and chased along the riverbank, but the young fella's stallion covered the terrain faster than the rest of them. When they last saw him he was rattling across the Grange bridge at full stride. By then he must have concluded that the only hope of rescuing you was to cut across the meadow and engage the river on the far side.

'Three hours later Jamie met Simon on the driveway with you in his arms. Jamie said you were barely recognisable. Your hair was caked with silt from the river and your clothes were torn to shreds. That night, in those conditions, you could never have known that Paul almost lost his life in the struggle to save *your* life. Afterwards his condition deteriorated, and he was probably delirious when Simon hatched his conspiracy to hijack the credit for saving you. It was a charade that would condemn you to a nightmare for what should have been the best years of your life, or perhaps forever, who knows. Sadly, what's done is done and cannot be undone. It was a dastardly act of betrayal and afterwards, when the young fella recovered from the fever . . . by then the treachery was complete. Simon, the consummate coward, had triumphed, and walked away with the most beautiful girl in the land.'

He stared at her but his thoughts seemed far away.

'Jamie reckons Simon grasped the opportunity when he came across the two of you lying in the field unconscious. Later, when it all died down, he went back to the place where they discovered Paul, and there in the grass he found strands of your hair buried in the silt from the river. Jamie said Paul was unconscious that evening when they brought him up to the mansion, but he distinctly remembers seeing his hair caked with the same silt and his clothes torn in exactly the same way as yours. Simon was soaked and shivering but otherwise clean as a whistle. It doesn't take a detective to figure the whole thing out, but Jamie just didn't piece it together at the time, not until much later, and by then it was too late.'

When he had finished telling the story he closed his eyes and emitted a deep sigh. The emotional effort had taken a lot out of him, far more than he realised. He sat back feeling tired and old, yet sure in the knowledge that in telling her the truth of what happened that night, he had done the right thing in the end.

And then he felt her arms around his neck, ever so gently. And when he looked up she was kneeling beside him, tears in her eyes, lips quivering. She kissed him lightly on the cheek.

'You're such a good man, John Considine. This can't have been easy for you.'

She laid her head on his shoulder and cried. He put his giant arms around her and held her, the outpouring of emotion that his words had caused wracking through her body as she sobbed her heart out. He felt her hot tears streaming down his shirt, but still he held her as she cried and cried.

Eventually she eased away from him, sat back in her chair and dabbed her eyes. She looked up at him and smiled briefly.

'Send me the bill for the dry cleaning.'

'You'd better believe it.'

They sat in silence for a time. Nothing they could say would belie the deadly seriousness of this life-changing moment.

'You OK with all of this?' he asked eventually.

She nodded her head and seemed to compose herself slowly.

'Do you ever see him?' she asked, her tone sounding low and vulnerable. 'Where can he be after all this time?'

She spoke so quietly, her voice thick with emotion, a fleeting glimpse, he thought, into the heart of this highly controlled, super-sophisticated ice-queen.

'He's in London.'

She stared at him wide-eyed. He took a long sip of his beer.

'I didn't plan on telling you the rest of it,' he said in a matter-of-fact tone. 'But the media are gonna to be crawling all over this, so what the hell. You'll hear about it soon enough.'

Until then she looked drained, pale, emotionally washed out, but now he saw a hint of alarm in her eyes. He heard the words catching as she spoke.

'John, please . . . tell me he's . . . OK.'

In the years ahead, whenever he looked back on their meeting that night, this would always be the defining moment for John Considine. He couldn't pinpoint exactly what it was – just a trace of something in her voice, a look in her eye, the faintest tremble of her hand as she lifted her glass. Yes, whenever he thought about it afterwards, that just *had* to be it. In the end it was always the eyes that gave it away. This woman, undoubtedly the most beautiful woman he had ever seen in his life, this woman who could have any man she desired, who could walk into a crowded room and ignite the atmosphere. This woman was in love.

'He's OK,' he responded casually. 'This is all about business, and I've been sworn to secrecy, but I'll tell it to you if it's what you want to hear.'

He saw the flash of relief in her eyes. A faint 'get on with it' smile flickered across her lips. He sat back in his chair and dug his hands into his pockets.

'The Bannon operation crashed six years ago – this much I think you know. The banks shut the company down, grabbed the assets and wheeled in an army of receivers. As to the reasons why, let's just say for now that aside from the meltdown in the UK property market, there were several contributing factors that rendered the collapse inevitable. One of those factors was a breakdown in relations between the company and the London construction unions, London historically being the powerhouse of the Bannon operation. I'm highlighting the union problem for reasons that should become apparent when you get to understand what's happening right now.'

He paused and glanced at her. She smiled briefly and nodded, the shock of the earlier revelations temporarily compartmentalised. Right now she seemed pretty much focused on this part of the discussion.

'Paul formulated a rescue package for the Bannon UK assets in receivership and recently presented it to the company's receivers. I'm not privy to the detail, but I *do* know that it has been endorsed by Beauchamps, one of the oldest, most conservative, most prestigious merchant banking houses in the City. Don't ask me how he succeeded in convincing them, but that's what's happened, and right now it seems he's back in control, for the time being at least.'

In spite of the inner turmoil he knew she must surely be feeling, she sat there poised and in control, legs crossed, hands clasped tightly.

'I assume you'll be with him on all of this.'

'You'd better believe it.'

From the faint smile on her face, he could see that she was pleased with this.

'It seems such a daunting undertaking. Is it likely to succeed?'

'I haven't got a clue, is the honest answer, and I'm not sure if anyone does. The banks have given their approval, and in order for that to happen those guys need to be convinced it's worth something better than a shot to nothing. The obstacles are so far beyond the norms of standard business practice, I reckon the average guy would run a mile from this. But this guy ain't the average guy, and nothing seems to faze him. We'll just have to wait and see.'

'Wait and see exactly what, John? I still don't get it. And you mentioned the media. What is it with the media?'

'Those guys'll be crawling all over this,' he replied, a little too quickly, she felt, the hint of tension in his voice so out of character for this man.

This must be deadly serious, she thought as she studied him; his demeanour preoccupied, his expression tense; a rare unguarded glimpse into the soul of a man most found impossible to read. But then, quick as a flash, his eyes hardened and his gravelly tones shattered the silence.

'At this particular moment there are four thousand men on the march into London from all corners of England, Scotland, Ireland, Germany and further afield. I know this because I'm part of a team that's making the whole thing happen. The unions and the cops are also aware that there's a situation developing – it is impossible to mobilise such a vast force without interested parties getting to hear about it – too many people on the peripheries, accountants, bankers, lawyers, you name it, the whole shebang. The unions hate the Bannons, always have done. It's vindictive, it's personal, it's spiteful, and it's orchestrated by one of the nastiest fuckers on the planet – a labour boss named Ben Bradshaw.

'Bradshaw runs the biggest construction union in London and he hates the family. This guy was instrumental in the demise of the Bannon Group and he'll do all in his power to spike any attempt to try and kick-start the operation. He probably already knows that a refinancing deal has been struck with the banks and he'll be pissed that no attempt has been made to engage with them at any level. This union hates being marginalised, especially by this family, and they're sure to react angrily. During the past five years they've maintained a token picket outside Bannons' largest London construction site in Croydon town centre, which gives you some idea of the depth of their intent. It also sends a message to all the other operators in the London area – keep us onside or we'll wipe you off the radar, just the same as the Bannons. Lately they've been steadily increasing their presence on the Croydon picket lines. Late last night we took a count and they've already ratcheted the numbers up to twelve hundred. You sure you're following all of this?'

'Yes. Everything.'

He stared at her and for the first time noticed a subtle change. Her eyes were bright and focused. Her earlier trauma pushed aside and forgotten, at least for now. He knew of course that she had been born and raised on the estate lands at Grange

Abbey and that a part of her life was inextricably linked to her association with this family. The mansion had been unoccupied and empty for almost a decade, its shutters closed to the world, its rooms languishing in darkness and dust behind the weight of the receivers' padlocks, its corridors silent and still, with the ghosts of a glorious past stalking their cavernous spaces.

It would be impossible for her not to be aware of all of this. The fortunes and subsequent misfortunes of the Bannon dynasty had been exhaustively reported in the press and on radio and television channels across the land. Whatever personal misfortune Francesca had been subjected to at the hands of Simon Bannon, and whatever demons she had been forced to confront during those intervening years, he knew that her innermost emotions would forever be formulated by the memory of those early years spent living on Grange Abbey.

'I understand all of what you're telling me, of course. I'm familiar with most of it. How could I not be? I was a part of it for a period of my life I so often wish I could forget forever, and yet I know I never will.'

Suddenly some faraway thought, some long-forgotten memory seemed to upset her. She covered her face with her hands and tears flowed in streams through clenched fingers. Immune from the vagaries of the world, there wasn't a lot left that could surprise John Considine, but that night he could only stare at her in anguished disbelief. Even during those dark days when he had first met her on the pier at Holyhead all those years ago, he couldn't recall ever seeing her behave like this. He sat silently and let her cry and cry, this ravishing woman he had sheltered and protected since that fateful night when her brother Jamie had consigned her smashed-up body to his care.

He had watched over her during the months of convalescence that followed, eventually placing her under the protection of Special Air Service veteran Nick Penn, whose father, Jason Penn, a decorated Second World War RAF fighter pilot, was one of Considine's top contracts managers in London. Nick, himself a recipient of the George Cross for defusing a three-hundred-pound car bomb in the centre of Belfast under sustained sniper fire, became her chauffeur and bodyguard when, a year later, following her astonishing re-emergence from under the scalpels of her brilliant plastic surgeons, Francesca had chosen to pursue the lifestyle of an international escort.

It was rumoured that she was the most sought after, highly paid escort in the world, and when he looked across at her it was pretty damn easy to see why. He remembered when she first told him what she intended to do with the rest of her life, and the look of relief on her face when he displayed not the faintest criticism.

'You've chosen a dangerous means of earning a living, darlin',' he recalled saying to her.

'We need to construct an unbreakable steel band of security around you to make sure we get you safely home at the end of the night.'

And now he studied her as she cried her heart out, the soft shadows of the lamplight washing across her face. He couldn't imagine what kind of demons she was exorcising. The context of their discussion had stirred emotions buried in the depths of her subconscious, never intended to be revisited. He waited silently until she finally composed herself. She dabbed her moist, reddened eyes and gazed across at him.

'I love him,' she said simply, ever so quietly. 'I've loved him since I was a little girl.'

Her eyes were cast down. She looked forlorn, upset, vulnerable. He sat and stared at her for an age.

'Then he's the luckiest man in the world,' he said eventually in his matter-of-fact tone. 'He may not even know it, but that's what he is for sure – the luckiest man in the world.'

He watched her as she clasped and unclasped her hands.

'Don't tell him I said so,' she whispered.

He gave a nonchalant shrug of the shoulders.

'Old Johnny's good at keeping his mouth shut.'

'Thank you – it's what I want.'

They sat a while, submerged in the aftermath of the cold, heart-wrenching reality of her turbulent past laid bare before her for the very first time.

'I must go', she said eventually, 'but one last question . . . '

'Go ahead. Shoot.'

'These men you speak of, the ones who are on their way to

London from all of those places. I assume they travel at Paul's behest.'

'You assume correctly,' he replied.

'What's this all about John?' she asked quietly.

He wheezed, then gazed up at the ceiling thoughtfully, then back at her, his eyes granite-hard, and when he spoke, his tone was chillingly calm.

'You still don't get it, do you?'

She stared at him uncomprehendingly.

'No John, I still don't get it. What is he planning to do?'

He stubbed his cigar and sighed a weary sigh.

'He's planning to storm the picket lines at Croydon.'

30

Frank Bannon's promotion to group chief executive was spectacularly contagious, and the Bannon organisation surged ahead, riding on the back of its new leader's meteoric maverick style. The company's profits soared, its balance sheet powering from strength to strength as the production lines ran full tilt and revenue piled in. Each year turnover outstripped all previous years, to become the highest ever recorded, and the asset value soared in the equivalent accounting period, further ingratiating Frank with banks and stock-market traders eager to align themselves to a name synonymous with glamour, success and the aphrodisiac of youth.

In the spring of 1967, Frank's five-year-old stallion, Accelerator, won the Cheltenham Gold Cup, coasting in seven lengths ahead of the strongest field assembled for the race in the preceding ten years. The horse powered past the finishing post to rapturous acclaim from a delirious thirty-thousand-strong Irish contingent. Frank's smiling face was flashed across the television screens of the world as he graciously accepted the coveted trophy from Queen Elizabeth, the Queen Mother. Later Accelerator went on to win the Epsom Derby and the King George the Fifth Stakes, to record his fourteenth successive win.

Then they brought the great horse back to Ireland, to Grange Abbey, where he had been born and bred as a foal. He was to remain on the estate for ten days prior to competing in the Irish Grand National at the Leopardstown racetrack in the south suburbs of Dublin, his final race before being put out to stud. The meeting was an all-ticket sell-out with racegoers packing the stands early to witness the event.

Frank instructed Jamie Sinclair to take charge of affairs at the Grange from the moment the horse entered the grounds.

The stallion's English trainer, Henry Adamson, expressed his satisfaction with this arrangement, having visited the Grange on a number of occasions previously. The stallion, accompanied by an entourage of training staff, stable lads, security personnel and the Bannons' resident veterinary surgeon, entered the Grange at seven on a bright Sunday morning, having earlier completed a one hundred and fifty mile road journey to the ferry port of Fishguard in Wales. They had landed at Rosslare in County Wexford at five that morning following a smooth four-hour crossing, and as they passed through the towns and villages, crowds were already lining the roads to wave at them as they drove by. A security vehicle led the twelve-strong motor contingent on the two-hour road journey from the ferry port to the Grange, together with vans and trucks containing the training staff and equipment, and finally the horsebox transporting Accelerator.

At dawn that morning Frank and a party of two hundred guests landed at Dublin Airport in high spirits, and were driven to the Grange in luxury coaches. They arrived to a carnival atmosphere. The driveway was buzzing with vehicles moving in and out. The white canvas marquee glistened in the early morning sun, and up at the mansion the doors to the veranda were thrown open to welcome the guests on arrival.

The following morning the stallion was led onto the gallop before a host of excited onlookers. Henry Adamson took the young jockey Robbie Foley aside and instructed him to take it nice and handy.

'Run him at an easy gallop, Rob, nothing too strenuous, ten minutes out and ten minutes back. It's all we need to do today.'

Four horses and their riders accompanied Accelerator onto the gallop, and all went according to plan that morning. A later examination by the resident vet pronounced the stallion fit and well, and afterwards, when he was groomed, fed and watered, the mood was upbeat, and the countdown to the big day officially began.

The party started in earnest when James and Catherine Bannon arrived on the estate from their home in the south of France. Frank had decided to stage the ultimate corporate event, an international showcase for the Bannon Group, with absolutely no expense spared. The family feted their guests with a mouth-watering, unending display of food, and the bars flowed with an array of drinks including Guinness on tap, served side by side with Pol Roger, Frank's favourite champagne. All day long, guests from across Europe converged on the marquee, immersing themselves in the carnival atmosphere, mixing, drinking and socialising with the crowds thronging the Grange. In the adrenalin-charged atmosphere, the expectation became immense. The highlight of each evening, the formal banquet in the marquee, was a lavish presentation on a gargantuan scale, the crowning glory a sixteen-piece band to serenade the thousand guests into the early hours.

And while all of this was taking place up at the house, out in the stables Jamie Sinclair's hand-picked team of his best stable lads kept close watch over their priceless guest, the wonder-horse Accelerator.

Always among the last to leave the bar, Frank was invariably in his office in a rear annexe of the mansion each morning before seven. With less than three days to the big event, his London acquisition team had been working feverishly to sign off on a parcel of land in Milton Keynes, a newly designated satellite town in Buckinghamshire. The deal would add a further four thousand plots to the company's growing land bank, and matters were finally beginning to click into place. Frank had spent the morning on the telephone discussing the finer detail with Johnny Greenfield, his land agent in London, when there was a knock on his door. He saw Jamie Sinclair and Henry Adamson standing in the corridor and waved them through.

'I've got to run, Johnny boy, so go and do it like I was saying earlier. Ask for reduction of a hundred grand, or else they give us an extra nine months on the closing. Settle for six if you've got to. Six on the contract or a hundred off the price is effectively the same thing. If they're not willing to move, tell them to fuck off.'

He replaced the receiver and turned and appraised the two men.

'You're looking pretty fucking glum, Jamie. Please tell me my horse is OK, because right now it's all that matters.'

Jamie glanced at Henry Adamson. Frank Bannon wasn't renowned for his patience.

'The horse is fine, Frank – it's the jock that's causing the problem. Robbie hit a fence on the gallop this morning and broke his collarbone on the way down. He's in an ambulance right now on the way to hospital.'

Frank yawned and flicked nonchalantly through some paperwork.

'So why come to me with this?' he asked in a bored drawl. 'I'm paying you and an army of guys to make sure the stallion races on Saturday, so by my reckoning this one's down to you, Jamie, even if the solution seems pretty damn obvious to me. Either Robbie rides him with a strapped collarbone, or we find the next available pilot. It is for you to decide.'

'Frank, if it was that simple I wouldn't be standing here wasting your time. The problem's not the rider. It's the horse.'

Frank's tolerance level was notoriously low. He pushed the paperwork aside.

'Get to the point, Jamie. It's beginning to sound like a fucking riddle.'

Jamie drew a deep breath, his normally cool demeanour fraying under the scrutiny of Frank's steely stare.

'Accelerator's a brilliant horse, Frank, but he's also one temperamental son-of-a-bitch. It's probably that temper of his that makes him as good as he is. But it's also what's causing the problem. Obviously the stallion is happy to let Robbie Foley ride him, but he kicks up an unmerciful stink if another pilot tries to climb on board.'

Frank listened with growing frustration, his impatience turning to anger as he stared at the two men.

'Calm down Frank,' Henry Adamson interjected in his thick, Yorkshire accent. 'We've a real problem on our hands here. It's an unusual situation, although not unique in the industry. On rare occasions I've come across situations where replacement jockeys, even the best ones, simply fail to gel with the animal, and the results are catastrophic.'

Frank seemed exasperated.

'Don't fucking tell me to calm down,' he retorted testily. 'You guys are responsible for failing to anticipate this and God only knows what the fuck else. I sincerely hope one of you jokers has a plan B, because I'm telling you now that if this doesn't get resolved, there'll be blood on the floor.'

They stood quietly as he contemplated them.

'Begin by getting Robbie out of that fucking hospital at the earliest possible time. Fill the fucker with morphine and get him back on board the stallion. If that's what we've got to do, then let's go do it. The stakes are pretty fucking high here, so much so it hardly bears thinking about. I don't *give* a fuck what it costs to do it, just so long as you get Robbie back on board. This horse must run, gentlemen, and, more importantly, this horse must win. Nothing less will satisfy me, and you can both interpret that any way you fucking want.'

They shuffled nervously but Frank was in a sour mood. He glanced at them.

'Are you two fuckers still here?'

Jamie turned to go but Henry Adamson held his ground.

'Frank, Robbie Foley's never going to ride the horse, so you can forget about it right now. His collarbone is fractured in two places and what we failed to tell you is he suffered a concussion when his head hit the ground. Right now the guy's in cloud cuckoo-land – even his doctors don't have a clue when he's likely to resurface. We think we have a solution to the problem; it's a long shot, but for the life of me I just can't figure it any other way.'

Frank suppressed his frustration and forced himself to calm his nerves. He wished he'd had a sniff of that little white powder his latest girlfriend Lavinia had introduced him to recently. He was also beginning to miss Lavinia and her long legs wrapped around him as he shagged her brains out all night, every night. She'd gone to one of those girly shower parties in Paris – was it the Plaza Athenee, he couldn't quite remember. He reminded himself to give her a call and tell her to bring him some of that magic potion when she arrived at the Grange for the Friday-night festivities ahead of Saturday's race. Assuming of course that there still *was* a fucking race. He pressed a button on his intercom.

'Grace, bring a pot of fucking coffee and three mugs.'

He sat there quietly contemplating the two men, gleaning a vestige of satisfaction from their discomfort before finally motioning them to sit down. Grace arrived carrying a tray with china cups and a silver coffee jug. They watched her as she poured. It was hard not to: she was an attractive twenty-one-year-old brunette with curves in all the right places.

'Thanks, Grace,' Frank smiled, winking at her, thinking perhaps that Lavinia's late arrival might yet prove a blessing in disguise.

'You're welcome, sir,' she smiled back.

The door closed and Frank sipped his coffee.

'OK guys, plan B. Let's have it.'

Henry gave Jamie an 'over to you' look.

'The stallion belonged to your kid brother,' he began. 'He broke it in as a foal, when most of the other guys had given up on the foul-tempered son-of-a-bitch. Back then the stable lads were too scared to approach him, but as we all know, Paul has a way with these things. One afternoon he climbed into the paddock, saddled the horse and took off, and that was about it really. The stallion cleared the paddock fence and galloped off into the sunset. Nobody was sure if they'd ever see them again, and then hours later Paul walked him back into the yard and handed the reins to Robbie Foley. "Hey Rob," he said, cool as a cucumber, "take him inside and wash him down." In those days the stallion went under a different name, Ricochet.

'The months passed and he grew stronger, tougher, faster – still a cranky, unpredictable son-of-a-bitch, except when Paul and, rather surprisingly, Robbie, was around him. There was some sort of rapport between Paul and that animal – I can't explain it – you'd have to see it to believe it. Then the day before he returned to boarding school he asked Robbie to take care of the horse during the time he was away. Back then Robbie was still a stable lad, small in stature, but feisty, always feisty. The family have lived on the estate all their lives.'

Frank drained his coffee and poured himself another cup. His mood seemed to lighten.

'Jesus, Jamie, you couldn't fucking make it up. Continue this yarn of yours.'

Jamie glanced at Henry, who smiled tensely and nodded.

'The morning before he departed for school, just before sunrise, he saddled the stallion and gave Robbie a leg up. Then he hit the horse a slap on the haunch and off they went, the two of them. I've been around horses all my life, Frank, and don't ask me to prove it, but I'd swear the stallion figured it out that Paul wasn't always going to be around to look after him, and in his absence he needed somebody to do that, and *that* somebody was Robbie Foley. Crazy it may sound, but I'd swear the horse seemed to sense that the arrangement was in his best interests. Robbie's been stable boy to the stallion going on two years. He wasn't afraid to be around him, and in the end that's probably what nailed it. The following month we raced him in a point-to-point at Clonmel and he cruised in for the win without breaking a sweat. Three weeks later we entered him in a novice chase at the Galway Races and he won by seven lengths; and then people began showing interest, and that's when I called you in London. Afterwards, on your instruction, we brought him across on the ferry and delivered him to Henry's yard in Newmarket. And that's about it, Frank. I'm kinda hoping you can figure the rest out for yourself.'

Frank stared at Jamie with a growing sense of disbelief and slowly straightened in his chair.

'Where are you going with this, Jamie? Please tell me you're not thinking what I think you're thinking.'

A bead of perspiration trickled down the side of Jamie's face.

'We've run out of options Frank,' he responded tensely. 'Other than Robbie, who's out of the picture, there is one other person the stallion will tolerate. One person with the skill, the know-how and the bottle to take him across the line next Saturday, and that one person happens to be your brother.'

'I don't fucking believe this,' Frank gasped, 'and even if I did believe it, which I fucking don't, my kid brother has never ridden a competitive race, and we're talking about the Grand National! Are you both out of your fucking minds!'

'I'm with Jamie one hundred percent on this, Frank,' Henry Adamson interjected quickly. 'The situation ain't exactly ideal – far from it. There's no chapter in the manual to cover this eventuality. So let's forget about the blame-game; we simply don't have the time. The advice we're giving you now is the best advice we can give, and it's the only advice available. If you want the stallion to race on Saturday, then this is what we absolutely must do. We need to ferry the young fella down to the Grange as quickly as possible, and if he turns out to be as good as Jamie seems to think he is, then we're in with a shot. Put him in the saddle and let's see what happens. If we don't like what we see, then we pull the horse and hold him back to race another day. But if we do like what we see, then I reckon it's game on. The buck stops with you, Frank, but you need to make your mind up real fast.'

The forthright Yorkshire man, reputedly one of the top three trainers in all of England, could be relied upon to call it straight – most of the time. Frank guessed he was probably too old to be intimidated, which, when he thought about it, was probably what he admired about him anyway. Henry had said his piece in a matter-of-fact, no-nonsense way. Frank regarded him pensively.

'It's too early in the morning for this shit,' he sighed, draining the last of the coffee into his cup. But Frank's mood had lightened. He sat and stared at both of them for an age as he pondered the options, then a smile broke across his face.

'OK you pair of fuckers, let's do it your way!'

They emitted a collective sigh of relief.

'So, what the hell are we waiting for! Let's chase down the little fucker!'

He pushed open the door to the outer office.

'Grace, get me the Monsignor.'

'Certainly, sir.'

'Oh and Grace . . . '

'Yes sir.'

'There's something I'd like you to do for me later. If you wouldn't mind staying back a while this evening . . . '

'With pleasure, sir.'

His telephone buzzed and Grace connected him.

'Good morning Charles. How are yah?'

'And a very good morning to you, Frank. How may I be of assistance?'

The cranky fucker, Frank mused, always so matter-of-fucking-fact. But the Monsignor did listen patiently while he explained the background to the problem.

'Charles – bottom line – we need my kid brother to pilot the stallion on Saturday and we need to get him down here as quickly as possible.'

The Monsignor seemed to ponder this.

'I just wonder have you really thought this through, Frank.'

'*Sure* I have.'

'And presumably you're comfortable with the concept of pitting a young, inexperienced amateur into the toughest race in the season, against the best jockeys in the land, most of whom would happily kill him rather than let him win.'

Frank tightened his grip on the receiver.

'I've just run out of options. If it wasn't sheer necessity, I wouldn't be making this call.'

The silence at the other end was telling.

'I'm not thrilled with that response,' the Monsignor replied eventually. 'You're obviously content to expose your brother to the risk of serious injury or worse in order to have a shot at the golden prize. I just wonder if you've really given this matter due consideration. And besides, there's another little problem. We don't really know where he is right now. He left yesterday with some others from fifth year on a character-building survival trek in the Wicklow mountains. You remember the sort of thing. It's part of the curriculum. They could be anywhere within a forty-mile radius.'

'Well, fuck to that!'

The Monsignor smiled, barely.

'We're sending a coach to rendezvous with them at a designated collection point this evening. The plan is to have them back in the college around midnight, assuming they actually find their way down off the mountain.'

Frank's mind was racing. This really was the worst news. Another vital preparation day lost, leaving barely two days to get ready for the race. These were the tightest of margins.

'Best let him get a night's sleep. We'll come by there first thing in the morning.'

'If that's your final decision – '

'Yes it is. Like I was saying earlier, we've just run out of options.'

'Then there's nothing more to be said, but remember, I still have reservations.'

★

The news of Robbie Foley's fall spread like wildfire through the breakfast rooms of Grange Abbey. Most of these people were racing fanatics who readily understood the far-reaching implications of this latest unwelcome news. In the racing world, a successful horse-and-rider partnership was a combination not to be tampered with, the horse in this case a highly tuned instrument, trained to the optimal level, an unpredictable, temperamental racing machine. The mood at the Grange was subdued as they agonised over this latest twist, along with the hitherto unthinkable possibility of withdrawing the horse from Saturday's field.

As the day wore on a rumour began circulating that the family was working flat out to try and source a replacement jockey. With lunch in full swing, Frank sauntered into the marquee, climbed the podium and took hold of the microphone. The venue looked to be about a quarter full with, several hundred guests scattered about.

'Good afternoon ladies and gentlemen,' he began. 'By now you'll be aware that Robbie was injured on the gallop this morning, and has been ruled out of participation in Saturday's Grand National. We wish him a speedy recovery and I'm delighted to say that the news from the hospital is good. Robbie's expected to make a full recovery, though unfortunately not in time to participate in the big race. The only solution available is to try and find a suitable replacement, and all I can say right now is that there are grounds for optimism. Accelerator is a temperamental son-of-a-bitch, and the challenge for all of us is to find him a partner with the necessary courage and ability to extract another great performance from this unique animal. This, ladies and gentlemen, is our absolute priority, and we will shortly be making a further announcement. Thank you and good day.'

★

In the early hours of the morning Jamie drove the jeep through the deserted village of Castleknock and turned in beneath the ivy-clad arches of the college. Frank sat in the front beside Jamie, with Henry Adamson and John Considine seated behind. It was a dark, gloomy morning as they sped along the driveway and skidded to a halt on the gravel turning-area beside the main front entrance. The Monsignor stood waiting to greet them.

'Welcome to Saint John the Baptist, gentlemen. I just wish I felt more comfortable regarding the purpose of your visit.'

Frank placed a hand on his shoulder.

Charles, if at any stage along the way I get a bad feeling about this, I'll abort. You have my word.'

The Monsignor led them through to the reception area and pointed to a door at the far end.

'Your brother is waiting for you. I haven't told him what this is all about. I decided I'd leave that dirty little task to you.'

Frank pushed open the door and the others filed in behind. Paul sat in a chair at the end of a polished mahogany table, dressed in the uniform of the fifth form: white shirt, red and blue striped tie, navy school blazer and grey slacks. The four men sat in a line along the table, Frank taking the chair nearest him. He poured coffee from a decanter and handed each of them a cup, then turned to his brother.

'You're looking pretty good, kid. How in the hell are you?'

Paul stared at the others and yawned.

'Frank, I crawled into bed three hours ago, so why don't you just tell me what this is about before I fall asleep.'

'That's my boy,' John Considine drawled. 'Straight to the point. No fucking about.'

Frank smirked.

'Don't they teach you any fucking manners in this place? We're here because we need you to help us solve a problem. Robbie Foley took a tumble on the gallop yesterday.'

'Yeah . . . so . . . '

'Well it's a bit fucking unfortunate, because he's due to ride the National this Saturday and now obviously that ain't gonna happen. And there you have it.'

Paul stifled another yawn.

'There I have what, Frank?'

Frank glanced at the others, then turned to his brother.

'Ain't it obvious? We want you to pilot the stallion in the National.'

Paul glanced at him and took a sip of his coffee.

'I must be still asleep, Frank, because one of us is dreaming.

Either you're dreaming or I'm dreaming.'

'This ain't no dream, son,' Henry Adamson interjected. 'We're here today because there's nobody else capable of staying on board the stallion long enough to make it across the first fence. We've been through all the options, and we've reluctantly come to the conclusion that you're the only one who can do it.'

Paul turned to the trainer.

'Has anyone told you I've never ridden a competitive race, and you're actually suggesting I ride the National in two days' time?'

Adamson shrugged.

'It's a long shot, for sure,' he replied, 'but pulling the horse at this stage is somewhere down there between a last resort and a financial catastrophe. Factor in the stud value and we're talking silly figures here, son, and besides, everyone keeps telling me you can do it!'

Frank nodded in agreement, then turned to his brother.

'Listen, kid, there are a thousand people down at the Grange right now willing us to find a solution to this. Mom, Dad, your uncles, all of them are there. Obviously the Monsignor doesn't approve, and I've told him that nobody's going to put you under pressure. Just say if you don't feel you can do this, and we're outa here.'

In the silence that followed, the only sound was the ticking of the old grandfather clock in the far corner. Nobody spoke – there was nothing left to be said. He sat staring at the ceiling, hands in pockets, legs stretched out, then yawned and turned to his brother.

'Frank, you are full of crap – Mum, Dad, your uncles. Where do you dream up this shit?'

He stared at the four deadpan faces, then swallowed the last mouthful in his mug.

'I'll need to walk the course at least once.'

The audible gasp of relief said it all. Frank grabbed his brother and pulled him close, slapped him on the face, kissed him on the forehead, then turned to the others and grinned.

'*That's* my boy!'

31

Later that morning a spokesman for the family confirmed
to the media that the Bannon stallion Accelerator would run
in Saturday's Grand National, with the replacement jockey
confirmed as amateur rider Paul Bannon, the seventeen-year-
old brother of the owner, Frank Bannon. The news caused a
flurry among the guests at Grange Abbey, and a less-than-muted
response from the wider media, where the wisdom of placing
an inexperienced, unknown amateur jockey on board a priceless
racehorse was soon the subject of intense debate and speculation.

Initial betting forecasts drifted steadily from odds of two-to-
one-on to evens, then two-to-one, finally settling at three-to-one,
late in the afternoon before the race.

Back at the Grange Paul made his way to the stables and
saddled the stallion, then walked him through the paddocks out
onto the gallop. Henry Adamson watched nervously during this,
the defining moment. He insisted that only key backup staff and
family members should be present in the workout area. Three
horses and their riders waited as Paul led the stallion onto the
gallop. Jamie gave him a leg up and Henry offered him a crop,
which he declined.

'I've never laid a whip on him and I ain't gonna start now.'

Adamson turned to Frank who shrugged dismissively.

'I'll leave it up to you, son, but this one's a real handful.'

Paul nodded to the other riders.

'You boys take the lead and I'll follow on.'

When they were off and running, he squeezed his knees and
the stallion responded instantly. The spectators watched him
turn onto the gallop and canter into the grey morning mist. When
they came around for the first time Paul broke from the others
and eased Accelerator down off the gallop.

'Something the matter?' Henry Adamson inquired nervously.

'I need Jamie to release the left stirrup two inches.'

When it was done he checked the adjustment.

'Yeah, feels better.'

'Take him at a steady gallop, son,' Henry instructed. 'Three full circuits.'

The old trainer watched intently as they cantered back onto the gallop and completed two circuits. On the final circuit, he turned to Frank.

'The boy sure knows how to ride,' he smiled, his demeanour tense, 'Centre of gravity pretty much perfect, negligible movement in the saddle. So far I like what I'm seeing.'

On the Saturday morning, when the odds drifted out to four-to-one, Frank began spread-betting fifty thousand across seven bookmakers on both sides of the Irish Sea. The preparations were complete, the markers laid down. At ten on the morning of the race, the Bannon entourage rolled out through the gates of Grange Abbey and turned onto the Dublin Road.

Accelerator received a tumultuous welcome when the cavalcade crossed the southern outskirts of the city and turned in the gates of the Leopardstown complex. The crowds lining the parade rings cheered when the stallion was unloaded and led the short distance to the stable complex for the pre-race preparations. In less than four hours Accelerator would be brought back out onto the track and pitted against an international field of thirty-one runners in the richest race ever run on Irish soil.

All morning, excitement levels rose to fever pitch as everyone waited impatiently for the clock to run down. Then, with only minutes remaining, there was a roar of anticipation when the English raider Runaway Bay led the field out into the parade ring. The crowds thronging the paddocks cheered wildly when Accelerator was led in behind the French horse LeVoillier, a previous winner of the Prix de L'Arc at Longchamps. The jockeys mounted up and cantered past the stands on their journey to the starting line. The starter called them first time, the tape went up and suddenly the race was on.

That morning the country awoke to clear blue skies, and by midday soaring temperatures had created a carnival atmosphere among the overspill milling around the hospitality tents. Out on the course it was a different story. The warm air and the saturated ground combined to create a misty fog that hovered over large sections of the track. The only stretch still visible was the area fronting the stands, where the great hulking structures lining the course had somehow contrived to dissipate the murky haze.

Paul galloped out in the middle of the pack and manoeuvered the stallion into a position third from the back of the field. The lead jockeys were setting a cracking pace and four horses came down heavily on the treacherous ground as they rattled across the first ditch.

They turned out into the country on the first circuit and disappeared into the all-encompassing mist. Bathed in the warm afternoon sun, the crowd stood and watched the last of the riders fade from view and listened to the thunder of hooves recede. In the eerie, surreal atmosphere, all anyone could do was wait for them to re-emerge out of the fog as they rounded the course into the straight for the first time. And when they did finally appear ,with miraculously no other fallers, Accelerator had moved from the back of the field into joint seventh position, eliciting an ear-shattering roar from the stands as the racing pack galloped into view and thundered down the straight.

Frank and his entourage cheered from their private box in the enclosure, but their efforts were drowned in a wall of sound as the riders headed out into the country on the final circuit. He felt a knot in the pit of his stomach as he watched his young brother pilot the stallion against the greatest horses in the land. Persistent rainfall during the preceding days had predetermined that the going would always be heavy. The situation was exacerbated by the earlier races, which had left the track looking like a mud-bath and the jockeys splattered from head to foot. Frank found the tension unbearable as he strained through his binoculars to follow the pack. The concern etched on Henry Adamson's face did little to alleviate his darkening mood.

Knowing that the outcome would have a vital bearing on the stud-value of the stallion, Frank struggled to control his fraying nerves. He snatched a glass of champagne from the tray of a passing waiter and downed it in one gulp as the horses passed the finishing line and raced out into the country for the last time.

'Fuck!' Frank bellowed. 'Fuck! Fuck! Fuck!'

A lady in the adjoining box turned and glared at him.

'And fuck you too, you fat cunt!'

Her male companion stared indignantly, but then seemed to have a 'don't mess with Frank Bannon' moment, and quickly turned away. Frank stared tensely over a track that now resembled a river of mud, the lethal combination of the sticky ground and the enveloping fog consorting to make these the most treacherous conditions. He pondered once again the Monsignor's warning words, and silently contemplated the wisdom of allowing his young brother to participate in this most dangerous of races. The crowd seemed strangely anaesthetised as they waited tensely, their silence contagious, until at last the muffled thump of hoof on turf reverberated in the distance, growing ever louder as the racing pack advanced through the blinding mist.

The vast throng held its breath and stared into the place where the wall of mist ended. Then suddenly a lone horse exploded out of the fog and rounded the final bend at a stupendous gallop. A stunned gasp rippled along the stands, and a roar erupted as the crowd jumped to its feet and watched the stallion charge down the final stretch.

'And now we have our first definitive view,' the commentator's voice crackled through the speakers. 'And with still no sign of the chasing pack it's the Frank Bannon-owned stallion Accelerator leading the field, carrying the colours of the Bannon family, bred in Ireland and trained in England by this year's leading trainer Henry Adamson, ridden by amateur jockey Paul Bannon. And here come the rest of them, with LeVoillier in second place followed by Dead Cert in third, then Centurion, Prince Regent and Break for the Border, but barring a mistake at the last this is looking like a one-horse race.'

A roar from the delirious crowd reverberated in the air as they watched the stallion race up to the final fence and clear it effortlessly.

'And now he's over the last, and racing to the finishing line with a lead of twenty-five lengths, it's the Irish horse Accelerator who wins the ninety-sixth Grand National in spectacular style at odds of four-to-one.'

★

The celebrations began in earnest when Frank and his huge entourage converged on the Grange. These were the days Paul remembered most fondly, when his elder brother and his riotous group of friends returned to Grange Abbey. Frank invariably travelled in a disparate group made up of close friends, business colleagues, and low-life hangers-on. But whatever the mix, the party always seemed to last forever, and this day would prove to be no exception. All evening crowds flooded into the Grange in vast numbers, two thousand revellers cramming the marquee for the signature black-tie race-night celebratory ball.

When Paul and the entire fifth-form at Saint John the Baptist entered the marquee dressed in their school uniforms, they were given a sustained round of applause. All evening the band serenaded the drunken boisterous crowd, and at midnight Frank's favourite group, the Clancy Brothers, arrived on stage to rapturous acclaim. The country's most popular folk-group delighted the audience with a medley of their greatest hits, ending with Frank's favourite song, 'The Jug of Punch'.

Paul gazed across the smoke-filled marquee and surveyed the vast crowd. It had been a long day and the celebrations showed little sign of abating, but for him the race had taken its toll. He turned to Anthony Selwyn and Carl Jones.

'I've had it,' he sighed wearily.

'You look fucked,' Carl Jones grunted.

Anthony Selwyn glanced at him.

'It's way after midnight. You need to hit the sack right now.'

He yawned. 'One last drink up at the house and then I'm gone.'

The night was warm and balmy as they set out along the orchard path towards the glittering lights of the mansion. In the great central hallway a myriad of noisy revellers drank and sang, and mostly looked the worse of wear. The crowd in the bar cheered the young Irish tenor standing by the piano as he led the chorus with 'It's a Long Way to Tipperary'. John Considine stood to greet them as they walked in the door. He nodded to the barman.

'Francie, three of your best pints of stout for these boys.'

'Three pints comin' up boss,' the barman barked.

Just then there was a loud crash in the far corner, the contents of a table upended, with glasses and bottles tumbling to the floor. Considine turned to see a woman scream as the drinks spilled over her, champagne and red wine soaking her snow-white dress. The piano player ceased playing and the crowds rose from their seats. From where he sat by the bar, Paul could see the cause of the furore, his brother Simon sidestepping through the debris, weaving precariously across the room, knocking into revellers along the way. He was taken aback by the deterioration in his elder brother in the year since they had met, his appearance disshevelled, his skin blotched and purple. He watched him barge through the crowd until they stood facing one another.

'Ladies and gentlemen, your attention please!' he proclaimed in a slurred, condescending tone. 'The hero is among us – let us honour the hero!'

The crowd turned to see Simon wave a glass in mock salute, spilling the contents as it slipped from his grasp.

'Back off Simon, there's no need for this,' Anthony Selwyn muttered diplomatically.

'Shut your fucking mouth, Selwyn!'

Simon spat the words with venom. The crowd went quiet. Paul stared coldly at his brother.

'Get lost, asshole – it's way past your bedtime.'

Simon seemed momentarily rooted to the spot. He gave a perfunctory bow.

'Hardly a hero's response, but one that befits you nonetheless.'

Paul pondered him disparagingly.

'It's the only response you'll get from me. You're a disgrace to our family.'

He swivelled on his stool and turned away dismissively, his withering comment hanging in the air. His brother contemplated him with an air of mock aplomb, then turned and faced the room.

'My brother deigns to turn his back on me, this gallant recipient of our admiration, this consummate winner in most things for sure.'

He snatched a drink from the counter and brandished it in the air.

'Another resounding win today as he commandeered my brother's stallion to victory.'

The bemused onlookers could do little but observe. Simon teetered unsteadily, and then a leery smile creased his face.

'I toast the hero,' he proclaimed mockingly, 'although by rights I should be toasting myself, ladies and gentlemen, since it was I who beat him in the one race he yearned to win the most.'

He raised a hand to rally the attention of the room, then laughed crazily and downed his drink in one go.

'My little brother, I honour this victory of yours today, to add to the ones you've won before, and yet in our hearts we both know you'd give it all away for the little girl I snatched from under your eyes.'

Paul stared at the bewildered onlookers, then climbed from his stool and brushed roughly past his brother. Simon's crazed laugh rang in his ears as he walked from the bar without bothering to look back. Outside in the corridor John Considine's voice resonated down the cavernous hall.

'Some speech your brother gave back there, kid.'

He stopped, turned, and gazed at the big man contemplatively, then shrugged.

'It was what it was.'

'That's all you've got to say?'

'It's all there *is* to say.'

'I still can't believe you let him get away with it.'

'I had no option,' he replied quietly.

'How no option? I just don't get it, kid.'

He stared wearily at John Considine, his heart bursting in his chest.

'I had no option . . . because my brother spoke the truth.'

32

Six months later, at the culmination of Frank's fifth year as chief executive, the company recorded a profit of eighty-eight million on its UK operations, surpassing the most optimistic forecasts and enthralling the City yet again. Bannons were bucking the trend under Frank's driven leadership, across all levels of management and in all areas of activity. The soaring year-on-year profit announcements triggered a knock-on contagious effect on house sales across the southern counties of England. Purchasers queued outside Bannon show-complexes and signed contracts in their thousands, in what industry observers interpreted as a clear vote of confidence from a general public keen to be associated with an in-tune, successful, vibrant operation.

Bannon starter-home policy was predicated on acquiring land in the best locations, paying whatever price was deemed necessary to facilitate the transaction. Frank's land agents scoured the English countryside for the right product and tendered aggressively to beat off all competition. A successful tender triggered an in-depth analysis of each new acquisition to ensure maximum housing densities.

No detail was left to chance. Town-hall civil servants and council officials from planning through to administration were wined, dined, and rewarded with an array of perks that included cars, cash, discounted houses, exotic holidays, escort girls, expensive wines, birthday presents and Christmas hampers.

All board members were aware that the company operated a slush-fund to facilitate the doling of out hundreds of thousands each year in bribes to planning officials. In Frank's view, making his directors aware also made them complicit. Bribing public officials was then, and is to this day, an illegal practice, punishable by heavy fines or imprisonment or both. Frank's attitude to all of this was endearingly simplistic – 'If everyone else is playing the fiddle, then let's play the fiddle better than everyone else!'

During the early seventies, when the average price of a starter home hovered around ten thousand pounds, Bannons initiated a policy of allocating a multiple of four times the unit sale-price to cover the cost of show-home decor. Young buyers visiting a Bannon show-home for the first time would marvel at the lavish, luxuriously furnished show-homes, never realising that the sumptuous decor that dazzled them on arrival was impossibly beyond their reach. Once, when Frank was interviewed by *English House and Home* magazine for an article showcasing the company and its aggressive marketing strategy, the interviewer alluded to this policy.

'Frank,' the young female reporter inquired, 'this questionable policy of adorning your show-homes to a standard vastly in excess of the asking prices for the homes themselves has to be immoral, or at the very least misleading. Surely these eager young purchasers can never aspire to such extravagance. It's simply beyond their wildest dreams!'

'It's interesting that you mention the word "dream",' Frank responded thoughtfully. 'I'd be a hypocrite if I didn't own up to the fact that in the final analysis all we're really doing is selling a dream. I readily admit that none of our purchasers will ever afford the levels of luxury they encounter in our show-homes. In their hearts they know it. What they see they'll never achieve – simple as that.'

The young interviewer regarded him skeptically.

'So you're actually admitting to blatantly misleading your customers!'

'In a way, it's inevitable,' Frank replied without hesitation. 'Show-homes will always be in the realms of make-believe, simply because we're showcasing a product that doesn't exist out there in the real world. Our purchasers are buying into an aspiration that vanishes the day they turn the key in the door.'

'An aspiration . . . in what sense an aspiration?'

'Well . . . because we're showcasing the perfect scenario and any fool will tell you that the perfect scenario simply doesn't exist. In our show-homes there are no unpleasant odours, no unmade beds, no dirty dishes in the sink, no ashes in the fireplace, no rubbish. The rooms are spotless; the decor is beyond lavish. We're presenting a product that is real only in the sense that we've physically created it, but in reality is little more than an airbrushed pipe-dream. People aren't stupid, we know it and they know it, but it still doesn't dissuade them from purchasing one of our homes.'

'I imagine it's too late for them to do very much about it at that stage, but you still haven't answered my original question, Frank. I asked if you consider your marketing strategy morally wrong or misleading.'

'Morally wrong, of course not. Misleading . . . perhaps, but in the grand scheme of things it is an irrelevance, because our homes are cheaper on a square-foot basis than those of our competitors, and it's a proven fact that our resale values increase faster. Nobody loses out. Everyone's a winner.'

'Do you have any other tricks of the trade?'

'No, simply because there are none.'

By and large, Frank's responses were considered forthright. He didn't appear to skirt the issues, and after all, a house-builder or any other manufacturer of a marketable product could hardly be criticised for displaying his product in the best possible light.

When asked to comment on other tricks of the trade, Frank had denied their existence, because as far as the public was concerned this was always going to be a no-go area. In the fiercely competitive arena of show-home presentation, Bannons, the ultimate magicians, had mastered the art of trickery and deception.

To the untrained eye everything would have appeared normal. The skinnier presses, the narrower wardrobes, the shrunken furniture, all deftly positioned to create the illusion of space. In the raw, brutal reality of the real world, their product had morphed into a house of mirrors, skilfully presented and packaged, but ultimately designed to deceive.

33

In 1967 Frank's hastily thought-out purchase of two hundred acres on the outskirts of Guildford in Surrey forced the company's board to focus on innovative ways of making the figures stack up. An hour before the noon tender deadline, he received a telephone call from Giles Gilchrist, managing partner at Gilchrists, the London estate agency handling the sale. He took the call in the privacy of his office.

'Frank, the magic figure's one point seven.'

'You're kidding me. That's three hundred grand ahead of our best estimate.'

'I warned you this was always going to be high-end.'

'One point four is high-end. One point seven is daylight fucking robbery!'

'Don't shoot the messenger, Frank,' Giles responded smoothly. 'All I'm doing is fulfilling my side of our little arrangement.'

'I need more time.'

'Out of the question.'

'I . . . need . . . more . . . fucking . . . time!'

Giles sighed.

'And I need to terminate this call. You've got fifteen minutes.'

Frank slammed the telephone back on the desk and stared out the window. He didn't bother to consult with his board – there was little point. The decision was his to make, and his alone. He sat back in his chair, put his feet up on the desk, closed his eyes and dozed off. The telephone rang exactly fifteen minutes later.

'Frank, we're out of time. What's it to be?'

'We go at one point seven.'

He heard a click and the line went dead. He lit a cigar and silently pondered the little arrangement to which Giles had referred. Frank had earlier handed him the Bannon tender document, containing all the relevant information except for one glaring omission, the price, a detail left for Giles to insert prior to sealing the document. If this was the only way to do business in the cut-throat cauldron of housebuilding, then Bannons would not be found wanting. Gilchrists' payback for insider knowledge of the tender process was agency exclusivity. Everybody wins. Nobody loses. Except that Frank didn't doubt that Gilchrists had other 'peripheral' arrangements operating at various levels of the deal, including almost certainly an enhancement reward package between agent and vendor agreeing a split in receipts achieved north of the 'reserve' figure. And in this case he suspected the reserve figure was probably one point five million. The next telephone call from Giles came in the early afternoon.

'Frank, our vendors have joined me in the boardroom. I've taken the liberty of putting you on loudspeaker.'

'Hello everybody,' he replied, content to play along with this tedious little charade.

'I can now confirm that the sealed tenders have been opened in the presence of an independently appointed firm of chartered surveyors, and I'm delighted to inform you that Bannons have been successful in securing this extraordinary parcel of land. Congratulations and well done!'

In the weeks following the tender the company's architects began working the layout in an effort to try and make the figures stack up. Frank was faced with a tight contract turnaround, the terms stipulating a non-refundable deposit and a closing date exactly four weeks following the tender. Days before the contract was due to complete, he called a board meeting and asked his architect Charles Pritchard to report on progress. Frank's friendship with Charles dated back to their time at university. The two boys came from diverse but privileged backgrounds. Charles had been raised in the rural surroundings of Percy Hall, his family's sixty-thousand-acre estate near Eastbourne on the Sussex coast. Tall and gangly, handsome and articulate, he had learned the rudiments of rugby at Eton College, then later with the Oxford Blues under Frank's captaincy.

Now a part of the Bannon inner circle, Charles's academic

brilliance had paved the way for his secondment onto the Bannon board of directors. But Frank was a demanding boss and Charles knew that failure wasn't an option. He outlined the key issues and then began his summary.

'We've applied all of the permutations and combinations that served us so well in the past, and regretfully we're still coming in twenty percent shy of break-even. We've factored in every conceivable cost-saving mechanism, from bulk-buy discounts right through to sales-price uplifts, and despite everything we're still coming up short.'

When Frank seemed about to explode, Charles coolly held up a hand.

'Please . . . allow me to finish. I'm merely trying to explain that our traditional methodology simply will not deliver the numbers we require, and we therefore *have* to adopt an avant-garde approach. There's a young architect named Andy Carmichael we hired recently specifically to work on innovative, previously untried theories. He's in reception right now and I suggest we *at least* listen to what he's got to say, even if some of his ideas may appear somewhat . . . unconventional.'

★

Dressed in jeans and a T-shirt, with long brown hair drawn back in a pony-tail, Andy Carmichael had a scruffy, nonchalant, 'take me or leave me' style which Frank warmed to instantly. He sat in his seat and casually gazed around.

'Holy shit – is this a morgue!'

Frank glanced at him and yawned.

'Get on with the presentation, asshole.'

'Andy . . . ' Charles prompted.

The architect scratched his head and smirked.

'I'm guessing from the vibes that you guys are still trying to figure out how the company paid so much for this piece of land, and I'm assuming it's too late to do anything about all of that. The problem now is we've got to find a way to make the whole thing stack up and turn this fuck-up to our advantage. Everybody with me so far?'

'We're all fucking ears,' Frank drawled.

'OK, so let's summarise the dilemma. The company now owns a two-hundred-acre parcel of land, which, based on current planning densities, throws up approximately two thousand plots. That's our starting position and we already know we can achieve those numbers in our sleep, but it still ain't enough to justify the price we paid. Of course, with a little help from our planning pals we ought to be able to tweak the numbers up to two thousand four hundred, but it still leaves us with a unit cost twenty percent south of break-even. Not the best deal in the fucking world, Frankie boy.'

Frank glanced at him and sighed.

'You're already on borrowed time, asshole.'

The architect smirked.

'What I'm trying to say is we need to devise a formula to deliver sufficient numbers to help dig us out of the shit.'

'What figure have you in mind?' Charles asked.

'I've done the math, and I see no reason why we shouldn't be able to achieve three thousand six hundred units.'

There were a few skeptical mutterings and one or two disbelieving gasps. It seemed incongruous to suggest that the land could ever deliver a staggering twelve hundred plots beyond the accepted norms. Frank pondered the young architect with interest.

'Care to explain?' Charles Pritchard prompted quietly.

He slurped a glass of water, spilling some on the table and the rest on his T-shirt. The bemused 'get on with the story, you sloppy little fuck' expression on Frank's face seemed to say it all.

'Gentlemen, the formula for achieving these numbers is staring us straight in the face. We simply reduce the frontages on all our units by three feet and simultaneously increase the depth by five feet to bring the square footage back to up to the average norm. Then we roll the fucking things out onto the market as fast as we can.'

Adam Baldwyn, Frank's director of planning, looked bemused.

'Andy, it's an all-day-long non-runner. Our frontages are already down to the bare minimum. It's impossible to design any tighter.'

The architect stood and walked to the display board.

'Take a look at this, you'll soon realise that from now on we ain't going to be building the same old tired designs. Reducing the front elevation is the key to unlocking the entire conundrum. We can prick about all day with the rest of it, because from a cost perspective all other measurements have minimal significance.'

He took a look around and saw he still had their attention – for now.

'We scrap the traditional separation of hall and living room, and replace the old-style hall with an entrance lobby. We incorporate the stairs into the living room, and access the kitchen-dining area through a set of double doors in the living-room partition. This simple reconfiguration delivers the critical three-foot-frontage reduction we require, and crucially enables us to construct six reconstituted units for every five current-design units. Gentlemen, the humble starter-home that's been churned out in cities throughout the land since the Industrial Revolution becomes a thing of the past, and we end up with an extra twelve hundred units at Guildford. Believe me guys, it works, with only one proviso.'

'And that is?' Frank inquired.

'You've got to have the balls to do it!'

There was really no answer to that. They sat silently, weighing the options, pondering the rationale. Tristan Ballard, the company's bright young sales director, walked to the display board and surveyed the image thoughtfully. He shook his head.

'This proposal is below substandard, below the minimum requirement and below the industry norm. It represents little more than sleight-of-hand. It's reproachful and misleading in its integrity. We as directors have a moral duty not to delude our customers by engaging in questionable practice.'

The architect stared at him.

'You honestly believe that?'

'Yes I do.'

'Then go tell someone who gives a shit.'

Frank smirked and turned to the young architect.

'Tristan has a point. I need to think about this.'

'You need to think about finding a new sales director. This guy's a joke.'

'I stand by my recommendation,' Tristan Ballard responded tersely.

'Tristan, you're a tosser.'

The young sales director regarded him dispassionately.

'I rest my case.'

Frank nodded to Tristan, who sat.

'OK smartass, say your piece. You've still got the floor – barely.'

The architect ignored the others and directed his words at Frank.

'I've given you a formula for the future direction that this company needs to take, so now you've got two choices. You either lead the market or follow the leader. If you decide to adopt my strategy, then you lead the market. There's a narrow window of opportunity, like maybe two years max, because by then every fucker in the land will have either stolen your idea or copied it. And just to be clear, I actually don't give a shit what you decide, because I'm guessing there has to be some gullible fuck out there who's gonna buy into this.'

'A question,' Charles Pritchard interjected in his suave, unruffled tone. 'If, applying your methodology, we actually succeed in squeezing three thousand six hundred units onto the lands, we already know we'll be in breach of every planning guideline in the book, including, critically, the open-space requirement: there simply will not be sufficient land remaining to meet the mandatory guidelines for public open spaces. What's your response to that?'

The architect lit a cigarette and stared thoughtfully through the smoke.

'It's an interesting question, because at the end of the day someone somehow has got to find a way to justify the price we paid. And despite one or two of my earlier flippant comments, Frank Bannon is the man with the ultimate responsibility for ensuring that this company stays one step ahead of the competition. So when Frank lays down a marker, then the rest of us have to try and make sense of it, because, at the end of the day, it's what we're being paid to do. And even if it sometimes seems impossibly difficult, we just have to fucking do it.'

He stood and placed an ordinance sheet on the display board.

'Gentlemen, this is Guildford Town Centre, and the area coloured yellow represents the tendered land. Guildford has been recently designated a satellite town due to its close proximity to London, and this innovative designation bestows town-centre status on all lands within a one-mile radius of the town centre. The red circle represents a distance of precisely one mile from the centre of Guildford, and as you can clearly see, ninety percent of our land falls within that circle. And it's also the reason we'll end up achieving the numbers we require – because this new town-centre designation concept permits densities of up to twenty units per acre.'

He glanced around the table at the directors of the Bannon construction group as they silently absorbed the implications, wondering which of them would be smart enough to spot the elephant in the room. Jeremy Macefield, a quietly spoken non-executive ex-City merchant banker, was first to speak.

'Andy, why, in your opinion, was the town-centre status of the lands not highlighted by the vendor's agent as part of the tender process?'

He stretched in his chair and thought . . . *Bingo!* Then dug his hands in his pockets.

'Honest answer – I don't believe the vendors actually knew about it, because if they had, the guide-price would almost certainly have been adjusted upwards to reflect the enhanced value. And that's surprising, because the relevant documentation has been available for inspection at the town hall since the beginning of the year. It's actually out there on public display. But if I was Frank Bannon, the question I'd be asking myself is why my in-house planning guys failed to elicit the relevant information when it was most pertinent – in other words at the pre-tender stage.'

Adam Baldwyn regarded him coldly.

'Mister Carmichael, at all times my department meticulously represented the facts.'

'So how come you missed the most pertinent fact of all?'

Adam Baldwyn bristled.

'And who are you to question my competence?'

The architect seemed unfazed.

'You *have* no competence. You fucking idiot.'

It was a beyond-derogatory assertion, and yet nobody rushed to Adam Baldwyn's assistance.

'I'm happy to test the validity of Mister Carmichael's assertion,' he responded testily. 'And if something has somehow been overlooked along the way, I assure the board that those responsible will be dealt with severely.'

His statement hung in the air.

'It may be more serious than that,' Frank responded in his matter-of-fact tone. 'But let's not jump to conclusions until we clarify the situation by, shall we say, lunchtime at the latest. Thank you for your time, gentlemen.'

Frank stood and walked briskly from the room. By midday Adam Baldwyn's resignation was on his desk.

34

In the weeks following Andy Carmichael's board presentation, Frank instructed his architects to test the new floor plans on a four-hundred-unit Bannon development at Caversham on the outskirts of Reading in Berkshire. He felt certain that they'd stumbled onto something special here which simply could not be ignored, and rather than wait the two years it would most likely take to secure permission at Guildford, he decided to use the Caversham project as a prototype-testing opportunity.

The fifty-acre Caversham site, strategically located on the banks of the River Thames north of Reading town centre, had recently been reclassified a town-centre location in the Berkshire Development Plan, and Frank chose the location because his planning consultants considered Berkshire to be a more 'relaxed' planning environment. The density was ratcheted up to eighteen units per acre on the back of the same principles pertaining at Surrey. New reduced-frontage house designs were inserted in order to facilitate the vastly increased density. Two months later planning permission was issued for nine hundred and seventeen units with no draconian conditions attached, a whopping five-hundred-unit increase on what had initially been envisaged for the development.

Frank instructed his show-house crews to work around the clock, non-stop, seven days a week. Teams of bricklayers operating in three eight-hour shifts began working the ten show-homes under an integrated floodlight system designed to facilitate non-stop production. Seven days later the carpenters came down off the roofs as the tilers simultaneously moved up on top, while down below an army of plumbers, electricians, plasterers and carpenters spread out across the various units as Bannon gangers forced the pace under orders from their driven boss, Frank Bannon.

Interior designers moved in and applied the same lavish decor to all eight units, and on the twentieth day following the pouring of the foundations, Bannons' Carlton Hall development opened its gates to the general public. When Frank visited the complex on Sunday morning, his sales director informed him that two hundred and thirty-five deposits had already been paid and that the crowds visiting the complex were showing no signs of abating. Elated by this news, Frank imposed a twenty percent across-the-board price-increase and instructed his sales team to release the entire development.

He ordered his site agent, Barry Llewellyn, to commence construction of the entire nine hundred units and to proceed with maximum speed. Bannons would yet again prove themselves to be market leaders, and the design changes that were tested at Caversham would soon become the norm on all major Bannon developments across the southern counties of England.

A front-page article in The *Financial Times* made reference to the Bannon 'feel-good-factor' which had ignited an eight-fold increase in sales across the Home Counties. In the article, financial controller Steve Richie alluded to the fact that although sales in London continued to outstrip the rest of England, the company had noticed a real growth-spurt in Surrey, Berkshire and on the company's six-hundred house Regency Court development on the outskirts of Cheltenham. He described the performance in London, where more than four thousand 'Bannon' homes were under construction across fourteen separate locations, as 'robust'. He confirmed that the trading statement for the year to December would see an increase in pre-tax profit of one hundred and forty-seven percent, equating to one hundred and four million pounds, with revenue up sixteen percent to one point six billion, and the gross margin exceeding twelve percent for the first time.

Steve stated that following the resignations five years earlier of the three founding directors, the group had moved from a position of being heavily indebted to more than halving its borrowings to one hundred and forty-four million. The company's land acquisition policy was funded on borrowings of eight hundred and twenty-eight million owing to land creditors, with fifty percent falling due in the calendar year, the balance being paid as the contracted land was drawn down. When the interviewer remarked that the borrowing level seemed abnormally high, Steve stated that the company's land strategy was grounded on the back of securing great deals which would guarantee five years of housing stock in the Greater London area, the company's most lucrative theatre of operation. He said it was imperative to boost mortgage lending to fuel the upsurge in demand, which in turn would boost government revenue and contribute to the further stabilisation of the economy.

The *FT* update came less than a week after Bannons announced the abrupt departure of planning director Adam Baldwyn and the simultaneous appointment of Andrew Carmichael as executive director with responsibility for architectural design. The article stated that Mister Baldwyn had left 'with immediate effect' in order to 'pursue other interests'. Bannons' share price closed strongly, up 11p at 139p.

All hunky-dory, or at least that's the way it appeared. Except that by the end of his sixth year at the top of Bannons Frank's hectic schedule was gradually beginning to tell, with friends noticing subtle changes in personality and staff in head office commenting on his increasingly erratic mood-swings. The affable, outgoing personality that most found endearing could suddenly turn hostile, leaving loyal colleagues bemused and distraught following an unexpected, fiery outburst.

Everyone knew that Frank drove himself hard at work, and harder in the hours that followed. He led by example and rarely asked anyone to do anything he wasn't prepared to do himself. This, and an uncanny ability to remember the first names of almost everyone who crossed his path, endeared him to his vast workforce. Frank was hero-worshipped by the construction crews on the ground and it was these men who were the ultimate beneficiaries of his unfailing loyalty and above-industry-average remuneration packages. His charismatic personality seemed to lull an awful lot of people into the misconceived notion that he was their bosom buddy. Men spoke with a sense of pride whenever his name was mentioned at weddings, funerals, football matches and parties.

'Frank Bannon! *Sure* I know him. He's a pal of mine.'

35

Ben Bradshaw sat in his chair at the head of the table and stared sulkily at the six district-area coordinators assembled before him. A man who seldom displayed good spirits, he appeared, to judge by his sour disposition on this wet Monday morning, to be in a particularly dark mood. The old grey seven-storey building near the junction of the Caledonian Road and Balfe Street behind Kings Cross Station had for thirty-five years been head-office to the Building and Allied Trades Union, and Bradshaw's personal fiefdom since assuming its executive chairmanship eighteen years previously. During those years the union had on occasion been sued, cited, sidelined, ostracised, and even expelled from Congress for unacceptable practices and persistent, blatant breaches of Congress rules.

Bradshaw had begun life as a union shop-steward in Birmingham in the fifties, in the myriad office towers and city-centre shopping complexes promoted by the prolific property tycoon Jack Cotton. Cotton, operating below the radar, transformed England's second city beyond recognition before turning his attention to the West End and then to Manhattan, where his iconic Pan-Am Tower would rise fifty-nine storeys over the tracks and platforms of New York's Grand Central Station.

Born and raised in the ethnic suburb of Erdington on the peripheries of Birmingham, Bradshaw first became known to the police in his teens following an assault on a black bouncer at a late-night bar in Spark Hill. CCTV cameras captured Bradshaw stabbing the guy in the neck with a broken bottle, but inexplicably he was released from prison having served only two years of a seven-year jail sentence, an experience which nonetheless made him decide that it was time to vacate that city for good.

A thug with a temper, he became *persona non grata* even in those sections of the city under the control of the most powerful gang bosses. With the temperature in Birmingham too hot to handle, Bradshaw migrated south to London, using his network of union contacts to garner work as a shop steward in the Building and Allied Trades, the most militant union in the city's burgeoning construction sector.

Bradshaw didn't waste time putting his street-fighting skills to good use, cajoling and bullying his way up the line, and exploiting his popularity among rank-and-file members to mount an early challenge for the leadership, which he succeeded in winning by a margin of two to one. Persistent accusations of vote-rigging cast a shadow over the election process but the allegations remained unproven and ultimately fizzled out. Bradshaw had brazened it out, and in so doing helped copper-fasten the leadership from that day forward. With his position at the top of the city's largest construction union unassailable, he proceeded to run the organisation's two hundred thousand paid-up rank-and-file membership with an iron fist.

Operating on both sides of the law, the union maintained a vice-like grip on construction activity across the capital, showing scant regard for existing employer-employee agreements. The executive encouraged all action necessary to establish industry monopoly, eliciting accusations of bullying and intimidation from employer organisations across the city. Bradshaw manipulated the law to suit union-specific requirement, and engaged the foremost Queen's Counsel to defend his position in the courts.

The union's most debilitating ploy was the use of flying pickets, a tactic which left employers with little option but to petition the courts for a restraining injunction to prosecute specifically nominated picketers. But arresting and jailing union members in a country where union membership was considered a God-given right was always guaranteed to unleash a public outcry sufficient to make employers rethink the veracity of pursuing such an inflammatory strategy. The bottom line was that if you wanted to conduct business in London, the smart option was to sit down and deal with the union that controlled the city.

And so it was that Ben Bradshaw sat at the head of his

boardroom table on that Monday morning, his mood sour, his humour darkened by the exasperating knowledge that his Building and Allied Trades Union, the largest construction union in the city, with a stranglehold approaching a monopoly, had thus far failed to definitively establish that monopoly. One or two of the smaller family-run firms had opted to mount a resistance and remain non-union, but they were isolated and he'd get around to dealing with them eventually. These were small beer compared to the one sprawling maverick company operating with impunity across the length and breadth of the city, *his* fucking city, scuppering all efforts to unionise its vast workforce; this one national operator, the firm Ben Bradshaw despised the most.

Bradshaw viewed the Bannon group refusal to engage as a monumental insult to him and a slight on his union, a situation which cut to the very core and could no longer be tolerated. The time had come to deal with the matter head-on. He still recalled his one and only meeting with the old man James in the grounds of a parking lot beside a Bannon tower block on the Fulham Palace Road.

'I demand that this meeting is reconvened on your construction site,' he whined, 'in your site canteen, in front of the members I represent.'

He still remembered the way the old man coldly stared him down in front of the dozen union officials who stood with him.

'I've got three thousand men in this city and you and your crooked union represents none of them, and that's the way it is gonna stay as long as I'm calling the shots. So, say what you have to say and get outa my sight.'

There was no mistaking the undercurrent of menace in James Bannon's chilling delivery, no mistaking the disposition of a man used to having his way, no mistaking the steely stare of the eyes. Bradshaw was unaccustomed to this.

Usually employers learned early in the negotiating process that their interests were best served meeting this union's demands, or else face the prospect of a prolonged and damaging lockdown. Union negotiators took pains to make it clear to employer negotiating-teams that the terms of any deal struck following the initiation of strike action would be infinitely less palatable than what had been on the negotiating table to begin with.

In such circumstances all wages accruing for the duration of the strike would be exacted from the company, with national wage agreements set aside and replaced by a draconian formula based on average annual earnings. Worse was the stranglehold imposed on the company's day-to-day administration by the union's shop stewards, draining resources, exacting time-and-half, double-time, wet-time, travelling-time, tool-money, meal-money and holiday-money. Undermining the traditional role of management and dismantling the hated subcontractor system was the precursor to the union effectively running the show.

Well, it was supposed to work like that, this tried-and-trusted formula, this fail-safe mechanism, this intimidation-based strategy designed to usurp power and grab control. But Bradshaw could sense deep down that he was dealing with something inherently different with these Bannon people. He could sense it, but his antennae just couldn't quite grasp it, until it gradually began to dawn on him, the missing ingredient, so often camouflaged but in the end always bubbling beneath the surface at these fraught meetings – the fear factor. There was no other explanation; it simply *had* to be that. There was no fear with these people. They weren't trying to hide it or cleverly cover it up. It simply wasn't fucking there.

Two prior attempts to infiltrate the company by surreptitiously inserting union cardholders into the workforce had failed miserably. On each occasion the union's most militant members had been selected to spearhead a staged confrontation with site administration, followed by a demand for union recognition, but each time they'd been forced to abort. On the last occasion Bradshaw had exploded.

'Why are you fucks running away from this?' he screamed. 'This union wields the power in this city and you're allowing a handful of Irish rednecks to scare the shit out of you.'

And each time the response was pretty much the same.

'It's just the way it is down there, boss. They took us aside and told us that if we didn't leave voluntarily, then we'd never leave at all. Those guys were paramilitaries, boss, and they fucking meant it. They run the show like a military operation and they all answer to a guy whose name you'll be familiar with.'

Bradshaw sat back in his chair, cursed under his breath and stared grimly at the ceiling. They listened to the familiar grinding of teeth and watched a facial muscle begin twitching out of control.

'John fucking Considine,' he whined.

He turned to his second-in-command, Terry Hayden.

'Terry, what the fuck are we gonna do about the Bannons?'

It always began like this, every Monday morning. Hayden, a hard-nosed union enforcer and one-time bricklayer from Wood Green on London's northern periphery, had worked his way quickly through the ranks, using violence when necessary, but in the end getting there mostly on the back of his talent as a skilled, street-wise negotiator.

Recently he had begun to notice a slow, steady deterioration in his boss's mood. He stared at Bradshaw's fat, bald, blotchy, bleary-eyed face, the trademark denim shirt with sleeves rolled up, his fat ugly belly straining the buttons to their limits. Struggling to disguise his distaste, he pondered the beady-eyed specimen who stood a paltry five foot two in his bare feet, the smell of stale alcohol wafting off his breath, teeth rotting in his mouth behind a thin, evil scowl.

Hayden glanced briefly at the faces of brothers Mick and Tony Travis, the two psychopathic half-wits seated opposite him, then at Pete Ravenscroft, Percy Hanratty, and finally Roger Maynard who all sat gazing downwards, staring vacantly at empty notepads.

So this was it, he thought, the seven-strong committee of the notorious Building and Allied Trades Union, London's largest, most militant, most feared labour group. What a fucking joke, but this was it, and sad to say, the buck stopped right here.

He sometimes wondered about Bradshaw's personal life. As far as he was aware he had never married. In the five years he had known him he had never seen him with a woman, his social life broadly consisting of long, late sessions swilling pints in pubs with eager rank-and-file union members. No woman in her right mind would go near the stumpy little fucker, and maybe that suited a nasty little cunt like Bradshaw, who he'd always suspected was a fucking queer anyway. He glanced again at the assembled faces of this dysfunctional, psychopathic bunch of thugs, all with criminal records, all extreme racists, at least one a convicted rapist, all of them degenerate fucks in their own right. He sighed.

'Physically we've done fuck-all, boss,' he replied, his voice raspy and hoarse from his sixty-a-day cigarette habit. 'We've been monitoring the operation from the outside, obviously, basically trying to identify any weakness. The eldest son, Frank, is running the show these days since old man Bannon took early retirement and swam with a seriously heavy sack of cash. The son applies the same magic formula – heavy reliance on a motivated, extremely loyal workforce on the one hand and a great big one-fingered fuck-off to the unions on the other. Oh, and by the way, Bannons' average wage pay-out is way higher than the current average union rate across the city, which makes me sorta wonder should I be applying for a job there myself, boss. But seriously, do those guys need us? The answer to that question is a large fucking no boss.'

Bradshaw picked up a water decanter and took a long, thirsty sip, carelessly spilling a glass or two down the front of his shirt and another across the polished table top. Then suddenly he stood and hurled the jug heavily onto the table, smashing it to smithereens, drenching the surprised group with the contents.

'Why can none of you boneheads wake up and figure out a plan to deal with this!' he screamed. 'These fucks are operating outside the laws of the land and in defiance of this union. We need to stamp on them! Pussyfooting around this one rogue operator cannot, and will not, be allowed to continue. Let's show these cunts who really runs this city, and this time let's show them we mean business.'

Terry Hayden took a quick look around the table at the glum, sullen faces staring back, then turned to Bradshaw.

'Just tell us what to do, boss, and we'll get on and do it.'

Bradshaw sat down heavily and brushed the table with a sweep of his arm. His eyes darted around the room, settling nowhere in particular.

'This . . . Frank, the son you mentioned. Have any of you morons ever met him?'

'No boss. The union hasn't confronted the company since the time you met with old man Bannon. Every now and then we send them the usual bog-standard letter, but it's always the same bog-standard response – you've got no mandate to represent the workforce of the Bannon Group of Companies. Please desist from further wasteful correspondence. In other words, boss, fuck off, yours sincerely.'

Bradshaw thought long and hard before replying.

'Then it's time we had another little chat with these bastards. Issue a written request for a meeting right away. Pick a neutral venue away from prying eyes, like maybe a basement car park in one of our buildings. Inform them I'll be personally handling the meeting, along with two union attendants. Tell Bannon to do the same.'

'We're on it boss.'

'Mick and Tony, I want you boys to hand-pick a dozen of your most reliable, most trusted enforcers and have them waiting in the wings somewhere close by – a disused stairwell or whatever. Figure it out for yourselves, but let's just say that when this meeting is over, the Bannons will have no illusions about who's really running this town.'

He stood and stared hard at Terry Hayden.

'Set it up, Terry, and remember this time, no mistakes – we're going in prepared.'

36

John Considine cursed silently as he climbed the wooden staircase leading to the elevated site-office on Bannons' sprawling Chelsea Harbour tower-block development. It was five minutes to four and he was expecting the telephone call to come through at four on the button. The plaster on his fractured ankle was due for removal in a week's time, not a day too soon he thought, as he sashayed along the gangway, leaning heavily on his crutches. Four weeks earlier he'd caught his foot on a reinforcing bar up on level nineteen, causing him to hit the deck heavily. Three feet closer to the edge and his momentum would have taken him over the side and down into the basement twenty-one floors below. In the event, he ended up with sprained ligaments and a fractured ankle.

He pushed open the door of contracts manager Fran Ryder's office on the second level and made his way through awkwardly.

'Fran, give me ten,' he grunted.

'Sure, boss. Coffee?'

'Naw, forget it.'

He sat heavily in the chair and waited for the door to close. He glanced at his watch – two minutes to go. It was late autumn; a cold wet Wednesday afternoon in London. He stared out the window at the bleak, dark evening and pondered his predicament. But for this cursed ankle he should now be shooting pheasant on the Grange Abbey estate on this, the opening day of the season, although with a bit of the devil's luck he'd belatedly make the trip in a week's time. The sudden rattling of the telephone transported him back to reality. He picked up the receiver and listened silently, then disconnected. Twenty seconds later the telephone buzzed again.

'What's going down?' he muttered quietly.

'They're gearing up to meet with your man this Thursday, or if not, Friday, late afternoon, five, maybe six.'

'The venue?'

'Don't know yet. Neither do they, but it'll be one of their buildings.'

'I'll need to know the venue.'

'You'll know as soon as I know.'

'When will you know?'

'I'm guessing tomorrow, possibly Wednesday.'

'Anything else?'

'There'll be three officials including the big man, and they'll want three from your side, including your boy. All sounds fair and square, except that there'll be a welcome party waiting in the shadows – ten, maybe twelve hand-picked guys capable of inflicting real damage. The plan is if they don't actually kill him, they're gonna teach your man a lesson he'll never forget.'

The line went dead. He replaced the receiver and sat back in his chair, staring out the window, except that this time he wasn't contemplating shooting pheasants on an estate in Ireland. He felt the weight of the plaster on his leg and cursed his luck. Unfortunately, this was one job he couldn't contemplate handling personally. John Considine took his responsibility to this family extremely seriously. He actually liked Frank Bannon – most of the time. He was smart, brash and pretty tough, but besides all of that, his unwavering loyalty to James would always place an attack on a Bannon family member on a different level for him. And this boy under threat happened to be the eldest son of James, his greatest friend, a detail John Considine was never going to take lightly, because that made it personal.

But it still left him with a problem. He knew with certainty that if Bradshaw's goons didn't kill Frank Bannon, then they'd most likely do the next best thing, which would be to consign him to a wheelchair for the rest of his days. There was history here, and Bradshaw seemed determined to make the Bannons pay for having won the first round. And that sure left John Considine with one hell of a dilemma as he silently cursed his foot for the fourth, or was it the fifth, time.

He had already decided that this one would have to be

delegated. Even with both feet on the ground, he felt that, realistically, this was never going to be handled in-house. He lifted the telephone with a degree of trepidation. It was a call he didn't relish making, a course of action to be contemplated only in the realms of absolute necessity. Deep down he knew that there was only one man he could trust to ensure that Frank Bannon walked out of that meeting alive.

The response, when it came, was in the early hours of the morning, to his unlisted home telephone number. *These guys sure like to start early* he thought, *or did they ever fucking stop.* He lifted the receiver on the second ring.

'Duke of Devonshire – five this evening.'

The line went dead and that was about it – short and sweet. He knew the venue, of course. He'd been there once or twice. The Duke of Devonshire bar on the Fulham Broadway was a large, buzzy joint, always pretty busy, and not ideally suitable he would have thought, but such matters were not up for discussion. These guys always seemed to know exactly what they were doing. He didn't think much further about it until he hobbled up the front step and pushed through the double doors at a few minutes to five that evening. Even though the joint was already busy, he could immediately sense the presence. You could never really be sure about these things, but still, as he advanced through the gloomy space he counted at least a dozen of them, scattered around, all studiously minding their own business. He walked onwards through to the back section, to where a lone man sat in the shadows at the far corner table. He hobbled across, leaned his crutches against the wall and sat heavily into the only other chair available.

'Thanks for this,' he said quietly. 'You're a busy man. I appreciate it.'

'It must be important. You're no time-waster.'

'You travelled across last night?'

'I came when I got the call.'

He stared at the man seated opposite, the most notorious Provisional IRA commander in the land, reputed to have five hundred fiercely loyal soldiers under his personal direction, and so far as he knew never questioned, never captured, never

215

photographed. Stocky and handsome, articulate and educated, Frank placed John McRory in his early forties. He was a member of the army council and boss of the Provisional's greatest stronghold, the no-man's land surrounding the town of Crossmaglen in south Armagh. Operating below the police and media radars on both sides of the border, McRory was reputedly the mastermind behind the devastating campaign the Provisionals had waged across the province during the past seven years.

'I'll get straight to the point. This is about the Bannons.'

'I figured as much.'

'A couple of days ago Bradshaw requested a meeting with Frank Bannon, and you know I normally handle these matters, except . . . ' he nodded towards his bandaged foot.

'Our mole on the inside is telling us there'll be a surprise party waiting in the wings. The meeting's scheduled to take place in three days' time.'

'They haven't bothered you much. I assume our presence is a deterrent. Why the renewed interest?'

'Bradshaw hates the family – always has done. I'm guessing he wants to end the stand-off that's existed since the last meeting with the old man five years ago. Bannons are outside of his control and it's beginning to cause them one or two problems – perception problems. It's a monumental embarrassment, and besides, he's a psychopath, and that's always likely to make him unpredictable.'

McRory allowed himself the briefest of smiles.

'Oh, I think you can take it we'll be helping you on this one. Send the details through to the usual contact. It's a tight timeframe, so make it quick. Anything else?'

Considine struggled to contain his surprise.

'I'm grateful, of course, but we haven't discussed the cost factor.'

McRory stared at Considine thoughtfully.

'You're off the hook on this one. It'll cost you nothing.'

Considine raised his eyebrows.

'Care to tell me why?

McRory glanced at his watch, then briefly towards the

counter. Considine sensed movement, surreptitious, coordinated, imperceptible, but movement nonetheless. These guys were getting ready to depart. McRory turned to him.

'This boy has a younger brother completing his final year at Oxford. During the summers he works with the bricklayers and the ground crews on some of your Dublin developments. Last October there was an incident on a construction site on the north side of the city, one of yours. I think maybe a thousand houses?'

'I know the one,' Considine nodded.

'Two of our boys were on a mission north of the border and someone pointed a finger at them. When they crossed back into the south they were picked up and questioned by Special Branch, and during the interrogation they named your boy as an alibi. It seems these boys worked together for two or three summers and became buddies. A Special Branch detective visited the site and interviewed your boy, and he confirmed the alibi. Swore our two boys had been working on site all during the previous day and claimed they were with him all evening. They interrogated your boy for seven hours but he stood solid as a rock. In the end there was nothing the cops could do but release our boys. When they arrived back on site they told your boy that if there was ever anything they could do to show their gratitude, he need only ask.'

'So, what did he say?'

'He told them there was nothing he'd ever want from them because they had betrayed his friendship. What the hell is it with you guys – this loyalty thing. Anyway the incident happened more than two years ago, but our memories are long. The organisation never forgets, and now it is payback time.'

His eyes darted around quickly.

'Stay still,' he whispered.

Considine remained in his chair and stared at the tabletop. When he looked up again his companion had disappeared in the smokey haze.

37

Terry Hayden walked into the Britannia pub in Hammersmith at closing time on Tuesday evening. He picked out Bradshaw in the middle of a group at the far end of the bar. Bradshaw waved, then muttered something that seemed to raise a laugh.

'Care to join us for a drink, Terry?'

'No boss, but you asked me to keep you posted on the Bannon thing. Their side got back to us an hour ago and they've given the green light for six on Thursday, our preferred date.'

Bradshaw grimaced.

'Then this is it – the final showdown.'

'Yeah boss.'

'And the rest of the preparations?'

'The venue is an underground car park in Earls Court managed by our members. From five onwards the general public will be barred from utilising the lower levels. All vehicles still parked on those levels will be checked out thoroughly one hour before the meeting. There are six upper levels, with capacity for a hundred vehicles on each level, and they'll still continue to operate in the normal way. Shutting the whole place will draw unnecessary attention. We want people to believe it is business as usual.'

'And the other . . . arrangements?'

'The Travis boys have been working pretty hard on this. They've put together a tight ten-man backup hit-squad. These guys sound just about perfect – three East End gang enforcers and the rest of them hand-picked for their brawling skills. Tony said to tell you you'll be happy with the result.'

'Sounds like you've done real good. Let's roll it on and teach this spoiled brat a lesson he'll never forget.'

★

The three men stood and waited in Frank's office for the meeting to commence. The steady drone of traffic on Park Lane barely penetrated the plate-glass windows. The morning was dark and blustery, and across the street the huge trees in Hyde Park swayed sombrely in the breeze. At seven Frank walked briskly through the door and pointed to two leather sofas either side of a high-shine marble coffee table.

'Let's sit,' he said, pouring each of them a coffee. Then he motioned to John Considine. 'OK, Johnny, run it from the top.'

Despite the deadly content of the discussion his voice appeared rock-steady, with not a hint of jitters.

You really had to hand it to these Bannons, Considine mused to himself. He turned to Steve Richie and Charles Pritchard.

'The reason we're keeping this group tight is because all of us need to be clear about what's going down here. Bradshaw and his goons will never be happy until they exert control over the Bannon group of companies. The day they establish a foothold is the day this company begins to self-destruct – it's as serious as that. The modus operandi is, send in the shop stewards and hit the company with the whole shebang; new wage agreements including travelling-time, wet-time, holiday money, tool money, meal allowance, overtime, double-time, triple-time, you name it. And with our history they'll exact a heavy price on this company. That's the reason we've got no choice – there *is* no plan B to fall back on. We must be prepared to do whatever it takes to stop this union muscling in on our workforce.'

'Then why bother meeting them,' Steve Richie asked. 'Why not send them the standard two-word message and save all the hassle?'

'We could do that,' Considine replied. 'We've done it in the past and they've gone away for a while, but the difference is now they're insistent. They've endured five years of frustration since James told them to fuck off last time. They've been biding their time waiting for the moment, and with James out of the picture they'll reckon it's as good a time as any to test Frank's nerve.'

'My guess is if we refuse the meeting, we'll have pickets on all our sites by close of business, and even if we do meet them, that scenario could obviously still happen. And if it does happen, we'll deal with it head-on. I honestly believe that if we deliver a clear message today, directly to Bradshaw, if he's smart he'll conclude that the monetary cost of hitting us with a prolonged, widespread lockout will prove too damaging, too costly and way too much trouble, and achieve fuck-all in the end. In a confrontation situation they know we'll throw everything we've got straight back at them.'

'But sending Frank into the meeting,' Charles Pritchard interjected, 'aside from the obvious danger it poses, doesn't make a great deal of sense if they already know the answer we're going to give. It's bestowing a level of importance on the proceedings that these assholes don't actually deserve.'

'It's immaterial,' Considine replied. 'Frank's already made the call, so that part of the plan's not up for discussion. I'm just here to fill in the detail, as long as you guys are still comfortable with all of this?'

They both nodded.

'OK, that's good, because calling what's about to take place a meeting is stretching the bounds of credibility, especially when we already know that they've assembled a punishment squad to teach our boy a lesson. We're obviously preparing for the worst, and the worst is that they may even try to kill him. We'll be taking counter-measures to ensure it never comes to that, but still, this really is about as bad as it gets.'

'It's a nightmare waiting to unfold,' Steve Richie responded tensely. 'Why not cancel, and give ourselves time to consider the options, including, if necessary, negotiating with the bastards? We can drag it out forever and withdraw at any stage for whatever reason. We're pretty damn good at this sort of thing.'

Considine glanced at Frank, who gave an imperceptible 'I'll take it from here' nod.

'Steve, we've already weighed the options, and our best option is to press on with the meeting. If we back off now, it sends out all the wrong vibes. And besides, we've got counter-measures in place and we're ready to go.'

But Steve still seemed unconvinced.

'None of us can ever predict the outcome of an explosive

confrontation like this with a degree of certainty. Surely no balance sheet, or profit margin, or duty to shareholders is worth placing your personal safety, or possibly your very life, on the line.'

Frank stared at him thoughtfully.

'Steve, if this was about the bottom line then, sure, I'd agree with you, except that it *isn't* just about that. This is about defending the honour of my father's name, and the name of this family. Sometimes you've just got to stand up and fight for the things that matter deep down, and if that doesn't explain it then there's really nothing more I can say, because like Johnny said earlier, my mind is already made up.'

He glanced at John Considine in time to catch the tail-end of the faintest smile. Yes, he thought, you of all people would understand this.

'Noble words indeed, Frank,' Steve responded, with a hint of irony in his voice, but he knew there was little point in trying to further dissuade his stubborn boss. John Considine drained his coffee.

'Guys, we have to move on with this because Frank needs to be briefed one last time. We already know the meeting is a sham and they know there's nothing they can say that'll get us to agree to anything, which is why they're dispensing with the usual formalities in favour of the physical approach. It has proved successful for them in the past, and they've probably decided they need to ratchet it up a few notches when it comes to dealing with us. We already know from our contact on the inside that they believe this is their best prospect of bringing us to heel, and we also know their plans are pretty much finalised.'

★

Dressed in jeans, sneakers, T-shirt and black leather aviator jacket, Frank emerged from the elevator and sauntered across the car park beneath his Park Lane headquarters. Considine stood waiting with two men beside a black Mercedes 600SEL saloon. They shook hands. He'd been advised that two ex-SAS paratroopers would accompany him to the meeting, but you didn't need to be told that these guys were soldiers. They were both average height, stocky, fit, short haircuts, focused.

'You OK?' Considine asked. Frank nodded.

'Good, then meet the rest of your team, Nick Penn and Shawn Hunt.'

They nodded.

'Nick and Shawn will attend the meeting with you. They both know exactly what to expect. When you guys get there you'll sit in the middle, with Nick on your right, Shawn on your left. At some point in the meeting, probably early on, Bradshaw, or someone on their side, will say something derogatory to you, some kind of personal insult. Stay calm, but just be aware that this'll be the signal for the fireworks to begin. From then everything will start to happen pretty quickly. Shawn and Nick are trained to deal with these precise situations, so don't try and be a hero − otherwise you'll fuck things up. The plan is to get you out of there as quickly as possible. So do exactly as you are told. Stay calm and follow instructions to the letter.'

Frank gave an imperceptible nod. Considine took a final appraising look at him, then hobbled across and wrapped him in a bear hug.

'I'd be beside you if I could,' he whispered in his ear.

'That I know,' Frank replied quietly.

Considine turned to the two ex-SAS officers.

'Time-to-go time. So let's move it. Oh and one last thing . . . '

The two soldiers turned.

'Bring my boy back in one piece.'

★

The Mercedes eased silently onto the ramp and slowed to a halt, its progress blocked by a welcome party of five, maybe six heavy-set goons wearing yellow construction vests. These guys were there to make sure nobody moved in or out of the joint and it looked like nobody was standing around arguing the toss. Frank, sitting in the front passenger seat, eased down the electric window. A huge bearded guy strolled across.

'Frank Bannon?'

Frank nodded. The guy looked him up and down.

'You fat-cats sure know how to get your hands on a fancy motor Mister Bannon.'

Frank, elbow resting on the window, stared at him calmly.

'The rewards of hard work, buddy – I certainly didn't get it standing around wanking myself on a picket line.'

The guy gave Frank the hateful stare. Frank smiled pleasantly.

'Open the boot, Mister Bannon.'

Nick Penn released the lid and seconds later it slammed shut. They stood back and the car cruised down the ramp and across the floor, to where three men sat along a table positioned close to the far perimeter. Other than a dust-covered Transit abandoned in a side-bay and maybe a dozen cars parked randomly, the place looked empty. The Mercedes swept smoothly off the ramp and cruised across the floor into a centre bay yards from the table.

Bradshaw watched three similarly dressed men disembark and stroll purposefully towards him. He'd never met Frank Bannon but he recognised him immediately from photographs. He was taller than he'd expected, maybe six foot three, rangy like his old man. The other two were tough types – cold, unfriendly, expressionless. They took their seats quickly. Frank stared coldly at Bradshaw.

'Say what you've got to say,' he said in a harsh, hateful tone. 'I've already spent way too much time here.'

Bradshaw gave a nonchalant 'suit yourself' shrug of the shoulders.

'Mister Bannon, every worker has the right to union membership. It's the law of the land. It's a law you've chosen to ignore, and it's the reason our members on your construction sites have mandated this union to represent them. Your failure to facilitate the transition to unionisation will precipitate an immediate and damaging lockdown of all Bannon group interests across this city. My union has the wherewithal and the capacity to put you out of business in a matter of days. You can do this the easy way or the hard way, but either way the decision is yours, Mister Bannon. Just tell us what it's to be.'

Frank held Bradshaw's watery stare.

'My answer is the same one my father gave you five years

ago. And in case any of you assholes don't remember what that answer was, it's fuck you and fuck that rotten-to-the-core protection racket you call a union.'

Frank's icy tone reverberated in the musty silence. The temperature seemed suddenly to drop sharply. You could cut the tension in the air as the six men stared at one another in a coiled-up atmosphere of palpable hatred.

'Well I'm genuinely sorry to hear that, Mister Bannon,' Bradshaw replied eventually. 'They did tell me you were a brash fucker, but I honestly don't see much of that. All I see is a spoiled brat, born into a life of decadent privilege. A degenerate who fucks his way around this town and fucks everyone who stands in his way. Well, your fucking days are over, Frank, because you ain't gonna fuck this union. The only thing you've got that's big is your mouth, and your big mouth was bound to get you into trouble sooner or later.'

Frank showed no emotion. He'd been warned to expect this.

'I came to deliver a message,' he replied calmly, 'and I'm hoping I delivered it clear enough to penetrate even your thick skull. Do whatever you have to do, Bradshaw, because we're ready for anything you've got to throw at us, and we'll fuck it back at you so fast you'll never know what hit you. We've got a mole right in the heart of your rotten little union. We know every move you're gonna make a week before you make it, and that includes the reception party you've lined up for us today, you devious cunt. So go ahead – press the button anytime you're ready. Let's get the show on the road, asshole.'

Bradshaw and the Travis brothers looked stunned and made little effort to hide their surprise. They sat and stared blankly at Frank, clearly gutted by the realisation that someone, somewhere, within the organisation had been compromised by their most hated enemy. And yet as they absorbed the repercussions of what Frank Bannon had just articulated, Bradshaw regained his composure. He stared hatefully at Frank.

'Your father was a thief who played fast and loose with other people's money. A whoremaster who fucked with other people's lives, and when all is said and done the best he could do was to sire a piece of shit like you. When I look at you, all I see is a flawed pedigree. A spoiled brat who years ago should have been taught the lesson we're about to teach you.'

Suddenly Frank heaved the table and sent the three men toppling backwards off their chairs. The two soldiers moved with lightning speed and in seconds the Travis brothers lay motionless on the ground. Bradshaw scrambled to his feet and desperately tried to make a run for it but Frank grabbed him and pinned him against the wall. In his peripheral vision he saw a steel door burst open and a flood of men spill out onto the platform. Frank Bannon was strong and tough and towered over Bradshaw but he knew he needed to act fast. He held him in a vice-like grip and slammed his head hard into his nose, the spurt of blood and cartilage barely masking the look of shock and fear in Bradshaw's beady eyes.

'That's for my old man,' he snarled, 'and this one's for me.'

He grabbed his adversary's blood-spattered face and smashed his skull into the wall. There was a crack of bone and Bradshaw hit the ground like a sack of potatoes.

The last thing Frank remembered was seeing the whites of his eyes, and then came the blow. He saw it coming a split-second before it connected, barely time to move his centre of gravity fractionally sideways to lessen the impact. It clipped the side of his head on the way down – he felt a gust of air and then the baseball bat slamming into his shoulder. In the blur of the movement he caught a glimpse of the guy: white t-shirt, big belly, arms covered in tattoos, and then the searing pain down the left side of his body. He felt his knees begin to buckle and then he saw the guy gearing up to strike again. He swivelled a yard and threw himself on the ground, his damaged shoulder taking the brunt of the impact, aware that he'd have to keep moving or else die on the floor of this basement.

He glanced up and braced himself for the strike but then there was a low popping sound and the guy's face exploded in a haze of red mist. The blur of noise reached a crescendo and seemed to reverberate out of control. He glanced around and saw a stream of guys pouring from the back of the old Transit: he'd barely registered the dilapidated heap of junk when they'd cruised down the ramp minutes earlier. He tried desperately to focus on the outline of what looked to be a marksman leaning on the front bonnet. Then there was a series of rapid pops, a silenced weapon of some sort, impossible to tell. He pulled himself up on his good arm and tried to survey the scene.

There was a bunch of guys all dressed the same, black polo-necks, black trousers, black berets, swinging chains and wreaking havoc. One of Bradshaw's goons bolted for the stairwell but then there was a shotgun blast and the guy came flying backwards with half his head and brains missing, sawn-off barrels judging by the severity of the impact. *They must have someone positioned on the half-landing* he thought. He could see the two soldiers pinned against a wall, hands on heads, guns trained on them. Their role had been terminated. It was out of their hands now. They were spectators.

He pulled himself up and sat with his back resting against the wall. Bradshaw's goons were running around screaming but there was no escape route. He saw the six union guys from the entrance barrier marching down the ramp in front of four black-clad gunmen. The transit crew were about to complete the job. Frank saw guys wielding chains and counted three, maybe four bodies lying motionless. He watched the Mercedes being driven up the ramp and then suddenly the place descended into silence, with just one voice barking out orders. He saw weapons being gathered and placed in bags, then one final sweep of the floor and in an instant it was all over. They lifted him into the stairwell, then out a side-door into a disused alley. The ex-soldiers were bundled into a taxi and ordered to lie on the floor.

'Lay him down on the back seat,' were the last words he heard. Then a blanket was dropped on his head. Then darkness.

★

Frank was rushed by ambulance to the accident and emergency department of Guys Hospital, where surgeons operated at midnight on what was diagnosed as a severe fracture of the left shoulder resulting from an apparent mishap on one of Mister Bannon's construction sites. The following day he was discharged with his arm in plaster, driven straight to Luton Airport and bundled on a plane bound for Ireland, where he would spend the next four weeks recuperating at Grange Abbey.

★

In the aftermath of Frank's explosive meeting, the Bannon board of directors held their collective breath waiting for a reaction, anticipating the inevitable backlash from Ben Bradshaw's union. Notwithstanding Frank's tough words, nobody was under any illusion that an organised widespread union lockdown would be a devastating prospect for the company, possibly threatening its very existence.

The company's ability to stand alone against a determined national union onslaught was at best questionable, and at worst a bleak prospect to even contemplate. Yet nobody had any illusions that if hostilities ever erupted, it was going to be an all-out fight to the death, because it was a racing certainty that Frank Bannon would go down fighting to the bitter end.

In the event Ben Bradshaw and his union may have arrived at this same conclusion, having had a taste of the firepower at Frank's disposal. As the days turned to weeks without incident or reaction, the directors gradually began to relax and breathe normally. In the twelve months following the showdown with the union, the company powered ahead, and Bannon bricklayers laid seventeen million bricks on their London construction sites. Frank Bannon's abrasive, in-your-face style had sealed the day yet again.

The day following the showdown The *London Evening Standard* ran with a front page headline which read, 'Four Fatalities as Gangland Violence Flares in West London'. The accompanying article stated:

> Yesterday Scotland Yard detectives were called to the aftermath of a suspected gangland flare-up at a high-rise public car park in the West London borough of Hammersmith. A police spokesman described the level of carnage they encountered, on a lower basement

platform, as resembling a scene from an abattoir. Four bodies were discovered in a stairwell and taken to the coroner's laboratory for forensic examination. All four victims appear to have been executed gangland style. One of the victims has so far been identified but police say they are withholding the details until their investigations are complete. A spokesman did confirm that the dead man is a known gangland enforcer with East End connections. Police have cordoned off the scene and are treating the incident as a full murder investigation. A press briefing is scheduled for tomorrow at 5 PM.

38

What most people didn't realise during those early months in his sixth year at the helm of Bannons was the extent to which Frank's growing dependence on cocaine was helping to bolster his hectic lifestyle, a habit to which he had first been introduced on the London social scene, ten years earlier. Lately he'd begun spending more time on the city's hectic party circuit, still arriving in the office each morning before seven, and remaining there until the late evening, then on to the Dorchester or the Ritz for cocktails, and afterwards the George or Annabels until the early hours.

He was living life at a breakneck pace, indulging his coke habit when he felt the need to sustain energy, sharpen concentration, or postpone the inevitable onset of weariness. Still young, still handsome, and invariably the centre of attention, to an observer his lifestyle must have appeared action-packed and enviable.

Women loved Frank and gravitated towards him, eager to share his company and bask in the aura of glamour and excitement that had come to define him. In Frank they found a heady mix of wealth, power and success, and a suave personality to contrast the underlying sense of danger which seemed to attach to him.

He charmed women at every function he attended. His legendary reputation as an insatiable lover added cachet to his exuberant self-confidence and fueled his enviable success rate with the opposite sex.

Frank would laugh when people teased him about this.

'If I screwed all of the women they say I screwed, I'd be three hundred years old with the mickey of a sixteen-year-old stud.'

Despite these genial denials, Frank got through a vast array of women without ever seeming to permanently attach himself to any one girl. He frequently awoke in the master bedroom of his palatial penthouse in Chelsea and greeted the beautiful girl beside him with – 'Darling, forgive me but I've forgotten your name.'

★

Jenny Saunders, Frank's loyal forty-year-old personal assistant, rode the elevator to his tenth-floor penthouse and turned the key in the front door. It was Christmas Eve morning, and although 1973 would mark yet another action-packed year for the Bannons, she pondered fretfully the realisation that she still hadn't found the time for even the most rudimentary Christmas shopping. She walked in the door, casually brushing some snowflakes from her jacket, and gasped when she saw Frank's naked body lying face down in the entrance hallway.

With trembling hands, she held his wrist and registered the weakest of pulses. She immediately ran to the telephone and dialled emergency services. Frank was rushed to accident and emergency at Charing Cross Hospital where he was diagnosed with system failure resulting from the combined effect of alcoholic poisoning and a massive overdose of heroin. He was immediately transferred to intensive care and connected to a saline drip, a life-support machine and a stomach pump. Seven hours later the doctors advised Jenny, who had remained in reception throughout the ordeal, that although Frank was out of the danger zone, they had barely gotten to him in time to save his life. Breathing a sigh of relief, she finalised arrangements to have him moved to a private room. Then she telephoned John Considine.

'John, we must ensure that all of this remains below the radar. If the media get a whisper of what's happened, the effect on the company's share price could prove catastrophic.'

'Is anyone else aware of this?'

'Of course not.'

'Sorry, Jen. I just needed to ask.'

'I understand.'

'We tried calling him without success earlier and I guess we now know the reason why. You've handled this really well.'

'It has been quite an ordeal.'

'And your observation about the publicity thing . . . it's right on the button. Let's talk later.'

In the early hours of Christmas morning Frank was transferred to the exclusive Fairley Sanatorium near Ascot in Surrey, where he would spend the next seventeen days in rehab. Initially he was monitored around the clock, and as soon as he began showing the first tentative signs of recovery he was given a detailed warts-and-all prognosis. But Frank was a bad patient and casually dismissed the whole thing as a once-off freak incident. After three days of becoming increasingly bored and restless, he called administration and demanded that they arrange for his immediate discharge. His consultant, a vivacious Scottish blonde named Helen Cawley, called to his room soon afterwards.

'Your request for a discharge – '

'Yes, doctor?'

'Out of the question,' she added matter-of-factly.

Frank put down the newspaper he'd been reading and gave her a bemused stare.

'I'll decide what's out of the question, Doctor Cawley.'

She stared at him ponderously.

'Mister Bannon, do you have any concept of how lucky you are to be still alive? I've read your admittance-chart, along with the analysis of your lab results, and I assure you that neither makes for pleasant reading. If you are insistent on leaving, I cannot legally prevent you from so doing, but based on what I've read in your report I'll be surprised if you're not back in a month . . . if you're lucky.'

'If I'm lucky?'

'In my view it's far more likely you'll end up on a gurney in the city morgue, but, as you've correctly pointed out, it's your choice, Mister Bannon.'

Frank seemed momentarily taken aback.

'Doctor Cawley, I've no doubt you mean well, but to me, your prognosis seems over the top. And besides, I don't have a choice. I've got a business to run and that means only one thing – I'm outa here. If this is some kind of an attempt to try and scare me, forget it – you're wasting your time.'

'I'm a psychiatrist,' she responded coolly. 'I never exaggerate a patient's condition.

Frank smiled.

'In that case we'll agree to differ.'

She frowned and gave a perfunctory nod, as if she'd heard it all before. Frank sat on the bed, hands in the pockets of his silk dressing gown, and motioned her to an armchair, but Helen Cawley chose to remain standing.

'In this sanatorium we're used to dealing with the worst effects of substance abuse and personal neglect, and most of the time we can cure the physical symptoms relatively quickly. However, unless we can somehow rationalise the emotional catalysts that have driven a patient to a lifestyle founded on extreme abusive behaviour, then we really *are* wasting our time. All of the cases we see in this facility are extreme cases Mister Bannon, and when we measure the level of abuse in those patients who present themselves on a scale of one through to ten, you are right up there at the top of the pile.'

Frank bitched, moaned, and argued a little longer, but in the end he relented. His initial signs of recovery soon dissipated and he became disorientated. He felt drained and fatigued, and suffered withdrawal symptoms necessitating constant monitoring and a radical reappraisal of his medication. He attended daily two-hour one-to-one sessions with Helen Cawley, which he found debilitating. But as the days passed and he entered the second week, his symptoms gradually began to improve and he started to feel alive and energetic for the first time.

He actually found himself looking forward to the gruelling daily sessions with Helen Cawley. Surprisingly those hitherto-mind-numbing, unending question-and-answer marathons had morphed into something far more thought-provoking and revealing.

'When did you begin to slide so rapidly downhill?' she asked him one morning.

Frank considered carefully before giving his answer. From the outset she had insisted that his responses should be completely forthright, or otherwise their discussions would prove futile.

'I've given that question a great deal of thought these past few days,' he responded tentatively, 'and I'm still not entirely sure I know the answer, but my best guess would be the day they asked me to step up to the mark and stand in my father's shoes.'

Helen stared at him appraisingly, then glanced at her notes. She was so attractive, he mused, his eyes tracking the hemline of her skirt as it rode up her shapely thigh each time she crossed her long, gorgeous legs. She was cool and elegant, and as the days wore on he found himself falling under the spell of her suave sophistication.

'Stand in your father's shoes . . . How interesting. Have you any idea how this rationale may have inadvertently propelled you on the path that would ultimately lead you here?'

'Oh, the answer to that is easy,' Frank replied immediately. 'I never thought I'd be man enough to fill them.'

'Mmmm, an interesting response . . . except that by then you'd pretty much proven yourself in that regard.'

'You haven't met my father.'

She smiled quizzically.

'Frank, you've turned a daunting challenge into an overwhelming opportunity, and despite the physical and mental cost you've endured along the way, you've made a remarkable recovery. It is testament to your innate resilience. Do you now feel you have the confidence to go back out there and face the big bad world you so recently left?'

'Yes I do,' he replied breezily. 'I realised it a few days ago.'

'Sounds like a eureka moment.'

'Yeah, you could say that.'

'Was it something in particular that motivated you to arrive at that conclusion?'

'Yes it was.'

'Care to share?'

'*Sure*. It was when I realised I'd fallen in love.'

'Fallen in love!' she responded with evident surprise. 'How wonderful,' adding conspiratorially, 'may I inquire with whom?'

He pondered her thoughtfully.

'With you, actually.'

Her smile froze on her face, and she calmly held his gaze betraying little hint of a reaction. She contemplated him carefully before replying, 'Frank, I'm your doctor. It's my job to look after your physical and mental well-being. I'm flattered by your lovely sentiment, but I should warn you that the ethics of my profession are very clear; there are strict parameters governing the whole area of the doctor-patient relationship. Emotional attachment between patient and physician is not uncommon – we come across it all the time – we've been warned to expect it and we're trained to deal with it. This clearly is one boundary that I am forbidden to cross. Doctors have been struck off in the past for so doing. In another few days your convalescence will be complete. It is imperative that we stay focused during these latter sessions and absolutely not digress into the fraught area of personal attachment.'

Frank smiled.

'Good speech, Helen, to which I say, screw the theory shit and let's focus on the reality of what I've just said. I'm in love with you, more so than with any other woman I've met in my life. I'm not just another whacko like all the other whackos they wheel in and out of this facility every day of the week, and I'll do whatever it takes to prove it. Helen, I don't have the time to play silly games, and that's the reason I'm saying it as it is. If it comes down to a question of ethics, then let's resolve the ethics issue by terminating the doctor-patient relationship right now.'

Helen sat back and stared at him with chill detachment.

'Please try and be realistic. Put your personal feelings aside and listen to what you're proposing. It is simply not possible on a number of levels, not least of which is the fact that our professional relationship is already very much on the record.'

Her marked coolness didn't appear to deter him. He stared at her thoughtfully.

'Is it because you're married, or in a relationship or whatever – do I look like I care? Of *course* I don't. I've learned to trust my instincts, and right now my instincts are telling me that there's a frisson of chemistry between us. I sense it and I'm pretty sure you sense it. Otherwise I doubt we'd be having this conversation.'

She stared at him dispassionately, then stood abruptly.

'I don't wish to discuss the matter further,' she responded coldly, 'and besides, we've run out of time – this session is at an end. I shall see you tomorrow at the same time. Until then, good day.'

She walked across the room briskly and disappeared through the door.

★

The atmosphere was strained when they began their final two-hour session on that last afternoon. It was a crisp, sunny day and Frank suggested that they utilise the conservatory. They sat in deep-cushioned armchairs and gazed silently through the windows to the gardens beyond. A sprinkling of snow from an earlier fall still lingered on the lawns and peppered the branches of the cypress trees straddling the boundary.

He turned to her.

'Helen, first and foremost I owe you an apology – you were brave to come here today. I'm scheduled to leave in the morning, but before I do so, I need you to understand that all those things I said to you yesterday were said straight from the heart. It may well be difficult for you to hear this, but I've been bitten by the bug so bad I can't even think straight. In my life I've met thousands of great girls, but none of them have affected me so profoundly as you have. I'm a man accustomed to having his way but meeting you has made me realise that the illusions of power, wealth and privilege are incidental in comparison to those precious things in life that matter most of all. There is no emotion that can transcend the love between a man and a woman. I'm in love with you – simple as that.'

She stared out across the garden and flicked a strand of her shoulder-length, ash-blonde hair behind her ear, her expression serious, her eyes troubled. When she spoke, her words had a poignant ring.

'My husband is an alcoholic,' she began quietly. 'We've been married nine years, and for most of those years my personal life has been imbued with tragedy – witnessing day after day the destructive merry-go-round of serial substance abuse up close and personal. Colleagues in whom I've confided have commented that it instils in me the edge they claim I possess in dealing with such matters, but I'm not entirely sure about that.'

She sat back and closed her eyes. Frank held his breath.

'I divorced my husband amicably four months ago. In the beginning everything seemed fine – he was charming, engaging, articulate, but it didn't take long before our relationship began to implode. When I look back I realise that the rare happy memories I had were outweighed by the myriad miserable ones. As my career became steadily more successful and his descended into oblivion, he began drinking more and more. In the early days I was much too busy to notice, and when eventually I did notice, it was too late – the deterioration was irreversible. Jeremy was no longer interested in eliciting comfort from me. He made it clear that he blamed me for putting my career ahead of his and for neglecting him when he needed me most of all.'

She stopped and gazed languidly through the window.

'When we finally parted, I swore I'd never again expose myself to the misery of living with an addictive personality. Then you come along, Frank Bannon – charming, gorgeous, worldly, enviable in so many ways, and yet sadly, an addictive abuser, the personality trait I've come to dread the most. I'm sorry, but there it is.'

He leaned forward and looked into her eyes.

'But surely you must realise that all of this is behind me. You've witnessed my recovery during these last seventeen days. You have *got* to trust me, Helen. Those days are gone forever.'

She glanced at him and smiled faintly.

'If only it was that easy, but sadly I know too much about these things. All my past experience, and everything I've learnt as a doctor, tells me otherwise. It's an irrefutable fact that ninety percent of prior substance abusers become repeat offenders. Which is unfortunate for you, Frank, because it basically means that the statistics are loaded against you. I take no pleasure in telling you that typically you possess the classic addictive traits. The personality type can sometimes prove difficult to decipher, but in the long run the symptoms are easy to identify – driven personality, workaholic, hyper, unpredictable, an unremitting approach to life.'

She smiled.

'Sound familiar?'

He stared at her thoughtfully, then nodded slowly, as if the truth had finally dawned on him.

'So I'm damaged goods, to be avoided at all costs, to be left to my own devices, no longer fit for human consumption. That's what you're really saying.'

This time when she returned his gaze there was a twinkle in her eye. She smiled widely.

'Oh stop feeling so sorry for yourself – you'll have me crying in a minute.'

She took his hand in hers.

'Frank, I wouldn't have said it like this if deep down I didn't truly believe you have the strength to confront the reality of your situation head-on, and that in the long run you'll prove strong enough to face down that reality. That is the challenge.'

He gazed at her, struggling to rationalise the nuances of what she had just said, uncertain whether he was listening to the psychiatric jargon of a trained consultant or the words of a woman damaged by life's experience – a woman who had nonetheless come to occupy his every waking moment.

When Helen crossed her legs, which she appeared to do with alarming regularity, the soft, silky sound of her stockings sent a frisson of excitement coursing through him. He couldn't begin to imagine the heavenly delights that lay beneath the bog-standard outfit she always seemed to wear – black skirt cut slightly above the knee, white blouse with the top two buttons undone, black stockings, black heels. Every facet of the beautiful psychiatrist enthralled him – her faintly pouted lips, her blonde, shoulder-length hair, her sparkling blue eyes.

He found himself endlessly trying to fathom what was really going on in the razor-sharp mind hidden behind those eyes.

'Don't shut me out, Helen. Don't file me away in the "case closed" section of some dusty drawer in your office, discarded for ever more, never to be revisited. I swear to you that whatever else this life holds for me, the circumstances that propelled me through the gates of this sanatorium have forever been consigned to history. This experience has forced me to confront the futility of my reckless existence, and make me wonder how, in the midst of all my troubles, at the lowest point in my life, I had the good fortune to meet a fabulous girl like you.'

She smiled, shook her head from side to side, and closed her eyes, silently contemplating some deep inner thought. Then, to Frank's profound astonishment, she leaned slowly towards him and kissed him full on the lips, her tongue warm and sweet in his mouth, her soft long fingers caressing his face.

Then she moved her moist lips close to his ear and whispered softly, 'Call me in exactly three months – not a day before, and only if you're still clean. This is the challenge.'

He sat mesmerised, and watched her walk the length of the conservatory to the far door without once glancing back.

★

Six months later Frank Bannon married Helen Cawley at a lavish ceremony in front of two thousand guests at Grange Abbey. Most of those who had known him previously sensed a subtle shift in personality during the months following his period in convalescence. The volatile mood-swings, the erratic, unpredictable behaviour that had come to define his personality, seemed now to have been discarded.

Frank no longer drank alcohol, and no longer smoked his beloved Montecristo cigars. Instead he sipped ice-water, and yet still managed to retain his genial, fun-loving personality even while partying into the early hours. He certainly hadn't lost his zest for life, and yet his friends still detected a clear and profound shift in him, which none could quite explain, but all agreed was definitely for the best.

When, in the months leading up to the wedding, he finally introduced the ravishing Doctor Helen Cawley into his social circle, gradually the penny dropped. Frank Bannon, legendary city poster-boy, international tearaway, and London's most eligible bachelor, had finally . . . finally . . . fallen in love.

The announcement of Frank's engagement in *The Times* created a minor media frenzy, culminating two months later in an army of photographers descending on the tiny church in the village of Straffan to record the society wedding of the year.

In trademark Bannon fashion, the international guest-list was feted and entertained for four days and nights in lavish style at the sumptuous mansion. End-of-year results announced the previous February confirmed that Bannon group profits had for a third year in a row broken the hundred million mark, with the latest indicators pointing to another bumper profit in the year ahead. Separate from all of this, the group had under Frank's six year stewardship assembled a portfolio of unencumbered prime West End freehold properties, delivering an annual rent-roll in excess of thirty million pounds.

Against the backdrop of this stunning dual fiscal achievement, Frank and his bride entered the marquee, led by a lone piper to the sound of rapturous applause ringing in their ears. In a move that surprised some and delighted others, Frank chose his younger brother to be Best Man for the occasion, and when the bride and groom were seated, and the applause finally died down, Paul stood to address the crowd.

'Ladies and gentlemen, on behalf of my brother Frank and his gorgeous wife Helen, it is my honour to welcome all of you to this wonderful celebration. In a departure from the normal tradition of delivering speeches after dinner, Frank wishes to say a few words before dinner is served, and as all of you are well aware ladies and gentlemen, Frank Bannon usually gets what Frank Bannon wants. But first a toast to the bridegroom and his beautiful bride Helen.'

Two thousand people stood and clinked their glasses, and when Frank finally stood, the applause lasted all of two minutes. It was a truly tumultuous welcome and Frank, always so cool and in control, seemed uncharacteristically emotional when he reached for the microphone.

'Ladies and gentlemen, for this warmest of welcomes, I thank you from the bottom of my heart. I stand before you today, humbled by the sincerity of the reception you have extended to Helen and me on this most magical of days. In all my life I never imagined that I would be so fortunate to win the hand of such a marvellous woman, and for her to embrace me as her husband, it brings me happiness beyond my wildest dreams.'

The applause rippled in waves through the vast, enthralled crowd.

'My life has been enriched by the good fortune that dictated that my path would cross with each one of you assembled here today, and by the honour your presence bestows on this wondrous occasion.'

The crowd listened in raptured silence, hanging on every word, touched by the irrefutable sincerity of Frank's potent sentiment.

'It is a strange mix of life we each of us live, ladies and gentlemen – filled with joy, with sorrow and with endless surprise. The inevitability, the richness, the unpredictability of this mesmerising landscape that our time on this earth offers, guarantees no certainty other than the opportunity to march right out there, grab life and live it to the full – and nobody can ever say I didn't give it my best shot.'

There were a few laughs, whistles and cheers.

'But those were the good old days, and now, at last, I'm a married man – happier than I could ever have thought possible in my wildest dreams. And yet ladies and gentlemen, this happiness I speak of is tempered with just a hint of sadness. What did I say earlier about this life we lead – a heady mix of joy and sorrow intricately intertwined in one fateful package.'

In this huge marquee, packed with guests from across the world, you could hear a pin drop as Frank Bannon delivered his speech at a temperate, measured pace, in soft tones not normally associated with his in-your-face, signature brash delivery. They watched and waited while he took a sip of water, and gazed across the vast crowd as if struggling to gather his thoughts.

'Four weeks ago my doctors confirmed to me that I am dying, ladies and gentlemen.'

His words, like the crack of a rifle-shot across the room, stunned his guests into a mesmerised paralysis. He allowed himself the briefest of smiles.

'I've been given three months to live, six at the outside. My condition has been diagnosed as advanced lung cancer, for which sadly there is no cure.'

No longer able to contain their shock, an anguished sigh reverberated in the air, filling the furthest reaches of the marquee in a vocal outpouring of sadness and muted disbelief. How could such tragedy befall this man, who possessed everything any man could desire from a life, and who now appeared to be telling the world that the one gift he could no longer possess was the gift he cherished above all others, the gift of life itself.

Frank gazed across the distraught gathering.

'Despite the profound implications of my diagnosis, Helen has insisted that our marriage should proceed as planned. I have tried to explain to her that she'll be a wife for a very short time, and a widow for much longer, but in the end nothing would dissuade her. Her final words on the matter were "You stick to the bullshit; leave the medical crap to me!"'

The ripple of laughter in the room soon evaporated into silence. Frank turned to his wife and smiled.

'Helen, I thank you for all that you have given me, but especially for your unconditional love. I shall love you until the moment I draw my last breath.'

Helen took his hand in hers and kissed it gently, then looked up into his eyes and silently mouthed the words, 'I love you, darling.'

The effect on the crowd was profound. The silence permeating the marquee was broken only by intermittent sobs; the sadness, the poignancy, the anguish of the occasion devastatingly etched on the collective emotion of the stunned assembly.

'For obvious reasons it is incumbent on me to inform you that I have today submitted my resignation to my board of directors, and the board has confirmed that it has been unanimously, if reluctantly accepted. Our new chief executive is one of my personal board appointees, my loyal colleague and great pal Steve Richie. Steve has asked that I remain as non-executive chairman, which I have readily agreed to do, at least until a new chairman can be nominated.'

At this point Frank seemed to momentarily lose his composure. He closed his eyes and bowed his head, then straightened up and smiled a thin smile.

'I ask for your heartfelt assistance and support in making this gathering a joyous occasion for Helen and me. Please do not allow the sadness of my words to impact on this marriage celebration, nor on the festivities which my family have laid out for you in the grounds of our wonderful Grange Abbey. Sooner or later death visits all of us; it is an intrinsic part of this life we lead, and life, as always my friends, is for living. We, of all people, must not be found wanting.'

When Frank placed the microphone on the table and sat

back in his chair there was a paralysed silence, and then like a cannon-burst the marquee erupted in a thunderous wall of noise. The barrage of sound melted into a chorus of chanting as the two thousand guests stamped their feet and called out his name.

'Frank! Frank! Frank!' they cried as men and women stood side by side with tears in their eyes, inextricably linked in their grief and abject sorrow. Frank, knowing he needed to stand one last time and acknowledge the power of the response, turned to his brother and said, 'Help me with this, kid.'

Then, to the delight of the crowd, Frank and Paul stood together, arm in arm, tears in their eyes; two brothers standing proud and strong as the applause thundered in their ears.

★

When the wedding festivities finally drew to a close, and the last guests had departed, Frank and Helen lingered on at Grange Abbey. The marquee was dismantled, the catering crews packed up and gone, the mansion cleaned, polished and lovingly restored to its former stately elegance. The days were sunny and warm, the evenings mild and bright, and Frank was enraptured with his new wife. At the end of the second week, a few days before their pre-planned ten-day honeymoon trip to New York, Helen turned to him one morning.

'Darling, I cannot imagine living a day without you.'

Frank gazed at her and was alarmed to see that her eyes were moist with tears. He held her in his arms, contemplating the enormity of the trauma his condition must be exacting on her mental equilibrium, and marvelling at the monumental commitment she had been so willing to make on his behalf.

'My darling, as long as I have a breath of air within me, I swear I shall never leave your side'.

She leaned up and kissed his lips, afterwards resting her head on his shoulder.

'I'm so sorry, my love,' she whispered. 'I promised to be brave and strong for you and yet my heart is breaking. The thought of losing you . . . '

She laid her head on his shoulder and began to sob quietly.

'I'm with you now, my darling,' he whispered gently, stroking her hair and clasping her in his arms.

'We'll be together for all the blissful days that lie ahead of us. We'll pack the memories of two lifetimes into those days and cherish every waking moment of our time together.'

She clung to him so closely he could feel her warm breath, her beating heart, her face moist against his. She gazed up into his eyes.

'Frank, would you be awfully disappointed if we didn't travel to New York. I can't imagine anything more wonderful in my life than to be right here, right now, with you. I do so love this house, and now that we have it all to ourselves, there is nowhere in this world I'd rather be. This place is so enchanting; so breathtakingly beautiful, my darling, I so wish we could linger here all the days of our lives.'

And so they remained at Grange Abbey, in the mornings taking long leisurely strolls through the woods and fields; in the afternoons sitting in the walled garden, sometimes quietly reading, sometimes talking together for hours in the sultry summer evening heat.

Then, as the days grew shorter and the evenings darker, they mostly sat by the fire in the library, never wanting for anything more than each other's company and companionship, their love for one another transcending all that the wide world might offer.

Sometimes friends and family chose to visit, but none stayed long. The warmest of welcomes was extended to all of those who came there, but after a time most seemed to sense the plaintive, the unspoken tragedy that lingered in the air; a sadness that tore at the heartstrings and in the end was impossible to ignore. Most just wanted Frank to know that they were still there for him and always would be. Visitors to the Grange during those sad days were loath to stay longer than was appropriate, and most slipped away discreetly with a heavy weight in their hearts.

★

Frank died at midday on the Sunday of Christmas week 1974, almost a year to the day since he had first met Helen Cawley at the

Fairley Sanatorium. James and Catherine, Paul and Simon, stood by his bedside, and Helen held his hands in hers in the moment he drew his last breath. He was thirty-two years of age. In the little chapel a mile below the village of Straffan, the congregation stood shell-shocked as they carried his coffin down the aisle, the lone soprano's haunting voice filling the air with the words of the hymn 'Nearer My God to Thee'. Grown men and women cried openly as they stood side by side in a heartfelt, outpouring of grief.

They buried him in the old graveyard behind the orchard at Grange Abbey, in a private ceremony attended by the Bannon family and all of the other families living on the estate. Father Barry McGovern, the local parish priest, recited a decade of the rosary and blessed the coffin with incense and holy water. The wizened old padre had been asked to deliver the homily; he took a deep breath before beginning, his words catching as he spoke.

'Frank Bannon, I baptised you when you arrived in this world, and I bless you now as you leave. In between, you straddled the earth like a colossus, scaling heights about which the rest of us can barely dream. Sadly, now that you are gone this world is a lesser place, those of us left behind who were enriched by your presence, now diminished by your passing. Great dynasties are so often tinged with tragedy and despair, God in his wisdom bestowing upon them the fruits of the earth in abundance, then tearing at the strings of their hearts lest they forget the order of all things. A light went out in our hearts when you drew your last breath, at the end of a life too short, leaving behind a vacuum filled with grief, beyond human comprehension, beyond human understanding. Frank, we bless your memory. We mourn your passing. We shall miss you forever. With sadness in our souls we bid you farewell as we consign you to eternity and the care of Almighty God.'

Three hundred mourners stood silently as the coffin was lowered into the damp, dark ground. They watched grief-stricken as the gravediggers lowered the casket and mounded it with sodden black clay. Later, when they dispersed into the gathering gloom, Helen stood alone by her husband's graveside, a solitary figure in the winter's fading light, lost in the layers of her private desolation. Finally, she knelt and placed a single red rose on her husband's grave, then turned and walked away.

39

In the end it was a lethal dose of high-octane grasping greed that brought the whole house of cards crashing down. Steve Richie's four-year tenure as financial controller had been universally applauded, and few were about to argue with Frank's dying wish that Steve should become his successor at the top of Bannons. It soon became apparent that the new chief executive intended to enact a seamless continuation of the brash managerial regime that Frank had indelibly stamped on the company, imparting more of the same aggression, style and panache of his enigmatic predecessor.

Steve initiated an acquisition strategy that reached beyond any funding policy previously envisaged, while simultaneously displaying a determination that impressed most observers and discouraged substantive criticism. He spearheaded an eighteen-month foray into the market, deploying a dazzling array of purchase mechanisms, together with an army of legal advisors to sift through tenders, private bids and associated documentation. The end result was that Bannons were left struggling to fund a staggering two-billion spending spree on housing land in the Greater London area. A monumental sum for a company which for the first time in its history had a non-family member at its helm. In the event, Steve's fledgling corporate regime ran the gamut and brazened it out, dismissing criticism as non-productive and accusations of recklessness as a sign of weakness. But even as the company traded into its third year, with Steve firmly in the driving seat, it was becoming increasingly apparent to anyone on the peripheries that something in the system was fatally flawed.

His acknowledged expertise in accountancy had stood to him during his years as financial controller, when Frank and his father had led the company forward, but the fundamentals that had worked so well in the past had somehow become discarded along the way.

Steve and his directors rarely left their Park Lane headquarters to visit the company's construction sites, opting instead to rely on a sophisticated monthly reporting system presented by an army of newly appointed regional directors. Early one summer morning, John Considine strolled into his office and handed him an envelope.

'What's this, John?'

'My resignation. Oh, don't look so surprised – it's nothing personal. I've served my term, that's all. Time to move aside and make way for a new generation with a new managerial style.'

Steve was taken aback.

'Don't be daft, John. You're part of the fabric of this company. We need your wisdom and experience now more than ever before. Let's talk about this again in twelve months' time.'

'Steve, my mind's made up,' Considine responded pragmatically. 'I'm a Bannon man – always have been. The problem for me is that the Bannons are all gone now. Old James left us a long time ago, and Frank is dead and buried.'

He stood and heaved his mighty frame out of the chair.

'My role is at an end. I wish you well.'

Steve watched the door close behind John Considine, and afterwards sat silently in the early morning stillness of his luxurious office suite, staring into the distance, feeling strangely vulnerable. What would Frank Bannon have done, he wondered, as he leaned forward, elbows on the desk, massaging his temples to ease the tension he'd been feeling more and more lately. He couldn't quite fathom the sense of foreboding in the base of his gut, even though he was acutely aware that changes in management policy introduced under his leadership had begun to implode, and as the weeks turned into months he despaired of finding a solution. The malaise within the organisation was deep-rooted and difficult to diagnose, and would ultimately be blamed on him.

Across the sprawling company, Steve's leadership style had precipitated an innate sluggishness at all levels of management.

The remote head office now seemed far removed from the day-to-day business of laying bricks and pouring concrete. The company was no longer run with the regimental, hands-on ferocity applied by James and Frank. The vast administration framework they had so painstakingly created had slowly begun to unravel. The Bannon construction empire was no longer run by builders willing get their hands dirty and mix it with the tradesmen, but instead by number-crunchers; faceless men in suits who seemed content to interpret the bigger picture from the rarified atmosphere of head office.

Steve and his board failed to comprehend the extent of the deterioration until it was too late. The heat of the past ten years had dissipated from the market, especially in the housing sector, where soaring land prices had finally tipped the end-product over the edge, beyond the reach of the hapless first-time house purchaser.

Out on the construction sites, a debilitating loss of efficiency led to sluggish house completions and production targets undermined by blinding incompetence. Worse again was the gradual erosion of corporate reputation in the City of London, the one place where reputation mattered most of all.

During the seven months since John Considine's departure, Steve often wished he still had access to the great man's wisdom and expertise, but that option was no longer available. In truth, he had chosen to ignore him most of the time during his tenure, when he had sought to impose his own particular stamp on the company. Big John had most likely concluded that Steve and his team considered him surplus to requirement – the unwanted residue of a bygone era.

On occasion when he had contemplated lifting the telephone and dialling his number, he had concluded that there was little point – John Considine would never be enticed back. The sudden clanging of the telephone snapped him out of his reverie. He glanced at his watch and saw that it was already past eight o'clock: where had the first hour gone? He lifted the receiver.

'Yes, Nicole.'

'I have Sebastian Beresford on the line for you . . . again.'

'Have you told him I'm here?'

'No, but he telephoned three times yesterday. He seems . . . insistent.'

Steve knew that Beresford, the chairman of the National Bank of Westminster, the company's primary lender, would never make direct contact except in a matter of the utmost importance. What could it be this time, he wondered – knowing that he simply couldn't ignore him indefinitely. He recalled Frank Bannon's policy of always dealing first with the problems you dread the most, but that seemed easier said than done, and lately Steve found himself plumbing more and more for the easier option, except that on this occasion he sensed he'd just out of options.

'Patch him through, Nicole.'

There was that sinking feeling in his gut again, at one time intermittent, but now pretty much always there.

'Good morning, Sebastian. How nice to hear from you – '

'Didn't your secretary tell you I tried calling on a number of occasions yesterday?'

'Well, yes she did, but – '

'I don't much relish being ignored,' Beresford added tersely.

'I do apologise . . . '

'Apologies are academic at this stage. Matters have progressed beyond all of that, which is why I need to get you over here right away; you and your financial controller . . . '

'Carruthers?'

'Yes, that's it, Carruthers. I'll expect you in precisely one hour.'

'That doesn't give us a lot of time . . . '

There was a click at the far end and the line went dead.

When Steve and Marcus Carruthers arrived at the bank's headquarters they were kept waiting another hour before being summoned to the boardroom. Sebastian Beresford motioned them to a seat and barely bid them the time of day. Steve recognised two of the men in the room as affiliates of the bank's corporate-property section – the other three he'd never seen before. None stood to shake hands. Beresford sat in his place at the head of the boardroom table. The bank's chairman was seventy-one years of age, sophisticated, tall, thin, and always impeccably dressed. He wasted no time getting to the point.

'Gentlemen, I've summoned you here this morning to relay some rather distasteful news.'

His refined, upper-crust accent had an appropriately sombre ring to it.

'After a lengthy and careful deliberation, I regret having to inform you that the bank is no longer in a position to extend financial support to the Bannon group of companies.'

Steve gasped.

'Sebastian, are you out of your mind – '

'Please . . . allow me to finish,' he motioned with a wave of his hand.

Steve wondered had he heard correctly.

'This decision is bound to come as a shock to you both, but sadly, events have taken on a life of their own since I tried unsuccessfully to engage with you yesterday.'

When Steve attempted to interrupt, Beresford ignored him.

'Late last evening the bank appointed Garfield Craig as official receivers to the Bannon group of companies.'

Steve gaped open-mouthed, but no words came out.

'Giles Prendergast from Garfields is here to brief you on where matters stand currently.'

Prendergast, sitting opposite Steve between two colleagues, nodded gravely.

'Earlier this morning Garfields oversaw the cessation of construction activity on all Bannon construction sites in the London region. My colleagues are currently overseeing the removal of your head-office staff from their positions with immediate effect, taking with them only their personal belongings and leaving the rest behind. My understanding is that the vast majority of your personnel are at this moment co-operating with the orderly transfer of control to my colleagues. We envisage re-employing some key staff to assist with the implementation of the receivership for as long as it is deemed necessary to do so, after which period their appointments will be terminated.'

He hesitated briefly while one of his colleagues whispered in his ear.

'I can also confirm that in the past few minutes the entrance gates to all of the company's development sites in the London region have been chained shut, hence the delay in engaging with you earlier.'

'Thank you Giles,' Beresford responded smoothly. Steve looked crestfallen.

'A similar exercise is scheduled to take place in Ireland and across the group's various other interests. All of which means that, from your perspective, this is effectively the end of the road. Your role as chief executive is terminated forthwith, and as of now the Bannon group as an entity is a thing of the past.'

Steve sat there shell-shocked, staring at his trembling hands. Despite all his earlier misgivings, this scenario was beginning to sound worse than his worst nightmare. He turned and stared vacantly at Beresford.

'At least explain the rationale for initiating such . . . drastic action. Surely we're entitled to know that much.'

'I should have thought it was obvious,' Beresford responded brusquely. 'The bank believes the company is patently insolvent, and is no longer capable of honouring its commitments. Our primary concerns are with the group's loan-to-value covenants, its inability to service future funding requirements and its vulnerability to creditors. The company's current level of exposure is unsustainable and has been constructed without the bank's approval. Ultimately the bank is of the view that we simply cannot countenance an expenditure of two billion on future land acquisition by a company that is no longer fit to pay its bills.'

Steve looked dazed and disorientated, his demeanour crestfallen, his voice rasping and unsteady.

'Our cash flows are tight for the very reason that we've committed two hundred million of our in-house funds to enable our land transactions to complete, and if we fail to complete, we forfeit our in-house deposits. Sebastian, you simply cannot permit this to happen.'

Beresford stared incredulously at Steve.

'How on God's earth could you countenance committing two hundred million in non-refundable deposits without prior funding approval for the balance, and then expect the bank to cough up one point eight billion to enable the completion? Your rationale simply beggars belief, because if that is what you've done, then I fear that your money really *is* gone. The bank's receivers will endeavor to recoup some or all of it, but if what you are telling us is correct then don't rate their chances.'

Steve walked away from the bank's headquarters, and wandered the streets of the City feeling dazed and distraught. He realised that the wheels had been set in motion, and there was no going back. The year was 1979 and the construction phenomenon that had been created thirty-four years earlier by James and his two brothers was finally at an end. The BBC's one o'clock bulletin was first to announce news of the collapse, confirming the rumours that had been circulating like wildfire in the City.

★

Two months later, a mini-bus carrying a team of accountants, and a truck filled with tradesmen, drove in the gates of Grange Abbey. The farm-workers and staff who had lived on the estate all of their lives were given ten days to pack their belongings and leave. It took all of a month to secure the mansion, itemise the contents, board up the windows and padlock the doors. When the last key was turned, they loaded their vehicles and drove down the driveway, stopping by the main entrance to pull the great gates closed. A steel chain was threaded through the bars and the padlock snapped shut.

40

He sat on a train in Oxford Station and stared absentmindedly out the window. It was the day before his twenty-first birthday, the last day of June, the summer of 1971, the hottest since records began. His years at John the Baptist seemed but a distant memory. Paul was now at the end of this his penultimate year at Christ Church College and at the beginning of a long, hot, hazy summer on the run-up to completing his final year at Oxford. The train lurched forward and gathered speed, and soon the idyllic, sun-drenched countryside was hurtling past. The invitation from his parents to join them at Genevieve, their sumptuous villa on Cap Ferrat had arrived a week earlier. At Waterloo he boarded a cab to Heathrow just in time to catch the late-morning flight to the south of France. Henri, his parents' driver, was waiting to meet him at Nice Airport.

'Bonjour, Monsieur Paul,' he announced cheerfully. 'Suivez-moi, s'il vous plait.'

From the airport they drove bumper-to-bumper down the Promenade des Anglais, then out along the coast road to Cap Ferrat. The sun glistened on the water and the bougainvillea glowed deep purple on the narrow lane leading to the gates of the villa. He stepped onto the gravel driveway and glanced up to see his mother waving from the veranda.

'Oh, how wonderful! My handsome baby has arrived,' she laughed. 'Come and join us. We're about to have lunch.'

Henri took his travel bag and Paul walked through the shady villa, climbing two flights to the south veranda. His father sat with his brothers, Matthew and Charles, either side of him under the shade of a large umbrella, while draped on a lounger beyond them sat the hulking frame of John Considine.

He recognised the dapper, bearded figure of his father's

business associate Henry Hyland at a telephone by the bar, deep in conversation. His mother embraced him, then hooked her arm in his and led him to where they were seated. A waiter offered them flutes of champagne.

'So tall and handsome,' his mother smiled, 'and twenty-one tomorrow. Does it get any better!'

She surveyed him proudly and raised her glass.

'To a young man with the world at his feet, may fortune follow you all the days of your life.'

Henry Hyland strolled across and clinked his glass.

'I'll second that,' he smiled. 'What a pleasure! I've heard a great deal about you.'

He remembered meeting Henry and his glamorous wife, the former fashion model Rebecca Sands two years previously at a summer party at Grange Abbey. He knew that the brothers held him in the highest regard.

'I once overheard my father telling a group of people that you are the undisputed wizard of the London property scene. High praise coming from him.'

Henry raised his eyebrows in mock-surprise, then nodded towards James.

'I learned a trick or two from him, you know.'

He placed a hand on Paul's shoulder and whispered, 'If ever you need my help, call me – don't hesitate – I'll be happy to assist.'

'Thank you. I'll bear it in mind.'

Afterwards they moved across the veranda and ate lunch at a table overlooking the ocean. Then in the late afternoon his father led him to his study and they sat alone.

'I'm proud of you,' he said matter-of-factly, his piercing blue eyes staring at his son from across the cavernous desk.

'I wish I could say the same of all my sons,' he added wistfully, then swivelled his chair and gazed distractedly out the window as if pondering the irony of his words. Paul sat silently.

'I look at you and I'm happy with what I see,' he said, turning back to him. 'We all are: your mother, your uncles, old Johnny out there.'

He seemed uncharacteristically reflective, but then his eyes twinkled mischievously.

'And twenty-one tomorrow – time to look the world straight in the eye.'

'I'll give it a shot, but you're a tough act to follow.'

His father smiled a world-weary smile, acknowledging the compliment. He took a cigar from a box on the desk and lit it.

'Considine told me you saved the life of that little girl. To this day he doesn't know how you did it. Recklessness beyond comprehension, he calls it. Bravery beyond belief.'

'I couldn't leave her to die in the water,' he said simply.

They sat in silence, his father observing him thoughtfully.

'He also told me about Simon's . . . intervention.'

'He told you that?' Paul inquired quietly. His father nodded.

'Old Johnny and I have no secrets, but I'm guessing you know that.'

'The dogs on the street know it,' he replied.

James smiled, but his smile faded in a flash.

'Don't ever call that son-of-a-bitch a brother,' he said bitterly. 'No brother of yours would have done what he did.'

The venom in his father's tone startled him.

'Frank's the only brother you'll ever have. The only brother you'll ever need.'

He listened to his father's words, his pulse racing as he struggled to fathom the conundrum lingering in their tantalising vagueness. But that particular discussion ended as soon as it had begun: his father had moved on. He watched him reach into a drawer, extract an envelope and place it on the table.

'Your twenty-first-birthday present. A sterling draft for ten million pounds. Go on. Take it.'

'Ten million,' he whispered.

James nodded.

'Oh, don't be surprised – it's not unique – your brothers received the same before you, and I'm giving you the same advice I gave to each of them, which is to utilise it sensibly. Still, having said that, it comes with no conditions. It's yours to do with as you please, so stick it in your pocket and let's get back and join the others.'

They stood and embraced one another, and when he turned to leave, his father held his arm.

'One last thing.'

'Yes, father.'

He placed a hand on his son's shoulder and steered him towards the door.

'Old Johnny is fond of you, but you probably know that.'

'I'm fond of him too, father.'

'I'm glad to hear it, because Johnny's a wonderful friend to have, and someday you're going to need him. And whenever that day comes, don't hesitate to make the call.'

41

The Foxhunter bar at the Allendale crossroads a mile from
Avoca village was strangely quiet that evening, the dozen or
so patrons scattered along the counter studiously minding
their own business. It was a winter's night in late October, and
Alphonsus Kilcoyne, the proprietor, sat silently dusting off
bottles, paying scant heed to anyone. In these parts it was best
to keep your nose out of other people's affairs, and Alphonsus
judiciously avoided meddling in his customers' lives.

But then the door opened and a gust of wind and leaves
swirled in from the dark autumnal night. Adam Gilbert and
Rex Chalmers staggered to the counter, looking drunk and
disshevelled from the day's excesses. Alphonsus cursed under
his breath.

'Fucking Gilbert,' he sighed, 'and he's drunk again.'

Gilbert spelled trouble and it was looking as if tonight would
be no different.

'Shift your ass, mister. You're sitting on my stool,' he barked
at a farm labourer seated in the far corner. The customer, a
gangly fellow in his early twenties, quietly staring at nothing in
particular, turned briefly to Gilbert.

'Stool's taken. Go find another.'

Gilbert stared at him.

'Sure, sir. Sorry, sir. Beggin' your pardon of course.'

He gave a mock salute and a cursory bow, then turned
and slashed his riding crop across the young labourer's face,
catapulting him onto the floor.

'Get off my fucking stool when I say so,' he snarled, 'and
take your fucking drink with you.'

He upended the glass, drenching the young labourer with
the contents, then stood back and watched him scramble to

his feet and make for the door, hands clutched to his eyes. He straightened the stool and sat on it.

'Two pints, Fonsie, and make it fast.'

Fonsie slid from his stool and did as he was bid. The other customers barely paid heed, knowing better than to engage with the master of Cloneen Priory, the estate Gilbert had inherited following the death of his father. Part of that inheritance had included the old Foxhunter at a crossroads on the periphery of the estate grounds. Fonsie watched his new landlord survey the room, his countenance flushed, his sprawling, rotund belly wedged against the counter.

'Your two pints, Master Gilbert,' he smiled, placing the drinks on the counter. 'Enjoy.'

Gilbert spat on the floor and glanced around the room, almost daring anyone to look him in the eye. Fonsie backed away quietly, but judging from the evil scowl beneath the ragged white beard that covered most of his landlord's face, it was shaping up to be one of those nights. Just then the door rattled open and three strangers stepped into the dimly lit tavern. Gilbert's gaze followed them as they walked to the far end of the bar and sat along the counter.

'Three pints, barman, at your leisure.'

'Coming right up, sir,' Fonsie nodded.

'And another two at this end,' Gilbert grunted, his gaze fixed on the three strangers as they settled in their seats. He watched them sip their drinks slowly, silently, wordlessly. They were hard types for sure, their clothes dark and rough, faces unshaven, cloth caps pulled low over their eyes.

'Something the matter, Adam?' Rex Chalmers inquired. 'You seem . . . on edge tonight.'

'Nothin's the matter,' he snapped.

Rex pondered him curiously and stared into the shadows to where the three men sat. There was a stillness about them he found vaguely unsettling – a stillness which seemed to perturb his companion more than him. He thought about it and decided probably nothing to it. Strangers often came through these parts, seldom lingering. He heard the scrape of a stool and turned to see his friend walk slowly in their direction, stopping by the counter a few feet from where they sat. Fonsie placed a pint in front of him. He drained half of it.

'Another!' he barked.

'On the way, Master Gilbert.'

He stood staring directly at them, but they paid no heed. They seemed oblivious to his presence. He pulled on his cigar and blew the smoke in their direction.

'Would you boys be here for me?' he asked.

The dark-haired man in the middle raised his head and observed him with mild curiosity.

'We're just minding our own business. Expecting company?'

'Maybe.'

'Well, good for you then.'

Gilbert laughed loudly.

'Oh I doubt it,' he roared, his deep baritone resounding through the bar. The three men observed him silently.

'Oh yes, sir, I doubt it very much. You see, sir, I've been expecting a visit for a long long time – all of thirteen years, to tell you the God's truth. Yes sir, if the truth be known sir, thirteen years since the day I tried to drown that little cunt Sinclair. The bitch needed to be taught a lesson, sir. I even tried to fuck her once – almost had her raped good, except she bit me on the nose and made a dash for it.'

He pointed with his finger and grinned.

'I've even the teeth-marks to prove it.'

The dark-haired stranger pondered him coldly.

'Just rewards for being a naughty little boy.'

Gilbert bristled at the insult, but the man's stare was deathly still. He stubbed his cigar and downed the remainder of his drink.

'Your face seems . . . familiar. You boys from around these parts?'

'No, sir. Just passing through on our way to catch the ferry in Dublin.'

'She'll hardly sail in this tempest. Yis'll be lucky to ketch it tonight.'

The stranger gave no reaction, just nodded towards the window.

'That your horse hitched up outside?'

'What if it is?'

'Oh, nothing meant sir. Just that it's a fine specimen.'

Gilbert squinted hard at him, struggling with his memory.

'Dammit, you remind me of someone,' he grunted, sliding off the stool. He stood and squinted at the cold-eyed stranger.

'She'd a brother . . . Jamie, a gangly fella, long gone from these parts, but I'd surely recognise him . . . '

The stranger continued to observe him with the same icy stare. Adam gave an involuntary shiver, then slowly pushed his stool away and returned to where Rex Chalmers sat alone.

And yet still as he sat he seemed strangely discommoded, all the while on edge, gazing into the corner to where the three men sat, eyes darting to and fro, until at last there was a rattle of stools and they stood to leave.

Two hours later, when the clock struck midnight, Adam Gilbert and Rex Chalmers downed their last drinks and Fonsie Kilcoyne breathed a sigh as he bolted the door behind them. He gazed through the tiny window and saw Chalmers mount his animal, then turn south towards the village of Avoca. He watched Gilbert check the beretta he always carried, stuff it into his coat and ride out in the opposite direction, towards the old Priory.

It was a dark, moonless evening, and the old roof creaked under the cold northern breeze rattling through its ancient tiles. He heard the clatter of the horse's hoofs grow faint as Gilbert cantered into the darkness out along the Priory road.

The young upstart commandeering his stool had annoyed him for sure – how dare the cheeky little fucker. And then those strangers had irked all evening. There was a familiarity about those three. He'd swear it, but as hard as he tried, his damned brain was so muddled from drink he couldn't figure it. His mood darkened. He whipped his horse into a gallop, checked the gun in his breast pocket and rode onwards into the black night.

They heard the echo of hoofs above the howl of the wind as the horse rounded the turn onto the narrow road leading to the Priory gate. They took their positions low in the ditch and pulled down hard on the thin steel wire, stretching it between two stout tree-trunks on either side. It gave a low, whirring twang as it tightened in mid-air, spanning the narrow lane between the two sturdy ashes.

They waited in silence, the noise of the hoofs growing louder, the crack of the crop whipping the animal to a gallop. Now, rounding the last bend, they could see the looming dark shape of horse and rider clattering down the centre of the cobbled laneway. Then suddenly he was beside them, the horse racing forward, the wire snagging the rider just below the neck, momentarily suspending him in mid-air as the animal galloped on.

An eerie scream pierced the darkness and suddenly he rocked backwards onto the rough hard surface. They scrambled up from the ditch and pinned his arms and legs. By then the winds had eased and his anguished cries reverberated in the stillness of the cold, starless night. Suddenly he tore an arm free and made a grab for the gun, but they ripped it from his grasp. Then a blow from a steel boot crunched into the side of his head, knocking him senseless.

Straining under the dead weight, they carried him through the open gate into the field and down the slope towards the stream on the outer border. They struggled through the mud in the low corner where the cattle came to drink their daily fill, and laid him beside a feeding trough brimful of cattle-dung and slurry. They took a moment to catch their breath, then, nodding to one another in the darkness, in one swift movement they lifted his heavy frame and tossed him into the freezing water. Instantly awakened by the shock, he tumbled and spluttered in the churning black fluid, the blood-ooze from the jagged line on his neck spreading a dark stain across the surface. He struggled frantically to escape the stinking putrid stench, but they turned him on his back and pinned his neck with a pitchfork. He screamed in agony and stared helplessly up at his tormenters, tears in his eyes, his mouth a snarl of pain. The man holding the pitchfork was strong – he snared his neck in a vice-like grip, rendering the tiniest movement impossible. And then he heard the scraping sound.

He gagged as the pitchfork cut into his neck, plunging him back down into the suffocating stench, filling his nose and mouth with black poison. When his lungs were about to explode, the pressure eased just enough to allow him to break the surface – and there it was again, that strange, grating sound. He blinked to force the putrid water from his eyes and then for the first time he caught sight of a thick slab of solid concrete inching its way slowly forward. Suddenly the nature of his dilemma began to dawn on him. He bucked violently and gazed beseechingly at his captor.

'Oh Jesus, God have mercy on me whoever you are. Have pity in your heart to forgive me, whatever sin I done!'

The pitchfork tore into his neck forcing, him to gag, convulse and gulp mouthfuls of the poisonous water. In the darkness he could hear the scraping of the lid and see its shadow looming inch by inch, further and further, until, with the tiniest gap remaining, suddenly the pitchfork was pulled roughly away. He struggled desperately to keep his mouth above the surface, suddenly aware that the grating sound had ceased – a glimmer of hope in the depths of his despair. The man leaned close and stared into his eyes.

'This is where you die, you evil cunt. You guessed correctly earlier – it was you we came to visit. When your ugly head sinks forever into this filthy grave, the world will be a better place.'

He stared upwards into cold merciless eyes, knowing that there would be no reprieve from this concrete hell-hole. There was something frustratingly familiar about this man, but what in the hell could it be?

'We left a gap of air at the top. We wouldn't want you drowning too quickly.'

The stranger raised his arm and the slab began shifting remorselessly forward, and suddenly the realisation dawned on him. His eyes widened.

'You!' he rasped. 'I recognise you now you heartless bastard – '

The slab crunched into position, leaving him isolated in the darkness of his watery tomb.

42

In normal circumstances the staff up at the Priory paid scant heed to the non-appearance of their unpredictable boss. The old Priory had become dilapidated and forlorn in the period since the Colonel's passing, his fiefdom whittled down to a skeleton crew comprising Tom Fogarty the yard manager, Ivan the kitchen boy, and the Colonel's loyal housekeeper Martha. The once-sizable stud farm had deteriorated following the sale of the yard's prize stallion to discharge one of Adam's gambling debts. Since then, the Priory lands had been set to local farmers, Adam living off the rental income from these, and a handful of meagre properties skirting the edge of the estate.

His three staff were well accustomed to their boss's erratic lifestyle and seldom batted an eye when he didn't show for days on end. Adam's reputation as a cruel, drunken buffoon was acknowledged across the length and breadth of the county. His frequent absences from the estate provided a welcome respite for his beleaguered workers.

Ivan Carter strode across the fields as the first light of dawn filtered above the horizon. He lived in his parents' cottage at the end of a country track that meandered down to the back of the old Priory yard. The winds had blown out during the night and the morning was calm and still as he mounted the paddock fence and sauntered up to the house. A rustling of branches startled him out of his reverie. He turned and stared along the hedgerow to where Adam's horse stood saddled beneath a large oak, quietly munching grass. He skirted the hedge until he was close enough to grab a rein, gently patted the animal's neck and led him up to the yard.

'Where'd he come from?' Tom inquired.

'I found him grazing in the paddock field, saddled and all, but ne'er a sign of the squire.'

'Walk him to the stables, Ivan. I'll saunter on up to the house.'

In the kitchen he heard Martha humming away quietly.

''Ere a sign of the squire, Martha?'

'His bed's not been slept in,' she frowned. 'I haven't seen sight of him since he left with Master Chalmers last evening.'

Two days later the search began in earnest, with hundreds of local volunteers downing tools and manning police search-lines across the county. Trained divers probed rivers, streams and lakes, even dredging the old limestone quarry beyond the ridge up on the south riding. Hedges, ditches, watercourses, remote farm buildings, and outhouses were scoured meticulously, all to no avail. By the end of the third week, with still no hint of a lead, the police opted to scale down the operation and set up a 'missing persons' file, which they stated would remain open 'indefinitely'.

The community soon settled back into its age-old routine, and with the passing of each week the mystery of Adam Gilbert's disappearance faded in the local consciousness, soon becoming little more than a topic for intermittent discussion in the village bars. In the following weeks, Rex Chalmers was questioned exhaustively by police, but he swore that the last time he saw Adam was at midnight on that fateful night in the Foxhunter.

Police officers spent hours quizzing Fonsie Kilcoyne, but his story was more or less the same. Yes, there had been an altercation with a customer early in the evening, but such incidents were not unique in the turbulent world of Adam Gilbert. The investigating team followed every lead meticulously, but uncovered little of significance, and gradually the trail went cold.

A month following Adam's disappearance, Maggie, Tom and Ivan finally vacated the old Priory. No last will and testament could be processed for as long as his disappearance remained unresolved. No distant relatives showed up to lay claim to an inheritance, and no legal document came to light. The windows at the Priory were eventually boarded up, the property abandoned to the rooks occupying the huge trees shadowing its walls.

Then one morning in early April, when the memory of the incident had all but faded, Ivan Carter walked into the Avoca station and asked to speak with Shawn Butterley, the duty sergeant. They led him through to the small back office, where Butterley appraised the slight, skinny kid from behind his untidy desk.

'So you've finally come to confess, Ivan. You murdered the fat fucker.'

'Not quite sergeant, but I think I seen something. I'm not rightly sure – '

'So, out with it, Ivan.'

'Sarge, you said if there was anything – '

'Yes, yes, yes Ivan, spit it out boy!'

'Anything at all – '

'Holy Jaysus Ivan!'

'It's just that yesterday when I was walking the fields behind the Priory, down by the stream at the old watering hole where we used to feed the cattle . . . '

'Yes! Yes! Yes! Yes!'

'In the summer when the stream ran dry we'd fill the cattle trough with water – '

'What are you rambling on about . . . '

'It's covered sarge.'

'Covered! Jesus boy – '

'Sealed solid with a concrete slab. Doesn't make sense sarge, and the strangest thing, there's the mother of all smells . . . '

Later that day a team of local men raised the slab and stared into the bloated face of Adam Gilbert glaring up at them, his skin black as coal, his stomach distorted and blown, the filthy, stinking water rancid with the evil stench of decay.

The discovery was immediately reclassified as a murder investigation when the Dublin 'Murder Squad' officially took charge of the inquiry. The body was left untouched under a loose tarpaulin in the place it was discovered, the immediate area cordoned off with crime-scene tape, and a young guard posted at the scene pending the arrival of a forensic team in the late afternoon.

Detective Jerry Greenfield, a veteran with thirty years' experience in the murder squad, was assigned to the investigation. He and his team began sifting through the evidence, reviewing the witness statements and interviewing anyone with even a tenuous link to the incident. Greenfield had a disarming personality and a jovial disposition which belied a razor-sharp brain, traits which went some way towards explaining his near-one-hundred-percent success rate.

The old Priory was opened up, and a meticulous, room by room search conducted over a number of days, but it turned up little of value other than confirming that Adam Gilbert did indeed live like the pig most people attested him to be. Greenfield soon came to realise that any number of people would happily have ended Gilbert's days, the emerging picture that of a sadistic, evil buffoon whose premature passing none in these parts had reason to mourn.

The detective interviewed scores of people during those first weeks of the investigation, including Martha Staunton, the housekeeper, Tom Fogarty, the yard manager, and young Ivan Carter, the last three employees to vacate the Priory. His team chased down the staff who had been dismissed in the period since the old Colonel passed away, and contacted the various police constabularies whose paths had crossed with Gilbert down the years. Greenfield interviewed Rex Chalmers and Fonsie Kilcoyne exhaustively, to no avail, and yet still, at the end of it all, some inner nagging instinct kept drawing him back to the Foxhunter bar at the crossroads below the old Priory. In the grainy depths of his inner thought-process the same instinct seemed to be telling him that if there ever was an answer to this puzzle, then the solution lay within the ancient walls of the remote tavern.

He stood leaning against the bonnet of his car savouring the sun's heat in the early spring morning until he saw Fonsie unbolt the door and step out onto the gravel forecourt. The detective glanced at his watch. It was a minute to ten.

'Like a bad penny,' he smiled, but the barman just gave a shrug of the shoulders.

'I'm brewing a mug, detective. Care to join me?'

'I surely will, Fonsie.'

Jerry Greenfield liked Fonsie Kilcoyne. He was ramrod straight, reliable and at all times co-operative. They sat by the counter and drank their tea in the deserted bar.

'Let's go back one last time to that fateful night, Fonsie. I get the feeling I'm missing some frustrating little detail.'

'Not a problem, detective. You go right ahead.'

The detective lit a cigarette and took a sip of his tea.

'Gilbert and Chalmers arrived around nine, on horseback – correct?'

Fonsie nodded.

'Wasn't that unusual, Fonsie? Those boys travelling on horseback in these modern times?'

'Not really, detective, well, at least not in these parts. The Priory lands stretch for miles in either direction of the Foxhunter forecourt. One big estate borders the next. Those old places can still be managed pretty effectively on horseback.'

Greenfield nodded slowly.

'Take me through the events of the night one last time, Fonsie, nice and slow.'

Fonsie sat back in his chair and sighed.

'I'm not sure if there's anything left to say that I haven't already told you, detective. There was the incident with the bar stool, and when the young lad left the tavern, Gilbert and Chalmers drank heavily all evening. The other customers paid scant heed, same as they did most nights. Adam Gilbert was real bad news, detective: troublesome, unpredictable, a regular pain in the ass. Most sensible people avoided him, except for – '

'Except for what, Fonsie?'

'Well . . . except . . . for the stranger.'

'The stranger?'

The barman scratched his head and stared out the window.

'There were three of them, as I recall; came in out of the blue sometime after eight. I omitted to mention it because it didn't seem important at the time.'

The detective took out a pipe and filled it. Fonsie nodded towards the end of the bar.

'Sat in yonder far corner.'

Greenfield tamped down the tobacco and lit up.

'So what's making you recall this incident?'

'I don't rightly know, detective. They arrived in and Gilbert seemed, I dunno . . . agitated, strangely out of sorts. I thought

I heard him ask if they were there for him, or words to that effect.'

Now Greenfield was on full alert.

'Carry on, Fonsie – this could be important.'

'I didn't get all of it, detective, but then I heard Adam say he'd been expecting someone to come for him – ever since the girl.'

'What girl was that Fonsie?'

'The Sinclair girl, detective – Gilbert called her the cunt – made some comment about attempting to drown her, or rape her, or words to that effect. Like I say, I didn't pick up on all of it.'

Fonsie went on to tell Gerry Greenfield that rumours had been circulating for years about an incident up on the Grange Abbey estate in the north of the county, ten, maybe twelve years previously. During one of those annual hunt balls that used to take place up there, some of the competitors swore they saw Adam Gilbert shunting a lady rider and her horse into the swollen Liffey. Fonsie assured the detective that a number of people on the estate that day claimed they witnessed it with their own eyes.

'I ain't no detective but I'm convinced it must have taken place,' he said reflectively. 'There were too many people telling the same story for it not to be believable. Afterwards Gilbert's name was blackened across the length and breadth of the county. Didn't seem to bother him much, detective, and he never denied it, but after the incident the old Colonel was rarely seen in public. Some of the locals maintain the shame of it did for him in the end. Then people began moving their business away from the Priory stud, so much so that in the end it was down to a bare trickle. That fateful day would prove a turning point in the fortunes of the Gilbert family.'

'Sure appears that way,' Gerry Greenfield replied absentmindedly, but his thoughts were already racing ahead. He felt a shivering sensation in his bones, the same feeling he always felt at the first tentative signs of a breakthrough.

'Grange Abbey, you say, Fonsie – the Bannon place?'

'Yes, detective. Well in those days it used to be, but it ain't any longer. Their fortunes also took a turn for the worse. Business went belly-up and the old house was abandoned years ago – still empty, far as I know.'

The detective took an envelope from an inside pocket and extracted a folded sheet of paper which he spread out on the counter. Neatly printed in the centre were the four letters 'B - A - N - I'.

'This make any sense, Fonsie?'

The barman stared at the sheet and shook his head.

'Like I said earlier, I'm no detective.'

'Well then, I guess this is where I come in,' Greenfield responded quietly. 'And as everyone now knows, Gilbert's body was discovered in a slurry-filled cattle-trough with a three-ton concrete lid on top – heavy enough to require the combined strength of four men to lift it off. The lid was placed on the grass while the forensic team carried out their work, and later the body was removed for post-mortem – the eventual verdict, death by drowning. The coroner concluded that Adam Gilbert may have survived in that hell-hole up to an hour before he finally succumbed. There were other injuries of course, some serious, but in the end it was death due to asphyxiation caused by drowning. A week later we revisited the kill-site and the slab still lay in the place where we dropped it. We looked around one last time and as we were leaving, almost as an afterthought, I asked the guys to flip the lid over, and there, scratched on the back, barely discernible but there nonetheless were the four letters 'B - A - N - I'. Until now we couldn't figure it out, but guess what, Fonsie, I think you've just helped me unravel the mystery.'

'How so, detective?'

Greenfield stared at the barman and smiled grimly.

'My belief is that before he died, at some stage Gilbert saw his killer and recognised him. When they placed the slab on top of him, he began scraping the name of his murderer into the underside of the concrete before he disappeared beneath the surface forever.'

'The murderer's name is Bani, detective?'

'Not quite, Fonsie. Let's just say Gilbert started on the name but never got to finish it.'

It slowly began to dawn on the startled barman.

'You can't think he scraped those letters with his bare hands, detective. Surely that's beyond belief.'

'But not impossible, Fonsie. Gilbert used the edge of a gold signet ring he wore on his right index finger. The flesh on the finger was heavily serrated, practically hanging off – raw down to the bone. He must have badly wanted to deliver that message.'

Shortly afterwards Fonsie walked the detective to his car, both of them in reflective, sombre mood.

He sat in the car and pulled down the window.

'You've been a real help. I appreciate it, but there is just one last question.'

'Sure, detective.'

'This guy – the stranger that spoke. Do you recall him saying anything else?'

The barman thought for a minute.

'I recall he said something about catching a ferry in Dublin, but that's about it, detective.'

'Can you describe him: his age; anything?'

'I didn't pay much heed; they were rough types for sure and they sat in the shade most of the evening. But if you're asking me to guess, I'd say late twenties – thirty at most. And in a strange kind of way he was a different kettle of fish from most of the other guys I've seen Gilbert confront in the bar of the Foxhunter.'

'Different in what way?'

Fonsie glanced at Greenfield and frowned.

'There was no hint of fear in him, detective, and this is me guessing again, but I'd almost swear it was the other way around.'

Later, when Greenfield checked the ferry movements out of Dublin Port, he found that there were none that evening and none the following day. He ran a routine check on the port of Rosslare forty miles to the south and discovered that a 7AM ferry had departed for Fishguard in Wales the morning after Gilbert's disappearance.

He sat in his chair and stared out the window, clicking his biro absentmindedly on and off, exasperated by the knowledge that there was no passenger manifest requirement between Irish and UK ports, rendering passenger identification impossible.

'Now aren't you the cute one,' he mused, 'sending the bloodhounds on the wrong scent.'

★

Two days later, in response to a routine inquiry, Gerry Greenfield received a telex from Roddy Peterson, a detective affiliated to the records section of Scotland Yard with whom he had dealt on a number of occasions, listing the names and addresses of five Paul Bannons currently domiciled in the UK. Greenfield quickly dismissed three of them in the age range of forty-five to seventy.

A Reverend Paul Archibald Bannon, an Anglican minister based in a rural village outside Cirencester seemed unlikely. But that still left one on his list, which, based on his discussions with Fonsie Kilcoyne, and on research into records of surviving members of the Bannon family with an original address at the Grange Abbey estate in north Kildare, seemed perfectly to fit the target profile.

Greenfield stared at the last remaining name, Paul James Bannon, the Penthouse, Hans Crescent, Knightsbridge. *I wonder,* he thought, as he tapped his pen reflectively, again feeling that tell-tale tremor building up inside.

That evening a letter was dispatched by registered post. It read:

Dear Mister Bannon,

We are currently investigating the death of one Hector Adam Gilbert, late of the Cloneen Priory, Allendale, County Kildare, whose body was discovered on the thirteenth day of April 1978 in a field in the township of Briarly near Avoca.

Mister Gilbert was reported missing in early October 1977, and the discovery of his body has upgraded the status of the inquest from a missing person's inquiry to that a full murder investigation.

As part of this investigation we are anxious to establish your whereabouts on the night of Monday the seventh of October 1977. Your co-operation in this matter would be appreciated.

In pursuance of this my colleague Detective Dan Sweeney and I are anxious to interview you as soon as it is practicable to so do. For the record I wish to categorically state that at this stage of the investigation you are not a suspect in the inquiry.

Signed,
Detective Gerry Greenfield

Three days later a response by registered post confirmed the availability of Paul Bannon for interview at his Hans Crescent address at midday on the Friday of the following week.

They boarded the Thursday-night ferry from Dun Laoghaire to Holyhead and caught the night train to London, arriving in Euston at seven on the Friday morning. They ate breakfast at an all-night cafe on the Euston Road, then caught the underground to Knightsbridge, arriving in Hans Crescent with fifteen minutes to spare. The apartment complex, in a quiet street off the Brompton Road, was red-brick and formal – Greenfield guessed on the higher end of the high end. They announced themselves to the porter, who buzzed them through immediately.

'Gentlemen, Mister Bannon is expecting you. Please take the lift to the seventh floor where someone will meet you.'

The lift opened into the hallway of a luxurious apartment adorned with white high-shine travertine marble floors, deep Persian rugs and ornate gilt mirrors. An attractive brunette wearing a plain black dress and black high-heeled shoes welcomed them. She smiled pleasantly.

'Good morning, Mister Greenfield. If you gentlemen would care to follow me, Mister Bannon will be with you shortly.'

She led them through to a vast rosewood-panelled lounge furnished with cream carpets, cream couches, gold-leaf chairs and gilt-framed paintings of colourful hunt scenes, tastefully interspersed with dramatic oils depicting bullfights and flamenco dancers. There were views across the roofs of Knightsbridge to Hyde Park in the distance, with Harrods department store in the foreground. She served coffee from a silver tray on a low ornate table. Then the door opened and a man walked into the room.

'Good morning, detective Greenfield. I trust you had a pleasant journey. I'm Paul Bannon.'

'Mister Bannon,' the detective smiled, standing to shake his hand. Gerry Greenfield endeavoured, as he always did, to formulate that vital first impression. Paul Bannon was about six feet two or three, possibly fourteen stone, ruggedly handsome, suave, and dressed impeccably in a tailored business suit with white shirt and grey tie. He stared at him with interest and wondered if he was looking into the eyes of a man capable of perpetrating one of the most savage murders he had encountered.

'Thank you for agreeing to meet with us so promptly,' he smiled.

'Not at all, detective, please tell me how I can be of assistance.'

The voice was polished, the eyes open and direct, the demeanour that of a man with little to fear.

'Mind if I smoke?'

'Of course not.'

He lit a cigarette, sat back in his armchair and blew the smoke to the ceiling.

'As I explained in my letter, we're investigating the murder of Adam Gilbert, late of the Priory estate near Avoca in south Kildare. Were you acquainted with the deceased, Mister Bannon?'

'Yes I was, detective'.

Greenfield seemed surprised.

'Oh really.'

'I'm originally from Kildare, detective. After a time, you get to know everyone.'

'Were you friendly with the deceased, Mister Bannon?'

'No, I was not.'

'Did you like him?'

'No, detective, I did not. Few did.'

Greenfield sat back and smiled amiably.

'Did you kill him, Mister Bannon?'

'Of course not.'

'Did you have motive to kill him?'

'I didn't kill him, detective.'

'So you say . . . but my question was, did you have motive?'

Greenfield stared hard into his clear blue eyes but saw nothing to arouse suspicion. This guy wouldn't break easily.

'Many years ago there was an incident on our family estate which almost ended in tragedy. Adam tried to drown one of our guests – and almost succeeded. It was a nasty incident, detective, but it hardly constitutes motive.'

Gerry Greenfield stared at the ceiling thoughtfully.

'Ah yes, I'm familiar with that story. If I'm not mistaken the girl's name was Francesca Sinclair.'

'That is correct.'

'And if we need to speak with her . . . '

'I have no idea where she is, detective. We lost contact a long time ago.'

Greenfield continued staring at this implacable man. Had he detected the faintest hint of yearning in those few words?

'Mister Bannon, can you account for your movements on the night of the seventh of October last – the same night Adam Gilbert was murdered?'

'Yes I can, detective. I visited a colleague at his home early that evening to discuss a business strategy. Later we had a couple of drinks and played cards for a while. When I looked at my watch it was late – after three if I recall correctly – and rather than travel home at that late hour my friend invited me to stay.'

The detective raised his eyebrows in surprise.

'I'm impressed with your recollection, Mister Bannon – the ability to accurately pinpoint your movements on one particular night almost nine months ago?'

The response was smooth as silk.

'I keep a diary, detective, and besides, your letter contained implications which I understandably chose not to ignore. I made it my business to establish my movements for the night of Adam Gilbert's murder.'

'This . . . friend to whom you refer. Is he in a position to corroborate your version of events?'

'Yes, he is, detective. And in anticipation of your visit today, I asked that he make himself available to meet with you and bring with him a sworn statement detailing the events I relayed earlier.'

He pressed a button on the telephone and lifted the receiver.

'Anna, we're ready now.'

The man who walked into the room was mid-sixties, dressed in a navy suit, white shirt and navy tie, his dark tightly cut hair greying at the temples. He was a hard type, and Greenfield watched him cross the room with an effortless poise that belied his nineteen-stone bulk. He sat and casually threw an envelope on the table.

'It's all there, detective – signed, sealed and witnessed. If you've any questions, I'll be more than happy to answer them – otherwise I'll be on my way.'

That night, as the ferry churned through the choppy waters of the Irish Sea, Greenfield sat by the bar and contemplated the day's events. Dan Sweeney sipped his whiskey and turned and surveyed his brooding boss.

'What are you thinking, Jerry?'

The detective sighed a weary sigh.

'I'm thinking that this all feels too neat and tidy, and that's the reason I've got the old familiar feeling.'

'What feeling is that, Jerry?'

The detective took a long sip of his whiskey and signalled the barman for two more. He turned to his friend and smiled wryly.

'We've been played.'

★

The murder of Adam Gilbert was officially labelled 'unsolved' and as the months passed Greenfield moved on to other matters. Then one afternoon, almost a year after his visit to Paul Bannon, the telephone rattled on his desk.

'Detective Greenfield?'

The accent was English; London definitely; a smoker's voice, hoarse and raspy.

'Yes it is. How can I be of help?'

'I'm not sure if you can, detective. I'm just following up on an inquiry you made a year ago through Scotland Yard concerning a fellow named John Joseph Considine. Am I talking to the right guy?'

'Yes, you are.'

'The name's Dave Richards – Detective Chief Superintendent Dave Richards. I'm with the Metropolitan Police here in London. The Yard forwarded me your inquiry.'

'Thanks for getting back to me superintendent. It's a routine follow-up linked to an unsolved murder in Ireland a while back. The file's still open.'

'What's your interest in Considine, detective?'

'He was the alibi for a suspect in the case.'

There was a silence on the other end of the line.

'Are you still there Superintendent?'

'And the name of the suspect . . . let me guess. Would it be Bannon?'

Greenfield sat rigid in his seat and gripped the phone.

'Yes, but . . . how could you possibly know?'

There was a chuckle at the far end. The sound of a cigarette lighter clicking and smoke being inhaled.

'It wasn't all that difficult, detective. My path crossed with your Mr Considine way back, almost forty years ago. Back then I was a young rookie full of ambition, making my way up. I climbed the ranks and I suppose you could say I got there in the end. Down the years I've been keeping a sort of watching brief on John Considine. Way back then we arrested him on suspicion of murdering a guy in south London. We were pretty certain he did it, detective, but we'd no option but to drop the case. Considine produced an alibi, a witness who swore he was with him on the night of the murder.'

He heard the superintendent draw on his cigarette.

'The alibi was a guy called James Bannon.'

Greenfield listened in silence. Dave Richards emitted a rasping chuckle at the other end.

'A word of advice from a wily old scout, detective. Get on with your life and forget all about it.'

'I'm not sure if I can do that, detective.'

Richards coughed heavily and cleared his throat.

'I'm telling you now, you're never going to crack it.'

'How can you be so sure?'

'Because they've covered their tracks. This is just payback time. They're smart, they're clever, and they're thick as thieves. Listen to the advice I'm giving you, detective, otherwise . . . '

'Otherwise . . . '

'Otherwise . . . you'll end up being as dumb an ass as I was!'

43

Jane Leslie, Anthony Selwyn's secretary at Beauchamps, yelled after him as he walked briskly from the office to the boardroom on the seventh floor. It was a typically chaotic morning in London's oldest, most prestigious merchant bank, the loan-book racing ahead on the back of sustained lending and renewed worldwide demand.

Sir Nicholas Selwyn, recently appointed British ambassador to Washington had through contacts in the upper echelons of the civil service, secured his son a position in the bank's investment department, pooh-poohing Anthony's reticence to the use of influence over a preference to earn the right to get there himself.

'Don't be naive,' Sir Nicholas had counselled pragmatically.

'In the City it is *who* you know, not *what* you know. You'll have ample opportunity to prove your worth in time.'

Anthony's refined personality and brilliant analytical brain soon caught the attention of the bank's senior directors, ensuring that he became at twenty-four years of age the youngest director in the bank's history. He hesitated when he heard Jane call his name.

'I've got Paul Bannon on line one.'

He pointed to the telephone extension nearest him. It buzzed immediately.

'Better make it quick. I'm late for a meeting.'

'My father's given me something to invest.'

'How much?'

'Ten million.'

'Fuck.'

'Exactly. When can we discuss?'

'I'm in meetings until midday. Sometime after that . . . '

The trauma of being bullied at Saint John the Baptist soon became a distant memory in the aftermath of the notorious fight at the Wall. Afterwards Anthony Selwyn, no longer an outsider, was welcomed into the school's elite inner group, enjoying its camaraderie and its protection, and nobody thought to argue the toss.

Within the school's hierarchy, Anthony could see that his new-found friend exuded the natural attributes of a born leader. He radiated an innate self-assuredness born of a lifetime of privilege, displaying unique skills on the rugby field in a school where such qualities would always be considered paramount. The epic fight at the Wall had been consigned in the annals of school folklore as the greatest fight ever seen in the memories of the thousand boys who had witnessed it explode before their eyes.

Another month passed and the cup season began in earnest. Saint John's won their first three matches with relative ease, but the team was bedeviled by a series of injuries. Paul was elevated from the bench to play fly-half in a semi-final clash with Sacre Coeur. Saint John's lost out narrowly to the team that went on to lift the trophy. The result was another bitter disappointment for the famous school, and it marked yet another season without a win, to add to the previous three.

Not since the famous team captained by Frank Bannon had John the Baptist College savoured the sweet spoils of victory. In the winter of sixty-seven, team captain Carl Jones's father died tragically in a motor accident, forcing Carl, an only boy, to depart the college prematurely to oversee the running of the family's thousand-acre dairy farm in south Tipperary. The awarding of the vacant team captaincy to Carl's closest friend Paul Bannon met with broad approval in the school. Initial murmurings of disapproval as to the veracity of entrusting the captaincy to a fifth-year student were soon quelled by a new sense of purpose that seemed to develop around the team. The players quickly recognised they had a captain who was fast, fearless and led from the front; whose infectious enthusiasm steeled them to once again contemplate the possibility of snatching victory from the ashes of humiliation and defeat.

In mid-January Saint John's were drawn in the first round of the Senior Cup against the formidable and fancied Belvedere College. The school held its collective breath as the teams faced one another in the driving rain in front of a packed stadium in the Dublin suburb of Donnybrook. The game descended into a dour, bad-tempered mud-fight, with Saint John's scraping through to the next round following a controversial penalty in the dying seconds of the game. Two weeks later they defeated Gonzaga by nine points to secure their place in the quarter-finals. The next outing, against a talented Terenure College side, was a bitterly contested affair, with Saint John's closing out the highly fancied south Dublin team in injury-time to win by a point.

A newspaper article the following day captured the prevailing mood under the headline: 'Mud-fight at Donnybrook Clinches Narrow Victory for John the Baptist Brawlers'. Two weeks later Saint John's routed Clongowes Wood College, winning by seventeen points to secure a place in the cup final against their bitterest rivals, Sacre Coeur College.

When the referee blew for the start of the match, the tension, already high among the eight-thousand-spectator sell-out, quickly reached boiling point out on the pitch when the teams crashed into one another from the kick-off, triggering a full-on brawl involving all thirty players. Fists flew for almost five minutes before the beleaguered referee and his linesmen finally succeeded in prising the players apart.

The Sacre Coeur decision to run the ensuing penalty resulted in a try in the corner, which their place-kicker failed to convert. The match descended into a dogged affair dominated by a brutal forward battle up front, the dour mood out on the field a stark contrast to the deafening war-songs of the rival fans packed into the west stand. The eight cheerleaders from John the Baptist banged their war-drums with split-second precision as they stood facing the fifteen-hundred-strong contingent crammed into the terraces. The tension on the field instilled a lethargy into both teams and the game became a forgettable, error-dominated affair, the score remaining unchanged into the dying minutes.

Then, from a line out on the Saint John's twenty-five, number eight Richie Reynolds fumbled the ball and the referee awarded a scrum to Sacre Coeur ten yards in front of the John the Baptist posts. The noise from the Sacre Coeur end reverberated across the stands as the ball rolled into the scrum, but at that critical moment, against all the odds, Frank Brilly struck against the head and the ball flew back on the John the Baptist side. Scrum-half James Brennan gathered the ball and raced through the blind-side, running the length of the pitch to score a try in the corner, leaving the teams level. The John the Baptist war drums exploded into action, their old anthems filling the air as the fifteen-hundred boys bellowed their hearts out.

And so it was, like so many things in life, that it would come down to the last kick of the match, to seal a famous victory or face a life-sapping replay in two weeks' time. Paul teed the ball up in the mud out on the far touchline and surveyed the posts, conscious that rugby conversion kicks didn't come much harder than this. He knew he could handle the distance, but he also knew that in this atmosphere, in these surroundings, in front of this crowd, a successful conversion was hardly more than a shot to nothing. This would need to be deadly accurate, and with the wind blowing directly from behind the posts it would also have to be a clean, firm strike. He'd done it a thousand times in practice in less fraught circumstances, and even then with a kick such as this there was always likely to be a margin of error of something approaching ten percent.

He planted the ball firmly in the sticky mud in an effort to counter the effects of the wind, then stepped backwards and stood hunched and rigid, legs apart, eyes levelled at the posts. He took a deep breath, then ran forward and struck the ball. The crowd fell silent, all eyes straining to follow its trajectory as it somersaulted through the cold, late-afternoon air. The thump of leather on leather still resonating in his ears he watched it travel high, then hang motionless on the wind as it cleared the wake of the stadium. In the packed stands they watched with bated breath as it fell from the sky almost vertically, the wind forcing it back on its path until it tumbled down and clattered onto the crossbar. Nobody moved in the all-embracing silence until the two linesmen glanced at one another and raised their flags together. Then the place erupted.

Long after they were gone, a lone figure sat in the deserted upper stand as the floodlights were finally doused and darkness enveloped the stadium. She stood slowly and walked quietly down the steps, her scarf pulled tightly around her, wishing that the cold, bitter wind would numb her senses and chill her breaking heart.

44

In his office on the seventh floor of the iconic Beauchamps tower in Threadneedle Street, Anthony sat at his desk and watched his friend gaze absentmindedly across the grey waters of the Thames.

'Admiring the view or contemplating a corporate raid?'

'I wish,' he replied wistfully, then turned and smiled.

'Let's take it one step at a time.'

He tossed the draft on the table. Anthony studied it approvingly.

'I mentioned this to the board this morning,' he said matter-of-factly. 'It went down rather well.'

'Well enough to warrant a bonus . . . '

'The thought never crossed my mind.'

Paul pondered him cynically.

'Remember who it is you're talking to.'

Anthony smirked.

'I assume you've given some thought as to what I should do?'

Paul stared at him pensively.

'Place five on twelve-month call and the rest in stocks and shares – medium risk. If the balance falls below eight we meet and discuss.'

'That it?'

'Not quite. I'd like you to park it in a shelter, a trust or whatever – you decide what's best.'

'Tax efficiency from the get-go.'

'My father's advice, so . . . yes is the answer.'

'I'll make the necessary arrangements.'

Paul glanced at his watch.

'And now I must go. There's a car waiting to take me to Heathrow.'

Anthony walked him to the elevator.

'We haven't discussed a fee. A deposit of this magnitude warrants a degree of discount.'

Paul shrugged.

'Charge the norm.'

'Are you sure? That's extremely generous.'

Paul pressed the elevator button, then turned to him.

'Someday I may need to avail of your expertise.'

'You'll always be welcome.'

'I know that.'

★

Four years later, on a sunny Saturday afternoon in the summer of seventy-six, Anthony Selwyn married his long-time secretary Jane Leslie in the church of Saint Mary Abbots in Kensington. The lavish reception in the Ritz Hotel was attended by more than three hundred guests. The festivities began with champagne cocktails on the terrace, and then dinner in the sumptuous dining room, at the end of which Anthony's best man Paul Bannon stood to address the gathering.

'Ladies and gentlemen, it is an honour and a privilege for me to deliver this speech today. Anthony and I have known each other a long time. Our friendship has endured the rough-and-tumble of our school days in Ireland, our university days at Oxford, and the present-day cauldron that is business in the City of London.

'He may not have been the most accomplished rugby player, ladies and gentlemen, but he soon discovered his true niche up in the stands, as arguably our most robust cheerleader, fervently leading the chant to the beat of the John the Baptist war-drums. Often when we had nothing left to give, those voices rising from the grandstands, led by the raucous tones of Selwyn, gave us the strength to dig a little deeper and scrape victory from the jaws of defeat.

'Anthony's brilliance in business has been acknowledged by his co-directors at Beauchamps, who wasted little time catapulting their dynamic protégé onto the board of the City's most illustrious merchant bank. And yet it now appears that our multi-talented young banker may have been donating less than his full attention to the nuances of those non-stop trading screens at Beauchamps.

'Yes, ladies and gentlemen, while his clients slept soundly in the knowledge that their investments were being assiduously monitored, alas it would appear that Anthony's true focus was otherwise deployed in the direction of the stunningly beautiful, Miss Jane Leslie.'

This brought laughter and applause from the assembled guests.

'To the directors of Beauchamps, most of whom are here to celebrate this day, please be assured that despite Anthony's split-focus during these past few years, you really had little to worry about; his brain operates at a level three times faster than most others I've encountered . . . '

The day continued with each speech accompanied by warm applause and a toast to the couple. Then the band began to play, and the wedding guests partied and danced into the night, the singer's captivating voice filling the room with her velvety tones.

Late in the evening Anthony drew his friend aside and whispered, 'The directors have expressly asked to meet with you.' He led him to their table and introduced Angus McMaster, William Fraser-Bryant, Andrew Stevenson, Stefan Morton-Browning and Robert Goldsmith.

'And last but not least our chairman and his wife, Sir Kenneth and Lady Blaine-Rutherford.'

Sir Kenneth, thin and suave, with silver hair impeccably slicked back, looked toned and tanned for a man Paul placed somewhere in his late sixties. He greeted Paul warmly.

'It's my pleasure to make your acquaintance,' he smiled. 'The Bannon group is one of the great dynasties of our time. Please let us know if ever we can be of assistance.'

'Thank you sir – someday I may do just that.'

'Then I shall look forward to the opportunity of extending our services to you.'

Later, in the cocktail bar, Anthony took him by the arm and led him to a corner table. The waiter poured champagne. They clinked.

'It seems your meeting with Sir Kenneth went down rather

well. He spoke to me afterwards and instructed me to "tell your young friend we're at his service".'

They clinked again.

'The old fox can spot talent a mile away, and then sometimes, out of the blue, he'll disengage for no apparent reason. None of us quite knows why, except that he invariably calls it right.'

Paul couldn't have known it then, but a time would come when Sir Kenneth's offer of assistance would prove critical in mounting one of the most ferocious corporate struggles ever witnessed on the streets of London, the sheer savagery of the encounters rendering a nation shocked, bemused, bewildered and enthralled.

★

'Aren't you going to introduce me, or must I do so myself?'

It was a voice he recognised instantly and one he'd despaired of again hearing. He spun round and smiled broadly.

'Good grief, you managed to make it in the end – how wonderful!'

Paul watched the ecstatic bridegroom embrace the woman who had just walked into the room. He took her by the hand, then turned to him and beamed.

'You must meet my sister Natalie!'

They shook hands.

'Natalie lives in Manhattan these days. We feared an air-traffic dispute at Kennedy would prevent her making the trip.'

She smiled.

'I hopped on a train to Chicago and flew out of O'Hare. Otherwise I'd still be sitting in departures.'

Paul gaped open-mouthed at the ravishing beauty before him, and then the memory of that night at the disco in Laurel Hill half a lifetime ago came flooding back. It slowly began to dawn on him that he was staring at the world-renowned British actress Natalie Selwyn, her latest film, *The Chameleon*, currently breaking box-office records on both sides of the Atlantic. She glanced at him and smiled. The waiter handed her a glass of champagne.

'We meet again,' she whispered. And then in the way it sometimes happens, their eyes locked, and in that moment they stood oblivious to the crowds thronging the hotel, who had already begun to notice her presence. Her eyes sparkled blue under long, shimmering lashes; her chestnut hair and pale, perfect skin accentuating the fullness of her deep-crimson lips. She wore a simple black figure-hugging cocktail dress cut above the knee, with matching black heels and a solitary string of white pearls around her neck.

'I feel I already know you,' she said simply. 'Anthony has told me so much about you.'

Just then a man pushed through the crowd and positioned himself between them. He was tall, distinguished and very drunk.

'Ah, there you are, Natalie. I've been searching for you everywhere. I'm beginning to believe you really are a chameleon.'

She glanced at him irritably, then turned to her brother.

'You haven't met my fiancée Rupert Cavendish.'

He stared in astonishment.

'You're . . . engaged!'

She smiled faintly and nodded.

'Good God, you never told me – how marvellous! We must make this a dual celebration!'

'Sorry, old chap,' Rupert interjected. 'Out of the question, I'm afraid. Contract stipulations and all that sort of thing. The studio masters in their wisdom have decreed that the *hoi polloi* must be kept in the dark, at least for the foreseeable future – better for the box office, apparently.'

Rupert Cavendish was tall, blonde and handsome in a blue-blooded sort of way, with a brash confidence and an aristocratic air which hinted at old money. An elderly lady approached clutching a cocktail menu.

'Please may I trouble you for an autograph, Miss Selwyn. I do love your films so much.'

Cavendish appraised her dismissively.

'Piss off, you decrepit old tart.'

'Rupert!'

'Oh for God's sakes, Natalie. One ought to be able to enjoy

oneself in the Ritz without being bloody well accosted.'

The woman appeared visibly shaken.

'I'm so sorry,' she stammered. 'I just thought . . . '

'Are you still here! How incredibly annoying!'

Natalie brushed him aside and flashed her famous smile.

'I do apologise for my friend's behaviour. I shall be more than happy to sign for you.'

Rupert snorted, then seemed to notice Paul for the first time.

'And who the bloody hell have we here?'

Paul regarded him dispassionately, then turned to Natalie.

'You must please excuse me. So nice to have met you.'

*

Later in his Hans Crescent penthouse he sat by the cocktail bar and poured two glasses from a bottle of '59 Chateau Margaux. The sultry sound of Carly Simon's haunting voice lingered low in the background. He handed the girl a glass and watched as she sipped.

She leaned forward and whispered in his ear, 'Mmmm, I've always been partial to a good vintage.'

He kissed her and savoured the moist rich taste of wine on her lips. He drew her close and kissed her again, and then the telephone buzzed. He picked it up and glanced at his watch, but all he could hear was the sound of laughter and music. And then, 'Hey! Is that you?'

The voice was hoarse and indistinct.

'Anthony . . . '

'Christ, am I glad I caught you!'

Even with the clamour of noise in the background his tone sounded perplexed and slurred.

'Anthony, it's two in the morning. Shouldn't you be in bed by now?'

'Is it really that late? Jeez . . . '

'Wherever you are seems pretty hectic.'

'Yeah, it's a blast.'

He glanced at the girl.

'That's good, Anthony. Just as long as you're OK . . . '

'I'm wonderful . . . everything's wonderful . . . we're having a ball, well . . . except for the scene with Cavendish earlier – really sorry, old chap.'

'Oh, that. I've forgotten about it hours ago.'

'I'm glad to bloody well hear it. You're sure?'

'*Sure* I'm sure.'

Anthony sounded out of it. The girl lit a cigarette and inhaled deeply.

'Your voice seems a little . . . strange. Is Jane with you?'

'Yeah, yeah, yeah of course. Jane's fine, she's not the problem. It's Natalie and Rupert. They'd an almighty flare-up earlier. Fucking hothead stormed off and left her standing on her own.'

This just wasn't making any sense. He took a deep breath.

'Anthony, it's way past your bedtime . . . '

'I know, I know!'

'Why don't I call you in the morning . . . '

'Wait! Don't hang up . . . I'm trying to explain . . . Natalie insisted on having your address. She wants to apologise.'

'Apologise for what!'

'She'll tell you when she gets there.'

He listened with growing disquiet.

'Anthony, you're not seriously suggesting she's coming here . . . '

'Why do you think I'm bloody well calling!'

He turned away from the girl and spoke quietly.

'Anthony, I've got someone with me. You need to cancel straight away. Let's do it tomorrow . . . '

'It's too late for that, and besides she flies to New York in the morning. She's on her way to you right now – might even be there already. I'm sure you'll think of something . . . '

He stared at the receiver as the line went dead, and then at the seductive blonde escort sitting next to him on the bar stool. She couldn't have been more than twenty-one or so but she had a world-savvy air about her. She sipped from her glass and smiled.

'I'm guessing it is . . . *time-to-go* time.'

He shook his head slowly.

'I'm sorry, I can't believe this – '

'Don't be. I get the drift. I'm a big girl. Shit happens.'

'I'll make it up to you.'

She leaned over and bit his earlobe.

'Ouch!'

'Promise?'

'I promise.'

She grabbed her coat, draped it around her shoulders and blew him a kiss.

When she was gone, the intercom sounded almost immediately.

'A Miss Natalie Selwyn to see you.'

'Thank you, Michael. Send her up.'

Seconds later she stepped from the elevator and sashayed past.

'Your friend didn't look happy,' she whispered.

She strolled through the apartment, casually glancing about, then dropped her stole on the carpet and sat by the bar.

'What a wonderful place, and the music . . . '

'Just a makey-uppy late-night mix.'

'Sounds really good.'

'Champagne?'

She nodded towards the Margaux.

'A glass of your wine would be nice.'

She took a small mirror from her clutch and checked her make-up. His eyes tracked the hem of her dress to the top of her thigh as she crossed her long, gorgeous legs. She lit a cigarette. He handed her a glass. She sipped.

'Mmmm . . . nice.'

She set the glass down and glanced at him.

'Rupert can be such a prick.'

He gave a vaguely non-committal shrug.

'It seems you tolerate him.'

She smiled briefly.

'Yes in a way I suppose I do. When one exists in a kaleidoscope of smoke and mirrors, one's vision can so easily become blurred. I live in an artificial world populated mostly by hypocritical types – a make-believe world filled with insubstantial people, devoid of substance and sincerity. I suppose, for me Rupert instils an air of realism into that contrived, surreal vacuum. Whatever he is, he's not like them. So, yes, I tolerate him.'

She was a rare beauty – sophisticated, glamorous, sexy, and yet, he decided, tantalisingly aloof. Her relationship with Rupert Cavendish seemed incongruous at one level, but he imagined this lady seldom dropped her guard and trusted others sparingly.

'Why are you here, Natalie?' he inquired gently.

The music switched from Nina Simone to Françoise Hardy's 'All Over the World'. The neon from the bar-light reflected in the smouldering pools of her eyes.

'I'm not entirely sure,' she replied quietly. 'I've been thinking about you all evening. I guess I just wanted to be with you a while longer.'

She glanced at him then slid from the stool.

'Please dance with me. I've always loved this song.'

He held her hand and led her to the floor in the low shadowy glow of the light. The velvet tones of the beautiful French singer played softly through the speakers. She laid her head on his shoulder and pressed her body close to his. They moved slowly, silently through the room.

'Déjà vu,' he whispered.

She looked up at him and smiled for the first time.

'That first dance of ours was so . . . so nice.'

He breathed the intoxicating aroma of her perfumed hair and felt the warm steady thump of her beating heart. Outside, the early-morning lights of the West End shimmered in the clear night sky as they swayed in a slow tantalising embrace. She gazed at him, her eyes shining blue with flecks of liquid gold, her lips slightly parted.

'Please take me there,' she whispered.

He gazed into her eyes, mesmerised by her beauty, enchanted by her vulnerability, spellbound by the magnetism of her sexuality. He led her to the bedroom and turned the lights down low, then held her and kissed her in the solitude of the early dawn, his every nerve thrilling with the anticipation of what was to come. She turned and lifted her hair and with trembling hands he unzipped her dress. She wriggled her shoulders and let it fall to the ground. She was wearing nothing else. He stared at her startling body naked before him.

'You are so . . . heart-stoppingly beautiful.'

The faintest trace of a smile crossed her lips. She unbuttoned his shirt and unbuckled his belt and then he took her in his arms and laid her on the bed. He held her and kissed her, then lay beside her and caressed her. He gently parted her thighs and felt her wetness through his fingers. She sighed and ran her hands through his hair, then guided him to her, sucking in air as he entered her. He felt her tremble beneath him, and suddenly their orgasm surged on a wave of exquisite, lingering, explosive delight. Afterwards she lay breathless in his arms, her skin shimmering pale in the first faint light of dawn.

'In my life no man has made me feel like that. I wish this night could last forever.'

He kissed her and held her and gazed into her eyes.

'And I wish you didn't belong to somebody else.'

She placed a finger on his lips and whispered in his ear, 'Tonight I belong only to you. So let us not talk about reality or unreality, at least until tomorrow, because who of us knows what tomorrow brings.'

In the early morning they descended the elevator to the underground garage. She sat beside him in the Mercedes and laid her head on his shoulder as he drove through Knightsbridge and Kensington to the M4 motorway and onwards to Heathrow Airport. As they approached the terminal, she turned to him.

'Stop here, my darling.'

He eased the car to the curbside and switched off the engine.

'There'll be the usual hullaballoo. Where were you? Why didn't you call? You can't just disappear . . . '

She stared into the rainy grayness of the morning and sighed.

'Shall I tell you why I hate leaving you?'

'You don't have to leave.'

'Yes I do.'

'But why?'

'Oh, you know – the usual: prior commitments, studio deadlines, contract stipulations and all of that. But I do hate leaving you because . . . '

'Because of what, my darling?'

She gazed at him in silence for all of a minute, then whispered,

'Because I've fallen in love with you.'

She opened the door and suddenly she was gone. He watched her hurry to the terminal and disappear in the misty morning rain.

Later, back in his apartment he found the note, a single folded sheet of paper tucked beneath her pillow. He sat on the edge of the bed, lingering in the remnants of her presence, the aroma of her scent, the crushing sense of emptiness he thought he'd never feel again. And then he realised she must have written it while he slept. He read silently.

My Darling,

When you find this note, I shall be somewhere far above the Atlantic thinking of you. Last night I fell in love with a man whose heart burns for another. I sensed it in the depth of your eyes, in the elusive sadness that lies hidden beneath that suave, sophisticated, handsome exterior, barely perceptible, yet unmistakably there. What a lucky girl she must be. I wonder, does she even have a clue?

Alas, it seems we are both actors, you and I, and when all is said and done there are no words left for me to say, except perhaps to tell you, that if ever you should break her spell, if ever it should happen, wherever it should happen, I'll be waiting there.

N.

*

A year later Anthony telephoned him in the early hours of a snowy December morning. 'Congratulations, Mister Bannon. You're about to become a godfather! Jane gave birth to a baby girl in Guys a minute after midnight.'

'Anthony, what wonderful news! Sounds as if everything worked a treat.'

'Yeah, well except for me. I'm afraid I caused a bit of a stir. They had to administer smelling salts when I fainted!'

'You didn't!'

'I bloody well did!'

They laughed until they cried.

'What an honour to be chosen ahead of bolshie old Rupert,' Paul said, wiping tears from his eyes, 'Aren't brothers-in-law usually the first to be asked?'

'Are they? I'm not sure to be honest. Anyway it's academic. That relationship is history. Didn't I tell you? Natalie finished with Cavendish a week after the wedding.'

45

Anthony Selwyn's daughter Alexandra was christened in the church of Saint Martin-in-the-Field near Trafalgar Square on a cold, sunny, Saturday morning in late January 1979. Her christening, at the very start of the new year, coincided with persistent rumours pertaining to cash flow problems within the beating heart of the Bannon construction empire. Each week, amid speculation that the construction giant was about to implode, another damaging story emerged, with even an eleventh-hour rescue plan being mooted in the financial sections of some business broadsheets.

The rumours ran unabated into the heart of the summer, and then, on the morning of the thirtieth of June, *The Times* finally confirmed what the dogs in the street already appeared to know. The front-page headline read, 'Bannon Construction Group Collapses, Shares Suspended, Receivers Appointed'.

Business editor Brian Allenby went on to describe how 'Bannons, Britain's third-largest construction company, has been forced into receivership, placing the future of five thousand jobs at risk following Britain's biggest corporate collapse in post-war history.'

The article ignited a media-frenzy, which rolled out interminably in the months ahead, and sent shockwaves through the beating heart of the City.

Television news bulletins broadcast endless images of Bannon employees blockading entrances to building sites, thwarting every effort to impose the receivers' authority. In a public display of defiance, hundreds of workers staged a sit-in at the company's Park Lane headquarters, while out on the street protesters waved placards proclaiming 'No Surrender!', 'Receivers Out!' and 'Bannons Forever!'

Property listings on the London Stock Exchange saw values drop eleven percentage points across the sector, fuelling speculation pertaining to further imminent collapses in an industry now perceived to be dangerously over-leveraged.

Myriad theories abounded as to the root cause of the Bannon demise, with most pundits concluding that the problems were company-specific and ought not be construed as a symptom of the underlying health of the wider industry. Others highlighted the particular problems associated with an expansion strategy now perceived to be akin to reckless trading.

As the weeks and months passed, the inner workings at Bannons were microscopically dissected from every conceivable perspective, with particular focus on a lack of managerial direction in the wake of Frank Bannon's sudden resignation four years earlier. In the months leading up to Christmas the furore surrounding the collapse seemed gradually to dissipate, when the workforce appeared to embrace the inevitability that there was no future for the company in the short term, no appetite for a management buy-out, and no likelihood of a rival takeover. After months of disruption and turmoil, the receivers finally wrested control of the assets, and began focusing on a solution which would be predicated on an orderly break-up of the company's myriad interests.

The sit-in at the company's headquarters lasted eighteen weeks, then suddenly one morning it was over. When the shambles left in its wake was eventually hoovered up, the Park Lane property was sold on the international market to a private offshore investment vehicle specialising in luxury apartment conversions.

Most of the company's London development sites remained chained and closed as the valuation process began in earnest, and the surveyors cast their measuring tapes across the remnants a long-gone dynasty.

★

The collapse of the Bannon empire faded from the front pages, and as the months became years, apart from the odd intermittent reference, the story receded in the public consciousness. The wider construction industry shuddered in its wake, and others followed a similar course as the recession bit hard and the industry ground to a halt. Some emerged unscathed to live another day. Others disappeared forever. In the survival of the fittest, the weak had been weeded out in the wake of the most damaging construction recession of the post-war years.

*

Then, early one summer's morning in the fifth year following the collapse, Anthony Selwyn's private telephone rang in his office.

'Hi, it's Paul.'

He gasped.

'Christ almighty! Where the hell have you been! I've tried endlessly to contact you.'

In the years since the collapse, there had been zero contact between the two of them. Paul Bannon had disappeared off the radar – and now this.

'When things started to unravel I took some time out to figure a strategy.'

Anthony didn't attempt to hide his bitterness. 'You could have at least tried to make contact. You could have lifted the telephone.'

'It wasn't part of the strategy.'

He felt his temper rising with exasperation.

'Damn your strategy! I'm your friend, Paul, not just a number on a slide-rule to be slotted into a fucking strategy.'

But he hardly seemed fazed.

'Don't judge me, Anthony; I don't have time for this. Events have overtaken us. We need to move on . . . and we need to meet.'

He gripped the telephone tightly as if it might somehow absorb his sense of frustration and annoyance. The Bannons could be cold as ice but on the other hand their loyalty knew no bounds.

'Don't judge me,' he had said, the message in the dismissive tone flagging a reminder, if one were needed, that seemed to say, 'No man stands in judgement on this family.'

He sat back in his chair and sighed.

'When do you wish to meet?'

'I'm in reception right now.'

He studied his greatest friend as he sat opposite him in the boardroom, no apology given or explanation proffered, his body tanned and fit, his tall frame draped nonchalantly across the chair. One might almost think that nothing had occurred that a good night's sleep couldn't rectify. He watched him take a sip of his coffee and extract a folder from his briefcase.

'I'm sure you know the most of it, but what you may not know is that when the receivers moved in, they also took Grange Abbey. It appears it got mortgaged somewhere along the way.'

Anthony was stunned. He sat back in his chair and nodded his head in disbelief. His greatest friend paused a moment to allow the news to sink in, then stared at him with ice in his eyes, and said simply, 'I want it back.'

'Please don't tell me they took Grange Abbey,' he muttered, 'along with all the rest.'

He gazed at him mystified and wondered how on earth they could have allowed their beloved Grange Abbey to get caught up in this whole complicated, evil mess. Whether accidental, or by arrangement, it was beyond comprehension, beyond belief, and in all probability downright careless. Another smart-ass lawyer sliding yet another sheet of paper across Frank's desk among the myriad others requiring his signature. It was so heartbreakingly easy to lose track.

Paul seemed to read his thoughts.

'For the record, Frank had no hand in this. Simon signed it away as part of a security package on the Irish land-bank facility without seeking prior clearance.'

Anthony stared at him.

'Un-fucking-believable. What on earth could he have been thinking?'

'I don't know, and I don't care. Like I said earlier, I just want it back.'

Anthony's mind was already in overdrive.

'The London receivers are Franklins. We've dealt with them in the past, which ought to help. The Irish receivers are Thorntons,

297

but my inclination is to bypass them and deal through London. Franklins will always make the final decision. And tactically I'm presuming you wish to remain anonymous.'

'Of course.'

'And the price-range . . . '

He slid a folder across the desk.

'It's all in there – everything you need to know. Stauntons brought it to the market a year ago as a private-treaty sale with a price-tag of two million. There was a handful of viewings – one hotel operator, a wealthy American with Irish connections, one or two Germans – but in the end, no bites.'

'How much are you willing to pay?'

Paul glanced at his watch, drained his coffee, then stood and stared thoughtfully at his friend.

'Whatever it takes.'

Seven months passed before he heard from Anthony again, and then one November's evening, in the early hours of the morning, his telephone buzzed.

'Good evening, Mister Bannon, Mister Selwyn wishes to speak with you.'

'Patch him through.'

The connection was immediate.

'We're in the middle of a deal that's taking longer than anticipated, which is why all of us are still here, but very briefly, you'll be pleased to know we've managed to secure the Grange.'

There was a brief if telling pause.

'When I didn't hear I was beginning to fear the worst.'

Anthony could sense the apprehension in his friend's voice.

'I used my power-of-attorney to extract the necessary funds from your account and I nominated one of our in-house lawyers to buy the place in trust. The deal closed yesterday. Congratulations.'

Again, silence at the other end, then finally,'I always knew I could rely on you for this.'

'It did take some manoeuvring, but the final price was six hundred grand. And the other good news is that the ten million you gave me to invest all those years ago is worth seventeen today.'

The audible sigh of relief at the other end seemed to say it all. Nobody knew better than Anthony Selwyn how much all of this would have meant to Paul Bannon.

'I guess I owe you a drink.'

'You owe me nothing. This one is, shall we say . . . on the house!'

He replaced the receiver and contemplated what had just been achieved. The future of Grange Abbey had been secured. The vital first piece of the jigsaw. Its importance could not be overestimated.

When he sat back and thought about it, the retrieval of his beloved family home helped copper-fasten the growing certainty in his mind that it would soon be time to turn his thoughts to other issues, to matters as important as life and death itself. He absolutely believed that the challenge that lay ahead had been ingrained into his destiny, its future mapped out before him on a path he was born to travel.

The journey upon which he was about to embark would be tantamount to a declaration of open war on the most militant, most organised, most powerful construction union in the land. The clashes on the picket lines would make the excesses of all previous corporate confrontations pale into insignificance, and rank as the worst peacetime violence ever to take place on British soil.

46

When Frank Brilly left Saint John the Baptist in the late summer
of sixty-eight, his destiny had never been in doubt. The only
son of Frank and Mercy Brilly, and brother to four sisters who
idolised him, all of them living and working in London, Frank
hopped on a plane one Sunday evening and reported for work at
his father's Camden headquarters the following day. Stocky and
outwardly dour, he exuded a menacing streak, which belied his
insubstantial stature and marked him out as the most destructive
hooker ever to play on the rugby fields of John the Baptist. Early
in the autumn season Frank joined the London Irish Rugby
Football Club and delivered a series of startling performances
that catapulted him through the ranks into the first-team squad,
his technique, competitiveness and explosive speed riveting the
attention of the club selectors.

Frank soon became embroiled in the cauldron of construction
that was London in the late sixties. Brilly Concrete had started
out in the post-war years pouring foundations and floor slabs
on James Bannon's construction sites. From there the company
expanded into the production of multi-storey carcasses for the
leading national contractors operating across the length and
breadth of London.

Frank worked side by side with his father's steel-fixers
and form-work crews, manning the drag-lines and the electric
shovels, feeding aggregates into the massive silos and pouring
concrete with the toughest gangs. By the mid-seventies Brillys
had been instrumental in altering the face of London's skyline,
with Frank junior setting the hitherto-unmatched deadline of 'a
floor a week' on the major tower blocks – much to the delight of
the contractors and their promoters.

When his telephone rang early one February morning in the

spring of 1984, the uncompromising boss of London's concrete gangs would be asked a favour he would find impossible to refuse.

★

The five directors of Beauchamps took their places at the boardroom table, their presence this morning at the behest of Anthony Selwyn, the Bank's head of international investment and corporate lending. Anthony's foresight in identifying a niche to enable Beauchamps' Middle Eastern clientele to diversify out of oil-based revenue into London commercial property had underscored his reputation among the wider banking community as one of the City's most savvy practitioners. Billions of Gulf State money flowed into London during the late sixties and early seventies, the lion's share washing through Beuchamps as its routing bank, a phenomenon universally credited to Anthony's far-reaching initiative. His knowledge of the tax-specific nuances of the offshore worldwide banking system was regarded within the tigh-knit, secretive world of banking as being second to none.

Investors moving funds through the City could take comfort in the knowledge that the requisite structures had been fine-tuned to shelter future profit in 'special purpose vehicles', or specifically tailored companies with nominee directors in remote, far-flung colonies of the Empire.

Among the great off-shore destinations of the world, the City of London was by far the most influential, most powerful, most far-reaching of them all. Its geographical off-shore tentacles offered a myriad of tailored tax options to assist the world's leading legitimate corporate interests in sheltering vast tranches of money, far in excess of that held in taxable circulation.

The City, the ultimate facilitator, was hardly concerned as to the nuances of mundane legitimacy, and displayed equal enthusiasm for the tax-specific requirements of the world's global crime syndicates. Its pact with the gangster Meyer Lansky in the aftermath of Castro's rise to power in Cuba transformed its Cayman offshoot into a trove for the vast illicit funds of the

American Mafia, an arrangement which exists to this day.

His star in the ascendancy, his personal fortune already measured in millions, with his trademark air of confidence, Anthony stood to address his colleagues.

'Good morning, gentlemen. I thank you for your time.'

They shuffled their papers and began to focus in earnest. Sir Kenneth waved a hand in the air.

'Your presentations are invariably dynamic,' he interjected, 'but when I studied this morning's synopsis, I decided it was one I really shouldn't miss.'

Anthony acknowledged him with a brief smile.

'You are most welcome, sir.'

The wily old goat rarely missed a beat. His analytical brain and razor-sharp acumen were attributes that many envied and few could emulate. Glancing briefly at his notes, Anthony gathered his thoughts, then closed the folder.

'My presentation this morning carries with it an element of risk beyond the remit of this bank's normal practice, but one which I'm eager to propose nonetheless. It is a speculative, leveraged, off-market, private-sector proposal, which is presaged on the injection of a large tranche of risk capital into an SPV. The end result, at least on face-value, seems less than clear – it would be remiss of me to pretend otherwise. And it may therefore seem incongruous that the structure which I'm about to endorse will carry with it my strongest, most positive recommendation.'

A typewritten synopsis headed 'Bannon Group Restructuring Proposal', similar to the one to which Sir Kenneth had referred earlier, lay before each of them. A cursory glance around the table confirmed that most had chosen to listen rather than read.

'The synopsis before you envisages the extraction from the Bannon Group receivers of the remaining Bannon Group assets, along with a subsidiary financial package for the recommencement of the business within all the usual parameters of our lending criteria, including guarantees, cross-guarantees, fixed and floating charges over all assets, et cetera.

'From the outset I wish to acknowledge a personal interest in this matter as distinct from a personal involvement, of which I have none, and in any event am constrained from so doing under standard banking governance guidelines. However, in the interests of clarity, I wish to state that I am acquainted with the Bannon family and in particular with Paul Bannon, the promoter of this morning's presentation. Paul and I have known one another since our school days, when we first became friends and have remained so to this day.'

He surveyed the room quickly – all of them seemed relaxed, so far no questions.

'Mister Bannon has identified certain assets which he wishes to retrieve from the receivers. These are summarised on page three of your synopses. You can study them at your leisure but for now I suggest we utilise the overhead screen.'

The lighting dimmed; the screen descended silently; and the overhead projector activated seamlessly.

'The assets have been arranged in the order of their importance. The first of these comprises a block of six thousand 'ready-to-go' residential and commercial plots, located in the Greater London area. As you can see, these have been independently valued at three hundred million.'

Anthony noticed several directors, including Sir Kenneth, begin scribbling on their pads.

'Next we have a tranche of seven thousand residential plots spread across the Home Counties, currently ensnared in the planning process, and valued on the same basis at two hundred and ten million. There are two thousand plots in the Greater London area with residential zoning only, valued at thirty million, and four thousand unzoned plots in the Home Counties valued at ten million. Finally we have the complex matter of construction work-in-progress across the entire land holding. This has been painstakingly valued at forty million. The total valuation for land and works-in-progress amounts to five hundred and ninety million. Is everybody following so far?'

Nods of assent.

'Any questions?'

No response.

'In the interests of clarity, let me remind you that all of the listed valuations are receiver valuations. At various times during the past years the receivers have attempted to market the assets at precisely the values quoted above.'

'You did say "receiver valuations"?' queried Robert Goldsmith, his tone sounding puzzled.

'Yes, I did.'

'As opposed to bank-book valuations?'

'Yes, of course.'

'But surely bank-book values offer a more pertinent benchmark.'

'I'll come to that later, Robert,' he responded in a 'shut-the-fuck-up-and-be-patient' tone of voice.

Goldsmith frowned. Sir Kenneth raised a hand.

'If Mister Bannon is seeking to fund the entirety of the listed assets, it presupposes that there are currently no other punters in the market.'

'Sir, that is correct.'

Sir Kenneth appeared to reflect on this a moment before nodding, 'Please continue.'

'Gentlemen, the total asset value is five hundred and ninety million, but Mister Bannon's explicit advice is that the real value may be considerably less. The majority of the six thousand plots with planning consent will see their permissions expire within the next twelve months. The term 'wither' is used within the industry to describe this phenomenon. As a consequence, he is of the view that the value of those plots needs to be reduced by forty million. The seven thousand plots currently in the planning process will require re-analysis, reprocessing, updating, and in most cases withdrawal and resubmission. Mister Bannon believes that this necessarily equates to a valuation reduction of thirty million.

'A further adjustment of fifty percent in the value of work-in-progress is deemed appropriate in order to accurately reflect the effects of construction deterioration, vandalism and all of the contingent difficulties associated with starting cold on existing, partially constructed platforms. Then, last but not least, he advises a contingency-sum reduction of twenty million to facilitate the restart operation.'

Anthony poured water from a crystal decanter and sipped.

'Gentlemen, the proposed adjustments equate to a reduction of one hundred and ten million. Mister Bannon is convinced that few experts on either side will argue greatly with this figure. However, assuming that agreement is ultimately reached around the requisite reductions, then this becomes the point at which he believes substantive negotiations will begin.'

Anthony paused and took another sip of water. His co-directors were silent, their facial expressions and body language indicating that they remained fully focused.

'The Bannon funding proposal is predicated on a cash injection of twenty-five million by Paul Bannon and a further twenty-five million by Paul's father James in the form of loan capital with an unspecified or perpetual repayment date. Seventy-five million is available through private venture-capital funds directly under the control of the Henry Hyland property empire. There are legally binding commitments covering the venture-capital element, which effectively means that it can be triggered at Mister Bannon's behest.'

The reference to the famed, reclusive property investor initiated one or two murmurings of approval, and raised eyebrows from Sir Kenneth. Anthony was aware that the legendary developer's name was revered in most of the elite City finance houses. He noticed Sir Kenneth staring at him intently, a hint of a smile on his patrician face.

'Mister Bannon intends to utilise this one-hundred-and-twenty-five million to fund the purchase of the listed Bannon Group assets at a revised price of three hundred and twelve point five million, crystallising a residue funding requirement of precisely sixty percent, which he proposes to borrow from this bank. This presupposes a further thirty-five percent downward adjustment following a successful negotiation around the earlier itemised revisions. Mister Bannon is confident that this will be achieved. You are all aware that he is a long-standing customer of ours and he is firmly of the view that this makes Beauchamps his logical first funding choice. Needless to say, he holds this bank in the highest regard, and he is most anxious that we give due consideration to the proposal I have outlined to you this morning. Based on my knowledge of the participant, and my unwavering confidence in his ability to deliver, this morning's proposal carries with it my unequivocal recommendation. I thank you, gentlemen, and I shall be happy to field questions at your leisure.'

William Frazer-Bryant, the rotund, affable head of the dealing room, was first to respond. 'Anthony, one wonders at the veracity of the receivers' dismal success-rate in the marketing of the assets over a four-year period – it simply beggars belief. One might at least have expected a degree of interest, and yet this appears not to be the case. Surely this at least raises a question-mark around the commercial viability of today's proposal. Is it that the assets are perceived to be below par, or stressed or damaged in a manner not readily apparent – a toxic blemish that may even have triggered the receivership in the first instance? Is the market not indirectly insinuating that the Bannon residue is either pie-in-the-sky or a pig in a poke?'

Anthony switched on the overhead projector and a map of London displaying the Bannon assets highlighted in red immediately appeared.

'There is nothing wrong with the assets,' he replied smoothly, 'and as we can clearly see, most are located west of the river in affluent, densely populated areas – Chelsea, Knightsbridge, Kensington, Hammersmith – it just doesn't get much better. The largest physical asset is Croydon town centre, and this has been the subject of a prolonged and bitter dispute between the Bannons and the London construction unions. The letting agents are adamant that given half a chance, they could fill the floor space in the seven high-rise office towers three times over. The development footprint straddles an area of approximately one square mile, and this unsurprisingly is the location upon which the unions have chosen to "concentrate" their focus. The relationship between the Bannon family and the London unions is fraught.

'So much so that notwithstanding the demise of the Bannon empire, the unions have persisted in maintaining a picket on the Croydon development to this day. It is tantamount to a declaration of war, and it is indicative of the depth of hatred between the unions and this family. It is plausible that this in itself may constitute a deterrent to some prospective purchasers. Who knows?

'My personal view is that any perceived lack of commercial interest has more to do with the impact of reduced activity in the marketplace and, by implication, the receiver's failure to reflect this reduction in their current quoted price levels. Those guys need to get real and pitch the product at a level commensurate with current depressed activity, because, quite frankly, aside from this, I am not aware of anything untoward or sinister.'

'Interesting you should say that,' Frazer-Briant responded thoughtfully, 'particularly since it's common knowledge in the marketplace that some prospective purchasers have been "deterred" from substantive engagement with the receivers' agents. I am reliably informed that there exists a level of intimidation in the market around the Bannon assets, orchestrated by subversive forces, which has effectively scuppered even the most determined expressions of interest. I assure you my sources are impeccable.'

There were murmurings of disquiet and expressions of surprise on one or two faces. Frazer-Briant was a highly respected, forthright board appointee, not prone to delusional exaggeration.

'I'm absolutely not aware of this,' Anthony responded coolly, 'but if William's information turns out to be correct, then I say to you, what business is it of ours? It merely serves to strengthen our client's hand – simple as that.'

Even the imperturbable Sir Kenneth seemed taken aback.

'Surely you're not suggesting that the bank should in some way condone such . . . unsavoury practice!'

'No sir, I am not. However, the reality is that first and foremost we are a bank. It is the business of a bank to lend money, and that is why I say to you, let us mind our own business. If external forces consort to create a more amenable climate in which to enable the business to be transacted, then why look a gift-horse in the mouth!'

On the surface at least, his co-directors appeared to be struggling with the implications of Anthony's brash, take-it-or-leave-it rationale. His nonchalant dismissal of their concerns around 'sinister forces' lurking in the background seemed to cast a shadow on the day's events. And yet notwithstanding all of that, he sat cool as a cucumber and brazened it out.

Sir Kenneth's face was inscrutable, and deep down Anthony knew that the great man regarded him as his protégé, or possibly his successor. He had to hope that his casual disregard of the board's plausible misgivings would be sufficient to carry the day.

'Anthony,' Sir Kenneth said eventually, 'in light of your earlier stated interest in the business of the Bannon family, standard protocol requires that I must ask you to vacate the room to enable us to consult.'

'Certainly sir,' he replied, gathering his papers. He knew of course that this token lip-service was normal connected-party procedure, a cosmetic age-old deferral to the system of checks and balances. Standards must be maintained, and even the flimsy Chinese walls of modern-day banking had to be *seen* to be maintained.

'Before I leave you sir, I should tell you that Mister Bannon is in the building and is available to join you at your leisure.'

Sir Kenneth nodded tersely.

'Give us some time to try and reach a consensus on this.'

'Of course, sir.'

An hour later Sir Kenneth's secretary summoned them to the boardroom. Anthony introduced Paul to the board. Sir Kenneth wasted no time getting straight to the point.

'Paul, thank you for joining us this morning. Anthony has presented a thought-provoking synopsis of your proposal to re-take the Bannon Group assets. Let me begin by asking, what on earth makes you believe you can acquire five hundred and ninety millions' worth of assets for the ludicrously low figure of three hundred and twelve million? By any reckoning, it seems incongruous.'

Paul smiled thinly.

'You've asked me the one question I cannot answer,' he replied, 'because the answer to *that* question will emerge from a negotiation which should commence only when the entire funding package is in position. In the absence of clarity, I'm guessing that the book value is somewhere around the three hundred million mark, and if the receivers are offered something in excess of this, my belief is they'll be tempted.'

'So you're asking us to adjudicate on this proposal based on little more than a hunch,' Robert Goldsmith suggested.

'In a way, yes.'

'It seems that what you're really asking is for us to step in and effectively assume the lion's share of the risk,' Frazer-Briant added.

'No, that is not what I am asking. If the debt-purchase negotiations are successful at the levels indicated, then the bank's risk will be capped at one hundred and eighty seven million rather than the current asking price of five-ninety. At one eighty seven the assets are extremely marketable. Construction recommencement will only enhance them further.'

'On the scale of lending risk, construction is considered extremely high-end,' continued the suave, dapper, impeccably dressed Frazer-Briant.

'You ought to know it better than most,' Paul responded smoothly. 'The name Frazer-Briant is emblazoned on the tower-cranes of most of the larger midland cities.'

'Then we're in agreement,' Frazer-Briant smiled.

An hour later, following an exhaustive session of questions and answers, Sir Kenneth finally turned to Paul.

'I'm happy with most of what I've heard,' he began, 'and I have to acknowledge that Anthony's canny dropping of the name Henry Hyland into the mix will have done you no harm at all. In fact, any doubts we may have harboured have been somewhat assuaged by the substantive involvement of arguably London's most astute property developer. For that alone you deserve to be congratulated. Nonetheless we're talking vast amounts of money here, and we have a duty to our shareholders to exercise restraint.'

He glanced up from his notes to try and gauge a reaction, but Paul's face was inscrutable.

'The bank is prepared to lend you the necessary funding subject to the following three non-negotiable provisos attaching to the term-sheet. Firstly, in order to reflect the risk element of the proposal, the bank will require an arrangement fee of ten million to be discharged up front. Secondly, all outstanding balances will be levied at a rate of eleven percentage points above the existing cost of funds, with interest charged quarterly to your account. Finally and most importantly, in order for the bank to justify this inflated level of funding, we will be insisting that you furnish a blanket, across-the-board personal guarantee. All of these are conditions precedent, cast in stone, and are strictly non-negotiable. And if you are willing to accept these, then I see no reason why we cannot proceed to the next stage.'

Paul struggled to remain calm as he absorbed the implications of all that he had just heard. He had always assumed that the interest rate would be higher than the norm, but it was the punitive level of the arrangement fee that genuinely shocked him. His mind raced across the permutations, and he swiftly concluded that in the overall scheme of things the initial pain of the arrangement fee would be swallowed up in the level of the debt reduction achieved, assuming the purchase negotiations proved successful. The request for a personal guarantee also surprised him, because based solely on the criteria contained in the presentation, the bank was never going to be over-exposed on the strength of these figures.

Nonetheless he knew that banks always sought to enhance their security, and he assumed that their insistence on a blanket personal guarantee was designed to keep him on the hook during the riskiest phase of the arrangement.

The directors of Beauchamps, the most prestigious and oldest merchant bank in the City of London, stared at him impassively from their positions around the boardroom table, professional shylocks each and every one of them. He fought to suppress a growing sense of excitement and spoke in a calm, measured tone.

'I believe there is the basis for agreement subject to one or two minor clarifications which shouldn't cause undue difficulty.'

He caught the sparkle in Sir Kenneth's eyes, the imperceptible raising of the eyebrow, and the thinnest of smiles on his sharp, intelligent face. There wasn't a lot of wriggle room here, but he suspected that these guys wanted to do the deal – so, maybe just a tweak or two.

'The proposed interest rate is by any standard draconian. However, I'm willing to accept it nonetheless, because frankly I expected as much. I also accept the ten million arrangement fee, subject to the understanding that the bank never seeks to question my modus operandi or undermine my strategy, even if this should lead to outright media hysteria. I have to be permitted to conduct my business in my own intuitive way, free from any form of external interference, or otherwise I shall be forced to fund this project elsewhere. Gentlemen, please understand that this is not a threat. I am also willing to provide you with a personal guarantee, on the sole proviso that Grange Abbey, my family's home in Ireland, is excluded from the documentation.'

'Oh for God's sakes, this is ridiculous,' Andrew Stevenson responded irritably. 'Why on earth should we be asked to exclude anything? A personal guarantee is precisely what it says, an uninhibited line of recourse to the personal assets of the borrower.'

Paul regarded him impassively.

'My brother's body lies buried in the grounds of that house, and as long as I'm alive no bank or individual will wrest it from my family.'

His expression unflinching, his delivery relaxed and resolute, his demeanour restrained, Paul spoke with singular yet unmistakable intent under the steely gaze of the Beauchamps board. Had he called it about right? Negotiating with these guys was never going to be easy. The silence seemed interminable but in the end it was Sir Kenneth who broke the impasse.

'Gentlemen, I do believe we have a deal. Get our legal people to prepare the paperwork as quickly as possible. I want this signed off by close of business.'

He stood and walked around the table to where Paul sat. They shook hands.

'May I be the first to offer you my congratulations.'

'Thank you sir.'

'And your lawyers are?'

'Solomons, sir.'

'Mmmm, an interesting choice. Gentlemen, we'll need to dot our "i"s and cross our "t"s.'

47

He'd been living there alone these past thirteen years since she had departed with the boy, existing in this silent place with its stripped-down walls and empty rooms, the contents long since consigned to the city's pawnbrokers, the paintings packed up and sold under the crack of the auctioneer's gavel.

There was nothing left in this place to remind him of her other than a single tarnished photograph, and the house itself of course, precluded from disposal by a complicated Bannon trust, as otherwise it would be gone the way of the rest. He gazed often at the solitary photograph he still retained in a locker by the bed, the gilt frame corroded, the glass shattered from myriad falls and blows.

Sometimes when he stared into the remnants of an empty bottle, he pondered whether she was dead or alive, and where on earth she might be, but then he'd grab another and raise it to his lips to cauterise the memory. He no longer cared a jot what the contents of those bottles might be, his sole concern to try and assuage the fear that was always lurking there. No amount of drink could blunt the memory of all that had taken place, or lance the bitterness that consumed him all the hours of the day.

In the silent emptiness, the distant slamming of a door set his heart racing. He scampered to the bed and dug beneath the mattress until he felt the cold steel of the gun he kept hidden there. He strained to hear, but there was nothing, only stillness in the vacuum of his blurred reality. Now the house was quiet again, not even the faintest sound, and yet still he waited, crouched by the bedside, not daring to move, hearing nothing but the laboured rasping of his own breath.

What in the hell could it be? He wondered. A delusion. A nocturnal presence. A figment of his tortured imagination.

In the cloudy swirls of his consciousness he could no longer differentiate between reality and illusion – it barely seemed possible. Then he felt that fear again, the cold, relentless fear that was always lurking there.

The sound of steps echoed in the chill gloom of the corridor, drawing ever closer, ever louder, until they stopped beyond the door. He wedged himself against the headboard and levelled the gun with quivering hands. The fear that was always there welled in the pit of his stomach and filled his mouth with sulphurous bile. He saw the handle turn slowly, and then the door open, and then the silhouette of a man standing motionless in the watery light. He gasped in disbelief.

'You!' he seethed. 'How dare you set foot in this house! I'll happily blow your fucking brains out.'

The shadowy figure moved forward into the stench-filled room.

'We have unfinished business. Did you really believe I'd let you get away with what you did to her?'

He levelled the gun and depressed the trigger, but the hammer clicked harmlessly into an empty chamber. Suddenly it was snatched from his grasp and a blow to his face rocked him sideways. He tumbled onto the floor and scurried to the corner, then glanced furtively at the door and thought about making a run for it.

'You can try, but you'll be wasting your time.'

The man held up the key for him to see.

'This is the end of the line for you. There can be no escape.'

In trepidation he watched the man load the chamber with bullets.

'I removed them when I saw you leave earlier to collect your daily supply.'

He began crying bitterly, a wretched, eerie, mournful wail. Tears filled the grizzled chasms of his cheeks.

'Cry all you want. Your tears are wasted on me.'

His lips contorted in an agonised mutter.

'You made me soil myself,' he whimpered.

The man levelled the gun and stared at him with hatred in his eyes.

'It's time to make peace with the demons in your soul.'

He stared at him beseechingly.

'How can you do this? You, more than anyone, should have compassion in your heart for me.'

He felt the cold steel of the barrel nudge into his forehead.

'You had none for her. Expect none from me.'

He screamed a silent scream and held up his hands in subjugation.

'Have pity on a broken soul.'

The sound of a single gunshot reverberated like thunder in the room. Simon slumped to the floor and lay still. The gunman tossed the weapon on the bed and walked away silently, like a ghost in the darkness.

One month later, an anonymous caller reported a fatality at a house called 'The Brambles' on Dublin's Ailesbury Road. The police forced the lock and discovered the heavily decomposed body of a man in an upper bedroom, later identified from dental records as one Simon Patrick Bannon. The rats had had a field day, and a forensic investigation quickly concluded, from the orientation of the body and the location of the weapon, that Simon Bannon had been murdered by an intruder. The investigating detective appealed publicly for the anonymous caller to contact them one more time, but no such contact was ever received. With no witnesses and no leads, the murder remained unresolved and the investigation ultimately proved inconclusive.

48

They came down the M1 from the Scottish cities of Glasgow, Edinburgh, Dundee and Dunfermline, travelling in cars, buses, trucks and jeeps. They boarded trains in Liverpool, Birmingham, Manchester and Newcastle, bidding farewell to their wives, their girlfriends, their children, their mothers – not knowing when they'd be back, not knowing how long it might take. They abandoned their commitments, handed in their notice, cancelled contracts, descended the platforms, and joined the march to the south.

They crossed from Ireland on the evening ferries out of Larne into Stranraer, from Dublin Port into Liverpool, Dun Laoghaire to Holyhead, Rosslare to Fishguard, Cork into Swansea, boarding the night train from Holyhead into London's Euston Station. Hundreds arrived by plane out of Belfast, Dublin and Shannon into Heathrow, and on transatlantic flights out of New York, Chicago and Boston. Others travelled through the port of Antwerp en route from Hamburg, Dusseldorf and Berlin.

When the call finally came, they downed tools in their thousands and travelled across the continent of Europe to the designated rendezvous point in the London borough of Camden. London's Metropolitan Police discreetly monitored their arrival through the hubs of Euston, Victoria and Waterloo.

Detective Sergeant Jack Ringrose sat and listened intently to the information coming down the line from Tony Stringer, his counterpart in MI6.

'They've been coming in all week, Jack. Our intelligence-gathering exercise indicates at least five thousand on the march.'

Ringrose whistled.

'Five thousand! You're kidding me!'

'It's a coordinated operation with one or two loose cannons

315

in the mix. So far we've identified a couple of hundred hard cases with paramilitary connections and a handful with criminal records, but most of these guys have no previous history. Still, it adds up to one helluva lot of bad guys gathered in the one group.'

'What's this all about, Tony?'

'Right now we don't have enough to call it, but we do know that Considine is coordinating most of it, and Frank Brilly's outfit is slap-bang in the middle of all this, which leads us to conclude that the Bannon construction family *have* to be calling the shots. The word on the street is that they're planning to restart their London operation sometime soon. A movement of labour on a scale as vast as this suggests their plans are pretty imminent.'

'Has anyone broken the law?'

'Not that we're aware, but interestingly, the unions have been ratcheting up the numbers outside the Bannon operation in Croydon. They've gone from two hundred up to two thousand in the past few days, and the numbers are rising.'

'Bradshaw?'

'Yeah.'

'Nothing illegal in that, is there?'

'No, nothing illegal, but it's potentially explosive, Jack. Bradshaw and the Bannons have history.'

Jack Ringrose pondered the implications.

'OK, Tony, let's monitor the situation during the coming days. Something's got to blow here, and until it happens we'll just have to sit it out a while.'

49

Ben Bradshaw sat in the wheelchair to which he had been consigned since the encounter with Frank Bannon eleven years earlier. That day his plans had backfired badly, because one crucial eventuality had been overlooked: the Bannons had come prepared. Pre-warned by a mole at the very heart of the union, the outcome of that failed ambush on Frank Bannon had been disastrous, to say the least. The damage inflicted to the base of Bradshaw's neck from a near-fatal blow had left him devoid of feeling from the waist down and consigned to a wheelchair for the rest of his days.

Seven long months in hospital had rendered him embittered and prone to mood-swings, but at least he had managed to resurface, with control of the union still in his grasp. In the weeks following the confrontation with the Bannons, his second-in-command Terry Hayden, had resigned unexpectedly, and although it had never been proven conclusively, Bradshaw's instincts told him that the sudden departure of Hayden as good as confirmed that the snitch had flown the coop.

He had long suspected that Terry Hayden harboured ambitions to wrest control of the union, so in the end his disappearance was probably the only positive to emerge from the whole sorry saga.

And yet now it seemed that, after all these years of relative peace and quiet, that the Bannons were at it again. All the information accumulated during the past months confirmed it: a formidable force in the process of being assembled at the behest of this latest Bannon, with the evil fingerprints of Considine splattered all over it. But then nobody, not even the Bannons, could put together a force of such magnitude in Ben Bradshaw's city without him getting to hear about it. This much he had learned from the Bannons: infiltrate the fuckers the same way they had infiltrated him, with hopefully the same lethal results.

When that low life snitch Hayden had departed, he decided not to replace him, instead promoting the broody, psychopathic Percy Hanratty to the key position. Hanratty, a second-generation Liverpool-Irish brickie, had, like himself, done time, a nine-year stint in Belmarsh for raping a twelve-year-old schoolgirl in a park on her way to school. Bradshaw never quite knew what was going on inside Hanratty's weird brain, but at least he knew which strings to pull to ensure the creepy bastard stayed in line.

'Do we know where they plan to strike first Percy?'

'Yeah, we do boss. All the latest information points to Croydon. We think they're gonna try and bust it open next Tuesday morning.'

Bradshaw stared down the table, past the Travis brothers, Pete Ravenscroft and Roger Maynard, a blank, faraway look in his eyes.

'We can't allow them to do that Perce,' he said eventually.

'No boss.'

Hanratty glanced nervously at the others but found no comfort there. *These fucks were always going to let you swim on your own*, he pondered bitterly.

'No Boss,' Bradshaw mouthed silently, his leery stare panning across the assembled group, until finally settling back on the ill-at-ease Hanratty.

'Care to share your thoughts with us, Perce?'

Hanratty's beady eyes darted around furtively.

'My . . . thoughts boss?'

Bradshaw regarded him dispassionately.

'Like maybe telling us how the fuck you plan to put a stop to this?'

Hanratty cleared his throat and clasped his clammy hands together.

'There's only one way in and out boss, and right now we've got three and a half thousand men manning the line, and they sure as hell ain't no bunch of schoolgirls.'

Tony Travis sneered audibly.

'Still can't get them out of his mind boss.'

Bradshaw's murderous stare made his grin melt instantly.
'Sorry boss.'

'Increase it to seven thousand,' Bradshaw barked, 'and remember who we're up against. There's no meaner fuck out on the street than that ugly brute Considine, and in case you bunch of mutton-heads need reminding, take a look at what the bastards did to me.'

50

The eight men gathered in the office suite on the mezzanine level of a cavernous warehouse in Stockley Park took their places at the boardroom table, for what constituted their fifth and final meeting. Paul Bannon sat and waited for the others to settle, these seven men he had so painstakingly chosen to spearhead his effort to retake the assets seized from his family.

He nodded to each of them as they took their allocated seats, sure in the knowledge that he'd made the correct choices. They were men from different backgrounds with different temperaments, cobbled together for their divergent skills with one important common denominator: their unswerving loyalty to him, and his unfailing trust in each of them.

He had studied them as the weeks rolled out, the early, inevitable personality clashes gradually giving way to an unspoken bond of mutual trust, as each began to appreciate the particular skills of the man seated next to him. And so at this final meeting, on the eve of the assault on Croydon, he knew that they were primed for action at precisely the right time. He pondered the options and realised that he was well pleased with the choices he had made.

John Considine was always going to be an integral part of this elite little group. They had met separately during the months leading up to this, and Considine had assured him that despite his years of absence from the day-to-day rough-and-tumble of the business, he was keen to play his part and deliver on whatever he was required to deliver. When Paul asked him to recruit two and a half thousand operatives, Considine's response was simply to inquire how soon they'd be needed.

'A lot of the old crew will be pleased to get the call,' he informed him casually. 'Some have been hoping it might come.

Others have been expecting it to come. Right now they're scattered across the continent of Europe, but no need to worry about that, because you can't underestimate the loyalty these guys hold for the family. It goes all the way back to the old man, to your brother Frank, and right now they're ready to deliver that same loyalty to you. My chargehands are already out there, active in the market, chasing these guys down, and the feedback from everywhere is – just say when.'

Paul's choice to spearhead the operation was always going to be the lethal Saint John the Baptist hooker, now king of the London concrete industry, his old school pal Frank Brilly. They had also met frequently, and during those meetings Frank had assured him that he'd bring another thousand workers in from the Brilly concrete gangs.

'The unions may try and sever the concrete supply at source,' Paul suggested.

'Count on it,' Brilly replied.

'It has got the potential to cause a real problem.'

'The unions control the national suppliers, so, yeah, it could in theory cause a problem, but we can bring a shit-load of pressure to bear on those guys. Brillys are the largest suppliers of concrete into London, with Whelans not far behind us. And if it comes to the crunch, we're ready to draw from our own quarries. We're a non-union outfit, the same as you guys, and eleven of our concrete-manufacturing plants are within cracking distance of the metropolis.'

'I wasn't aware of that, Frank.'

'Some of them are a long way out, but we'll roll it in from a hundred miles if we have to. It's already set up. We've got the manpower and the capability to wheel it in non-stop, twenty-four-seven. Let me worry about this – you just figure out the rest.'

'That's a big piece of the problem solved.'

'Oh and by the way, when I mentioned Whelans earlier, it was for a reason. They're our biggest competitors in London which is why we're not exactly bosom buddies.'

'I thought it was more like sworn enemies.'

'And that's the really strange thing. I had a visit from Vincent

Whelan recently, the old man's eldest son. He's been running the show, along with his four brothers since the old boy stepped down. Last week he walked into my office cool as a breeze, and asked to speak with me: He said,

"I hear Bannons are planning an assault on Bradshaw's union. I'm guessing you've got it all figured out, but we'd really like to be a part of this. I can deliver six hundred of my best guys at short notice."

'When he was leaving he handed me a card with a telephone number. He said,"Just make the call – the response will be instant."

"No need for me to call," I replied.

"I'm accepting your offer right now, and when the air clears, you and me need to sit down and figure a way to put an end to this rivalry. We've been cutting the ground from under one another at every tender process. There's gotta be a better way."

"I'll be happy to do that Frank. Let's sort the Bannons out first." '

Anthony Selwyn had volunteered to sit at the conference table and act as Paul's advisor, confidante and vital conduit into the banking world. He'd already spent endless weeks developing cash flows, refining deadline dates, and gearing up the money supply to cover all eventualities. When, one day, Paul inquired as to how he could afford the vast amount of time required to oversee this demanding process, his answer was straightforward in its simplicity.

'I want to see you succeed in this because, more than anyone else, I know how important it is to you. But from my perspective it's equally important that this thing delivers, because it's the largest speculative private funding package that the bank has dealt with. I brought it to the board as a concept which carried my clear and unequivocal imprimatur, which effectively means that in the City I'll be judged by the success or failure of this venture. So I guess you're stuck with me. My reputation hangs in the balance here.'

Paul smiled ruefully.

'You're a great guy, Anthony. Not having you on board was never an option.'

Even John Considine's stony features registered surprise when Steve Richie first took his place at the boardroom table, clearly a part of Paul Bannon's inner circle. When the shit finally hit the fan for the Bannon Group, Steve was universally scapegoated for calling it wrong, but Paul remembered a discussion he had once had with his brother Frank late one evening at Grange Abbey. During their discussion, Frank had confided that there was no one in the world he trusted more than Steve Richie and that his loyalty to the Bannon family was beyond reproach. Steve was always going to be his brother's choice to take over at the top of Bannons when Frank eventually decided to call it a day. Paul remembered him crying his eyes out at Frank's graveside, inconsolable. The turmoil in the years that followed, as Bannons somersaulted out of control was an experience no one was likely to forget, least of all the ultimate fall-guy Steve Richie whose reputation lay on the scrapheap. The consequences of a flawed decision-making process had ultimately proven catastrophic, but Paul brushed all these matters aside when he decided to give Steve a call. Foremost in his mind was the one trait that mattered most to the Bannons; he lifted the phone knowing that Steve Richie's loyalty had never faltered.

'Even after all that's happened you're asking a loser like me to come on board? Are you aware that people no longer even want to be seen socialising with me?'

'I have my reasons,' Paul said simply. 'I'm in charge now and I want you back in as financial controller. You *know* this family and you *know* this company. We've all made mistakes along the way, and if you've learnt anything from yours, then your experience ought to prove invaluable as we face the future together. What do you say, Steve?'

'If you're really sure.'

'*Sure* I'm sure.'

Steve's voice seemed to catch on the hint of a sob. He took a moment to compose himself, and then said simply, 'When do I start?'

Another member of Frank Bannon's old board of directors, Andy Carmichael, sat opposite him in the restaurant nonchalantly chewing gum. Paul had finally tracked him down to the Paris headquarters of the French national contractor Lafayette PLC on the Place Vendôme. He had expected this one to be more difficult, but as they sat having dinner in Chez Francis at the Seine end of Avenue Georges V, Carmichael's response was unequivocal.

'I loved working for that brother of yours – we all did. We'd have followed him through the gates of hell if he'd asked us, which thankfully he didn't, although sometimes it fucking felt like it. Never a dull moment on the Frank Bannon express train. I'm getting the feeling that this venture of yours is beginning to sound like more of the same, and if that's the case, then I say bring it on. I'm with you on this, out of loyalty to Frank of course, but also because the word on the street is that you're the smartest of them all. I wouldn't miss this for all the tea in China, mate.'

He stared at the young maverick architect, smiled and shook his hand. If he'd harboured any doubts about this choice before they met, he left their meeting with none. Once again it was that magic word that sealed it: loyalty.

Jamie Sinclair was probably the one who was most surprised to receive the call. In the months following the collapse of the Bannon Group, he'd been recruited by a wealthy Irish racing dynasty to oversee a large stud operation in Tipperary. When the call came, it was a voice from a long-forgotten past, but one he recognised instantly.

'I never thought I'd hear from you again. You've been maintaining a low profile.'

'We cut the cord with a lot of people. It's impossible to stay in touch with everyone.'

'You still OK?'

'*Sure* I am. How about you?'

'I've recovered from that fucking blow you gave me, physically anyway. Inside, well . . . that's another story. There are wounds that never heal.'

'We must let bygones be bygones Jamie. What's in the past stays in the past. It's time to move on.'

'There's not a day in my life I haven't thought long and hard about the consequences of my actions, – the nightmare I foisted on my sister, the destruction of our friendship, everything. If I could wind back the clock, I now know I'd have done it all so differently, but that's an option I no longer have.'

There was a silence at the other end.

'Where is she, Jamie?' he asked quietly. 'Is she dead or alive?'

'I don't know. She never contacts me.'

The silence was interminable, so long that Jamie couldn't tell if he was still there.

'What happened was a catastrophe, Jamie, but neither of us can change the past. What's done is done. It's the future that concerns me now. I'm compiling a team to grab back the Bannon Group assets. I want you to come on board and be a part of this.'

This time the silence was at Jamie's end, and when it eventually came, the reply was simple.

'When do you need me?'

'Straight away.'

The steely-tough Bannon ramrod took a long, deep breath and fought to control his emotions.

'I'll hand in my notice today.'

51

The two traffic cops sat in the patrol car on a slip-road adjacent to junction seventeen on the M25 four miles north of the sprawling satellite town of Croydon. It had been unusually quiet on the midnight shift along the Surrey-Sussex border, the only incident a mini-van driving erratically in the early hours. When they had pulled him in, the driver, an elderly guy, smelled of alcohol and seemed the worse for wear. He apologised and said he'd recently lost his wife of forty years to cancer following a prolonged illness.

'Sir I sympathise with your predicament,' Constable George Allenby responded. 'Go sit in the police car and my colleague will take you home. I'll follow behind in your van, but next time we may not be so lenient.'

They dropped him off at his house, an isolated cottage in a quiet village a mile off the motorway.

'I'd hate to end up like that poor old sod,' his younger colleague Danny Goodwin remarked later as they sat parked in a siding under the branches of a large spruce.

'Unlikely in your predicament, mate, with, what is it now, five sprogs and another on the way. You and the missus ought to be well looked after.'

It was five-thirty on the Tuesday morning at the end of an August bank-holiday weekend, and traffic was light.

'Looks like the country's decided to take an extra day's holiday,' George Allenby muttered in his nasal West-Country tone. 'Two more boring bloody hours to go,' he added with a yawn, sinking low into his seat and closing his eyes.

Heavy droplets of rain hammered noisily on the windscreen as the first light of dawn began to slowly reveal a soupy grey sky. Allenby turned to his young partner.

'Wake me up if anything happens, Danny,' he grunted.

Danny glanced at his colleague and nodded. They'd been partners for three years and worked well together, often taking turns at cat-napping, especially on these long, boring, nocturnal motorway stints. That was just the way it worked on the motorway detail. He stared out across the empty lanes at the now-shiny wet surface. The country must have woken up, he mused, taken one look out of the window and gone back to bed – lucky bastards. His balls were itchy, his legs were cramped, and his partner was beginning to smell. Isn't life fucking great, he thought, absent-mindedly pondering the unseasonal lack of traffic – eerily quiet, even for this time of morning.

It was then that he first heard it in the distance, a low rumbling growing steadily louder, like the revving of a powerful engine as the driver changed through the gears. He glanced down the empty motorway in the direction of London where the road curved out of sight. He lowered the passenger window and felt the cold morning air on his face, and then suddenly he saw it, an articulated truck with a flatline trailer attached, its headlights flaring through the early-morning mist as it powered down the straight. The six men seated in the driver's cabin barely glanced in his direction as the big Scania thundered past, its dual trailers laden with an array of construction equipment and tower-crane parts. He watched the tail-lights disappear in the distance, then turned to see a fourteen-wheeler loom into view, the grinding of its engines shaking the ground beneath them as it growled along the southbound carriageway.

From then the stillness of the early morning was shattered by the unbroken screech of engines as they rolled out of the mist and down the straight on their journey south. Allenby stirred in his seat, blinked, and stared out at the advancing convoy.

'What going on?' he grunted.

'Beats me, George,' Danny replied. 'I was about to wake you. The first one appeared not long after you nodded off. I've counted seventeen so far.'

Now fully alert ,they watched another fourteen-wheeler rumble past, its engines screaming under the weight of its immense cargo. A convoy of six-wheeler personnel carriers followed on, their platforms covered in grey tarpaulin, the rear sections open to reveal gangs of men crowded inside.

'Forty-seven . . . forty-eight . . . forty-nine . . . by my counting this next one's number fifty.'

'Time to call this one in, Danny. Get on the blower. Go do it now!'

Allenby stared at the advancing convoy, its sheer scale reminiscent of army footage, although he was pretty certain this wasn't the army – these guys sure didn't look like soldier boys.

'Tango-Two-Seven to headquarters – over.'

'Headquarters to Tango-Two-Seven – over.'

'We have a convoy of heavy vehicles moving south towards Croydon, passing junction seventeen – over.'

'How many vehicles – over.'

'Seventy-seven so far – over.'

A pause.

'Roger, Tango-Two-Seven. Follow them and ascertain their destination. We'll notify the Highway Authority and get back to you – over.'

'Fucking great,' Allenby sighed. 'Let's do it.'

52

Archie McMaster sat in the jeep with his three companions and sighed quietly. The union executive had ordered him here ten days ago to strengthen the line, in anticipation of an expected onslaught from the Bannons. He stared distastefully at the three goons seated with him, and pulled down the window to allow the thick fog of cigarette smoke to disperse. There were already five thousand men on the line. The numbers had been ramped up from just over two thousand in the past ten days. He glanced back towards the site entrance, and estimated the numbers this morning to be less than a thousand – helluva lot of no-shows, but hard to blame the fuckers really. The end of a bank holiday was always a non-starter, and the majority of these guys had been pulled at short notice from sites all across London, most of them reluctantly.

Everyone knew that the prospect of earning real money was massively curtailed by a union call to picket-line duty, but most of these guys had the sense to realise that this particular union didn't take no for an answer. The union looked after them pretty well most of the time, and they knew that they could rely on members from other jurisdictions to answer the call if ever their own particular predicament warranted such action.

If you knew what was good for your health, then you sure didn't mess with Ben Bradshaw's union.

Archie had been raised in the slums of Dundee, where he soon learned the hard way that you had to fight to survive in this world, which was OK, because fighting was something that came naturally to the young man. He left home in his early teens to work on the big construction projects in central Glasgow, on government programmes for the development of high-rise apartment blocks designed to replace the notorious slums of that city.

From there he migrated south to London and signed on as an enforcer with the Building and Allied Trades Union, a task for which his background and tough demeanour made him ideally suited. Along the way Archie had inflicted a lot of pain and damage in the line of duty, and yet, despite his fearsome reputation, he had somehow succeeded, albeit only barely, in keeping his nose out of prison. He was a canny, street-smart Scot who knew how to connect with the hard guys, and on this occasion he'd done just that to facilitate the task in hand.

His brother Billy sat beside him in the back seat, with two of his old pals from Dundee, Sonny McArthur and Pete Livingstone seated up front. Archie sat there – bored and brassed off. These picket-line assignments were arduous, and he was beginning to despair that this was just another wild-goose chase ordered by those psychopaths in head office.

Still, he wasn't planning to go anywhere; his orders were clear and explicit, delivered straight from the man at the top – stop these fuckers in their tracks. Under no circumstances allow them to recommence operations on site. Show them early on that there ain't no future for them in this town.

Like most others in the rank-and-file membership, Archie was well aware that the Bannons were this union's most hated enemy, responsible, if you could believe the rumours, for consigning the old man to his wheelchair. Archie had always regarded Bradshaw as a nasty piece of work, unequivocally down there with the lowest of the low, and in Archie's world that placed you close to rock-bottom.

Still, every man needed to recognise on which side his bread is buttered, and when this union issued instructions to use whatever means were necessary to deliver the goods, to Archie McMaster that covered all the options, including violence and murder if necessary.

But so far it had been a no-show, not much so a whisper during the past ten days. So maybe these guys had already got the message, same as the rest of the fat-cats operating in the London region, which was – don't fuck with this union, or else do so at your peril. A hard core of ruffians out on the picket-line had been tooled up with everything from knuckle-dusters to iron bars to baseball bats. Anyone who had the audacity or the stupidity to move against this line would soon have second thoughts.

A waft of cool air made him decide to roll up the window. He yanked the collar of his bomber-jacket around his ears, pulled his woolly hat down over his shaven head and settled into the seat.

'Next time you fuckers need a smoke, get out of the fucking van,' he rasped.

No one answered back, but then, he wasn't expecting a response. He squinted through the rain-smeared windscreen and scanned the horizon for the umpteenth time. He pushed his seat back and was about to doze off when something in the distance caught his eye. He rubbed the mist from the windscreen and focused on the headlights of a line of vehicles coming down off the intersection onto the main drag leading up to the site entrance.

'We've got visitors,' he said tersely.

The first faint drone of the engines reached his ears as the lead truck turned onto the straight and advanced remorselessly up the hill in their direction.

'What's going on, Archie?' Pete Livingstone inquired. 'This mean anything?'

He stared out along the road and pondered the question.

'This mean anything?' he muttered rhetorically. 'I reckon this means it's showtime.'

An hour earlier he should have suspected something amiss when a BBC TV crew began setting up a position on a gravel platform fifty yards north of the main site entrance. *How could they have known a situation was about to develop,* he mused. The usual way probably, a tip-off from the cops, although there wasn't the faintest sign of a police presence, at least not yet. But as he surveyed the line of vehicles looming steadily closer, Archie knew that the cops were never going to be too far behind.

'Shouldn't we do something, Archie?' his younger brother Billy asked excitedly. Archie stared at him blandly.

'Yeah, like how about shut the fuck up and let the thousand guys out there on the line do what we expect them to do – earn their fucking keep!'

He scanned the picket-line and saw most of them shuffling from one foot to the next in anticipation. Dumb fucks, brave in a pack, useless on their own. The approaching convoy had set the adrenalin running high but Archie was keenly aware that his bosses up in London had demanded a far greater presence than this.

They'd have it soon enough, but the big question was could these guys hold the line until the cavalry arrived. In most cases a thousand-strong picket line should have been sufficient to intimidate the hardest adversary, but he'd been warned that these Bannons were different. Well, they were about to find out, he thought, as he turned his attention back to the BBC crew on the hill.

Union policy towards the media was to keep the buggers sweet; butter them up and get them on side. They were mostly fucking lefties anyway, natural allies except for, well . . . except you never really quite knew. They run with the hare and hunt with the hounds, and ultimately pin their allegiance to the whim of the masses – whichever way the wind blows.

Behind this debacle, the mother of all public-relations battles would no doubt rage, as fierce as anything you might witness out here on the line, to win the hearts and the minds of the public, and massage them into extrapolating the outcome in a particular way.

The final battle, the battle of big business versus a powerful construction union would be acted out in the boardroom, with only one conceivable outcome – the winner takes all.

But Archie McMaster wasn't being paid to fight that particular fight, and so he turned his attention once again to the business at hand. In accordance with specific instructions, the picketers had spread out along the length of the north perimeter upon which the main site entrance was located. The entrance had been padlocked shut, using heavy-duty chains and a backup line of steel stanchions embedded in the ground at intervals fronting the main gates. The massive silo, towering eighty feet into the sky from its location beyond the perimeter, had been systematically sabotaged and was virtually unrepairable. Thousands of gallons of water had been pumped into the cement at the bottom of the cylinder to foil any attempt to restart the mechanism.

The inside of the silo was now a clogged-up, solidified mass, rendering any attempt to retrieve the equipment a practical impossibility. The silo complex represented the beating heart of the entire operation, and in vandalising the apparatus beyond repair, Archie McMaster and his merry men had well and truly spiked the blood supply to the main artery.

He watched the lead trucks fan out either side of the entrance, the crews spilling out in their hundreds to take positions in what looked like a prearranged, preplanned exercise. Judging by the scale of this operation it was beginning to look like these guys had come not in their hundreds but in their thousands. Archie listened to the incessant bark of the chargehands patrolling the main drag, and quickly realised that this was going to be no picnic. It was a well-organised, well-supervised operation. He felt a nagging sense of foreboding as he watched them spread along the line and inch ever closer to the perimeter. It was a sight to behold as they spun left and right in their thousands, closing down the gap under the supervision of their twelve fiery chargehands. None appeared to be empty-handed. From where he sat, Archie had a clear view of an array of equipment that included shovels, pick-axe handles, iron bars and lump-hammers.

They stood quietly, in contrast to the tidal wave of abuse being hurled at them from the strikers manning the union line, and as the minutes passed without incident, the picketers responded to the non-activity like it was some kind of moral victory. Even Archie began to wonder if the prospect of breaching the line had somehow given the leaders of these men pause for thought, but just then he detected a knee-jerk movement directly opposite the main gates. Three men emerged from the ranks and walked forward until they stood facing Barney Wigglesworth, Archie's nominated leader on the picket-line. The noise from the picketers slowly began to abate.

Wigglesworth, a hard-case Geordie gang-member, was as violent and unpredictable a psychopath as any Archie had met. He had a formidable reputation as a construction-union enforcer, and along the way had spent four years in Barlinnie on a charge of manslaughter. Archie had travelled north to Newcastle to recruit him, and when Wigglesworth presented himself at headquarters the following Monday morning along with a dozen of his associates, he knew that his journey to the north had been worth the effort. Archie sensed that events were about to take a seismic turn for the worst.

'OK guys, change of plan,' he grunted. 'Let's get down there now!'

He climbed out of the jeep and moved quickly along the line, edging forward into a position close to Wigglesworth. He was now able to assess the three men who had stepped forward. He immediately recognised Paul Bannon from file photographs retained at union headquarters. He studied him with interest. He was a big, lean, rangy guy weighing maybe fourteen stone, with an imposing, athletic presence. Frank Brilly stood to his left and regarded Wigglesworth as if he was nothing more than a piece of dog-shit. Archie was already familiar with this menacing little fuck, the so-called concrete king of London, whose doors had been slammed in the face of all attempts to introduce union representation. The Brilly outfit didn't come under the jurisdiction of the Building and Allied Trades, so it was never going to end up being their problem.

And yet here he was, blatantly standing shoulder to shoulder with the union's most hated enemy, so maybe this was the opportunity to finally make Brillys part of the problem. He filed that idea in the back of his mind on a to-do list under the heading, 'Let's fuck Brilly', then turned his attention to the man standing on Bannon's right. If he he'd been a betting man he would have put this guy down as a soldier. All the tell-tale signs were there: the hard stare, the short-cropped hair, the super-fit, muscle-bound physique. In the face of this potentially explosive scenario, none of these three looked like they gave a fuck about the consequences of what lay before them – or maybe they were just good actors.

You really had to admire it when you saw it. A lifetime spent out on the line had trained Archie to smell the fear factor, but on this wet grey morning in Croydon there wasn't as much as a whiff. He watched Bannon step forward and narrow the distance between himself and Wigglesworth. He stood before him and stared calmly into his eyes.

'You're trespassing on Bannon property. I'm ordering you to leave now before it's too late, and take the rest of these scumbags with you. I'll only ask you once, you fucking piece of shit.'

The words were delivered with crisp, clear, unequivocal intent. The big union enforcer stared at him incredulously. Then he turned to the guy beside him with an 'is-this-guy-for-real' expression – but turning sideways proved to be his first and last tactical error. The blow to his right ear hit him like a train, an iron fist delivered with electric speed. Wigglesworth was a pretty tough guy but he hadn't braced himself for a hit like this. His legs buckled and he went down instantly, hitting the ground like a sack of potatoes. A seismic heave reverberated across the narrow space, and in one rippling movement the men on either side of the line crashed headlong into one another.

From their position up on the hill, the three astounded television crew members watched the scene explode before their eyes.

'It's a battlefield down there! Let's go live! Now!' Jonathan Fredricks, the young BBC outside-broadcaster, commanded urgently, sensing that this could be the beginnings of something really special.

'OK Johnny, we're live in five!' his cameraman responded and the sound engineer gave him the thumbs-up.

They held their breath and watched the opposing lines collide with fists flying and the sound of weapons ringing in the air. The thousands of men massing in the spaces behind flooded through the gaps, and down the line, the fight spread along the full length of the perimeter and raged out of control. Jonathan Fredricks struggled to retain his composure, his normally calm voice sounding nervous, frayed and barely audible above the shattering commotion. In the distance the scream of police sirens filled the air. He glanced back quickly and counted four cars closing rapidly, with headlights blazing and strobe-lights flashing.

Constable George Allenby watched through his rearview mirror as the approaching police cars sped along the ramp and pulled up to where he and a nervous Danny Goodwin sat waiting a hundred yards back from the unfolding melee.

'The cavalry has arrived,' he muttered cynically, as they disembarked the vehicle and approached the eight police officers led by Sergeant Ron Phillips from the Croydon constabulary.

'Morning, sergeant.'

'Morning, George. What in the fuck's going on up there?'

'Not really sure sarge, but a Saturday night rumpus in downtown Croydon it ain't. They've been at it full-on for the last hour.'

'Have you made an approach?'

Allenby stared at him, wondering if he'd heard right. Is this fucker out of his mind or what the fuck!

'No, sir. Not yet, sir. We thought it best to maintain a watching brief and await further instructions. I'm guessing there's at least five thousand of them up there. We didn't think a two-man approach would have much of an effect, quite honestly.'

Phillips stared at him quizzically but didn't register anything other than honest concern on his big rural face.

'Well we can't just stand here scratching our balls, can we?'

'No, sir.'

'I'm going to call it into the Yard,' he said tersely. 'This is a public disturbance on a scale beyond our remit. In the meantime, we'll make a concerted approach utilising all five cars.'

Which minutes later is precisely what they did, but all to no avail. In the end it was a fucked-up strategy that left them with four injured police officers, three cars overturned, two blazing out of control, and ten badly bruised egos.

53

Detective Chief Superintendent Jack Ringrose assessed the early reports on the deteriorating situation in Croydon with growing concern and quickly concluded that the local constabulary was way out of its depth on this one. The news that five patrol cars had been written off, with police officers down and injured, made matters immeasurably worse, and he hardly needed to hear that a BBC crew was already at the scene filming the unfolding drama, blow by blow. He cursed under his breath – a tip-off from the local constabulary no doubt. Unfortunate for him, but terminal for the snitch if Ringrose ever succeeded in having him rumbled.

Earlier he had ordered two hundred officers in full riot gear to be deployed in a convoy of police buses. He breathed a sigh when his second-in-command, Detective Inspector Charlie Sherwood, radioed confirmation that the police convoy was already approaching the scene.

'I'll be with you in fifteen, Charlie,' he responded, killing the radio and booting his unmarked car up to a hundred miles an hour.

Sherwood turned to see a bulldozer powering down the back of a low-loader and moving in a straight line towards the main site entrance, engines roaring as the driver rammed the throttle to the floor. The strikers swarmed forward wielding crowbars and baseball bats, but a protection detail on either side of the cabin beat them back each time. He watched the driver lower the blade and smash through the stanchions like they were matchsticks.

Sherwood glanced back and felt a wave of relief when he saw the lines of riot police taking positions a hundred yards back. They were already in formation with helmets fastened, batons drawn, and shields positioned, preparing to advance under the barking orders of supervising officer Detective Sergeant

Dwayne Saunders. The sound of steel on steel made him spin round, in time to see the dozer demolishing the entrance gates, releasing a dust-cloud of debris a hundred feet into the air. The dozer thundered forward and the fighting raged out of control, with the opposing lines locked in a pitched battle on both sides of the entrance. Ringrose stared tensely at the unfolding scene, and quickly concluded that the Bannon onslaught was a carefully thought-out clinical exercise, planned and executed with military precision.

He watched his officers splay out in front of the entrance forcing the picketers back, but by now the construction crews were clambering in their hundreds across the gap into the relative safety of the construction site on the far side.

Ringrose grimly surveyed the aftermath of this latest skirmish. He had a bad feeling in his gut. His radio crackled into action. It was Dwayne Saunders sounding tense.

'We need ambulances chief. Some of our guys are down injured, and we have a fatality. Not certain, but it looks to be one of the union boys.'

'How many injured, Dwayne?'

'At least twenty seriously chief – it's a fucking battlefield up here on the front line. And chief . . . '

'Yeah Dwayne.'

'I reckon you need to ramp the numbers up to a thousand. Otherwise we're fucked.'

That evening the BBC broadcast the unfolding drama at Croydon in graphic detail to a shocked nation. The cameras panned in on scenes of a full-on pitched battle across the entire building-site perimeter, with scant evidence of a police presence. Confirmation that a second striker had lost his life added a grave extra dimension to the appalling scenes of blood and mayhem beamed across the land for the world to see.

The following day the union ratcheted up the presence at Croydon and ferried in an extra three thousand protesters. The depleted numbers on the first morning had sent Bradshaw into a fuming rage that lasted all of an hour.

'He'll fucking explode if we don't get this sorted,' Tony Travis said to Archie McMaster as they stood and stared at the gaping hole in the line and the hordes of construction workers pouring across the breach. Even Travis, who thought he had seen it all, stood mesmerised by the intensity of the onslaught, now made infinitely worse by the confirmation that a second picketer had lost his life, and scores on both sides were down injured.

He saw a group of ambulances parked on the carriageway, their crews reluctant to engage without confirmation of safe passage, unachievable while the fighting raged on, and who could really blame them. This was war without the Geneva Convention, and those guys weren't being paid enough to risk their lives; that meant that the rescue operation was on hold, indefinitely. He stared with grudging admiration at the fiery Bannon chargehands as they imposed order in the midst of chaos, their men pouring through the breach to the Bannon gangers on the far side.

As dawn broke on the third morning, a thousand riot police positioned themselves on both sides of the entrance, facing the picketers with batons drawn. But with six thousand enraged picketers manning the line, it was gearing up to be another one of those days. The strikers screamed abuse and hurled missiles at anything that moved.

Tony Travis saw a line of trucks turn onto the approach road, and realised at the same time as the picketers that this was a construction detail transporting vital materials. When they loomed up the main drag, the strikers smashed through the police barriers and converged on the advancing convoy. The lead truck crawled forward and missiles rained down on the teams of men positioned on the side gantries, but they held the ground and beat the strikers back with steel bars. The police struggled to clear a path but they were hopelessly outnumbered and ultimately became swallowed up in the mêlée.

It took the convoy's twenty-eight trucks all day to negotiate the perilous final journey to the site, and when the last truck rumbled across the entrance, the gates were slammed shut.

Travis stared back to the hill at the growing media presence gathered there, inevitable really considering the graphic images beamed across the airwaves the previous night.

★

It all began again at dawn on the fourth morning, the swollen numbers on the line desperate to stop the Bannon roller-coaster in its tracks. Archie McMaster surveyed the scene grimly, but with thousands having already crossed into the far side, he had a growing sense that Bannons had grabbed the initiative. He knew that this would ultimately come down to a war of wills between a powerful union and a maverick contractor, with little the authorities or anyone else could do to sway the outcome.

The strikers poured onto the entrance road and formed a solid human wall a hundred yards deep, forcing the convoys to halt and break the vital umbilical cord to the construction site. Their frustration turned to hatred as the guards up on Brilly's trucks lashed out with a ferocity that even the most hardened union veterans had never previously encountered.

★

The second week passed without major incident, with both sides digging in and consolidating their positions. A sense of realism pervaded, following the growing realisation that this wasn't about to end soon. The lull that followed round one was merely the precursor to what was shaping up to be something other than a leisurely walk in the park. It wasn't long before the shit hit the fan.

As the blockade entered its third week, a young apprentice picketer was crushed beneath the wheels of one of Frank Brilly's convoy trucks and died instantly. The police bussed in hundreds of officers in response to a frantic media and public outcry. But with no attempt to mediate and with no appetite to engage, the union blockade at Croydon intensified, with no hint of a let-up on either side of the line. Ambulances ferried the injured to the accident and emergency units of all the nearby hospitals, but the strain on resources was finally beginning to tell. The chief registrar of the Royal Surrey County Hospital, Doctor Michael Davenport appeared on ITV's *News at Ten* and appealed directly to the government to intervene.

'Our medical staff are being forced to deal daily with the endless flow of victims in this dispute. The injuries we are seeing are appalling. Our facilities are overcrowded and our wards are reminiscent of a warzone. I would ask our Members of Parliament how long they intend to stand in the wings and allow this catastrophe to continue.'

In the wake of his appearance, the media labeled the dispute a national scandal and focused on the government's inability to resolve a situation which was haemorrhaging out of control.

At prime minister's question time, the Labour spokesman for the Environment, Roy Dudley, raised the matter yet again.

'Prime Minister, this is the fourth occasion on which I've implored your government to intervene in the appalling debacle at Croydon, and so far you have expressly refused to do so, despite the dangers it poses to the wider community, to the basic rule of law, and the very real prospect of further loss of life. The country is justifiably appalled by the scenes of violence beamed daily into homes across the land, and every day that this dispute is allowed to continue poses further questions around the effectiveness of this government.'

The barrage of noise which followed from both sides forced the Speaker to intervene.

Finally, the Prime Minister stood to respond.

'Mister Speaker, my right honourable friend complains that matters in Croydon appear to be out of control, and yet the Metropolitan Police have assured me that this is patently not the case. The Home Secretary is adamant that the dispute has been contained, and I can confirm that the police have this morning increased their presence on the ground to more than a thousand officers. Nonetheless the government is facing a fundamental difficulty by virtue of the fact that this appalling dispute is being played out primarily on property which is not in public ownership. That in itself poses a legal, jurisdictional dilemma, which has been referred to the office of the Director of Public Prosecutions for clarification. Meanwhile we are faced with a dispute between two opposing sides, each of which believes it has a fundamental right to defend its position. The right of the Building and Allied Trades Union to mount a peaceful protest, and the right of the Bannon Construction Group to conduct their business in a democratic, free-market environment. This is a democracy, and the government simply cannot be seen to favour one side or the other. Our duty is to maintain the rule of law, and I am satisfied that the Metropolitan Police are doing everything in their power to do just that in these extraordinary circumstances.'

54

The chauffeur eased the Daimler into the forecourt of the Dorchester Hotel and drew up smoothly beside the main entrance. She stepped briskly from the car and nodded to the doorman. It was a warm, hazy evening, still sunny, as she walked through to the luxurious foyer, glancing briefly towards Christopher, at the concierge desk, who acknowledged her with his customary bow.

There was an air of excitement in the hotel, the restaurant and bars buzzing with activity, the music from the jazz trio in the cocktail bar spilling down the crowded foyer. She strode purposefully towards the elevator annexe, oblivious to the glances her electric presence invariably caused, but then something caused her to pause momentarily. She stared back towards the concierge desk and scanned the newspapers. The *London Evening Standard* headline read, 'Scores Injured as Croydon Construction Clash Claims Third Fatality'.

She glanced at Christopher.

'May I?'

'Please . . . be my guest.'

She rode the elevator to the sixth floor and hurried down the corridor to her penthouse suite overlooking Hyde Park. She threw her purse on the bed, sat in an armchair, unfolded the paper and began reading:

> Following scenes of violence which police chiefs
> have described as worse than any previous peacetime
> dispute, the Croydon stand-off between the Building
> and Allied Trades and the Bannon Construction
> Group entered its fourth week with no immediate
> sign of a resolution. Earlier today thousands of
> construction workers were involved in clashes with

striking picketers as the union hinted at further moves
to strengthen the protest . . .

She glanced at her watch and saw that it was seconds to nine
o'clock. She flicked the TV control just in time to catch the
beginning of the news. The cameras panned across hordes of men
converging on a convoy of trucks moving laboriously through the
entrance gates of a vast construction site. The next image focused
on a worker being dragged from a truck and beaten to the ground
by hundreds of angry picketers.

Amidst all the chaos, she could see police in riot gear
struggling to separate the opposing groups under a sustained
barrage of missiles raining down on them from both sides. She
listened to a young broadcaster struggling to make himself heard.

'I spoke earlier to the officer in charge, Detective Inspector
Jack Ringrose of Scotland Yard, to try and ascertain what efforts
are being made to bring this dispute to a conclusion.'

'Inspector Ringrose, we have an unconfirmed report earlier
of a fourth fatality. Our viewers are wondering when we can
expect to see an end to this impasse before it claims even more
lives.'

The detective responded with calm assurance.

'There are a thousand riot police on the ground and a further
five hundred on the way. The size and the sheer intensity of
this confrontation has taken all of us by surprise. We have been
forced to respond to a situation none of us could have anticipated.
The severity of the intent that both sides have demonstrated is
without precedent.'

She sat and stared at the images flashing across the screen, a
heaving body of men locked in a pitched battle across the length
and breadth of the site boundary. The camera cut to an earlier
image of a truck departing the site, surrounded, overturned and
set on fire, the driver scrambling from the cabin and whisked to
safety before the flames engulfed him.

'It's begun like Johnny said it would,' she sighed as the
scenes faded and the news bulletin moved to other matters. She
switched the television off and sat silently in her chair. She had
known the Bannons since she was a little girl, and in the depths

her heart she knew that when all was said and done, this violent picket-line with its thousands of protesting men would succumb in the end, their strength insufficient to break the iron will of this family. She sat motionless until she realised that her hands were gripping the seat so tightly that her knuckles were white and her heart was thumping in her chest.

So brave, so utterly fearless, the mastermind behind this chaotic confrontation; a man to whom thousands were willing to pledge their loyalty and place their personal safety on the line.

And you couldn't even know, she sighed, *that I still love you from the depths of my heart. How could you possibly be aware of it? This hidden love from this hidden girl who abandoned you that fateful morning when we lay together all those years ago. When I abandoned you as you slept, at that moment I forfeited the right to deserve your love.*

The soft knocking on the door snapped her back to the surreal world she had so carefully constructed around herself. She stood and glanced quickly in the mirror, took a deep breath and strode across the room.

'Darling,' she smiled, leaning forward and kissing the tiny but legendary Hollywood film director. 'Sooo nice to see you. Come this way. You look tired . . . '

55

In the end it was a Whelan chargehand, Mick McMillan, who volunteered to resolve the problem with the silo. When the extent of the sabotage was finally assessed, it left the production teams with a dilemma of catastrophic proportions.

For eighteen days the convoys had been stockpiling tons of material on site, but with the huge silo irretrievably damaged, the on-site production had ground to a virtual standstill.

While the union stand-off raged outside the hoardings, on the inside the management team had begun to grapple with a problem with the potential to render all their efforts worthless. Paul sat in the cavernous office they had constructed in the basement of tower seven and listened to the dismal news from his advisors.

'We've had to abandon the repair effort, Mister Bannon. It's a lost cause.'

Clive Dennison, the design engineer, glanced around the room gravely. His words hung in the air.

'We've succeeded in sourcing a second silo from a plant-maintenance facility in Düsseldorf, but the earliest we can expect delivery is in five weeks' time. It's a smaller silo, approximately two-thirds the capacity, but it's still a wide load, and that's gonna make transportation a logistical nightmare. As soon as it arrives in the port of Dover, the cops will have to close the motorway from the south coast up to Croydon to facilitate the transfer. We're probably talking a Sunday morning, all of which can be achieved if we plan the route meticulously, except . . . '

'Except what?'

'Well, sir, except that the union will get to hear about this – it's inevitable. And they'll do their damnedest to sabotage it from the moment it arrives in Dover all the way along the route up to Croydon. And even if we do succeed in getting it here, they're gonna throw the kitchen sink at us to prevent it crossing the line. They're never going to allow it, because they know that spiking the silo is severing the jugular, which basically means we'll be shafted. It's all about the silo, sir.'

Bernard Shanley, the plant yard supervisor, nodded in agreement.

'I agree with Clive, Mister Bannon. Even if we succeed in landing the equipment on site, it'll take a month to get it up and running – assuming we work around the clock with three crews on eight-hour shifts.'

The twelve men in the room sat silently, digesting the repercussions of this latest damning assessment. All eyes turned to Paul in anticipation of him somehow effecting a solution to this devastating setback. It was Vincent Whelan's laid-back voice that broke the silence from the far end of the room.

'One of my guys believes he can solve the problem with the silo. I wasn't going to raise it until everyone had their say, but in the absence of any viable alternatives, my man believes he can get that heap of junk you've got sitting out there working again.'

'It's simply not possible,' Clive Dennison responded dismissively. 'We've had three independent assessments from three different experts and they're all saying the same thing – the silo's a lost cause.'

Paul glanced at Whelan, then at Dennison, then back at Whelan.

'What's he proposing, Vincent?'

'He's sitting outside right now. I'd sooner have him explain it.'

They watched silently as Whelan's big London chargehand strode into the room and sat in a chair beside his boss. Paul knew you had to be tough to run a concrete gang for the Whelan outfit, and this guy ticked all the boxes. He was six two or three in height, maybe fifteen stone, all muscle, a cold hard look in his eye, red hair cut tight, and four days of stubble on his chin. Vincent Whelan didn't waste time with introductions.

'Mick, fill Mister Bannon in on what we discussed earlier.'

The chargehand lit a cigarette and nodded.

'It's pretty simple, Mister Bannon. We plan to set fire to the silo.'

There were groans of disbelief and a few 'what the fucks,' but McMillan paid scant heed. He stared down the table at the impassive expression on Paul Bannon's face and decided, to hell with the rest of these fucks, he still had the attention of the only man who counted.

'Calm down, guys,' Paul said impatiently, 'and let's listen to the proposal.'

He turned and nodded to the impassive McMillan.

'We've solved a few problems like this in the past, Mister Bannon. Usually with smaller equipment than that mother-fucker you've got sitting out there on the floor. But it makes no difference because the principle's the same. We'll just light a bigger fire in the belly of that big bastard and I reckon we'll get the result we want.'

'Explain the principle, Mick,' Whelan interjected.

McMillan pulled on his cigarette and inhaled deeply.

'Mister Bannon, we climbed the side of the cylinder yesterday and took a look down from the top. The silo stands one hundred and seventeen feet above the ground, and the bottom third is blocked solid with congealed cement. I'm guessing it has been like that for maybe two or three years. My proposal is to inject a combustible mix of high-octane gasoline and diesel down into the cylinder. Set it on fire and repeat the process until we crack the surface and weaken the deposit. Then we insert a wrecking-crew in there with jackhammers and smash it out in sections.'

'It's never gonna work,' Bernard Shanley drawled, his tone bordering on the derogatory. 'Anyone who knows anything in the industry will tell you that concrete hardens as it ages. After seven days it's pretty hard. After twenty-eight days it's at optimum strength. After two years, forget it.'

'Correct if we're talking concrete,' McMillan responded, 'except that what's down in that silo isn't concrete. It's cement, pure and simple, and cement requires a composite injection of sand and gravel to give it optimal strength. Otherwise it never really gets there. My plan is we run a relay of crews inside the silo, along with a second team of engineers on the outside working the electrics and the drag-lines, repair what needs to be repaired, replace what needs to be replaced, and I reckon we're good to go.'

They sat silently contemplating a solution that had already become a discarded impossibility. Deep in concentration, hands cupped under his chin, Paul stared at McMillan.

'How long will it take?'

'All depends . . . three days, three weeks, maybe longer – it's impossible to say.'

During all of this, his eyes had never left McMillan. He nodded gravely, then for the first time he stood and glanced around the table.

'We've run out of options – let's go for it.'

An hour later, as the clock struck noon, the three crews assembled and advanced on the silo. The great hulking carcass had stood derelict for years, its working parts seized solid from disuse, vandalism and the ravages of time. Now all of a sudden it became the focus of extreme attention, as the possibility of its rehabilitation became just that, a possibility – nothing more.

Earlier a scaffold crew had run a working frame up the blindside of the silo, hidden from the prying eyes of the picketers swarming the peripheries. In mid-afternoon a flaming torch was lowered into the cylinder and the liquid-soaked cement ignited, sending a pall of black smoke hundreds of feet into the sky. Just after dark the flame was doused and the first crew were lowered onto the surface. Suddenly the rattle of the jack-hammers filled the air, the sound amplified within the cavernous cylinder as the crew attacked the surface non-stop until McMillan sent a signal down for them to climb back out.

'Well, boys. Any luck?'

'Nothing so far, Mick. We may as well be scratching it with a nailfile.'

If he was disappointed, McMillan showed no sign, as he stared thoughtfully down into the dark cylinder from his position high on the gantry. He turned to Tommy Randolph, a mechanic from the plant-yard.

'Set fire to it again, Tommy, but make the mix more combustible, and let it burn for six hours this time.'

'Sure, boss.'

An hour later they lowered the torch for the second time and the black smoke bellowed out from the top with such intensity that the skies for miles around were darkened and the air smelled like poison. Six hours later the crew descended onto the surface. The roar of the jack-hammers filled the night air with deafening intent as McMillan's team attacked the surface for the second time.

But again the news was bad when, later, the crew reported that they had failed to make a dent in the stubborn material. He swore silently, then turned to Tommy Randolph.

'Same again Tommy. Repeat the process.'

At midnight Vincent Whelan appeared on the floodlit gantry as the crew doused the flames for the fourth time. He stared at the grease and soot on the blackened face of his chargehand.

'The council are threatening to get a restraining order to stop us polluting the countryside.'

McMillan frowned.

'Get Bannon's lawyers to delay the process, or bribe the fuckers.'

'We're doing all of that, but that's only going to win us a certain amount of time. This show's being beamed prime-time into every home from Land's-End to John O'Groats. How're we doing?'

'Not fucking great.'

'So what's the plan?'

'We stay with it. You're just gonna have to trust me, boss.'

'Do what you have to do. We'll hold them off at the gates.'

'Thanks boss.'

The following morning lawyers for the Department of the Environment initiated injunction proceedings in the London courts to force the Bannon group to cease all operations at Croydon, citing the scale of pollution generated by the ongoing works. The black cloud from the silo had crossed the Surrey border into north Sussex and was heading in the direction of the heavily populated towns of Brighton and Eastbourne on the south coast. Bannon lawyers opposed the application on the basis that these temporary adjustments were essential to enable on-site works to proceed, and that the livelihoods of five thousand construction workers depended on a resolution of the process.

Eminent scientific evidence and environmental expertise was proffered to argue that the works posed minimal danger to the environment and negligible long-term impact. Both sides took a day to deliver their evidence, and on the morning of the third day Quentin Trevellian QC delivered his summing-up for the Bannon defence. Frank Considine sat in the back of the court and waited for the judge to deliver his verdict.

'Mister Trevellian has raised some points-of-law which require further consideration. I shall therefore need time to reflect on the evidence in greater detail. I shall deliver my decision the day after tomorrow. The court is adjourned.'

'It's the best we could have hoped for,' Trevellian said to John Considine as they walked quickly from the courtroom. 'I advise you to use the time well.'

'Getting Trevellian was a master-stroke,' Considine remarked to Paul when they met for dinner later. 'The most famous lawyer in the land, and at such short notice – I just don't know how you did it.'

Paul smiled.

'Trevellian was my outside-centre when I captained the Oxford Blues!'

★

The first signs of a breakthrough came on the approach to midnight the following night, as the remorseless attack on the silo entered its sixth day, the gangs going down in relay every six hours. During all this time Mick McMillan never left the gantry, the crews on the ground acutely aware that his reputation was on the line with his plan to rehabilitate the great silo. All of them knew that the very future of the project hung in the balance, depending on the outcome of this all-or-nothing strategy.

They also knew that anything less than a result would be interpreted as a victory by the thousands of picketers on the line outside, and on the inside, where for the first time the Whelan crews stood shoulder to shoulder with the Frank Brilly outfit, they felt they had something to prove to the world. The seven-hundred-strong Whelan contingent never left the ground while all of this was going on. They sure as hell weren't going to let their London chargehand Mick McMillan be hung out to dry.

At dawn on the sixth morning the jackhammers in the silo suddenly ceased and Jerry Gavin, the crew leader, shouted up from below.

'Mick, you'd better get down here and take a look.'

McMillan heaved his big frame onto the ladder and arrived on the platform minutes later. Jerry Gavin stared at him excitedly.

'Mick, it just seemed to happen suddenly. There's a crack along the centre the size of your fist, and the rest of the surface is like a mosaic.'

McMillan stared at the blackened surface, studying every inch of it intently.

'There's still thirty feet of this shit underneath, but we just might get lucky,' he grunted. 'The water the fuckers dumped in here probably didn't permeate all the way down, at least not to the same extent. The congealing process may just have formed a barrier below the surface, inhibiting deep saturation. Let's break it up and start the extraction process. My guess is the further down we go, the easier it gets. Well done, boys.'

McMillan stayed on the gantries all the following day and watched the tower-crane driver lower the bucket precisely down the centre of the silo. The crews on the platform hand-loaded loosened blocks of cement into the bucket and signalled the crane operator to raise the first load. They worked non-stop into the night, and as the first light of dawn broke over Surrey and the bucket descended into the silo for the umpteenth time, the crew down below sent word up to McMillan to retrieve the jackhammers.

With the first ten-feet extraction completed, the density had begun to change, as McMillan had predicted. The silo crew sent up a request for shovels to be lowered down to dig out the remaining twenty feet of material. The service crews, the engineers and the electricians, swarming the base of the silo, watched in silence as Mick McMillan, having spent six nights on the gantries, finally descended the scaffold, his features blackened beyond recognition. Frank Brilly stepped out from the nearest group and shook his hand.

'Well done, Mick. You cracked it in the end.'

McMillan stared at him and nodded.

'Thanks, Mister Brilly. Those words mean a lot coming from you.'

'All the time you've been up there, we've been reconfiguring the mixing plant, stripping it down, replacing the moving parts. Right now we're about ready to run a test. What's the timeframe at your end?'

'The silo'll be empty in an hour. We've got a water pipe hooked up to a sluice valve ready to wash it down. Give it another hour to dry, then fill the fucker with clean material.'

56

On the Monday morning of the fifth week, with still no end to the dispute, the mood on the picket line had been buoyant following definitive confirmation that Bannons had opted to repair rather than replace the silo. The black cloud hovering in the skies above the construction site seemed almost a death-knell, reflecting the company's futile attempt to restart the operation. It was a gamble that seemed doomed to failure as with each passing day the union tightened its stranglehold and displayed no sign of weakening.

The dispute was now entering its sixth week, and barring the odd, random movement of men and materials, there had been little evidence of on-site production when the Travis brothers arrived at union headquarters for their weekly meeting.

'They were never going to get a replacement silo across the line,' Tony Travis explained eagerly. 'They realise it boss, five weeks too late, and now they're looking to repair the on-site equipment. The problem for them is we've fucked it so bad they'll be wasting their time. We've got them on the run boss. This'll be over sooner than you think.'

Bradshaw stared at Tony Travis disparagingly.

'What do you know, you fucking muttonhead? I've been telling you all along not to underestimate these fuckers. This ain't over by a country mile.'

'I agree with Tony, boss,' Percy Hanratty interrupted, a tinge of annoyance in his voice. 'Bannons are under siege and that's the way it's gonna stay.'

Bradshaw glowered angrily at his second-in-command, but decided not to push it. Hanratty might be a low life parcel of shit, but he was a smart son-of-a-bitch.

In the past four years the balance of power had shifted imperceptibly but decidedly in the direction of Percy Hanratty.

Bradshaw knew it coincided with his own immobility – his perpetual confinement to this cursed wheelchair, a fact which every day reminded him to despise the Bannons all the more. He knew Hanratty had been labouring surreptitiously behind the scenes, visiting the union wards, attending late-night meetings, socialising with the rank and file. He was aware that Hanratty had the goodwill of the union's board, including those two Travis fucks, as well as Ravenscroft and Maynard.

He needed to deal with this decisively and soon, which was why he'd secretly been planning his exit-strategy right under the noses of these boneheads. So far he was pretty sure he hadn't been nobbled.

Still, he wasn't envisaging an immediate exit, at least not until the Bannons had been put down for good. This latest spoiled brat was proving a stubborn opponent, a fact which annoyed Bradshaw but didn't surprise him. His brother Frank had been one tough son-of-a-bitch, although maybe not quite tough enough. At least Ben Bradshaw was still breathing while the man responsible for his paraplegic condition lay six feet under.

Bradshaw's stomach tightened when he recalled meeting the old boy James all those years ago. He'd never forgotten the look in the old man's eyes; the undisguised revulsion; the withering hate-filled stare. Bradshaw knew that this man would have killed him if he could, and might still do so anyway. His thoughts were interrupted by Hanratty's whining, high-pitched tone.

'Boss, if Bannons fail to get that silo operational, then they're fucked. The environmental guys are crawling all over them. The skies are black with the shit that's spewing out every day. It's an ecological fucking disgrace, boss and it'll break those fucks in the end.'

'What in the fuck do you know?'

Hanratty was on a roll.

'The media are having a fucking field-day boss. It's a blessing in disguise . . . '

'Don't claim credit for this one, Percy. Bannons manufactured this fuck-up all on their own.'

Hanratty glowered at Bradshaw thinking, *what a mealy-mouthed, ungrateful old fuck.*

'I disagree.'

'You fucking what?'

Hanratty could sense the annoyance, but decided, what the fuck.

'What's happening out there is a hundred percent down to the siege this union has maintained. It's taken the Bannons until now to realise that sourcing new equipment was always going to be a monumental fucking nightmare. The pressure from the line is what's done it in the end, forced them to rethink their strategy and try kick-starting the silo. And if you want to see what a badly thought-out strategy that's turning out to be, you just need to switch on your TV.'

Bradshaw stared grumpily around the table, trying to gauge the mood. He didn't really like what he sensed.

'Yeah, well, who knows? Maybe you're right, and then again – maybe not. It ain't over until that fat fucking lady sings.'

He turned to Tony Travis.

'So what's the latest, Tony. I haven't got all fucking day.'

Never comfortable under the spotlight, Travis glanced nervously at Hanratty, but all he got was a sneaky smirk.

'They've got that Whelan goon McMillan up on the gantry trying to figure a way out, but so far all he's done is set fire to the fucking sky. He's been up there non-stop for three days.'

'You telling me he hasn't been down, even to take a shit!'

'No boss, I swear – not even a shit.'

Bradshaw stared at him incredulously.

'He uses a chamber-pot boss.'

'And where did you glean that disgusting little gem of information?'

Travis gulped, coughed, and then gulped again.

'Every morning he hands it to one of his goons boss and they turf it over the edge.'

'Over the edge of what?'

'Over the edge of the hoardings, on top of our members, boss.'

'Fuck.'

'My sentiments, boss. These fuckers have fuck-all sophistication.'

Bradshaw gawped at him.

'And I suppose you went to Swiss finishing school, you fucking tart.'

Hanratty glanced around the table furtively.

'There's something else we need to discuss, boss.'

'Oh really.'

'Yeah really.'

'Get on with it, Perce. I'm all fucking ears.'

'Boss, the boys on the line are pissed about not getting paid. Last week, we cut their supplement by half, and it sure as hell didn't go down too well. And this morning Walter in accounts is telling me there's fuck-all left in the coffers for this week. Our boys are a loyal bunch of bastards, but at the end of the day they've got to eat, same as the next guy. If the guys on the line think we don't have the funds to pay them, I reckon they'll blow a gasket.'

Bradshaw yawned noisily.

'This whole fucking thing's a drain on resources, and Walter's got it right. There's only a few pennies left in the account. Simple as that.'

Hanratty stared at him in disbelief.

'Jesus boss, we've been collecting dues from these guys since forever. There's got to be millions in the account. I can't tell them we've got nothing left to pay. They'll fucking lynch me.'

'You'll think of something,' Bradshaw responded testily. 'Remind them that this union's been negotiating on their behalf forever, and they'd better maintain the siege or else negotiate their own fucking wages from here on in.'

They stared in disbelief as he spun his chair and exited the boardroom without further ado. Tony Travis was first to break the silence.

'If there ain't more money in the pot, we're snookered,' he stated flatly. 'I'll go have a word with that fucking clown Walter.'

'Maybe we really are skint,' Roger Maynard added gravely. 'We've been sustaining six thousand guys for all these weeks. Maybe the money really is gone. The boss might be right to expect our guys to maintain the siege.'

'Like fuck,' Hanratty replied. 'Eaten bread is soon forgotten. Unless this thing is funded, it'll evaporate before our eyes. The only loyalty these fucks have is to their wage-packets.'

57

The pressure on the police to impose a semblance of order increased with each passing week, their political masters demanding some form of decisive action to help stem the stream of violence. The resource allocation of fifteen hundred riot police appeared to provide a temporary respite, at least until the tragic death of a nineteen-year-old Glaswegian striker hit by a Bannon delivery truck exiting the site in the middle of the seventh week. The death of a fifth striker ratcheted the tension back up to fever pitch and left the politicians baying for blood.

The clamour for a response manifested itself in the issuing of a warrant for the arrest of construction boss Paul Bannon on a charge of inciting violence, constituting a danger to the public. The arrest ignited a media storm, the television images focusing on the prisoner being led handcuffed through the main gates by a dozen policemen, with riot police on both sides struggling to contain the enraged strikers.

From their position on the front line, Barney Wigglesworth and Archie McMaster watched the gates swing open and the police bundle their prisoner through. Sensing Wigglesworth was about to lunge, Archie held him in a vice-like grip.

'Are you out of your fucking mind! Relax!'

Wigglesworth glowered hatefully from behind the wall of riot police, but Archie held his shoulder firm, then turned his attention to Bannon, the focal point of this murderous wall of abuse. On the face of it he seemed unconcerned almost to the point of boredom as he strolled forward chewing gum, casually taking his seat in the back of the police van. When the doors closed Archie watched the convoy of vehicles speed away, sirens blaring, and couldn't help but feel a grudging admiration for his hated opponent.

'I swear I'll get him someday,' Wigglesworth grunted.

'Yeah, you and the rest of these fucks,' he pondered, as he watched the convoy fade in the distance.

Later in the day there was uproar on the union line following the announcement of Paul Bannon's release from custody on foot of a petition to the High Court by Queen's Counsel Quentin Trevellian.

★

She sat watching the late-evening news in her apartment by the Thames near Chelsea, the picketers screaming abuse, hurling debris, and waging all-out war with the cops. The strike was now entering its eighth week, the intensity of the violence showed no sign of waning and the public outcry escalated. She watched the cameras zoom in as the gates swung back and the police escorted him through.

She listened to the protesters vent their anger, focusing their collective hatred on this one man. Her heart skipped a beat as the camera lingered on the face of a man she had known half a lifetime ago. He walked through the midst of those chaotic scenes, his expression unperturbed, his demeanour calm. His nonchalant lack of concern seemed to anger the protesters to a level of murderous hysteria, but in her heart of hearts she knew they were wasting their time. No mob and no living person, would frighten this man.

58

Two seemingly unrelated incidents became the precursor to the first faint hint of a wavering in the resolve of the strikers as the stranglehold at Croydon entered its fifty-fifth day. During mid-morning break, while the picketers milled around the mobile canteens eating sandwiches and drinking mugs of coffee, the sudden burst of an engine ricocheted in the air and a cloud of smoke billowed into the clear blue sky.

Unable to see above the hoardings, the strikers converged on the lookout tower, a thirty-foot makeshift platform, which had been constructed beyond the entrance in the early days of the dispute. The lookout stared across the top of the hoarding and scratched his head, then turned to face the men milling around the base.

'The silo's back in action, the drag-lines, the electric shovels . . . everything!'

Two elevator cages packed with construction workers ascended the north face of the nearest tower block, the hated name 'Whelan' stamped across their jackets. The tower-crane bucket swung low across the sky and climbed steadily upwards, laden to the brim with freshly mixed concrete. The men on the ground stared in silence as the bucket panned across the twelfth-floor platform and dumped its load onto the formwork before resuming its journey back down the side of the building. Then after the speediest of turnarounds, the big bucket climbed back up to the top, with liquid concrete lapping over the sides.

After four years of stagnation and a deadly fifty-five-day lockout, the Bannon site at Croydon had at long last returned to full production. Paul watched from high up on the twelfth floor as the third bucket traced along the side of the building and dumped another load onto the platform. He turned to Mick McMillan.

'I've a lot to thank you for, Mick. You solved our biggest problem the fastest way.'

The chargehand stared at him.

'You guys would have figured it out in the end. Sheer necessity would have focused your minds.'

'Yeah, maybe, but it's a dual hit. Our production lines are back in action and we've driven a steel wedge through the morale of the men out there on the line.'

McMillan turned and spat over the side.

'Fuck the lot of them, Mister Bannon. They're getting what they deserve.'

The chargehand stared down at the sprawling mixing plant, the life blood of a construction site that stretched for a mile in either direction. The thundering roar of the giant mixer and the whine of the tower-cranes crisscrossing the skies made him ponder the irony of Paul Bannon's words, and the clear-cut, devastating message it sent down to the strikers below: you thought it was all over, but this fight goes on!

★

The recommencement of site-works at Croydon coincided with the publication of an article in The *London Daily News* under the headline, 'Internal Probe Reveals Union's Hidden Bank Accounts.'

The article, by investigative journalist Tim Robertson, read:

A recent inquiry into the financial affairs of London's leading construction union has uncovered the existence of hidden bank deposit accounts held in the name of Benjamin Robert Bradshaw, believed to be the same 'Ben Bradshaw' currently chairman of the Building and Allied Trades Union, a position he has held for the past fifteen years. The union has been recently embroiled in a much-publicised dispute with the Bannon Construction Group at Croydon town centre. The deposit amounts are understood to exceed seven million pounds. A union spokesman refused to comment . . .

The article created a furore at union headquarters when hundreds of picketers converged on the building screaming blue murder, and demanding an explanation as to why their wage packets had been unaccountably halved the previous week. Not being in full possession of the facts didn't prevent the union's shop stewards from quickly drawing the inevitable conclusion. If Ben Bradshaw had salted eight million pounds of union funds into a hidden deposit account, it went a way towards explaining why the coffers were empty, with sweet fuck-all left to fund the dispute.

All morning the union's downstairs reception remained flooded with noisy protesters baying for an explanation, but with the notable exception of the young, terrified receptionist Thelma, the place had long since been abandoned.

At dawn the following morning a convoy of trucks transporting washed sand and gravel exited the gates of Frank Brilly's aggregate quarry in West Sussex and began the journey north along the motorway to the Bannon construction site at Croydon. Seventy men sat alongside the drivers to protect the delivery on the final leg of its perilous journey through the union blockades. When the convoy crossed the Surrey border, a police patrol car pulled out ahead and escorted them the last few miles to the construction site. Fifty-six days had elapsed since Paul Bannon's lightning fist had taken Barney Wigglesworth down and precipitated the deadly clash that followed in its wake, the longest construction dispute in post-war history.

They exited the motorway at the Croydon junction and turned onto the ring-road to negotiate the final leg of the journey. The light drizzle they encountered crossing into Surrey had gradually worsened into what was now a teeming downpour. The police car switched on its strobe-lights when the first of the seventeen trucks turned into the one-mile stretch leading to the construction site. The lead driver saw the grey outlines of the seven towers materialise in the distance, their hulking shapes shrouded in mist, and as he advanced ever closer, he strained his eyes and gasped.

'They've gone! The strikers have gone!'

Up ahead the gates swung open and the police car peeled away, leaving the convoy to run the last stretch unimpeded across the empty spaces where the picketers had held the ground for eight ferocious weeks. The riot police were still there, standing in groups, helmets resting at their feet, their random presence and bemused expressions heightening the surreal atmosphere.

The lead driver yanked on a pulley and the horn from the big Scania bellowed hoarsely as the men up on the platforms downed tools and turned to watch them make their final approach. With all horns blaring the convoy crossed the line and rumbled through the gates to its final destination beside the aggregate pits scattered along the silo. Sustained cheering filled the air, the thousands manning the platforms acknowledging that this was the moment Bannons had beaten the biggest union blockade the country had ever seen.

The men seated around the boardroom table four storeys below the north tower ceased their conversation and listened in muted silence.

In the afternoon the banner headline in the early edition of The *London Evening News* proclaimed, 'Construction Siege Ends as Bannons Tough It Out Against Warring Unions'. The article read:

> The ending of the protracted construction dispute at Croydon was universally welcomed with the lifting of the union blockade earlier today. The bitterly fought dispute was marred by the loss of five lives and scores of others sustaining serious injury. Its resolution is believed to have been precipitated by revelations concerning the illegal movement of union-related funds into personal deposit accounts controlled by union president Ben Bradshaw. It is understood that these accounts have been frozen following the issuing of injunction proceedings in the High Court initiated by the union executive.

59

The Mercedes swept off Park Lane into upper Brook Street and drew up outside the restaurant. The maître d' met him at the door and shook his hand.

'You're the last to arrive, Mister Bannon. Your guests are already seated.'

He followed him down the stairs, across the crowded room to where the others sat at a large round corner table: Andy Carmichael, Jamie Sinclair, Steve Richie, John Considine, Vincent Whelan, Anthony Selwyn, Frank Brilly and at his specific request the chargehand Mick McMillan. He sat in the last empty chair between Anthony Selwyn and John Considine.

'Gentlemen,' the maître d' smiled, 'we have pheasant from the Highlands, which doesn't appear on the menu. It's one of Mister Bannon's favourites, and if anyone wishes to partake, then the good news is we have plenty in stock.'

Three months had elapsed since the ending of the strike, and in that time Bannons had commenced construction on four West End developments.

The topping-out ceremony for the seven towers at Croydon had been completed that morning, and with five million square feet already pre-let on long-term leases, Bannon's London agents had pre-sold the seven towers to the British Overseas Pension Fund in a deal which would singlehandedly wipe out all existing borrowings and render the remaining assets debt free.

A recently completed valuation of the debt-free assets by Timothy Hyland Associates, the London-based chartered surveyors, was rumoured to be in excess of two point four billion pounds.

Paul nodded to the maître d' when he returned to take the order.

'Everyone seems keen to taste the Scottish pheasant, Silvano.'

Grange Abbey

'Your usual wine, Mister Bannon?'

Paul nodded, and the maître d' stepped back smoothly to allow the waiters to materialise with plates of seared scallops and prawns, followed later by the roast stuffed pheasant with new English potatoes on the side, accompanied by copious quantities of '61 Chateau Margaux.

'God be with the days when we'd hop on a plane and shoot our own pheasant on Grange Abbey,' John Considine remarked, 'although this Scottish shit doesn't taste bad once it's been drowned in the Margaux.'

They laughed loudly.

'Gentlemen,' Anthony Selwyn said, 'our host has an announcement to make – he'd like you guys to be the first to hear this.'

'Holy shit,' Considine grunted. 'You haven't asked Ben Bradshaw to join the board of Bannons!'

They laughed again, loudly.

'Not quite,' he smiled. 'But you did mention Grange Abbey earlier, Johnny, and amidst all the carnage and destruction surrounding the businesses my father created, sadly we also lost Grange Abbey. It was what upset me most of all.'

He glanced across at Jamie, whose eyes were cast down. He could only imagine what Jamie Sinclair must be feeling right now – the Grange had been his home too. Considine, his napkin stuffed in his collar, sat silently in his chair, his expression grim. Paul placed a hand on Anthony's shoulder.

'And then one day I asked my greatest friend to retrieve it, and that is exactly what he did. He snatched it from the clutches of the receivers and delivered it back to me.'

He picked up a glass of Pol Roger and stared into the depths of its golden glow.

'Grange Abbey is the house where I was born. It is the land where I was raised, and its soil is the soil in which my brother Frank lies buried. For your abiding friendship, and for all of these things, I thank you, Anthony.'

He gazed around the table at these men who had stood with him during the ferocious confrontation with Ben Bradshaw's union, their faces solemn at the mention of his brother's name.

'In a few days I make a return journey to Grange Abbey for the first time, and when I make that journey I want you, the people I respect the most, the ones who helped me win the greatest fight of my life, to come there with me.'

There were a few nods and grunts.

'And besides,' he grinned, 'it's the beginning of the November shoot!'

'Done deal,' Considine bellowed.

Anthony Selwyn smiled contemplatively.

'Gentlemen, I offer you a toast to Grange Abbey.'

They raised their glasses and drank.

★

Later they moved from the restaurant to the super-charged atmosphere of the cocktail bar at Annabels. The famous club in Berkeley Square was heaving with late-night revellers gyrating to the sound of the Rolling Stones' smash hit 'Let's Spend the Night Together'. Considine sat on a bar stool and sucked on a Montecristo. Jamie moved through the crowd in his direction.

'Mind if I join you?'

'Be my guest,' he nodded, motioning to the seat beside him.

'Another drink, Mister Considine?' the barman asked.

'Scotch on the rocks by two, Marco.'

Jamie sat silently until the drinks arrived. He seemed preoccupied. They clinked.

'Somethin' on your mind Jamie?'

Jamie downed the whisky in one gulp and stared into his empty glass.

'I was wondering if you're still in touch with my sister.'

Considine glanced at him, surprised, then swirled his Scotch and slugged it.

'That what this is about?'

'It has been on my mind. I've been meaning to ask.'

Considine took his time replying. He stubbed his cigar and lit another.

'Only on rare occasions, and usually at her behest.'

His initial annoyance at Jamie's inclusion on the team had

mellowed during the Croydon stand-off. Jamie's work ethic had always been beyond question, but his reckless lack of fear during the interminable day-to-day confrontations with the most militant elements of the union had been a sight to behold, and ultimately justified his inclusion, or at least explained it. His initial misgivings were soon forgotten.

'I miss her after all these years,' Jamie said quietly, all the time studiously avoiding the big man's gaze. 'More so lately, if the truth be known.'

In the years since she departed, he'd often thought to ask as to her whereabouts. But John Considine was a fearsome man who treated him with disdain and made scant effort to hide it. Their time together during the confrontation with Bradshaw's union had forced them to tolerate and respect one another for the greater good. But beyond that, Jamie couldn't tell if it had sealed their friendship – with this man, you just never knew. He saw him nod to the barman and two more drinks materialised instantly.

'I'm uncomfortable discussing your sister with anyone, but especially with you, Jamie. None of us can rewrite the past, and no one knows it better than me. But that still doesn't alter the fact that you and the rest of them cut her loose and let her swim with the sharks.'

Jamie gave him a fleeting glance.

'You don't need to remind me. I do it myself every day of my life.'

'Do whatever you have to do, Jamie, but don't come looking to me for forgiveness.'

They were silent for a while and Jamie seemed forlorn. He stood to leave, but Considine held his arm.

'I can tell you that what's on the inside she keeps well hidden, and what's on the outside seems OK. When you delivered her into my care, from that moment she became my responsibility, and anyone who knows me will know I take my responsibilities seriously. She's been to hell and back, and I've looked out for her along the way as best I could. I've been there for her when she needed me, but her biggest problem is a problem I can't solve – that's the one she's got to solve herself.'

'And what might that one be?'

He gestured towards the end of the bar.

'She's in love with him.'

Jamie glanced to where Paul stood beside a beautiful brunette, smiling up into his eyes. He stared at them in contemplative mood.

'Seems like he's getting by.'

Considine shrugged dismissively.

'He lives his life the best way he knows how,' he replied. 'There are ships that pass in the night, and that lady's just one of 'em.'

60

The days turned into weeks; the weeks turned into months. The trip to Grange Abbey came and went, and Bannons' London operations forged full steam ahead. The management team concentrated on carving a ring-fenced strategy for the future, and the company emerged from the debilitating effects of the union siege, growing ever stronger as the production lines powered into top gear. The construction industry shook off the lingering effects of the seventies recession and the property market rose on a cocktail of increased demand, optimism, and a heady influx of international funds into London. And then, out of the blue, the call came.

'I regret having to belatedly tell you that your father was diagnosed with cancer last August. Your parents were adamant that nothing should distract you from your engagement with the unions. They expressly instructed that you were not to be informed.'

He was astounded.

'But that was six months ago. You've hidden this from me all that time!'

'I felt honour-bound to carry out your father's wishes to the letter.'

He stared into the distance, knowing that he could hardly criticise this middle-aged lady for her loyalty and integrity to a man who all the days of his life had been the recipient of those virtues. Suddenly forced to contemplate the imminent demise of the one person he had always considered to be immortal, his annoyance gave way to a profound sense of heartfelt grief.

'What shall I do, Janine?'

'You must come immediately – he's extremely ill.'

The lear jet accelerated down the runway at Luton Airport

and soared into the stormy grey skies. The telephone call from his father's secretary had spurred him into immediate action. He eased the bucket-seat into reclining position and stared absentmindedly out the window. *So typical*, he thought as he contemplated his parents' insistence that even the spectre of imminent death should be withheld lest it impact negatively on the business at hand.

The plane touched down in brilliant sunshine at Nice Airport and taxied to the VIP terminal. Janine was standing by his father's Bentley waiting to meet him. Customs clearance was routine. He flashed his passport and they waved him through immediately. Minutes later they began the short journey to the villa.

'How is he, Janine?'

'He knows you're on your way and he wishes to see you the instant you arrive.'

The vagueness in her response didn't mask the urgency of her words. They travelled the rest of the journey in silence, crossing swiftly onto the Cap and skirting the village of Saint Jean, its sleepy harbour dotted with myriad ocean-going yachts and cruisers. There were dozens of cars scattered along the entrance to the villa. A catering van pulled sideways to allow them to pass. The house itself was a hive of activity. His mother stood waiting by the door.

'My darling,' she smiled, 'it's so comforting to have you here.'

She leaned forward and kissed his cheek.

'Forgive us for keeping you in the dark about all of this, but your father was insistent, and . . . well, you should know what he's like.'

He smiled and hugged her closely.

'You look tired, mother.'

She gave an involuntary sob. He held her in his arms.

'I've tried to stay strong, especially for him. What else can I do?'

'You've always been his strength.'

She sighed.

'The thought of losing him is so painful, and yet one becomes strangely attuned to its inevitability. He's been clinging on to the last vestiges of mortality, so you must go to him now while there's still time.'

He glanced down the stairs, then at her.

'Still the same room?'

She nodded. 'It's what he wanted.'

He descended the stairs two levels, then walked to the end of the corridor and pushed the last door open. The room was bright and airy, the double doors to the terrace thrown open, the sun's rays streaming across the tiled floor, the sound of the ocean breaking on the rocks far below. A nurse seated by the bed stood to greet him.

'We've been expecting you,' she whispered. 'I'll leave you for a while. I'm outside if you need me.'

When the door closed he walked to the bedside and sat in her chair.

'Father,' he said quietly. 'It's me . . . Paul.'

The old man lay in the bed so still he could already have been dead. His emaciated face and hands were as pale as the stark white sheets. He held his shrivelled hand in his own and waited silently. The eyes flickered.

'Relax, I'm not dead yet,' he whispered.

'I'm glad to hear it.'

The hint of a smile appeared like a shadow on his lips. His head turned and he gazed up at his youngest son.

'Such a good boy.'

He could feel his heart bursting as he struggled to hold back the tears.

'My beloved son, I'm proud of all you've achieved.'

'You taught me well. No man had a better teacher.'

'What you did . . . in London . . . fantastic result . . . such a good boy.'

He stared down at the shrivelled face of the man he had hero-worshipped all his life. His voice faltered.

'Whatever good is in me I inherited from you.'

He felt his father's grip tighten with a strength that surprised him.

'You've done well, but your business isn't finished . . . yet.'

The intensity in his voice startled him.

'Not finished . . . '

His eyes flickered. His breathing sounded raspy and shallow. Except for the strength of his grip, he might have been dead to the world. He watched in trepidation his lips part in a barely audible whisper.

'You must . . . look after that little girl. I promised her . . . on the night of her wedding.'

He stared at his father, astounded.

'You promised . . . Francesca?'

He waved a hand dismissively, then nodded, barely.

'Wherever she is, you must . . . find her.'

He could hardly believe what he was hearing. The old man's eyes opened and he stared up at him.

'And then you must kill him.'

He gazed down into his ghost-like face, wondering if he had heard correctly.

'What did you say, father?'

'You must . . . ' his father's grip tightened, '. . . kill Bradshaw!'

He stared at him incomprehensibly, then saw his head tilt weakly to one side and his eyes close. The spectre of imminent death filled the room.

'Bradshaw's in jail, father – in Wormwood Scrubs, serving five years for embezzling union funds . . . '

He waved a hand dismissively.

'I know . . . I know . . . but you have to find a way. He belongs in . . . hell.'

His voice trailed off and his lips moved in a whisper.

'He tried to destroy my family . . . your brother Frank . . . and now you, the only son I have left. You must give me your word . . . '

He stared mesmerised at his father's fragile, emaciated carcass and pondered the last desperate wish of a dying man, his once-powerful voice barely audible, his breathing laboured . . . His eyes . . . closed.

He squeezed his wizened hand and leaned down close.

'I give you my word,' he whispered.

'And Francesca . . . '

'I will fulfil the promise you made to her.'

The flicker of a smile, and then his grip slackened. His father's sapphire-blue eyes stared up at him, but with the slackening of the grip, the life force had slipped away. He held his hand to his cheek and allowed the tears to wash over it.

James Patrick Bannon had drawn his last breath.

★

They walked along the lower cliff path, the breeze warm in their faces, the ocean still and calm, the sky cloudless and blue. It was mid-morning and he was scheduled to leave the villa in the early afternoon. Five days had elapsed since the burial, a private ceremony with barely a handful of close friends in attendance. Catherine seemed troubled, preoccupied, melancholy, the sadness in her eyes studiously hidden behind impenetrable Cartier sunglasses. She linked his arm until they reached the outer point beside the ocean where the property ended, and then she turned to him.

'Your father and I . . . we had no secrets.'

'I would never have thought otherwise.'

'Then if I ask you something, you must be forthright and answer me truthfully.'

There was a hardness to her tone which surprised him.

'But of course.'

Her gaze was steady and unflinching. He wondered where this might be leading.

'When you went to him that morning . . . did he say anything?'

He tensed but tried not to show it. How much could she ever really know?

'Nothing other than what you might expect. He asked me to find Francesca – to look after her. He told me he was proud of me . . . of what I had achieved . . . '

She reached out and took his hands in hers. There was an intensity about her that made him flinch.

'Is that all?'

'Yes . . . as I recall . . . '

'He told you to kill that hateful man Bradshaw.'

She had warned him to be truthful, but her question had

thrown him. His silence seemed to say it all. She smiled, but it wasn't a warm smile.

'I thought as much,' she said matter-of-factly. 'And of course you said yes to that.'

She didn't wait for an answer. Instead she led him through the trees to an old stone seat.

'Have I ever once asked you for anything in this life?'

'Never,' he replied.

'Never,' she said, 'until today that is.'

She removed her sunglasses and looked him in the eye.

'Your father asked you to find Francesca, and that you must do. But I am asking you – unashamedly begging you – not to carry out this shameful act. You promised your father, but your father is gone from the world. I loved him with every fabric of my being, but as God is my judge, he had no right to ask you this. Ben Bradshaw is not a threat to us – he never will be. Let him languish in jail for the rest of his miserable life.'

Something seemed to upset her. She turned away momentarily, and when she spoke her words had a pleading ring.

'You have to promise me this one thing, or otherwise you'll destroy whatever peace of mind is left for me in this world.'

He gazed at this wise, intelligent lady, knowing that there was only one answer he could give. His father was dead and gone and would never know.

'I give you my solemn word I will not carry out this act. It releases me from a promise I would have dreaded fulfilling.'

She looked up into his face and smiled.

'Thank you, my darling. You can take me back to the house now.'

The path meandered along the ocean's edge and climbed gently towards the villa. She linked his arm. They walked in silence.

'There's something I must ask you,' he said eventually, thinking there might never be another opportunity like this.

'Then ask,' she said simply.

'Something my father said to me.'

'Say what you have to say,' she said in the same gentle tone.

He led her to a seat on the shady side of the veranda.

'You remember my twenty-first birthday, when I came to the villa, and he invited me to his study . . . '

'Of course.'

'He handed me a cheque and afterwards we spoke for a while, and then he said a strange thing. He said to me, he's not your brother . . . not like Frank.'

He felt her grip tighten.

'Is that it?' she asked.

Her face was ghostly pale, but he knew this needed to be said.

'And then before he died he told me that I was the only real son he had left. A figure of speech, I wondered, or perhaps some deeper meaning. I shall never know the answer unless I hear it from you.'

She seemed to reflect on this for an age, and then she let his hand slip, and began speaking in a detached monotone.

'After the tragedy, your father and I swore we would never speak about this again – but your father is in his grave now. Frank is gone; Simon is gone; and you and I are all that are left.'

He listened to her words with growing trepidation. *After the tragedy, she had said. After what tragedy? What on earth could she have meant?* There was a black feeling in his heart about what was to come.

'It was Christmas morning and the house was busy with the comings and goings of the festive season. There were log-fires blazing in the hearths, delivery vans in the yard, and frantic preparations for an open-house reception after church. You can imagine the activity now, of course, but then you were only two years of age and barely able to walk. The morning was sunny and cold, and I can still remember the frost on the meadow infusing a magical air about the place. Maggie and the others had been busy since early morning – I hardly had time to catch my breath, until suddenly some deep-rooted instinct prompted me to glance out the window.

'I stopped and stared across to the river, to a solitary, childlike figure standing by the water. The air was crisp and clear, and the sun shimmered off the frozen land, but the river was such a distance away I could barely see. I stood rooted to the spot, until it gradually began to dawn on me that this child

. . . this distant, faraway child could only be Simon. He was barely six at the time, his brown curls stark against the snow, his eyes cold as a witch's shiver – always such a strange . . . silent little boy. I turned and ran quickly to the room where he and Nancy slept . . . '

'Nancy . . . '

She glanced at him with folded arms, and continued in the same detached monotone.

'Simon's twin sister . . . we never told you about Nancy.'

He stared at her, thunderstruck, hardly daring to breathe.

'When we adopted him from the orphanage he was one of a twin. The nuns seemed anxious that they shouldn't be separated . . . '

'Simon . . . adopted!'

She dropped her eyes and stared at her trembling hands.

'There were complications when Frank was born. Initially everything seemed normal, but then later I began to haemorrhage and I was rushed to intensive care. I almost died giving birth and I almost lost Frank too. Afterwards the doctors advised me never to conceive again or otherwise it could be fatal – a devastating setback for the two of us at the time. Your father and I craved more children, but all the experts assured us that another pregnancy would be catastrophic and must never be allowed to happen. Your father was insistent that my wellbeing should be paramount, and it was afterwards that we decided to adopt. We realised that there could be no more natural children, and so adoption seemed the logical next step. Two years later an opportunity arose and we embraced it – a heaven-sent opportunity to adopt a little girl . . . and a boy.'

She turned to him and smiled.

'Then afterwards, a miracle! I was pregnant again, and we held our breath until the morning you were born, and the house was filled with the magical sound of a baby crying.'

He listened mesmerised to a story he was hearing for the very first time. He stared at his mother as she sat silently, immersed in the realms of some long-forgotten memory. After an age he heard her sigh.

'Something made me go back to the window. I looked out,

and that was when I saw it . . . '

'Saw what Mother?'

Her mouth tightened in an anguished grimace.

'The pram,' she whispered. 'I saw the pram.'

Her lip quivered, and her voice descended into a trance-like rasp.

'He used to push her in the pram, everywhere – the corridors, the kitchens, all around the yard. It was a game they played all day, a childlike ritual acted out in their own little dream world. I walked slowly from the house, down through the fields, tracing the wheel-tracks in the frost. Then I began to run . . . and run . . . and run . . . '

She hesitated and her voice seemed to catch.

'When I arrived there, I was breathless. He turned and looked at me so serenely, a dispassionate smile on his small, angelic face. "Simon you must be so cold," I said.

'"No Mamma," he replied.

'I stared at the pram turned sideways on the riverbank.

'"Simon, my darling, where is Nancy?"

'He didn't reply, just kept on staring . . . kept on smiling. Then he turned ever so slowly and gazed into the water. I followed his gaze and I saw my baby staring back at me, her face suspended beneath the surface, her blonde hair flowing, her eyes wide and startled, still open but devoid of life.

'"Oh Simon," I cried, my heart-wrenching sobs echoing across the empty spaces, "what have you done to my little baby?"

'I covered my face with handfuls of frosted snow, but my tears burnt through and fell on the frozen earth. I turned to him and took his icy hands in mine.

"What have you done Simon? Why would you want to hurt my little Nancy?"

Even in the sultry heat of the Mediterranean he realised his mother was shivering.

'And what did he say, mother?' he whispered.

'He said . . . ' Tears welled in her eyes – he couldn't recall seeing her cry like this for his father. Perhaps she had mourned his passing somewhere in the privacy of her own grief.

'He said . . . "I never wanted to hurt her, mamma." I sank to my knees and sobbed the way I'm sobbing now. I screamed at him. "Then why did you *do* this?"

'He didn't reply; just kept staring at me. I shook him like a rag-doll and screamed at him again.

' "Why . . . did . . . you . . . do this!"

'He looked up at me and smiled.

' "Because I wanted to hurt *you*, mamma." '

61

'I wonder if we could meet . . . '

It was a voice he hadn't heard for almost a year, but one he recognised instantly. She heard him say, 'Guys, gimme five,' then the shuffling of feet and the sound of a door closing.

'Hi.'

'Hi.'

'Everything . . . OK?'

'Yes, but I need to see you.'

He glanced at his watch. Still only seven past seven. The early hour didn't surprise him. Her hours were . . . unconventional.

'Any time after six is good for me.'

'I'm at the Dorchester, the Park Suite, eighth floor. Shall we say for seven?'

'I'll be there.'

That summer the August temperatures in London soared into the mid-thirties. The streets teemed with visitors basking in the steamy summer heat – brown-legged girls with long hair and short skirts, young couples with children, flooding into Hyde Park, laughing, chatting and thronging the cafes along the Serpentine. He stood sipping champagne by the open door to the terrace, then turned and casually glanced at her. She seemed relaxed, serene, inwardly content, her expression bemused. She studied him and smiled faintly.

'You seem in a reflective mood,' she said quietly.

He shrugged.

'A little bit of yearning is all. I look across to the park and think, oh to be young and free again. I know I'd savour it all the more next time around.'

She smiled broadly, her eyes twinkling. She really liked

John Considine. She waited for him to sit, her eyes tracking him across the floor, all the time observing, her gaze never leaving him. He lit a cigar and sipped the ice-cold champagne.

'So, what's on your mind?'

Straight to the point, as always with him – jettison the bullshit and deal with the business at hand.

'A couple of things,' she responded flippantly.

He watched and waited, but she was in no hurry.

'I need your advice . . . '

He motioned with his cigar, 'I'm listening.'

But as if she hadn't heard, she seemed to take an age to gather her thoughts. Then eventually, 'I'm giving up the business. It has served its purpose. There's no reason to continue.'

He studied her, careful to hide his surprise, his expression noncommittal.

'I'm glad to hear it. When did you decide this?'

'About a month ago, when I first suspected someone was following me.'

He placed his glass carefully on the table, his focus sharper now. The lady wasn't prone to exaggeration, and that meant that this had to be for real. In the lawless, unchartered jungle in which she operated, her antennae were primed to sense the faintest whiff of danger.

'Do you have any idea who it might be?'

She twirled her champagne glass, pondering the contents.

'No I don't. It's hardly more than an intuition, but whoever it is that's out there is good – very good; highly trained; professional. I doubt most people would have noticed.'

'And this is why you've decided to quit?'

'No, of course not – it isn't the first time. It's just that this time it's coincidental.'

She spoke so calmly she might have been discussing the weather, but then this one was an expert at camouflage.

'I feel that there's a . . . malignant presence out there.'

'You can sense it?'

He didn't expect a response and he didn't get one; he already knew the answer, and he also knew that this needed to be dealt with – had to be dealt with, urgently.

'You mentioned there were a couple of things.'

'Yes I did,' she replied, standing to refill his glass, then her own. She closed the door to the terrace and sashayed across the room, the champagne flute in one hand, the other in the pocket of her tight blue jeans. She sat on an arm of the sofa and gazed at him.

'How is he?' she asked quietly.

He contemplated her as she sat there, poised and beautiful, her golden hair swept behind her ears, a stray strand hanging loose, barely thirty, he guessed, the look in her eyes reflecting a lifetime of experience far beyond those years.

'I rarely see him since the war with the unions ended. He maintains a low profile.'

He could see she seemed interested in hearing anything about this.

'Bannons has been transformed from a construction vehicle into a trading company with a rental portfolio to die for. Oh don't get me wrong – construction is still at the beating heart of it all, except that these days they farm the bulk of it out to independent contractors. It limits exposure to unforeseen elements, hostile unions, and so on. We beat them once, but they can always re-emerge. These days the company is an acquisitive private entity, targeting trophy assets in prime locations at prices vendors seem unable to refuse.'

She began to speak but then her voice trailed away. She sat back and gazed at him, her eyes glistening in the low rays of the evening sun.

'I want to see him,' she said quietly. 'It's the reason I asked you here.'

Somewhere in the farthest reaches of his mind he had known it would always come to this. He stared at her reflectively.

'It's been how many years . . . fourteen . . . fifteen? Does he even know you exist?'

This seemed to upset her. She turned her face away.

'He knows I exist,' she whispered.

He caught an involuntary quiver of the lip. The tenor of his words had thrown her. He apologised immediately.

'I never meant to upset you. I'm just a blunt old fool. Those words must have sounded harsh.'

There was a vulnerability about her he hadn't often seen. She glanced at him, then dropped her eyes.

'Is there . . . you know . . . someone?'

He lit another cigar and pulled on it heavily.

'From time to time, yeah – but never the same squeeze. I ain't no psychologist, but my guess is that for a man supposedly in possession of most of the things in life, emotional fulfilment sure ain't one of them. There's a barrier that no one penetrates.'

She nodded as if this was something she already knew.

'Please, advise me what to do, John.'

He stared at her thoughtfully, his mind racing.

'He's in the South of France these past few weeks . . . since Catherine passed away.'

'Catherine Bannon . . . dead!'

He nodded.

'A year to the day James passed. They recovered her body from the ocean a mile below the villa. Last time I visited she took me aside and confided in me that life had lost all its meaning for her the day James died.'

'Oh John, she was such a strong, charismatic lady. How unbearably sad for all of you.'

'Sad for the ones left behind,' he responded thoughtfully, 'but James and she had the most wonderful life, you know. When he died she held it together for a while, but we could all sense the grinding sorrow etched in the fabric of her soul. Her parting was a surprise to some, but not to me. For me it carried with it a certain . . . inevitability.'

She watched him stare wistfully into a cloud of cigar smoke, as if chasing some unspoken memory.

'You're sure you want to do this?'

Back to reality in a flash. This man didn't dwell on memories.

'Yes I am.'

'My advice . . . '

She nodded.

'You need to get down there and make it happen. He's got a cruiser moored in the bay, due to sail three days from now, Sunday morning to be precise. Doesn't give you much time.'

She stared at him wide-eyed.

'You're suggesting I simply arrive there unannounced!'

'You've got it in one.'

'You can't be serious!'

'Believe me, I'm serious.'

She gave him a cynical stare.

'It's not exactly what I had in mind.'

'Perhaps, but it's the best way'.

This wasn't making any sense.

'There's got to be a better way. What you're proposing sounds . . . preposterous.'

He gave a nonchalant shrug.

'Look, if you're asking me to set it up, I'll give it a shot, but I can't guarantee the outcome, and that's why it'll be better coming from you.'

She seemed to ponder this.

'Cannes is a big town. I wouldn't know where to start.'

'It ain't that big, and besides, you're pretty damn good at this sort of thing. Begin by checking out some of those fancy restaurants along the Croisette. He spends most evenings in one of them, Felix, Festival, the Palme D'Or. And then it's back to the cruiser – far as I know.'

She gazed at him, her mind in overdrive.

'I still don't see why you can't just set it up.'

'I can try, but you should listen to my advice.'

'What you're suggesting seems surreal.'

'Trust me – I know this man.'

She took a slow sip of her champagne.

'You'll at least tell me which cruiser.'

'You'll recognise it when you see it.'

She laughed in disbelief, then checked her watch and telephoned guest services. He heard her order a car for ten minutes. She replaced the receiver and made a face at him.

'You're being mischievous.'

He gave her a 'maybe maybe not' look. Sometimes this man could be . . . impossible.

'And you're quite sure I'll recognise it?'

'*Sure* I'm sure.'

Her look of frustration said it all. She stood and folded her arms.

'Is he aware you . . . looked after me?'

'Not from me he ain't. Remember, you're the one who made me swear not to tell. Unless he heard from Jamie, which is pretty unlikely – my guess is he doesn't know.'

'Jamie and Paul are in contact?'

'They teamed up during the union dispute. Paul recruited him into the core team. A surprising choice, I know, but in the end it all worked out.'

'I haven't spoken to Jamie since we parted on the pier at Holyhead all those years ago.'

'Doesn't surprise me.'

John Considine knew that Francesca was the consummate professional – the ultimate expert at concealing her emotions under a myriad of multi-layers – and yet her desire to reconnect with Paul Bannon was etched in the roadmap of her magnetic features.

'Francesca, I'm really trying to help you . . . '

She nodded.

'And when all is said and done, that is exactly what I'll do . . . '

'But you have to trust me. You must go there and make it happen.'

62

The assassin had been tracking her for seven weeks since first engaging with her in the arrivals hall at Gatwick Airport. The only available photograph had led to a crucial tip-off from an Arab source on the client payroll. She'd been identified checking out of the Royal Mirage in Dubai under an assumed name, then followed to the airport, where she boarded a British Airways flight bound for London.

He'd been hanging around for almost three weeks waiting for a call, but this interminable delay didn't overly concern him. He was a patient man, a loner, with neither personal nor family ties, a professional contractor with an impeccable track record. From time to time he studied the grainy photograph; not a definitive image, but the only one they'd managed to obtain. It had been taken with a precision telescopic lens showing the target with an unidentified male on the veranda of an ocean villa somewhere on the Californian coast.

The client instructions were pretty clear: kill her and produce unequivocal evidence, a body part being the preferred choice. This second requirement rendered the arrangement infinitely more difficult, but then the one-and-a-half-million-dollar price tag plus expenses, more than three times his normal charge-out rate, compensated for it pretty well. For whatever reason, they wanted her dead, badly it seemed, but these matters were of no interest to him. A long-distance shot didn't seem practical with regard to fulfilling the second part of the transaction. Unfortunate considering he'd successfully terminated his previous target, a dual hit on a husband and wife from a distance of six hundred metres. And then there was the added extra complication of the bodyguard who shadowed her pretty much most of the time.

When suddenly she appeared, walking briskly through the crowded arrivals hall, he depressed the shutter and reeled off half a dozen shots. Women were of no interest to him, but still he could see that she was a looker, cocky, proud, acutely aware of her surroundings. Then, just for an instant she stared straight at him, her sunglasses glinting in the bright overhead lights.

Had she succeeded in picking him out in the crowd? Impossible to be certain. He slid seamlessly behind the cover of a nearby pillar, only to re-emerge and find that she was gone. Was it paranoia? He doubted it. This was one smart bitch. He'd have to proceed infinitely more cautiously from now on.

63

The Air France flight from Heathrow touched down at Nice at two in the afternoon under a clear blue sky. She hurried through passport control and found her chauffeur waiting in the arrivals lounge. They drove along the coast to the Martinez in Cannes where she was ushered to an ocean-view suite on the seventh floor. Earlier, when she explained to Nick that this trip was personal, a mini-vacation, he had insisted on travelling nonetheless.

'My orders are to stay with you. Mister Considine has asked for the security detail to be strengthened with immediate effect. I contacted Terry yesterday. He's wrapping up an assignment in Berlin, but he'll be in London to meet us on our return.'

She knew that he was referring to Terry Clarkson, a former SAS associate of Nick's. He'd been utilised on occasion during Nick's vacation periods. She considered him to be extremely reliable.

'Mister Considine feels it's prudent to ratchet things up a notch. He wasn't thrilled when I told him I'd be working the French trip on my own.'

'Nick, it's a two-day vacation– '

'You won't even know I'm there – same as always.'

She stared at him thoughtfully.

'I'm not sure I've got this right Nick. It's almost . . . intangible.'

He shrugged.

'Let's run with your instincts. They haven't let you down yet.'

Cannes was busy that August, with temperatures soaring into the late thirties along the length of the Cote D'Azur. She sat on her terrace and gazed at the array of boats moored in the bay, then focused a set of Zeiss binoculars on the vast flotilla, but to little avail. All of the craft were facing out to sea, the pull of the tides taking them in a similar direction.

She wondered at the logic of John Considine's advice to go it alone on this one: however long she thought about it, she still couldn't figure it. It made no sense. And yet he'd seemed adamant, and so she didn't argue. The prospect of seeing him again after all the years left her feeling drained and nervous but she knew in her heart of hearts that this was something she could no longer postpone. Her sense of excitement was tinged with apprehension. The realisation that she was this close. That he was somewhere in some other part of this party town. Perhaps even right now in some other part of this famous hotel.

She rang down to room service and ordered a light lunch to the room, then later donned a tracksuit and worked out in the gym for an hour.

★

'*Marcel, encore deux bouteilles s'il vous plait.*'

'*Monsieur Bannon, je suis désolé mais je regrette de vous informer que je n'ai que deux bouteilles de Chateau Palmer soixante-et-un.*'

'*Pas de problem, Marcel. Ouvrez les deux.*'

'*Merci monsieur, d'accord.*'

It was the last Saturday in August and he sat at his favourite table on the terrace of Le Restaurant Palme D'or with his five guests. When the waiters arrived with the entrees he glanced at his watch.

'We'll need to leave in an hour to catch the fireworks from the cruiser or else we can stay here?'

'Definitely the cruiser,' Anthony Selwyn grinned. The others nodded their approval.

The previous evening Anthony and Jane had gazed out from the terrace of their suite high on the Hotel Splendido and watched the cruiser drop anchor in the deep lagoon outside the harbour at Portofino. Later Paul and his French girlfriend Monique joined them in the restaurant for dinner, and afterwards they drove down to the small harbour where the tender was waiting to ferry them back on board.

At sunrise they lifted anchor and sailed past the town of Santa

Margerita on the journey to the south of France. Paul's telephone buzzed when the cruiser anchored in the Bay of Cannes. It was Henry Hyland.

'What a coincidence! I've just seen you arrive. Rebecca and I are wondering if you could join us for sundowners at the Martinez Beach Club!'

Paul turned and saw Henry and Rebecca standing on the deck of their yacht three hundred yards further out, waving furiously. He smiled and waved back.

'OK Henry, if you're buying the drinks, then dinner is on me.'

Later they sat at a table by the edge of the sea and watched the sun cast a sorcerer's spell of molten gold across the waters of the bay, then slowly disappear behind the hills. The sky was bright with stars, and the music from the beach clubs carried in the air. The town seemed to heave with the excitement of the night all the way to the necklace of lights on the mountain road to Miramare.

The late evening was warm and hazy as they set out from the restaurant to the Carlton pier, to where the tender was moored.

She strolled along the Croisette in a snow-white linen dress, a flawless ten-carat solitaire held on a tiny chain around her neck, her sleek golden hair shimmering in the moonlight, her skin as pale as milk. Even in this Riviera paradise thronging with the most beautiful girls in the world, men and women turned to steal a glance at this tall vision walking alone on the crowded, floodlit pathway. In this playground of excesses, Francesca was the ultimate prize, a dazzling, heart-stoppingly gorgeous, delectable creature, tantalisingly out of reach behind an aura which seemed to say, 'Admire, but do not touch - it'll never happen'.

It was ten in the evening and the Croisette heaved with the sound of music and laughter. It was the carnival end to another long, hot, hazy, lazy season. On this last Saturday in August the beach bars were buzzing in anticipation of the fireworks display soon to commence out on the waters of the bay. She saw them before they saw her.

Suddenly he was there, in the middle of a group, strolling casually, hands in pockets, head bent slightly, listening to something someone was saying. But it was the willowy brunette linking his arm who caught her unawares. She hadn't expected that. She watched them draw ever closer and saw him glance in her direction, briefly. Now, barely a yard apart.

Suddenly he stopped dead in his tracks and stared at her, wide-eyed. Their eyes locked, and then in an instant she melted into the crowds and evaporated in the night. He stood gazing in astonishment at the place where she had been. His companions stared at him.

'You look as if you've seen a ghost,' Rebecca Hyland mused.

He turned and stared at them as if they were strangers.

'I must go,' he said absentmindedly to this bemused group of his closest friends. 'I can't explain it – but there's something I must do.'

Slowly he backed away and disappeared into the crowd.

She walked briskly in no particular direction, just needing to get away, her emotions in turmoil, her eyes brimming with tears. How could she have been so utterly stupid? How could John Considine have called it so unbelievably wrong?

She had visualised this moment for hours, days, weeks, half a lifetime, but in her mind it had always panned out differently. She always imagined it as a one-to-one reunion, but this had been nothing remotely like that.

How painfully naive I must be, she thought as she hurried through the night, fighting back the tears. *How could I have ever expected to find him alone, available, unaccompanied?*

She barely noticed the crowds thinning as she hurried along the marina into the relative tranquility of the park. She moved slowly now, passing the memorial to Jean Moulin, hero of the French Resistance, then sat on a park bench and gazed across the bay. She glanced absentmindedly at families with children, and young couples out for a late-evening stroll.

Her life had been a resounding failure in so many ways, with one or two notable exceptions. She had a son she idolised; she visited him as often as she could at Eton College, where he had been boarding these past four years. And then this searing love she had harboured for a man who seemed so tantalisingly, frustratingly beyond her reach. There and then she decided it had to end, this schoolgirl crush that threatened to destroy her soul – this heart-breaking, angst-filled, never-ending love.

'Is it really you, this vision before me?'

It was a voice she recognised from another lifetime, the words spoken softly so as not to startle – a voice from a distant summer in the prime of her youth. She continued to gaze across the dark, shimmering water, her hands gripping the edge of the seat to stop them trembling out of control. She glanced back and realised that he was barely a few feet away, half-hidden in the semi-darkness. She stood tentatively and turned to him, hands by her side, fists clenched.

'Yes, it's me,' she whispered.

He moved from the shadows and stared into the face of this girl he had adored all the days of his life.

'How have you been all these years?' he asked in the same low voice.

She gazed at him silently, her lip quivering, her cheeks stained with tears, her eyes glistening in the night. He held his breath, not daring to move, not knowing what to do next. He wondered if she had heard him, but then he saw her lips move and he heard the words, 'Lost without you.'

He felt his heart bursting in his chest.

'It is inconceivable that we should meet like this.'

'No,' she said simply. 'I came to find you.'

'You came . . . for me.'

Her lips formed a silent 'yes'. He moved half a step closer.

'I can't believe this is happening,' he whispered. 'Please, let me . . . hold you.'

She stood motionless, her eyes cast down.

'You may not wish to do so,' she whispered.

He seemed mystified.

'How can you say that?'

A shiver ran through her. She stared at him wide-eyed, her lips formulating a response that failed to materialise.

'Francesca, how can you *say* that?'

And then she whispered, 'You should know that I am nothing but a common whore who sells her body to the highest bidder. A prostitute who services men the world over. A woman with no shame. A woman with no soul.'

She stood before him, tentative, vulnerable and afraid, not knowing the effect that these desperate words might have, her heart thumping in her breast, her self-confidence evaporated in the warm night air. Then she heard his voice again, his tone low and gentle.

'And you should know that none of this matters to me. I have loved you since the day I first saw you. I have never loved anyone in my life but you. I will love you until the day I draw my last breath.'

Her lips quivered in a half-smile and a single tear ran down her cheek.

'May I hold you,' he whispered.

Suddenly she was in his arms, and in that instant the fireworks cascaded across the skies above Cannes. He gazed into her coral green eyes as the night erupted in a dazzling burst of colour.

'Can this be happening to us, or is it a dream?'

'It's happening,' she said softly. 'It's a dream come true.'

They stood in the shadow of the palms, oblivious to the world around them until the last of the fireworks faded in the sky. He held her and she melted in his arms, feeling utterly safe in the all-encompassing protection of his embrace. Time became meaningless as they clung to one another in the sultry August night, her perfume wafting in the air, infusing him with her breath, encapsulating him with her presence.

'Johnny told me I'd find you here,' she whispered. 'He said you'd be leaving soon.'

'I will not leave without you.'

She wondered had she heard correctly. How could it be possible? And then he took her hand in his and led her towards the lights of the Croisette.

★

The assassin stood still as a ghost. His dead eyes penetrated the darkness. He watched their every move and strained to hear the words they were saying, but they spoke so quietly it was impossible. He felt the steel of the dagger cold against his wrist, and contemplated taking them down in one lethal move, but on this last night of August there were people everywhere, and something about the man made him hesitate.

He thought he heard him say, 'I will not leave without you,' but then they were moving in his direction and he slipped seamlessly into the night.

★

'I saw you earlier with your friends . . . there was a girl.'
He nodded.

'The girl's a friend from time to time, an arrangement that suits us both. I have a boat moored in the bay. When I met you we were on our way there.'

'They sail with you tomorrow?'

'Tomorrow we go our separate ways.'

She stopped and gazed across the water.

'Your boat – he told me I should recognise it easily.'

'It's true. You will,' he said simply, offering no further explanation.

They crossed from the promenade into the crowded lobby of the Martinez. She turned to him and gazed into his eyes.

'When you said earlier about not leaving without me – there is nothing I'd love more.'

She felt his lips gentle on her cheek, and then, 'Francesca, in the morning . . . '

'Yes, my darling.'

'I'll be waiting for you.'

She listened to his words and felt herself engulfed in a wave of blinding, bursting love.

'Thank you,' she whispered, her heart thumping in her breast.

When she turned and walked to the elevator, he stood and waited until the doors closed behind her, oblivious to the scrutiny of the stranger standing in the dim light of the bar, watching their every move.

64

She wandered onto the terrace, her mind racing, her head dizzy with delight, her body quivering with the thrill of it all. She poured wine from a bottle of claret and sipped, then gazed across the Bay of Cannes in a whirl of shock and disbelief at what had just unfolded. She glanced down to where the binoculars lay, then picked them up and slowly scanned the water. *I should recognise it, he had said. Whatever could he have meant.*

The sound of music wafted on the still night air as she panned across the bay, not knowing what to look for. And then somewhere in the middle of the vast flotilla something caught her eye. She traced back slowly until the powerful binoculars picked up a sleek, white, triple-decked cruiser, its lights sparkling on all decks, lying solid and still in the water. She had spent some time on luxury cruisers, but rarely had she seen anything quite as startling as this. She guessed it to be all of two hundred feet long, and yet it wasn't its size that caused her to catch her breath – it was the golden scroll of letters emblazoned on its side. She stared, mesmerised, at the name, *her* name, *Francesca*, reflected in the water, glistening in the starlit night.

She steadied her hands and hovered over it for an age, her heart beating like a drum as she gazed in disbelief, and wondered how she could ever have doubted Frank Considine, her powerful guardian angel during all of those dark and desperate years. She pondered the momentous events of the evening as she lay on her bed, knowing that sleep would be impossible on this most wonderful night of her life.

In the first light of dawn she walked from the elevator, an elderly porter by her side wheeling a trolley laden with matching Louis Vuitton cases. She glanced across the foyer and saw him. He moved forward and stood before her.

'There are no words to describe how beautiful you look this morning.'

Her eyes sparkled with delight. She smiled and hugged him to her.

'I'm the luckiest girl in the world. I can't believe this is happening to me.'

'I couldn't wait to see you,' he said simply.

She leaned up and whispered in his ear, 'I lay awake all night and thought of you, and when I slept I dreamed of you.'

He held her in his arms and kissed her, then took her hand and led her from the hotel, across the Croisette to the end of the Martinez pier. A pretty blonde girl dressed in white T-shirt and navy shorts helped them board the tender, and a sailor dressed in matching attire spun the wheel and accelerated smoothly out into the water. She glanced at him as they moved across the shimmering depths of the bay, the wind ruffling his hair, his tanned face creased in a smile. A million thoughts raced through her mind as they skimmed the calm, still water, her world suddenly turned incredibly, impossibly upside-down, and right here, right now, standing by her side, the only man in the world she had ever loved. And then some faraway thought seemed suddenly to catch her unawares. She bowed her head and averted her gaze. He drew her gently towards him.

'What is it, my love?'

She rested her head on his shoulder.

'I'm sorry,' she replied. 'It's just that I am so hopelessly in love with you it frightens me . . . '

'Don't be afraid,' he smiled. 'There is nothing in the world for you to fear.'

He held her close to him, his heart so brimming with love for this breathtaking woman he felt it must surely burst.

They clung to one another until they edged beneath the shadow of the cruiser. He led her up the starboard gangway, to a vast suite with panoramic views across the bay on either side. She stared in awe at the splendour of her surroundings. The cruiser seemed suddenly to come alive, with men and women moving in all directions.

'This is your cabin,' he smiled, 'and I'll be in the one next door.'

A girl stood waiting to greet them. He turned to her.

'And this is Charlotte, my girl Friday. She's here to look after you.'

They shook hands.

'Charlotte has just become engaged to our captain, Philip Beresford.'

'Congratulations! How wonderful!' Francesca lifted her hand and stared in admiration. 'What a beautiful diamond!'

Charlotte beamed.

'Fancy a try?'

'Why, yes, thank you.'

Charlotte's bubbly personality was infectious.

'I finally get to meet the lady after whom our ship has been named.'

'I still can't believe it,' she smiled. 'When I first saw it I was . . . lost for words.'

'Then you must permit me to show you around. It's impressive.'

Later, when Charlotte escorted her up on deck, she found him seated with two men in business suits. They stood to greet her.

'Francesca, allow me to introduce two friends from London, Harry and Crispin Shand.'

They shook hands.

'It's a pleasure to meet you,' Harry smiled. 'I wish you bon voyage!'

He handed Paul a black leather attaché case.

'Everything is exactly as you requested. Once you've satisfied yourself as to the contents, we'll bid you farewell and be on our way.'

'Please give us a few moments, gentlemen.'

He stood and led her through glass doors to an inner salon, then sat her down and clicked open the attaché case.

'I apologise for this mystery,' he said, 'but certain matters have been delayed for far too long.'

She looked at him bemused.

'I've waited a lifetime to do this one thing,' he smiled, and then withdrew a black leather box from the attaché case and handed it to her. He took her hands in his and knelt before her.

'Francesca, I love you with every beat of my heart. And I swear on the lives of my mother, my father, and my brother Frank, to love and protect you all the days of my life. Will you marry me?'

She gazed at him dumbfounded, reeling from the words she had just heard, her expression startled, as she gazed enraptured at this man kneeling before her. He felt her hand trembling. She seemed traumatised.

'In a heartbeat,' she whispered, but her eyes were cast down.

'What's troubling you?' he asked gently.

She sat silently for an age, then gazed up at him.

'You cannot know,' she whispered, 'the . . . terrible things that have happened to me.'

She seemed forlorn. He felt her grip tighten.

'The past is gone,' he whispered. 'The future is all that matters.'

But it was almost as if she hadn't heard.

'Terrible things . . . that have conspired to make me incapable of ever having a child for you. My love, if I tell you nothing else, I have to tell you this.'

When she looked up at him there was a sadness about her that startled him.

'Francesca,' he said gently, 'all I've ever wanted is to have you by my side all the days of my life.'

He held her hands and gazed reassuringly into her eyes.

'Now,' he smiled, 'open it.'

She sat back slowly and clicked the case open, then gasped in disbelief. The solitaire resting on its black velvet display was a diamond of the most astounding quality. It sparkled in a cascade of blazing light that stunned her into silence. He lifted it and placed it on her finger. It fit perfectly.

'So mesmerisingly beautiful. It shines like . . . the sun. I cannot believe that this is happening to me. I simply cannot believe . . . '

She looked up at him and slowly it dawned on her.

'Shands, the Bond Street jewellers. Oh my God, I . . . ought to have guessed.'

'You like it?' he smiled.

'In all my life I've never seen anything so beautiful.'

Francesca gazed at the ring, her mind reeling from the seismic twist her life had taken in the hours since they had met. She felt her world spinning; a cocktail of reality and make-believe.

'We're ready to sail and they're about to leave. Shall we bid them farewell?'

She stared, mystified, at him. It all seemed surreal.

'Yes, but wait!'

She gazed at the ring, then wrapped her arms around him.

'I shall wear this ring as a dazzling symbol of my absolute love for you.'

She hugged him close to her and kissed him softly, and then they walked back out under the crystal blue skies of the bay. Harry and Crispin Shand were waiting to greet them. Charlotte popped a bottle of Pol Roger and handed each of them a glass. Harry Shand gave a dignified bow.

'Madam, my apologies for the subterfuge, but we were sworn to secrecy. A willing part of a small conspiracy with, I'm happy to say, more than a little help from the captain's fiancée – my brother Crispin's brilliant idea. She helped us to size you correctly.'

Francesca gaped at them and then turned to Charlotte and laughed.

'What a smooth operator! I'd never have suspected.'

A technician emerged from the deck below carrying a briefcase, and behind him two heavier men, obviously a security detail, both dressed in black suits with white shirts and dark ties. Crispin Shand walked over to her, lifted her hand, examined the ring and swivelled it slightly.

'Yes, it's the perfect fit for the perfect lady. We brought Jason, our head technician, along with us to fine-tune the detail.'

She turned to Paul.

'You arranged all of this in a matter of hours. How impossibly clever!'

'The stone has languished in our vaults for the best part of forty years,' Harry Shand interjected smoothly. 'Mister Bannon purchased it five years ago. When he telephoned us late last night and asked that we attach it to a platinum band, we proceeded with the utmost urgency. Jason came to our workshop at midnight and began the delicate process of piecing it together. Mister Bannon's jet was on standby at Heathrow and we flew to Nice at five this morning.'

She turned to Paul and embraced him.

'It's the most startling diamond I have ever seen.'

'Madam, this is indeed a special stone,' Crispin Shand smiled. 'It is a twenty-carat vvs flawless diamond solitaire of the most breathtaking quality, superbly cut by a master craftsman to the most exacting standard, purchased in its raw state from de Beers by our late father sometime in the thirties. It is befitting that it should be worn for the first time by a woman of such astounding beauty.'

She listened enraptured to all of this, then leaned forward and kissed him.

'Thank you my, darling,' she whispered softly. 'I shall wear it all the days of my life.'

65

Cannes receded in the distance as the cruiser sliced powerfully through the water on its journey to the open sea. The assassin tracked it through his binoculars from the ferry terminal at the end of the old-town pier. When it faded to a dot on the horizon, he returned to his hotel room and dialled a number. The telephone answered on the first ring.

Silence at the other end.

'We have a problem – an unforeseen development. I will need more time.'

'How much time?'

'I cannot say. Possibly six months.'

'This is . . . most unfortunate.'

'If you wish me to return the deposit – '

'Out of the question.'

'But – '

'You accepted our terms. You know the rules of engagement. You will complete the contract satisfactorily or we will send someone to . . . find you. Do you understand?'

'I understand.'

There was a click and the line went dead.

★

In the late afternoon Charlotte called Paul aside.

'The connection you requested through to Mister Considine – he's on the line.'

'Thanks, Charlotte, I'll take it in my office.'

He closed the door, sat in his chair and gazed out the window. He'd been through a war with the big man, and now this. He picked up the telephone.

'Thank you, Johnny.'

'For what?'

'For bringing her to me.'

'I'd a hand in it, for sure, but this is one determined lady. With or without me, she'd have got to you in the end.'

'My father asked me to find her but she came to me instead. I can never repay you for this.'

'You owe me nothing. You'd have found each other. It was meant to be.'

He stared across the ocean and smiled at the thought.

'She told me you've always been there for her.'

'I helped her when she needed it, and got to know her along the way. You'll find none better, but I'm guessing you know that.'

There was the sound of a match striking and he heard the big man inhale.

'The problem *now* is she's in trouble – the kind of trouble even I can't handle. She needs a more powerful man than me to get her through this shit. There's only one man I know who ticks all the boxes, and that man is you.'

Paul sat by the desk in his rosewood-panelled office as the cruiser powered through the waters of the Mediterranean Sea. They had left Cannes two hours earlier on a parallel course a mile out from the French coast. In the distance he could see San Remo with its grand casino and snow-white buildings rising into the hills. They were now cruising in Italian waters and on schedule to reach the harbour at Portofino in approximately four hours' time.

'Johnny, I don't know what kind of trouble she's in, and I couldn't care less. I'm just thrilled you brought her to me.'

'It's what she always wanted. She loves you, simple as that. She's been mixing with some of the nastiest lowlifes on the planet – not out of choice, but out of necessity. And yeah, I've been looking out for her just like you said, but there are evil forces lurking in the shadows. So ask me am I doing you a favour and the answer will always be yes. As long as you always remember that his package carries a health warning which says be on your guard from the get-go.'

He listened quietly to the words of a man he had respected in his life, a man in his father's steely mould who shot from the hip, with scant regard for the consequences and less for the fallout. But there was a chilly ring in John Considine's tone.

'Is she in danger?'

'Yes.'

'Mortal danger.'

'I believe so.'

The silence that followed seemed to last all of a minute. Considine knew better than to interrupt the thought-process of this fearless man he had come to respect more than any other. He waited in silence.

'It's good we're having this conversation. It's good you're telling me this.'

If John Considine had harboured any doubts about confiding in Paul Bannon, he knew by the deadly tone in which these words were delivered that he could now rest easy. He now knew for certain he'd made the right choice.

'There's something else I ought to tell you,' he said. 'It's a theory – a John Considine theory – but I'll share it with you anyway.'

He listened to him exhaling, blowing smoke from one of those big cigars he liked so much.

'My belief is that she instinctively sought you out at this time, because somewhere in the realms of her subconscious she knows that no other man can protect her from the evil fuckers that are out there. Oh don't get me wrong, she loves you like nothing I've ever seen, but she also knows she needs to be protected, and you're the boy she's chosen to do the business. I reckon she's made the exact right choice.'

He pondered the devastating implications lurking in the words John Considine had just articulated.

'I need to deal with this faster than I thought. Where's the best place to begin?'

'Begin by talking to Nick Penn. He's been shadowing her during all those times when it really mattered.'

His mind was moving swiftly now.

'We anchor off the north coast of Sardinia in two days' time. Get him out there.'

'I'll deal with it straight away.'

'And I want you out there with him.'

'Sounds like you intend to deal with this full-on.'

'Fucking right. Take the jet. Come on board at the Costa Smeralda and stay on board until we reach the Island of Capri.'

'OK, boss, consider it done.'

*

She stayed by his side from the moment the cruiser left the southern coast of France in its wake and entered Italian waters. She sat with him when he sat and walked with him when he walked. Once, when they summoned him to take a call, he saw the fleeting look of anguish on her face as he stood to leave. But then he turned to her and took her by the hand.

'What are we waiting for! Let's go!'

She smiled and slipped an arm around his waist.

'I love you,' she whispered as they walked.

In the evening they cruised through the waters of the Ligurian coast, past the town of Rapallo a mile off the starboard bow, and dropped anchor as the sun was setting on the lagoon outside the harbour at Portofino. The Splendido Hotel sat perched high on the hills above them. He turned to her.

'I thought we might have dinner there tonight if you'd like that.'

'Just the two of us?'

'Yes.'

'I'd love it.'

A water-taxi approached from the town carrying a group of men.

'Francesca, my lawyers are coming on board for an hour – just some routine business. Let's meet at seven for drinks before dinner.'

She hugged him close and kissed his cheek.

'I'll see you in a while, my darling.'

Later she answered a knock on her door, and a tall, auburn-haired, soberly dressed girl smiled at her pleasantly.

'Miss Sinclair, I'm Nicole Davidson, Mister Bannon's personal assistant in London. It's my pleasure to finally meet you.'

'Hello, Nicole.'

'Mister Bannon has already explained to you that he'll be engaged for the next hour or so. There are documents that urgently require his signature and some businessmen boarded the cruiser a short time ago. He has asked me to reserve a table at the Splendido for dinner at eight.'

'Yes, he mentioned that.'

'Miss Sinclair, Mister Bannon has also asked that you accompany me to his office at six forty-five this evening for a short meeting with his lawyers. I do apologise for the tight timeframe, but our lawyers are due to disembark the cruiser at seven to attend a function in London later this evening. Mister Bannon's jet is on standby at Turin Airport.'

'A meeting with his lawyers, you say. A matter that concerns me?'

'Yes, most certainly.'

'Well, if you're quite sure . . . ' she replied, sounding vaguely puzzled. Nonetheless she was there waiting when Nicole Davidson returned at precisely six forty-five. She led her to a rosewood-panelled office on the port side of the cruiser and introduced her to a rotund, balding, soberly dressed man standing by the desk.

'Miss Sinclair, allow me to introduce Mister Bannon's London lawyer, Jeremy Priestland.'

They shook hands.

'Please have a seat,' Nicole smiled. 'I shall return at seven on the dot to accompany you upstairs.'

Jeremy Priestland sat at the desk and waited for the door to close.

'Please Miss Sinclair, do not in any way be alarmed. Paul has asked that the matters pertaining to this discussion should be expedited with the utmost urgency. It is primarily the reason for my visit here this afternoon, along with one or two unrelated matters.'

She stared at him, mystified.

'Obviously I've no idea what this is all about.'

'I assure you that there is nothing the matter, Miss Sinclair. On the contrary, my instructions are to put in position certain arrangements which will prove beneficial to you personally, and all I need now in order to finalise matters is your signature.'

She nodded silently and waited for him to continue.

'I have on this desk a print-out of a deposit account which has been activated at the Zurich branch of UBS Bank, registered in your sole name, and I am instructed to present this to you for your exclusive personal use. Paul has made it clear that he wishes you to be financially independent, and has authorised that the mandated amount is to be activated with immediate effect.'

She stared at him, her expression dismissive.

'What you seek to do is impossible. I will not permit this.'

If her response surprised him, he didn't show it.

'Miss Sinclair, it is Paul's heartfelt wish that you accept these arrangements in good faith as his personal gift to you. Nothing could be simpler. All that it requires is your signature and I can take my leave.'

She ignored the fountain pen he flourished in her direction and stood to go.

'Don't shoot the messenger, Miss Sinclair,' he said, smiling in a vaguely condescending way. 'All I ask is a moment of your time. I've come a long way.'

She turned briskly and sat.

'The decision is of course ultimately yours, and I assure you that I shall at all times respect your wishes. All I am asking is that you consider this matter carefully. It is a magnanimous gesture which is being made for all the right reasons, and in the absence of a signature I fear my journey here today will have been wasted.'

She found the subtle application of pressure in his tone unsettling. Here was a man used to having his way. She stared at him disdainfully.

'You say these are Mister Bannon's express instructions.'

When he nodded she took the fountain pen and quickly signed her name to the document, then stood to leave. He cleared his throat.

'Miss Sinclair, I really ought to tell you that if you were to walk off this boat in the next minute and decide never to see Mister Bannon again, the monies lodged to this account are irreversibly yours to do with as you please. There are no strings. I thank you for your co-operation.'

She stopped and glanced at him coolly.

'I shall be meeting with Mister Bannon shortly and I shall thank him personally for his generosity.'

'Then perhaps, Miss Sinclair, I should appraise you in respect of the amount that has been lodged to your account.'

She waited impatiently for him to continue.

'The balance in the account is one hundred million pounds sterling.'

She gasped audibly and then appeared to falter. He rushed to her aid but she brushed him aside and caught the edge of a bookshelf to steady herself. She stood silently, her head bent forward, then turned to him.

'Thank you,' she said quietly, and left immediately.

★

Catherine Davidson met her on the outside and accompanied her up two flights of stairs to the stern deck.

'This is where I leave you,' she smiled. 'I trust you'll have a wonderful evening.'

He was sitting on a cream leather couch, sipping a cold beer, dressed in navy slacks and snow-white shirt, the dazzle of the late-afternoon sun reflected in his sunglasses. When he stood to greet her he could see that her face was pale and drawn, and when he embraced her he felt her trembling in his arms.

'Is anything the matter?' he whispered.

'You must forgive me if I seem ungrateful,' she replied, her tone disconsolate, her voice thick with emotion. 'Your generosity is beyond comprehension, and yet I feel that if I accept this astounding gift, it inadvertently casts a shadow over my motives in seeking you out. After all the endless years I pined for you, now that I've found you I dread the thought of losing you. I came in search of you alone, and nothing else but you.'

He held her in his arms and whispered in her ear, 'Francesca, there are no words to describe how much I love you, and that is why you must allow me to look after you as best I can because, more than anything else in the world, this is all I ever want to do.'

Later they sat on the terrace of the Splendido Hotel and ate dinner at a table overlooking the ocean, the warm evening air fragrant with the smell of honeysuckle, the soft sounds of the piano tinkling in the night. Two hundred feet below, in the dark waters of the lagoon, the cruiser lay on its anchor, its decks emblazoned with light. He held her hand and gazed into her eyes.

'That night when you came to me all those years ago . . . '

She held his gaze, her eyes molten liquid green, her perfume hanging on the breeze.

'Afterwards I pined for you all the hours of the day. There were times I felt I would rather die . . . without you.'

'I should never have left you,' she said softly. 'I was such a foolish girl, innocent in the ways of the world. Not a day of my life has passed since that day that I haven't thought of you, of where you are, of who you are with. During all those days I was pining for you too, my darling.'

Her voice faltered and she covered her face with her hands.

'And then when Johnny told me that you almost died saving me from the river, I thought my heart would burst with the weight of my despair. Down all the years my heart kept telling me that it was your voice I heard calling my name that night. The one voice I yearned for most of all. When Johnny told me that it was you who rescued me, I resolved there and then to someday search you out, to see if you might still want me the way I still want you.'

The skies over the Italian coastline were sprinkled with stars that night, the moonlight splayed across the water in a shimmering display of sparkling magnificence. The candles flickered in the summer breeze, and the soft strains of the piano carried in the warm night air. They lingered for a while, and when dinner was ended she took his hand.

'Darling, I love this magical place, but now I just want to be alone with you.'

At the small harbour in Portofino the tender lay waiting in the dark water. The air was still and the sea was calm as they slipped away from the pier and crossed the lagoon under the star-studded sky. Back on the cruiser, he led her to the door of her cabin, held her in his arms and kissed her goodnight. He gazed at this astounding woman, her eyes sparkling like emeralds, her hair shining liquid gold in the moonlight, her captivating aura causing his words to tumble out in a nervous, schoolboy stutter.

'You are the most gorgeous woman in the world . . . '

She smiled a smile of undisguised delight, her eyes full with love, her crimson lips slightly parted.

'Darling, you sound . . . so nervous. It's so . . . endearing.'

She took his hand and led him through the door of her cabin.

'Don't leave me,' she whispered. 'Don't ever leave me.'

They made love with the passion, the fervour, and the desire of all those lost and lonely years simmering just beneath the surface. She moved slowly, rhythmically, expertly beneath him, her body taut, her breasts heavy, her nipples hard against him.

His lips searched for hers; her tongue searched for his. He clung to her helplessly, his body at one with hers as she moved relentlessly, irreversibly, until all sense of control began to slowly slip away.

'Come with me,' she whispered. 'Come with me, my darling, deep within me.'

She entwined her arms around him, touching him, embracing him, her long golden legs caressing him, pulling him closer, drawing him deeper. His heart beat like a war-drum in his chest, then suddenly he was lost in the depths of her spell, in the overwhelming magic of the thrill, the ecstasy, the spell-binding intensity of the instant his orgasm released into her.

He heard her gasp as she clung to him, the depths of her desire cascading through every pore of her being. They lay beside one another, entwined in the stillness of the hour, bathed in the heat of a flame that had been ignited in the distant summers of their childhood. A burning flame that had withstood the ravages of time, of endless separation, of dark days and darker deeds. A flame that against the most desperate odds had stubbornly refused to die.

'I now know with life's certainty what I knew for the first

time as a little girl,' she whispered. 'I was born into this world to love no other man but you.'

In the enveloping stillness of the night, entwined in each other's embrace, the gentle lapping of the water lulled them to a dreamlike sleep. Then, sometime before dawn, as the first light filtered across the lagoon, he awoke and turned, startled, in her direction.

'What's the matter, my darling,' she asked.

He lay back on the pillow and held her in his arms.

'Just for one moment I imagined you were gone.'

She gazed at him, her lips parted, her eyes glistening, then placed a finger gently on his lips and whispered, 'I'll never leave your side all the days of my life.'

66

John Considine and Nick Penn stood on the ocean terrace of the Hotel Romazzino in Porto Cervo and watched the cruiser drop anchor a mile off the Costa Smeralda. Minutes later they saw the tender curve sharply in the water, then make for the harbour, leaving a trail of foam in its wake.

Francesca stood on the deck and gazed absentmindedly towards the glistening Sardinian coast.

'Is this really necessary, my darling?' she inquired quietly. 'I feel so utterly responsible for the upset I'm causing you.'

Since departing Cannes she had barely left his side, her mood darkening only once, briefly, when he alluded to the forthcoming meeting with John Considine and Nick Penn.

'You'll never have to face the world alone again,' he had reassured her. 'I'm with you now.'

When the two men finally stepped on board they shook hands and Paul led them to his office. They sat on cream leather couches. A pretty blonde waitress served coffee and water. On the wall was a framed photograph of three men dressed in matching white polo-tops, smiling broadly from the terrace of a restaurant in a sun-drenched street, the name 'La Rosetta' emblazoned on the wall behind them.

'Ah,' John Considine said, studying it intently, 'James with you and Frank in happier times. Where have all the good guys gone . . . '

'Eleven years ago,' he smiled, 'our parents' wedding anniversary at the Hassler. My father always liked to lunch in the dusty old side-streets of the Eternal City. La Rosetta was one of his favourites.'

He stared wistfully at the photograph and gave a shrug.

'But let's leave those golden days aside. There'll be plenty of time to revisit the past.'

He turned to Nick Penn.

'Johnny tells me you stood with my brother against Bradshaw and you took care of Francesca all these years. I'm grateful for everything you've done.'

'I'm a soldier, Mister Bannon. I did the job I was asked to do to the best of my ability. Well, at least that's how it all began, but things changed along the way. I admired your brother and I admire the lady – it's difficult not to.'

He gestured towards the photograph of the three men.

'I feel connected to this family. My old man served his time with your father, and over the years I got to know Frank quite well, and now you. Mister Considine tells me you're a fearless man, and as a soldier I can identify with that. It's an attribute that may prove useful, because this lady needs to be protected.'

'From what?'

The soldier hesitated briefly, but held his gaze.

'From her past, Mister Bannon.'

He sat silently contemplating this.

'She believes she's being followed. Has she ever mentioned this to you?'

'We review her personal security on a regular basis, so, yes is the answer. Security-wise she's been tutored by the best in the business – even holds a black belt in judo. So when she first told me she suspected she was being followed, naturally I believed her. She may even have seen him briefly – the guy shadowing her.'

'Have you seen anything?'

'No, sir, but this guy's a professional.'

'How can you be so sure?'

'Miss Sinclair operates in a danger zone most of the time: she's been programmed to sense danger. I feel certain she saw something the rest of us would have missed.'

'Any idea what this is about?'

'Difficult to say with certainty, but there was an incident some years back. She was lucky to get out alive. Some Arabs took her . . . '

411

He glanced at John Considine, who gave a reassuring nod.

'They smashed her up pretty bad, gang-raped her and recorded the whole Punch-and-Judy show on celluloid. When I got there I saw an array of knives laid out on a table, and you didn't need to be a genius to figure out what those guys had in mind. I terminated the four males in the building, destroyed the evidence and triggered an incendiary in the room. Then I got her out.'

'And you think it might be connected to this.'

'She's been living in a jungle, Mister Bannon, and there are predators in every jungle. It's difficult to be one hundred percent certain, so let's just say it's stronger than a gut feeling. Maybe I missed something – a telephone number scribbled on a piece of paper, a scrap of evidence that might have provided a connection – who knows? It all happened so fast. Those guys were one evil bunch of motherfuckers, and now maybe someone's out to balance the score.'

'So you're saying there's a hit out on her.'

'I reckon we ought to be working on that assumption.'

'What do you recommend?'

'Probably not a great deal more than what we've been doing up until now. If we begin by assuming that a determined assassin can get to virtually anyone, then we can build our plan accordingly. I've talked it through with Mister Considine and we both agree we ought to recruit a second bodyguard, which I've already done – a guy called Terry Clarkson. He's reliable – a soldier – I've worked with him before. The plan is for one of us to stay close at all times when she's on the move, like zero to a hundred yards, with the second guy operating on a wider one-to-five-hundred-yard sweep. Whenever she moves, we move, and whenever this geezer makes his move, we have to hope we get to him before he takes her down. It's extremely serious, Mister Bannon.'

Paul stared at Nick Penn in deathly silence, his blue eyes cold as ice. Again, the bodyguard held his stare.

'If it's as bad as I reckon it is, Mister Bannon, then we're about to participate in the deadliest game.'

When she walked into the room they stood to greet her. She sat and stared from one to the other, all of them grim-faced and tense.

'So, it's as bad as that?'

Considine winked at her.

'He plucked you from the jaws of death once before,' he said quietly.

Paul took her hand.

'Tell us about the guy, Francesca,' he inquired gently. 'Did you really get to see him?'

'Yes. For a millisecond.'

'Can you describe him?'

'Short grey hair, bald in front, Mediterranean features, Moroccan perhaps. Thin lips, long nose, average height, early thirties.'

'Anything else?'

'No, but I'm pretty sure he knows I saw him, and that'll make him extra careful in the future.'

The cruiser rounded the north coast of Sardinia and followed a south-easterly course into the late afternoon until the hazy line of the Italian coast appeared along the horizon. In the distance the towering mass of Mount Vesuvius stood bathed in the evening sunshine, the city of Naples straddling its slopes in a cloudy white mist of shimmering heat.

Up ahead of them the island of Capri, once the fabled paradise of the Roman emperors, and now a paradise destination for millions of tourists, sprang from the ocean, its sheer cliffs towering a thousand feet into the sky. The cruiser dropped anchor under the shadow of the cliffs in the deep green waters beyond the harbour.

67

The assassin stared at the telephone with his dead eyes. Fifteen seconds earlier it had rung at the pre-arranged time. When it rang again he picked it up and listened silently.

'You have disappointed us. We expected this matter to be resolved before now. It is . . . unfortunate.'

He held the telephone to his ear, devoid of feeling. Expressionless.

'There is a change of plan. We no longer require that you fulfil part two of the contract. Of course, your fee will be adjusted accordingly. Acknowledge, if you understand.'

'I understand.'

'This will make your task infinitely easier. Correct?'

'Correct.'

When the connection went dead, he replaced the receiver.

In the early hours of the morning his telephone rang again. He glanced at his watch and saw that it was approaching three. He picked up the receiver and listened.

'Hi, it's me.'

'Yes, hello,' he replied, immediately alert.

'We dropped anchor off Capri seven hours ago.'

'And?'

There was a brief pause.

'The second payment of five thousand. This will be in cash also?'

'Of course. As you requested.'

'In three days' time we return to Cannes.'

'Call me when you arrive. We can meet.'

'OK.'

Five nights earlier he had followed the guy to a bar in the old town and watched him drinking alone. He pulled up a stool next to him and smiled in a friendly, casual way.

'I'm guessing by the name on your shirt you're from off the big cruiser?'

The guy looked at him warily.

'What if I am?' he replied sullenly.

He held his hands up in a 'no harm meant' gesture.

'There's a guy on board who owes me money is all, fifty grand from a casino play six months ago. But then he sails the following day on the cruiser, and leaves me high and dry. Right now I'm just trying to collect what's due to me.'

'Your problem, buddy – nothing to do with me.'

The assassin stared into the mirror behind the bar.

'It's worth ten grand to me to track this joker down. I'll pay five in cash right now, and another five if you connect me with my man.'

The crewman turned and stared at him.

'You're carrying five grand cash in this dump.'

The assassin opened his jacket and flashed the wad.

'It just doesn't get much easier.'

The crewman thought about it.

'I reckon you've left it too late, pal. We're out of here at first light.'

'Makes no odds – I just need to know when you get to make it back here.'

'That it?'

'Like I said – it doesn't get much easier.'

'And the name of the guy owes you the money?'

'Wish I knew but the problem is he never told me. The only name I've got is "Francesca", same as on the pocket of your shirt.'

'This guy could be long gone. These jokers don't hang around.'

'My problem, pal, just like you said. All I need is the timetable for the return journey. The rest is down to me.'

68

The assassin had been watching the elderly couple for the past three days. They rarely left their penthouse apartment on the second line except for an hour each morning to go shopping off the Rue d'Antibes. He guessed they were both in their late eighties, definitely French, the husband wheelchair-bound, the wife stooped and frail, yet still able to manoeuvre him the short distance to the local mini-market. No one paid heed to them and they rarely spoke to anyone, not even to bid the time of day. Each morning they followed the same routine. They stopped and picked up a bottle of wine, some fresh bread, and a few other rudimentary items before setting out on the return journey.

On the fourth morning he climbed the escape-stairway to the top floor and entered the apartment with ease. By his reckoning they'd be due to return in approximately forty minutes. He glanced around quickly, listening for the slightest sound. The place was empty. He checked the two bedrooms in the rear section and saw that only one was in regular use, the other crammed with an array of discarded furniture and accumulated junk.

He moved along the corridor to the salon, taking in the bathroom along the way. Most of the furniture was old but not cheap, probably once upon a time even chic, but none of this was of interest to him. He walked across the salon and stared out the window. This was just about perfect.

From here he had an uninterrupted view of the deep-water moorings favoured by the bigger boats, five, six hundred yards out from the Croisette. The stretch of water nearest the shoreline was blocked out by the hulking condominiums and hotels straddling the front line. These he had already discarded because of the crowds, the in-house security, and the inevitable twenty-four-hour porterage. But this location, he decided, was pretty much perfect – quiet, shaded, the majority of the apartments in the complex unoccupied, probably until the late spring of next year.

He sat in an armchair and listened for the whine of the elevator in the corridor outside. He heard the key turn in the lock and watched the reflection of the old woman in the hall mirror, backing into the apartment, manoeuvring the wheelchair through. The old man feebly raised his walking stick and pushed the door shut. He waited and watched as the woman entered the salon the same way, pulling the wheelchair along. Once inside she swivelled it around, then stopped and stared at him silently.

The man appeared to have difficulty comprehending the situation, and became noticeably agitated, but the woman pondered him calmly, her eyes briefly registering the hand-held gun resting on his right thigh before returning her gaze to his face. She came at him with surprising speed and swung the grocery bag. He hadn't expected that, but in the end it proved futile. He shot her between the eyes and watched her collapse in front of him, dead before she hit the ground. The old man gazed down at his wife, then back at him. The assassin studied him with mild interest, noting the tears welling in his eyes, tears not of fear, but instead, those of a grief-stricken man. He raised the gun and casually shot him between the eyes. He jerked backwards in the chair, head lolling to one side, eyes open, a thin flow of blood streaming down his face from the neat little hole.

The assassin stepped over the woman and wheeled the man into the bedroom, then returned, laid the woman on her back and dragged her to a position on the floor beside her husband. He returned to the salon, picked a croissant from the floor and began eating it as he walked to the window and scanned the horizon. He sat in the armchair he had placed there earlier and stared into the distance.

Now it was all just a matter of time.

69

From the viewing platform in the town beside the Funicular, Paul and Francesca watched the cruiser slip anchor hundreds of feet below and head for the Port of Naples with John Considine on board. Later they strolled down the narrow streets to the buzzing terrace of the Quisisana and sipped cocktails in the late-evening sun.

Nick Penn had remained on the island to link up with Terry Clarkson, who had earlier touched down at Naples International Airport and would be returning to Capri on board the cruiser. The previous evening Captain Philip Beresford, his fiancée Charlotte, and sixteen of the crew joined them for cocktails at Al Piccolo in La Piazzetta, and afterwards dinner at nearby Villa Verde.

Earlier, in an emotionally charged reunion, Francesca was astounded when Jamie boarded the cruiser and embraced her. The others watched from a discreet distance as they shed their tears, made their peace, absolved one another and discarded their demons.

'I want Jamie to be a part of this,' Paul had said to Considine after the meeting with Nick Penn. 'It's another pair of eyes, and he more than anyone should have a vested interest in protecting his sister. Let's get him out here.'

Considine stared down the table at Francesca, smiling and laughing with Jamie, and realised what a wise move Paul Bannon had made. All of them had been impressed with Jamie's fearless stance during their war with the London unions, none more so than the implacable John Considine himself. Slowly, methodically, an impenetrable shield was being constructed around their precious cargo. These men would protect her against the enemy that was lurking out there if it was within the realms of human endeavour to do so. Of that he was now certain.

It had been a boisterous evening filled with camaraderie and song, but tonight they sat alone on the crowded terrace by the edge of the glamorous Via Camerelle. She held his hand and smiled wistfully.

'Since I came to you, my darling, I can't imagine a life without you, because my life without you already seems a million miles away.'

He held her hand and whispered in her ear, 'In all my life I never thought I could love like this.'

She rested her head on his shoulder.

'I wish I could embrace the certainty you instil in me. I dread to think that perhaps even at this very moment there are forces plotting to overwhelm us.'

'Signor Bannon, Signora.'

They looked up to find the maître d' of Le Rendez-Vous restaurant standing beside them.

'If you'd care to follow me, your table is ready . . . '

They sat together at a table in the far corner and watched the waiter decant the wine, then pour. The night was warm and sultry and the streets buzzed with the sounds of laughter and music. The candles flickered in the warm evening breeze as they gazed into each other's eyes, captivated by the magic of the moment, oblivious to the world beyond them.

They made love in their penthouse high up in the Quisisana, the terrace doors thrown open, the shutters drawn back, the still night air wafting in from the ocean below.

'So impossibly beautiful,' he whispered, 'so sweet, so sensual. I love you with every beat of my heart.'

She held him close and whispered.

'I love when you say these things to me. I love you beyond belief . . . '

70

The assassin watched the cruiser make its approach from the south in the early hours of Sunday morning, its bow cutting through the semi-rough waters of the bay with deliberate, graceful ease. He knelt behind the tripod, adjusted the binoculars and tracked it all the way into the bay until he saw the distant splash of the anchor hitting the water. He stared with a degree of surprise as he surveyed the scene.

For some inexplicable reason they had chosen a deeper mooring, three hundred metres further out from the last time, which, given his location one hundred and seventy metres back from the waterline on the Croisette, would make this a thousand-metre shot, placing it at the extreme end of achievability – still within his range, but only just.

He pondered the adjustment and quickly concluded that it still constituted the best opportunity he was likely to get. She was a clever bitch, this one. He guessed that she was on to him, and if she was sharing her concerns with those guys out on the water, then it was safe to assume they were already taking counter-measures – the choice of a deeper mooring appeared to confirm it. He needed to take decisive action before the bitch slipped out of his grasp forever. That time in departures when he thought he was being his usual careful self, she had picked him out from the crowd. He now knew it. He cursed himself again for his stupidity and decided it was time to get the job done and disappear.

Later he saw the tender leaving the cruiser on a course to the old town with one male passenger on board, but otherwise there was little sign of any activity. He moved across and examined the rifle perched on the second tripod, then gazed through the telescopic lens, adjusting the focus ever so slightly until the crosshairs were at optimum clarity. A little more waiting, he thought, a little more watching. It was all just a matter of time.

★

Terry Clarkson instructed the pilot to make for the harbour in the old town and drop him off at the ferry terminal. Nick's insistence that the cruiser be anchored further out in the bay had caused a degree of alarm, but had been acted upon without hesitation.

'If I seem paranoid I make no apologies. A marksman positioned on the roof of one of those apartment blocks will feel he has a shot to nothing inside six hundred metres. Anything beyond that's a helluva different ballgame. My guess is you'll be pretty safe out here.'

How could he have ever known that those last words would come to haunt him.

Terry's brief was to look out for anything vaguely suspicious. It was a game of cat and mouse with no beginning and no end; tedious, frustrating, never knowing when the enemy might strike. A wild-goose chase or a disaster waiting to happen – only time would tell.

He strolled the Croisette, meticulously studying each building from the relative cover of the pine trees, then turned and repeated the exercise. It was eight in the morning and with the season at an end the promenade seemed eerily quiet. The early-morning joggers barely glanced at him as he surveyed each building through high-powered binoculars from his position among the trees and shrubbery.

He quickly concluded that the block of buildings stretching two hundred metres west of the Carlton Hotel and two hundred metres east of the Martinez were prime positions for the execution of a single long-range shot. But so far on this cloudy grey morning everything appeared to be normal, a fact that did little to alleviate the bad feeling lingering in his gut. The wind blowing in off the Mediterranean was raising a ripple across the bay just as he trained his binoculars on the cruiser at the stroke of nine.

Now for the first time, he could detect real activity on the rear upper deck: six, maybe eight people moving about, most likely catering staff preparing to serve breakfast to the principles. He saw the lady with the flowing blonde hair walk from the salon across the deck to the rear guard-rail, sunglasses on, hair blowing in the breeze.

She stood gazing out to sea, hands resting on the guard-rail, head held high into the wind. He was about to turn away when there was a distant crack and a spray of red vapour filled the space around her. In an instant she was gone, the impact catapulting her over the side.

He stared incredulously, then swung around instantly, but there was nothing to be seen. His walkie-talkie crackled.

'Terry, she's down! It's fucking consternation out here! There's a marksman on the top floor, right side, the grey apartment block, second line, left of the Carlton. I swear I caught a glint of something, a flash of a lens. Go! Now!'

The traumatised crew watched him dive off the upper deck and appear moments later with her body in his arms. He held her in the water, thirty feet behind the cruiser, in the space where he had surfaced. The crew stared aghast at the scene below them, until it slowly began to dawn on them why he was making no effort to take her back on board. Francesca Sinclair, the love of his life, lay dead in his arms, the delirious expression on his face telling them that nothing Paul Bannon could do would bring her back.

★

The assassin disappeared like a ghost in the broad light of day, melting into the morning crowd, disappearing down the maze of streets behind the Rue d'Antibes, his escape route mapped out meticulously, a silent harbinger of doom and destruction – never to be seen again.

71

Amidst the chaos that ensued in the immediate aftermath of Francesca's death, nothing in the world, and no man, could console Paul Bannon. Those who tried to reach out to him were repelled, vigorously at first, then as the weeks and months passed, with a weary emptiness that the ones closest to him found impossible to penetrate.

Each day his disposition appeared to shift gradually; the outgoing, extrovert personality most of his friends once knew, replaced now by something entirely different. People now perceived Paul instead as an introverted loner, gaunt-faced, distant, unapproachable, his appearance unruly, his hair long and ragged, his pale, stubbled features bearing the haunted look of a grief-stricken man; a wretched, bitter, inconsolable figure, lost in the depths of irreversible, devastating despair.

He lived his vagrant life in a pall of the utmost gloom, severing contact with family and friends, his lonely, self-imposed isolation catapulting him deep into the realms of icy oblivion. Anthony Selwyn tried. Frank Brilly tried. Frank Considine tried. Jamie tried. They all tried.

But Paul had disconnected from his previous life, choosing instead to live in the devastation of his grief, beyond human contact, beyond human consolation. He eschewed all of the places that reminded him of her, preferring to inhabit a remote hinterland on the outer peripheries of his previous existence. The sadness that hung like a cloud over his fiercely loyal head-office staff seemed ultimately to steel them into running the business as best they could in the absence of their fearless, broken-hearted boss.

He lived in a no-man's land, anonymously, on occasion to be seen wandering the streets of London in the early hours, his tall frame hunched and emaciated, the weight of his grief destroying him like a cancer eating away at his inner core.

Seven months after Francesca's death, during a rare fleeting visit to his apartment in Hans Crescent, he shuffled past a pile of letters neatly arranged by Laura, his housekeeper, when something caught his attention. A hand-delivered envelope lay separate from the rest, with the words, 'Contents Most Urgent – Please Do Not Ignore', written in heavy black lettering. He stared at it absentmindedly, then picked it up, walked through to the kitchen and tore the envelope open.

It contained a single sheaf of paper from the London firm of lawyers, Pritchards, which read:

Dear Mister Bannon,

We have been trying in vain to contact you in a matter of the upmost sensitivity. Miss Francesca Sinclair was an esteemed client of ours, and it is with a heavy heart that we now find ourselves acting in the administration of her estate. In this regard we wish to engage with you in a matter of the most pressing urgency.

Prior to her untimely death, Miss Sinclair put in place certain specific arrangements, which we are now endeavouring to fulfil. As part of these arrangements, she entrusted to our care a sealed package, with instructions that it should be handed to you in the event of her death.

We respectfully request that you contact us, in order that we may satisfactorily fulfil Miss Sinclair's final instruction.

Yours most sincerely,

Steven Pritchard
Managing Partner

He held the letter in shaking hands and read it several times again. Then he stood, walked to the telephone and dialled the number.

★

The wayward appearance of the man who shuffled into the thirty-seven-storey City tower housing the offices of Pritchards on its top three floors caused a measure of concern at the marble-encrusted security desk in the ground-floor foyer.

'How may I assist you, sir?' the shaven-headed, sour-faced security attendant inquired haughtily.

'Mister Steven Pritchard.'

The attendant stared at the dishevelled individual dressed in trenchcoat, jeans and trainers.

'You have an appointment?'

'The fuck do you think, asshole?'

The attendant bristled.

'Your name, please.'

'Paul Bannon.'

The guy picked up the telephone and dialled.

'Natasha, I have a Mister Bannon in reception. Claims to have an appointment with Mister Pritchard . . . '

The attendant's demeanour gradually began changing to one of confused surprise.

'You say he . . . owns the building.'

He stared at the receiver, then at the shuffling tramp standing before him.

'Sir, if you'd care to have a seat . . . '

The glass doors of the high-speed elevator opened instantly, and a tall willowy blonde dressed in white blouse, tight grey skirt and black heels walked briskly towards him.

'Good morning, Mister Bannon, I'm Natasha, Steven's secretary. May I ask you to please come this way.'

They crossed the lobby and rode the elevator to the top floor. On the way she looked at him and smiled.

'Mister Bannon, her death must have been incomprehensible. I'm so dreadfully sorry.'

He stared at her for a few seconds as the elevator whirred to a halt.

'Thank you, Natasha,' he said quietly.

Steven Pritchard stood waiting by the elevator. He was tall, slim, late thirties, suave in appearance, with a premature head of meticulously groomed steel-grey hair. His face registered only the briefest hint of surprise at the gaunt, ghostlike apparition standing before him. They shook hands.

'Thank you so much for meeting with us,' he said. 'I've heard a great deal about you, principally from Francesca of course. Your reputation precedes you. Please, come this way.'

He followed them to a spacious corner office suite with full-height plate-glass windows offering breathtaking views across the river and onwards to the distant south coast of England. He walked to the window and stood a while before turning back to them.

'I remember we swivelled the top thirty floors forty degrees to maximise the view. I guess we got it right.'

'Was it your idea to do that, Mister Bannon?' Natasha asked.

'Yes it was,' he replied. 'I recall instructing my architects to spin the building, and they said it couldn't be done due to restricted site configuration, ground-level footprint, that sort of thing. I suggested they leave the first seven floors in the original configuration, then swivel everything from level eight up. There were one or two issues with services but in the end that's exactly what we did.'

'What a stroke of genius,' Natasha smiled as she poured coffee and placed it on the table in front of him. She watched him pick it up and sip with trembling hands. Steven Pritchard glanced at her briefly, then turned to him.

'Mister Bannon, there are no words to describe the pain and sadness we all of us felt on hearing the tragic news of Francesca's shocking demise. She really was our most esteemed client, and as the executor of her will I am privileged to say that she also considered me a friend, confidante and legal advisor during all of the last ten years. A month prior to her death she entrusted me with certain specific tasks to be expedited in the event of her death. At the time, little did we know how imminent that shocking event would prove to be. It is as if she had a premonition that something terrible might happen . . . '

He could see that the young lawyer was struggling with this.

'A great deal of what she entrusted to me pertains to you

in one way or another. I have here a sealed manila envelope containing a cassette upon which there is a taped, recorded message to which Francesca stipulated you should listen as soon as it is possible to do so. And because it has taken longer to reach you than we anticipated, I rather hoped you might adhere to Francesca's request during your visit with us today. As you can see, there is a cassette recorder on the table, and with your permission we will leave you in peace to listen to the contents, if indeed that is your desire. All other matters can be dealt with at a later stage.'

He watched as they discreetly took their leave, and when the door closed behind them he stared at the envelope, then tore it open and inserted the cassette into the recorder. Then in the depths of his despair he felt his heart bursting in his chest as the soft, silky tones of her voice filled the room.

'My darling Paul . . . my darling, darling Paul . . . I know that when you listen to this recording for the first time, that by then I shall have bestowed such profound and unspeakable sadness upon your life. In the midst of fearing the inevitable, I came to you at the end, because the sheer strength of my destiny propelled me remorselessly into your arms.

I have loved you all of my life, my darling, with a passion and a desire so strong that it nurtured me and preserved me during all my darkest days, during those lost and lonely years when I yearned for you each second of every day. And then how utterly magical it was for me to spend those golden days with you, my absolute love.

The knowledge that those evil forces that stalked my past world would relentlessly await their chance to move against me and strike a mortal blow, was of such profound insignificance when compared to the all-embracing love you bestowed upon me from the moment we met again on that wonderful night in Cannes.

Do not be sad, my darling, now that I have gone.

This you must promise me from the depths of your heart. Do not be sad, because to do so would only serve to diminish the searing, stunning love that passed between us.

You are so strong, my darling, I would die again a thousand times if I thought the memory of me would render you forlorn and weak. You must ensure that my legacy is sufficient to enable you to overcome this crushing grief, because, my darling, even after all that you have done for me, I need you still to be strong as I now entrust to your loving care my most precious possession.

That magical day, the most thrilling day of my life, when you asked me to marry you, and you swore to me it mattered nothing when I told you I could never conceive a child for you – when I heard those words, you made me the happiest woman in the world.

What I omitted to tell you then is that you already have a child by me. Yes, my darling, a child, *our* child, a beautiful boy, in whom the essence of all that was good between us lives on.

Our son is called James. He is seventeen years old, and I know in my heart of hearts that nobody in the world will look after him more lovingly than you, his wonderful father.

All those years ago at Grange Abbey when I came to you that night . . . and afterwards, well, you can guess the rest of it. And that is why I need you to be strong, my love; for you to live a life brimming with happiness and fulfilment; for you to care for our precious son, whose future destiny I entrust so willingly to your care.

Draw the strength you need from the depths of the sadness I know that you are feeling at this moment.

Live a happy and a carefree life, my love, for otherwise our time together will have been diminished by my passing.

Goodbye, my sweetheart. Pick up the broken pieces of your heart, because now you must be strong not just for the two of us, but for the love of our darling boy.

Afterwards, when they walked into the room, he lifted his head from his hands and stared at them with a vulnerability that melted their hearts. His eyes were swollen red from the tears that lay pooled on the glass table in front of where he sat. They stood silently and stared at this quivering, pathetic, broken man, the devastation of his loss etched bitterly on his gaunt, emaciated face. Then slowly, silently, he stood and buttoned his coat.

'She told me I must be strong,' he whispered. 'I don't know where I shall find that strength, except that somehow I know I must.'

72

In the dark depths of a freezing January night the distant ringing of a telephone rattled him out of a restless sleep, but the voice on the other end of the line startled him all the more.

He sat up, suddenly wide awake.

'Paul . . . Paul Bannon?'

'Yes, Nick, it's me – a ghost from the past.'

'I never thought I'd hear from you. It's been, what . . . almost a year?'

'Yeah, I guess.'

'Mister Considine told me her death . . . affected you . . . almost blew you away. I blame myself for all of it, Mister Bannon. I should have protected her . . . '

'None of us could save her in the end, Nick.'

'Yeah, but I was the one who failed . . . '

'You didn't fail, Nick. You bear no responsibility for what happened. You were there for her.'

Silence at the other end.

'Nick?'

'Except for the one time it mattered most of all.'

'I've made peace with my demons, Nick, and you must do the same.'

More silence.

'Nick?'

'Yes, sir.'

'There's something I need you to do . . . '

'Name it, sir. Anything.'

★

When Natasha Robertson arrived at the Hans Crescent apartment, barely a month after Paul Bannon's visit to Pritchards, she was taken aback by the frenetic level of activity there. Her watch said it was seven, but even at that hour of the morning there was an organised buzz about the place.

Beyond the opulently decorated foyer she could see through to a rosewood-panelled office where a dozen men sat at desks with telephones to their ears.

'Hi, Natasha,' the forty-year-old brunette standing by the elevator door smiled. 'I'm Rebecca Jameson, Mister Bannon's secretary. She glanced at her watch.

'He's still in the gym, I'm afraid, but in light of the urgency of the documentation, he has asked that I accompany you down there and have it executed without delay, if you'd care to follow me.'

The elevator descended to basement level and opened into a spacious gymnasium where there were three men dressed similarly, with army style crew-cuts, two of them running flat out on treadmills, the third man barking orders.

'OK, boys, we've hit the target – thirty minutes at eleven miles an hour. Now down on the floor. Fifty press-ups. Fifty seconds. Go!'

She watched as they powered through the exercise, and each time on the tenth movement the instructor shouted 'Hit!'

In the end the instructor glanced at his watch.

'Two seconds off the mark – take five.'

The two men lay face down, sweating profusely.

'Paul, when you have a minute,' Rebecca Jameson called. 'We need a signature.'

The man furthest away rose to his feet and ambled over. He was dressed in black tracksuit, black T-shirt and black trainers. Natasha studied him as he approached, her expression changing gradually to one of undisguised disbelief. He smiled faintly.

'Hi, Natasha. How lovely to see you.'

'I hardly recognised you,' she smiled. 'The last time we met you were . . . so different. The transformation is . . . amazing.'

He took the document and scrawled his signature.

'You and Stephen were good to me when I was at my lowest,' he said quietly. 'We've begun channelling some business through Pritchards.'

'I'm aware of it,' she replied. 'We're absolutely thrilled.'

'Perhaps we might have dinner sometime.'

'Yes, I'd be . . . delighted.'

★

The boy knocked on the door of the drawing room, entered hesitantly, and stared at the man standing by the fireplace. He stood for a while, walked forward, then seemed to hesitate again. The man looked at him and smiled. The boy was tall and wiry, his handsome face and deep green eyes tentative under a shock of unruly blond hair. The man walked across and stood before him.

'How did you get those?' he asked, pointing to a line of recently inserted stitches directly below his jawline.

'Rugby, sir. I lay on the ground too long and got stamped.'

'What's your position?'

'Outside-centre, sir.'

'Any good?'

'My coach thinks I have potential. I captained the junior team, sir.'

'Sounds promising.'

'Thank you, sir.'

They stood staring at one other silently.

'I know this can't be easy for you,' he said gently. 'Are you willing to give it a shot?'

The boy looked at him and seemed to lose his composure. He wiped a tear from his cheek.

'I do apologise, sir.'

'You have nothing to apologise about.'

The boy's expression was one of tentative, surreal curiosity. He held himself strongly but hesitantly, nervous and vulnerable.

'My mother told me she loved the two of us more than all others in the world. So, yes, I'm willing to give it a shot, if you're willing to do the same.'

He walked forward and embraced his son.

73

Terry Clarkson shot the guard at point-blank range the instant he stepped out of the rear basement door. He grabbed him by the collar and let him down gently, then clipped the silenced beretta back in its holster. Nick Penn moved swiftly from the undergrowth and advanced along the darkened corridor. Up ahead they could hear muted conversation and the low sound of a television coming from the half-open door to the kitchen.

Terry moved forward and peered through the narrow gap between door and frame, then held up two fingers. Nick crept past him and squeezed soundlessly through the gap. He took three steps into the room, then shot the guy seated at the table in the back of the head. The second guy turned and gasped in disbelief, but Nick put a finger to his lips and held the gun steady.

'Upstairs,' he whispered. 'How many?'

The guy stared silently, eyes glazed.

'Just fucking tell me, and everything will be OK.'

The guy was in shock.

'Last chance, asshole. How many?'

'Two others, and the family – the Prince, his wife and four children.'

Nick nodded, then shot him between the eyes. He slumped on the floor but the television drowned out the sound. They moved rapidly along the corridor towards the stairs in the gloomy light. Suddenly there was another guard in front of them. He let off a shot and Terry went down. Nick shot the guy in the chest, then ran forward and pumped in two more for good measure. He stared down at Terry.

'You OK?'

'Yeah, feels like someone hit me with a fucking sledge-hammer,' he gasped. 'The jacket took most of it. Go now, go!

I'll be fine. Go!'

Bannon appeared at the end of the corridor.

'The plan is, you come in later,' Nick rasped.

'Terry's down. I'm coming now.'

'OK, but stay behind or we'll end up fucked.'

Upstairs the sound of the gunshot was causing consternation. They could hear women and children screaming, the noise of footsteps, and the sound of men's voices shouting on the floor above. Nick raced up the stairs and saw two men disappearing into a room and slamming the door shut. He briefly glanced up the stairs at some kids screaming hysterically on the top landing, then smashed through the door behind the two men, rolled onto the floor and levelled the gun. They both stared at him wide-eyed from beside a half-open window. Neither was armed.

'Move a hair and I'll blow your fucking heads off,' he screamed. He saw their eyes stray to a second man who had just materialised through the door, and slammed it shut.

'Leave it open,' Nick commanded without taking his eyes from the two men.

'No need. Terry's in the corridor.'

Nick scrambled to his feet and glared at the two men.

'Which one of you fucks is in charge here!'

'It is me,' the younger of the two replied, calmly but visibly shaken. 'Where are my bodyguards? What have you done with them? You should know that the alarm has already been raised.'

'Your bodyguards are dead,' Nick snarled. 'Your security system is deactivated and there ain't nobody coming to rescue you.'

The older man panicked and ran to the window. Nick raised the gun and shot him in the head. Paul grabbed the last guy and threw him roughly into an armchair. He stared at the body of his dead companion lying prostrate on the floor.

'Who are you?' he screamed, his calmness deserting him. 'Why do you behave like an animal? If this is about money, I can make you very rich. Do you have any idea who I am?'

'You murdered someone who was once close to me. Someone I had sworn to protect. I'm here to exact vengeance on the man who ordered her death.'

He seemed to consider this with mild surprise.

'Then you are mistaken, this . . . person you say I murdered is a . . . woman?'

Paul stared into his eyes.

'You knew her by the name Aurora.'

The flicker of recognition lasted barely an instant.

'You are mistaken,' he screamed. 'I have never heard this name . . . Aurora.'

Paul knelt beside him.

'Oh, you know the name all right, and if you lie to me once more I'll put the gun in your mouth and blow your fucking brains out. Now, begin by telling me who you are. I need to be sure I've got the right guy.'

He glanced at him with a look of abject terror and turned to Nick, who shrugged.

'Tell him, asshole'.

The guy sounded petrified, his breathing laboured and sporadic.

'I am Iranian, but not of this illegal regime. I am from the lawful regime of the Shah. We have taken our families and our riches with us, and our homes are elsewhere now. Someday we will return to reclaim what is rightfully ours.'

'Did you order the hit on Aurora?'

'I will not tell you this until I know what fate lies in store for me and my family.'

'We are here to avenge a death, and someone must pay the price. If you answer me truthfully, then you can decide upon whom we shall exact our vengeance. You'll be given two choices, and you have my word that we will abide by whichever choice you make, provided you answer me truthfully. Did you order the hit on Aurora?'

The terrified Arab stared at him, his face stained with tears.

'These two choices you speak of . . . '

Paul stared into the dark, glazed pools of his eyes.

'Your life, or the lives of your wife and four children – it's the only choice you've got. Now answer me. Did you order the hit?'

The Arab cried out at the top of his voice, a sound that was not of this earth, a wailing, tear-filled, agonised rasp that penetrated all corners of the room. Eventually he took his hands away from his face and stared up bleakly at his tormentor.

'If this is the only choice I have, I authorise you to take them, all of them, and spare my life.'

He stared with disgust at this pleading, pathetic man.

'Did you authorise the hit on Aurora?'

'Yes I did,' he screamed. 'The filthy whore slaughtered my father and my two uncles. I swore vengeance on her from that day. The slut got what she deserved.'

Paul stood and shot him once in the head.

'We're out of here,' Nick shouted. 'Let's go, now!'

★

Some days later a paragraph appeared on page five of the *Daily Telegraph* under the headline, 'Iranians Slain in Luxury Kensington Mansion'. The article stated:

> In what appears to be a carbon copy of a similar incident at the same location ten years previously, six bodies were recovered yesterday from a house in an affluent Kensington suburb adjacent to Hyde Park. All the victims were males and were the subject of what police believe was a professional contract slaying. A police spokesman said it is too early to speculate on the motivation behind this latest outbreak of violence, but he did confirm that the property is owned by a Middle Eastern family with Iranian connections. A woman and four children, understood to be the family of one of the victims, were found unharmed in an upper-floor room of the house. The woman is under sedation, and police hope to interview her in the coming days. A police source speculated that the killings may be connected to an internal dispute involving international business interests between rival Iranian factions.

74

'Jamie, you and me, we've had our differences. But that's all in the past now. I've grown to trust you. I've grown to respect you. I even fuckin' like you these days.' Considine sat opposite Jamie, pulling on a cigar and sipping a glass of his beloved Midleton.

Earlier they had taken off from Luton Airport in Paul's jet and were somewhere in the skies halfway to Ireland. Paul sat next to Anthony and glanced up from the *Financial Times*, his interest suddenly piqued. Young James sat in the cockpit next to the captain. Paul glanced surreptitiously at Anthony.

'Sounds like Johnny's in a philosophical mood.'

'It certainly does,' Anthony replied lightheartedly. 'The Grange Abbey effect perhaps?'

They were heading to Ireland for the beginning of the November shoot and the all-round mood was good. Paul returned to his newspaper.

'You can never really tell with Johnny,' he muttered absentmindedly. 'He's a hard one to read.'

Jamie was a cool one but he seemed ill at ease in the presence of the big man.

'You know I hate loose ends, Jamie,' Considine continued in his deadpan, gravelly tone. Jamie sat quietly.

'There's something I've been meaning to ask you.'

'Oh no,' Paul smirked.

'Ask ahead,' Jamie responded.

Considine took a look towards the cabin door and leaned forward.

'You killed him, didn't you?'

Jamie glanced from Considine to Anthony to Paul, then back to Considine.

'Killed who?' he asked.

'Simon Bannon of course – who else? The cops never solved it and it has been bothering me ever since. Now, personally I'd no time for the fucker, but aside from all of that, unless someone convinces me otherwise I reckon this one's down to you.'

All of a sudden you could cut the tension in the air.

'Don't go there, Johnny,' Paul interjected, glancing surreptitiously towards the cockpit. 'Now's not the time.'

But Considine appeared unperturbed.

'I can account for everyone's movements other than yours, Jamie, and God knows you had reason enough to do it. I'm not here to judge you, the opposite in fact, because I saw what he did to her, and I reckon he got exactly what he deserved. The man that took his revenge on Simon Bannon will forever have my respect.'

'Johnny!' Paul warned, the panic in his voice evident, but Jamie just gave a dismissive shrug.

'I didn't kill him,' he responded evenly. 'I thought about it. I articulated it, but I swear on my sister's life I didn't do it. I'm a man of many parts, and there's not a whole lot I'll shy away from, but the one act I know I could never do is take another man's life, whatever the circumstances, whatever the crime. I haven't got it in me, and that's the God's honest truth.'

No one said anything to this. They all sat silently, bemused or shell-shocked – it was impossible to tell. The circumstances surrounding Simon's death had always been a moot subject. Considine continued to stare at Jamie contemplatively, until in the end he gave a nonchalant shrug.

'I hear the words you're saying, Jamie, but my mind's made up. I've got this one down to you.'

Jamie didn't reply. He sat silently.

'Then you've got it wrong.'

It was the voice from the cockpit that startled them. They turned together to see the tall gangly frame of young James leaning casually against the partition beside the cockpit door. The group had been so anaesthetised by Johnny's line of questioning that none of them noticed him until the moment he spoke. They all just stared at him.

'He didn't do it,' he said, cool as a cucumber. 'Jamie Sinclair wasn't the only one with a motive.'

He glanced at his father, a hint of uncertainty in his eyes, as if seeking some form of tacit approval amid the paralysis that seemed to grip all of them. Paul's face was a mix of pride and affection, the sheer unconditional love of an adoring father for his beloved son. It was as if that was all the boy needed to see, because a faint smile broke across his face, and then he just turned and walked back to the cockpit. They remained transfixed in their seats, the repercussions of the words they had just heard washing over them. The expression of baffled astonishment on Considine's stony face said it all. He poured a measure of Midleton and downed it in one go.

'Holy fuck!' he grunted. 'It runs in the family!'

★

Ben Bradshaw stared blandly at the flickering TV screen, not registering the content, his mind in a different place, far removed from the oppressive gloom of these grey walls. His parole would kick in in three days' time following the completion of four long years with remission in this stinking hell-hole. Some high-flying Hooray-Henry in Bannon's bank, Beauchamps, had chased down the accounts and nobbled the bulk of the cash, all except for the half a mil that lay hidden in a suitcase buried in the basement of his two-up two-down in Finsbury Park.

Luckily the fuckers had missed out on that one, and he reckoned it ought to be sufficient to see him through, assuming the rats hadn't had it for breakfast. He stared absentmindedly around the drab recreation hall with its harsh artificial light, its sickening sterile smell, and contemplated life on the far side away from this lowlife stench of a place. He heard the scraping of seats on the stone floor and swivelled around as far as he could manage. The rest of them had up and left, which was unusual to say the least. He glanced at the clock on the wall – seven minutes to seven meant another seven minutes of recreation time. Strange, he thought to himself – even the fucking warder has done a runner.

It was then he heard the door open and close again and the shuffle of footsteps moving up the room, eventually stopping in the space directly behind him. He struggled to turn but it was impossible. Then someone grabbed his head in a vice-like grip and whispered the words: 'Paul Bannon sends his regards' – the last words he heard before the screwdriver smashed through his skull above his right ear and sliced through to the far side.

That was the way they found him ten minutes later, slumped in his wheelchair, the screwdriver still buried in his brain.

75

The rugged features of Jack Randall, NBC's personable, seven o'clock news anchorman, flashed onto the TV screen.

'It's Oscar time again, folks,' he drawled in his signature, deep baritone, 'and with British actress Natalie Selwyn tipped to win Best Actress for her performance in the thriller *The Analyst*, in which she plays a rookie psychiatrist attached to the San Francisco PD on the trail of a serial killer, our reporter Connie Carstairs caught up with Natalie's father, Sir Nicholas Selwyn, Britain's ambassador to the United States, at Dulles International today, and asked him for a comment on his daughter's riveting performance.

'Listen to what he had to say.'

The camera panned in on a tall, distinguished, grey-haired man, impeccably dressed in navy suit, blue and white striped shirt and navy silk tie, accompanied by three soberly dressed associates all carrying attaché cases.

'Sir Nicholas, a comment, please, on your daughter's Oscar nomination ahead of tomorrow's big event.'

Sir Nicholas stopped and smiled casually.

'My daughter is a wonderful girl and of course I wish her well. I'm extremely proud of her and I shall remain so whatever the outcome of tomorrow's decision proves to be. And now if you'll excuse me . . . '

★

Caroline Carter rang through to her.

'It's your brother on line three.'

There was a click, then a muzzy, long-distance connection.

'Hello, Anthony.'

'Christ, Natalie! Getting through to you is like breaking into Fort Knox.'

'Oh really! And what did you expect?'

'A dedicated line for friends and family perhaps.'

'Mmmm.'

'I've seen the movie twice by the way and your performance is astounding. The media are raving about you on this side of the pond – newspapers, magazines, television. Your face is everywhere. You're the darling of Europe.'

Natalie Selwyn strolled through her vast suite on the seventeenth floor of the Peninsula on fifty-fifth and fifth and gazed absentmindedly at the roof of the Saint Regis on the far side of the Avenue.

Her secretary Caroline Carter sat at a desk in an adjoining room fielding calls from journalists across the world.

'Thank you, Anthony. It's good of you to call.'

'You sound pretty damned cool for a girl who's just been nominated for Best Actress.'

'I'm just a little tired is all.'

'I imagine it must be hectic.'

'It's all a bit of a whirlwind really. The film's grossed eighty million since it opened in the States five weeks ago. Everyone's happy.'

'I bet they are. So what's next?'

'We fly to LA later for the awards ceremony, assuming we ever get to make it out of New York. Caroline is limiting each interview to five minutes max, and now they're telling me I really need to get back in there. How are my four gorgeous nieces?'

'Excited and thrilled that their aunt is the most famous actress on the planet.'

'Make sure and give them my love. I can't wait to see them.'

'They implored Jane and me to allow them to sit up tomorrow night and watch the whole thing live. In the end we relented.'

'How sweet.'

The connection crackled with static.

'Natalie, are you still there . . . '

There was a gap and then he heard her voice.

'I really ought to go.'

'Good luck tomorrow, Natalie, and all our love . . . '

In the background he could hear people calling her name. Another brief pause, and then, 'How is he, Anthony?'

★

Anthony Selwyn had been half-expecting this. Lately his secretive sister had been making a habit of getting around to it at the tail-end of their conversations. She had recently turned thirty-one and was now arguably at the zenith of her fame. A month previously, *International Playmate Magazine* had voted her the sexiest girl in the world, and yet, despite everything, he suspected that her closely guarded private life remained an emotional blank canvas.

He remembered in the weeks following that sole encounter with Paul Bannon in London, sensing a subtle change he found difficult to fathom in his enigmatic, broody sister. He articulated it to his wife one evening over dinner at the Ivy.

'Darling, it's so obvious it should be hitting you in the face. She's in love. Your beautiful, uber-cool, super-sophisticated sister has been captivated by your best friend's smoldering charm and swept away by the power of his presence.'

'Good God, I hadn't thought of it. How clever of you!'

'Not really. Women's intuition more likely.'

'Should I try and . . . intervene?'

'It may not be appropriate.'

'You think not?'

'Not now, perhaps. Why not wait a while . . . '

Natalie had ended her relationship with Rupert Cavendish abruptly. A development which surprised a few but didn't unduly upset anyone other than the bombastic buffoon himself. Seventeen life-changing months had passed since then. The wheels of fortune propelling his beloved sister to the dizzy heights of worldwide fame and simultaneously thrusting his greatest friend into the darkest depths of despair. These thoughts raced through his mind as he pondered how he should best address her question.

'He seems at peace with himself now I suppose, but those first six months were beyond horrendous. He disengaged from the world and lived his life in the shadows, drowning in a tidal wave of the most abject sorrow. It was as if the will to live had been sucked out of him by a savage blow to the heart – like watching somebody slowly die of an incurable, wasting disease. I really thought he was gone, Natalie, beyond the reach of all of us, but then he discovered the boy and seemed to re-emerge from the depths of his despair. There's still a certain melancholy about him. And yet the realisation that he is the father of her son has somehow restored in him the will to live. You should see them together. He clearly adores him – they're inseparable. For a man who almost died of a broken heart, the transformation is incredible.'

The line crackled and faded and he thought she was gone, but then he heard her voice again.

'And has he . . . you know . . . met anyone?'

'I hardly think so.'

'It must all be so . . . desperately difficult.'

Even across the thousands of miles that separated them, Anthony Selwyn sensed a shattering loneliness in his sister's voice, which cut to the core of his heart. It astonished him that, even as she was this very moment the epicentre of the universe, the world's most sought-after woman, she still remained hopelessly, vulnerably, impossibly alone.

How did circumstances contrive to create such anguish against all the odds, he wondered, and yet almost inevitably it appeared they did. It seemed to go with the territory, a singular fate attaching to some of the great female icons of the world. Women for whom fame and circumstance were but a withering legacy, a passport to unbearable, impossible isolation. There and then he decided it was time to act.

'Natalie, please tell me if I'm reading this correctly, but what if I could arrange for you to meet with him. It may still be possible, but the difficulty is . . . '

'Anthony.' It was barely a whisper. 'There is nothing I'd love more.'

'Yes, but, . . . the difficulty is . . . '

'Yes, Anthony.'

'He's about to embark on an extended trip to Australia and New Zealand, departing the day after tomorrow, business and rugby combined. His son has been shortlisted to join the British Schools rugby touring team.'

'Oh, really . . . '

'Why don't I look into it right now and call you back. That's a promise.'

76

Paul Bannon sat at the head of the table in the apartment at Hans Crescent and watched the wall panel slide back silently to reveal a large flat screen. The lights dimmed, the automatic curtains swished shut and the screen flickered into life. The renowned architect Richard Rowntree, famous designer of high-end, high-rise buildings the world over, sat to his left along with a backup team of specialist consultants. A second team of structural engineers from the London-based firm of Ivan Brentwood Associates sat on the opposite side.

'We'll begin if you're ready, Paul.'

A mock-up, computer-generated aerial view of a forty-seven-storey glass tower, standing strategically on an in-fill site at the river end of the City, sprang into view, its unique octagonal shape glistening in a stunning montage of reflective glass and steel. The camera panned slowly around, revealing the building in all its glory, the sunlight glancing off its subtle angles. Then the light changed gradually from daylight into darkness, displaying a series of spectacular night-time views, the windows sparkling on all levels as the camera traced a path upwards, encapsulating the vast tower in its magnificence.

'Tell me you like what you see,' Richard Rowntree laughed.

'Yes I do,' he replied. 'The shape is spectacular, even if my agents are telling me the lettable floor space will be diminished as a result. But still. It's dynamic.'

'We've consulted exhaustively during the past months on the conundrum of reduced floor-space dictated by the outer contour of the building. Most experts are assuring us that a higher-square-foot rental level should emerge from the dynamics of the design, sufficient to mitigate the floor-space reduction.'

Paul stared at the building, deep in concentration.

'Let's run it one more time.'

As the image faded and the screen lit up again, Nicole walked discreetly up to him.

'Sorry to disturb, but Anthony has called in. Says he needs a quick word. Sounds rather urgent. I explained you were in conference.'

He continued staring at the image of the tower as it filled the screen, then turned to her.

'Hold him on the line. I'll be there shortly.'

'Certainly.'

When the second viewing reached its conclusion and the lights came on, he stood.

'Guys, I'm outa here but I'm giving you the green light on this. Let's get the show on the road.'

★

'Anthony, I'm connecting you.'

'Thanks, Nicole.'

'Hi.'

'Hi.'

'Nicole said it sounded urgent.'

'Not that kind of urgent, but I need your attention for five minutes.'

'It's pretty chaotic here. Can this wait until tomorrow?'

'I'm afraid not.'

His friend's tone surprised him.

'OK. Go.'

'I understand you're leaving the UK later. May I inquire as to your itinerary?'

'Are you serious?'

'Just fucking indulge me.'

He paused and took a deep breath.

'I'm en route to Sydney to spend a couple of days with my father's brother Matthew. Seems he's in a bit of a mess out there – needs some kind of financial assistance. Also there's an infill parcel fronting the harbour that looks interesting. Afterwards

I'm crossing to Dunedin. My kid is touring the island . . . '

'I know. I read about it somewhere. Do you intend flying directly to Sydney?'

'Jesus, Anthony.'

'Please . . . just answer my question.'

He stared in exasperation at Nicole, who offered one of her less-than-sympathetic smiles, which didn't surprise him. She really liked Anthony Selwyn.

'I fly to Paris this evening for three nights. There's a house on the Avenue Foch – been chasing it for years. I think I may have mentioned it . . . '

'You're staying at the usual place?'

'Of course.'

'Then I have a favour to ask of you.'

'Spit it out.'

'There's someone who wishes to meet with you.'

'Sure. Who is it?'

'I can't tell you that.'

'Jesus, Anthony.'

'Christ, Paul, I'm asking you this as your friend, so give me some slack and just do it. It's set up for the day after tomorrow, the cocktail bar at eight. And . . . please don't let me down.'

He stared at the receiver as the line went dead.

'Jesus.'

Caroline Carter was yelling instructions from the room next door.

'Let's go right now, everybody. We're ten behind schedule. C'mon, you guys, we're outa here!'

The porters grabbed the luggage. The makeup lady applied the finishing touches and began packing her equipment. The photographer grabbed the last few shots and everyone started to move.

The telephone buzzed as they were about to pull the door. Natalie ran back.

'Hello.'

'He's flying to Charles de Gaulle this evening. Spending three nights in Paris en route to Australia and New Zealand. I've told him there is someone who wishes to meet him, but I didn't tell him who it was, based on a discussion I had with Johnny Considine some time ago. Apparently when Considine set it up for Francesca, he advised her to just turn up unannounced, and in the end it all worked out.'

'But why? It seems rather strange.'

'I'm not quite sure. Considine told her to just do it, I think because, if he suspects he's being manipulated, it makes him . . . unpredictable.'

Judging by the breathy chuckle at the other end of the line, he guessed that his sister didn't need to think too much about all of this.

'And where have you arranged this . . . clandestine meeting.'

'The cocktail bar of the Hotel du Crillon. It's where he stays.'

'You're sure he'll be there?'

'Positive. He'll be pissed for not knowing in advance who

he's meeting, but trust me. When this guy makes a commitment it's cast in stone.'

★

It was a cool evening in Paris as he strolled past the Madeleine and crossed onto the Rue Royale. Passing Maxims he glanced at his watch – it was approaching seven forty-five as he rounded onto the Place de la Concorde. What the hell had gotten into Anthony, he wondered, as he walked into the Crillon's lavish foyer and stopped at the concierge desk.

'Bonsoir, Fabian. Y a-t-il des messages?'

'Rien, Monsieur Bannon.'

'Merci, bonsoir.'

On the approach to the diminutive cocktail bar he could hear the sounds of a piano tingling. He sat by the bar and glanced briefly at the sexy French singer standing beside the piano. She smiled and began to sing.

> *Let's waltz to the strains of the band,*
> *Darling, come take my hand . . .*

'Monsieur, comme d'habitude?'

'Merci,' he nodded as the barman poured his ice-cool beer.

> *Let's dance through the warm summer's night,*
> *Dance while the starlight shines bright,*
> *This feeling I feel seems so right . . .*

He sipped his beer, the sultry sounds of the girl's voice filling the room, and his thoughts began to stray. Elbows on the bar, chin resting on his hands, he gazed through the reflective glass and tinted mirrors to a place far beyond.

> *Let's talk about friendship gone cold,*
> *Friends who have died or grown old,*
> *Let's think about teenage romance,*
> *Saturday night at the dance . . .*

His mind drifting, his melancholic mood seeming to shut the world out, he barely noticed the atmosphere suddenly become super-charged.

> *My darling I've loved you through all of my days,*
> *I'll always love you, I'll love you all ways . . .*

The barman was staring at him, eyes wide, his mouth frozen in a half-smile.

'I believe you have an appointment, monsieur.'

Shaken out of his reverie, he turned and stared at the ravishing woman seated on the bar stool beside him, her hair sleek, her lips crimson, her molten blue eyes sparkling in the light . . .

'Natalie!'

David Delaney